Scar...ildhood.
Befo...ma
usherette and bookse.............................es,
Scarlett loves nothing.............................lay
.........RTHUMBER................................ck,
with large qua...........

Scarlett also writes novels under her real name Rowan Coleman. Currently she lives in Hertfordshire with her husband, five children and a very large collection of beautiful shoes.

To find out more, visit her website at:
www.rowancoleman.co.uk
Facebook or Twitter: @rowancoleman and
@scarlettbailey

Praise for Scarlett Bailey:

'Festive fun from the Queen of Christmas chick lit'
Fabulous Magazine, Sun on Sunday

'A delicious Christmas read!' Tricia Ashley

'I LOVE it! It was funny, romantic and the perfect book to snuggle up with – Scarlett Bailey does it again!' Miranda Dickinson

'Endearing and funny, we loved this gorgeously Christmassy romcom' *Closer*

'A light, fun and fast-paced chunk of chortlesome chick-lit' *Heat*

'An awesome Christmassy read with a lot of twists and turns . . . you can't put it down' Chicklit Club

Also by Scarlett Bailey:

Just For Christmas
Married by Christmas
Santa Maybe (digital short)
The Night Before Christmas

Writing as Rowan Coleman:

The Memory Book
Dearest Rose
Lessons in Laughing Out Loud
The Happy Home for Broken Hearts
The Baby Group
Woman Walks Into A Bar
River Deep
After Ever After
Growing Up Twice

The Accidental Series:
The Accidental Mother
The Accidental Wife
The Accidental Family

Scarlett Bailey

Two Weddings and a Baby

EBURY
PRESS

3 5 7 9 10 8 6 4 2

First published in 2014 by Ebury Press, an imprint of Ebury Publishing
A Random House Group Company

The Random House Group Limited Reg. No. 954009

Addresses for companies within the Random House Group can be found at:
www.randomhouse.co.uk

A CIP catalogue record for this book is
available from the British Library

The Random House Group Limited supports The Forest Stewardship
Council® (FSC®), the leading international forest-certification organisation.
Our books carrying the FSC label are printed on FSC® -certified paper.
FSC is the only forest-certification scheme supported by the leading
environmental organisations, including Greenpeace.
Our paper procurement policy can be found at:
www.randomhouse.co.uk/environment

Printed and bound by CPI Group (UK) Ltd, Croydon, CR0 4YY

ISBN 9780091953553

To buy books by your favourite authors and register for offers visit:
www.randomhouse.co.uk

For Debbie Ann Pookorny and Joel Llande

June 2014

Dear Debbie

Since the moment I met you, I have wanted to be with you, and it only took me eight years to make it happen! You have made me so happy, and I can't wait to spend the rest of my life with you, and our children.

So, Debbie, will you please make me a very happy man, and marry me?

With all my love, always,

Joel
xxx

Chapter One

It was raining, which seemed appropriate. Tamsyn Thorne's home town of Poldore was welcoming her back in exactly the same way it had bid her farewell more than five years ago – under a cloud.

'Nice day for it,' Tamsyn told the cabby, who'd picked her up at the train station, as she wiped away the condensation from the side window and peered out at the grey, wet Cornish town, shining in the summer rain. Poldore looked, as ever, as if it was tumbling down the hill towards the Atlantic – as if one good nudge might be enough to send it floating out to sea, like a sort of picture-postcard Atlantis.

'They reckon it's going to get worse before it gets better,' he mumbled. 'They were saying something about a super-storm on the news, whatever that is. Apparently we're getting all of everyone's weather in one go . . .' Tamsyn wasn't really listening. She was too busy looking, and taking it all in.

Poldore, the place where she had grown up, not knowing or caring about what world lay beyond the moors and the woods she roamed with her sisters and brother, when they were all little. And then later the place where she had first fallen in love, first kissed a boy in what was known as Kissing Alley behind the church. It was where she'd first stayed out all night at a party after telling her mum she was at a sleepover, lost first her father, then her best friend, then her brother, who had once been her closest sibling and who now barely spoke to her from one year to the next.

This was Poldore, and Tamsyn was back, against her better judgement, for a wedding, for her younger brother's wedding. Ruan Thorne, so close to her in age that he had felt like a twin for much of her life, was getting married.

Tamsyn was fairly amazed that she had been invited at all, never mind been asked, or rather told by her mother, who had expertly wielded all the emotional-blackmail weapons she had in her considerable armoury, that she was going to be a bridesmaid.

'You're sure Ruan wants me to be a bridesmaid at his wedding?' Tamsyn had asked Laura Thorne as she'd gazed out of her Parisian office window the day her mum called to tell her the news.

'He's having you as a bridesmaid,' Laura had told her. 'All of you girls, plus Lucy is going to be chief bridesmaid – you know she and Alex are best friends now? It's going to be so lovely. All my children back together in one place, first time in years. And as you know, it's my first proper visit back since, well, since we lost your dad and I moved to Suffolk with Keira.

I need you all there for me, Tamsyn. And there's nothing like a wedding to smooth things over, I always say.'

'Do you always say that, Mum?' Tamsyn had asked her. 'I'm fairly sure I've never heard you say that, and also, if you remember Keira's wedding, that was when Aunty Jean told Esther Hamble that she was a harlot and they haven't spoken to each other since, except to issue death threats and slanderous rumours.'

'Well, that's different and you know it,' Laura had said, and the tone in her voice was enough to tell Tamsyn that she was not about to be bested. Tamsyn had heard that tone a lot during her life, and for a good deal of her life she had ignored it and done what she pleased anyway. It wasn't until fairly recently that she had realised that when her mum spoke to her that way, it wasn't to try and contain or oppress her; it came out of a deep-seated worry for her child. God only knew that Tamsyn had given her enough to worry about, living out her role as the family's black sheep with quite some commitment, and yet her mother had always been there for her, whatever she'd done. Still, being a Thorne, she couldn't entirely shy away from an argument.

'"He's having" is quite a lot different from "He wants", Mum,' she pointed out.

'Well, Alex wants you all there,' Laura said. 'And Ruan would never say no to Alex about anything. That girl – she's made the world of difference to him,

Tamsyn. Maybe now is the time to set things right between you two. He's happy and settled, and so are you at last – it's all water under the bridge now, surely?'

Tamsyn had known there was no point in hesitating. If she'd said no at that moment, she would only eventually say yes at some point later in life, but it was more than the impossibility of saying no to her mother once she had her mind set on something. She missed Ruan, she regretted what had happened, and that was why she had left her highly successful and fashionable life in Paris and travelled all the way to Cornwall to wear a shop-bought, off-the-peg bridesmaid's dress which her sisters had gleefully told her entailed puff sleeves, and – God forbid – a great big bow. But it would be worth it, it would *all* be worth it, if she could know that Ruan had forgiven her. It was time, more than time to make amends to her brother. There was only one very slight obstacle standing in their way. It just so happened that in keeping with the family tradition, Ruan and Tamsyn Thorne were two of the most stubborn people ever to be related to each other in the history of mankind.

'You can drop me here,' Tamsyn told the cabby as they reached the top of the town. The Poldore Hall Hotel was where the wedding reception was due to be held, and where she had booked herself a room, politely declining the offer to stay with Alex or in Alex's mother's cottage. (According to Keira, Alex's mum, Gloria, was something of a force of nature.) The hotel was situated high on the hill overlooking the estuary with views out to sea and only a couple more minutes' drive away. Tamsyn was already late for the family dinner in the Silent Man, however, and she knew from experience that walking the steep and narrow streets of Poldore was always much quicker than trying to drive them. She was nervous enough about the prospect of being back in the fold of the whole family once again, and turning up late could easily be misconstrued as something 'old Tamsyn' would have done, the girl who didn't care about anyone or anything, including herself.

'You sure? It's really coming down out there now.' The cabby peered out of his window, as if rain rather bemused him. 'Seems like no one told the weather it's meant to be June. Forecast says it's going to rain like this for a week; there are even flood warnings in place, and they reckon it's going to get really bad tonight. Just hope the flood defences hold.'

'Shame,' Tamsyn said, smiling briefly as she handed him some cash. 'Not exactly wedding weather, is it? Still, whatever doesn't kill you makes you thornier . . .' She smiled at what had become the unofficial Thorne family motto.

'Or gives you a nasty cold,' the cabby smiled at her. 'Enjoy your stay in beautiful Poldore.'

'"Enjoy" is probably not exactly the right word,' Tamsyn muttered to herself as she slammed the car door shut and the cab pulled away. Well, this was it; there was no turning back now. It was time to face the music.

Pulling the collar of her white 1950s Chanel raincoat up around her neck, she snapped open the handle of her Louis Vuitton suitcase and took a moment to pause and look down at her home, its edges blurred by the rain. It almost seemed as if, the moment she stepped out of the cab, she'd stepped back in time and she felt exactly the same as she had as a teenager, kicking against the constraints of her Cornish life, desperate to break out. She couldn't wait to be free.

Hunching her shoulders against the rain, Tamsyn set off towards the harbour and the pub. Five days: that was all she had to make things right with Ruan. Five days, and then it would be back to Paris, back to Bernard du Mont Père, back to her career as a junior fashion designer at a leading cutting-edge label and back to her real life. And five days wasn't very long to fix a rift that had lasted five years, but she was going to try. Five days wasn't so very long at all. Especially if she could spend most of it drunk.

Her hopes of arriving at the family dinner in the local pub as a sleek, beautiful, totally transformed Paris fashion plate were being comprehensively dashed by the persistently heavy rain and the brutal wind that grabbed handfuls of rain and hurled them gleefully in her face. By the time she got to the Silent Man her hair, twisted into a chignon at the nape of her neck, would be frizzing itself into a wild frenzy and her black eyes, carefully lined with kohl, would soon mostly resemble the style statement of a panda. Oh well, Tamsyn thought, I'll always have my Louis Vuitton case – they can't take that away from me.

Her intention had been to go straight down to the pub, and not even look at Poldore's central church. St Piran's stood in the centre of a small graveyard, at the intersection of three roads, all of which eventually led back to the same place. Tamsyn started to hurry by, averting her eyes from the ancient building, as if somehow even acknowledging it would change things. But when the moment to walk past it actually arrived, she discovered she couldn't do it. It was impossible to pass by, her pace slowing even as she determined to hurry, rivulets of running water swelling into little streams around her feet. Eventually she came to a standstill.

How could she not say hello to her best friend? Her best friend, whose empty grave was one of the most recent in the graveyard, the last to be dug before the diocese declared that it was full.

Tamsyn stopped noticing the water drenching her as she remembered the day she'd heard the news that her friend was lost at sea.

There had been a fight, a fight between Merryn and

Ruan, and Merryn had gone out on her boat to calm down. It was something she had done a thousand times, a million times before. Like all of them back then, Merryn had learnt to sail practically before she could walk. Most kids in Poldore spent their lives on boats the way other children spent them on bikes. No one could have known that when the weather turned suddenly she would be taken by surprise. And even then no one would have guessed that Merryn – bright, funny, clever Merryn – the girl that used to make Tamsyn laugh so hard she couldn't breathe, would never come back from a quick little trip out around the harbour.

Tamsyn bit her lip as she found her way to Merryn's gravestone, the white marble shining like new amongst the old mossy stones that surrounded it. It was in a peaceful spot, set in the ground beneath the cedar tree. And there had been no coffin, just a small metal box of some of her favourite things, mementos that her family and friends had collected. Tamsyn had put a few things in, including a photo of the two of them as teenagers, sitting under this very same cedar tree. It had been on this very spot where she and Merryn had first tried their hands at smoking, where they used to drink cider on a Friday night, waiting for the boys they liked to walk by. Oh, how they had riled the vicar; he'd sent them packing a hundred times, but they would always come back. Hanging around in the graveyard, kissing boys in the alley that ran behind the church. The vicar had never been particularly sympathetic to their claims that it wasn't their fault, they didn't have anywhere else to go and it was impossible to get served in a pub in a town where everyone knew your name. They had been tearaways, the two of them, it was true. But they never meant anyone any harm; they had just been trying their hardest to feel alive.

For a moment as she looked down at the stone at her friend's name, etched into the marble, Tamsyn didn't care about rain, or the cold. Just for a moment it was that warm spring evening again, the evening Ruan had first noticed that Merryn – newly crowned the Queen of the May – wasn't just his big sister's sidekick any more. And it was here, under this very tree, where her brother had fallen hook, line and sinker for her best friend. At first Tamsyn had been a little jealous, but soon enough the three of them became a little unit, a band of dreamers and adventurers leading the town's youth astray, making campfires in the woods, forming new bands from week to week, writing terrible poems and reciting them under a full moon. Tamsyn had drawn a portrait of each and every one of her friends in black charcoal, and she still had them in a folder somewhere, all except one. The one she had drawn of Merryn was buried beneath Tamsyn's feet.

They'd had this idea that they were the first children of Poldore ever to really understand the world and what it was about. They thought that all of the generations before them had simply been sleepwalking. But even then the differences between Tamsyn and her brother had started to grate. She was always plotting ways to leave, and Ruan was always thinking of ways to keep Poldore alive. When their mother declared that she was leaving Poldore for Suffolk, to be near her eldest daughter Keira, who had been barely more than a child bride, nineteen-year-old Tamsyn had jumped at the chance to go with her. Soon after, she had escaped to university and then to Paris. Whereas Ruan had stayed, even taking on the responsibility for their baby sister Cordelia, despite the fact that he was only eighteen. It was inevitable, Tamsyn supposed, as she looked down at the plaque, that someday Merryn would have had to choose between them. She closed her eyes for a moment, trying to hide the tears that merged with the rain, even though there was no one there to see them.

'What on earth are you doing, standing there in the pouring rain?' A male voice, followed by a hand on her shoulder, startled Tamsyn so much that her wet, irresponsibly shod feet skidded out from underneath her for a moment, so that she wobbled like a baby gazelle, and was as much reliant on her captor to steady her as she was keen to be out of his clutches.

'What? What do you want?' she demanded, spinning to face the stranger, taking an unexpected slippery step towards him as if she was indeed fronting up for a fight.

'Oh, oh God, I'm sorry . . .' he said, squinting in the rain as he took in her face. 'I thought you were someone else.'

Tamsyn narrowed her eyes.

'Oh yes, that's your trick, is it? See a woman, standing alone in a graveyard, for God's sake, and use the old "I thought you were someone else" excuse as a trick to try and feel her up? What kind of a pervert are you?'

'I wasn't feeling you up, I was . . .'

'Assaulting me?'

'No, saying hello,' the man said, utterly unrepentant, his grin infuriatingly cheerful.

'I deal with far worse than you in Paris all the time,' Tamsyn warned him. 'Try anything and I'll have you on the floor in under thirty seconds.'

'Well, now you're being inappropriate . . .'

'How dare you, what do you mean? How am I being inappropriate?'

'Threatening to throw Poldore's vicar to the ground!'

'The what, now?' Tamsyn asked him, glad for a moment that the freezing rain had numbed her face into a mask.

'I'm Reverend Jed Hayward.' He repeated the information, offering her his hand. 'The vicar here in Poldore.'

'Well,' Tamsyn spluttered. 'You should be ashamed

of yourself. Grabbing a woman from behind. It's not very . . . vicarish, is it?'

'I . . .' Reverend Jed Hayward laughed out loud, which made Tamsyn want to hit him a little bit. No, actually quite a lot.

'I'm sorry. I thought you were my verger; she's due to come and take choir practice tonight. She's about your height, and in the rain I couldn't make you out clearly. Although, now I look at you, I can see you are quite different. We had a few things to sort out before I left, but she hasn't turned up. I promise you, I am a vicar and I wasn't trying to assault you.'

'You don't look like a vicar.' Tamsyn blinked the rain out of her eyes, to examine the supposed cleric. A man, in his mid-thirties, with a smattering of stubble, hair that was too wet to tell what colour it was, but with a fringe that fell into his eyes and rain running over high, Nordic-looking cheekbones. There was no dog collar, or anything as sensibly identifiable as a cassock. Instead he was wearing a shirt that must once have been white, an opaque veil that now clung to his torso, which, what with its well-defined pecs and an actual six-pack, was one that any of the male models that Tamsyn had worked with over the years would have been proud of.

'What does a vicar look like?' Jed Hayward asked her, apparently utterly unconcerned by the rain that punctuated every word a thousand times over.

'Not bloody gorgeous,' were the first words that popped into Tamsyn's head, but she bit them back just in time.

'Look,' she said, grabbing onto the handle of her case and remembering what she was supposed to be doing. 'Honestly, it doesn't matter. You're the vicar, you thought I was a – whatever it was you said, fine. I've got to go, I'm meeting my family, some of whom I haven't seen for several years and I'm already late, so . . .'

'So *you're* Tamsyn Thorne?' the vicar asked, catching Tamsyn off guard for the second time. 'You're the only sister I haven't met yet, the designer who lives in France. I've heard so much about you.'

'Have you?' Tamsyn asked. That normally wasn't a good thing.

'I'm officiating? At Ruan and Alex's wedding? You know . . . as the vicar.'

There was a moment when all that Tamsyn could do was stand there, hearing the rain thundering in her ears, acknowledging the wet seeping in through her boots to soak her freezing toes, and wishing that the wind might scoop her up and whisk her off to anywhere in the universe apart from right there, right then.

Instead, a whip of lightning cracked against the church spire, causing Jed and Tamsyn to take an instinctive step towards each other, so that they were standing chest to, for all practical purposes, bare manly chest. If Tamsyn had believed in any sort of celestial higher being, she would have put the lightning down to having improper thoughts about a vicar's chest, but right now it didn't seem like a terribly good idea to be standing underneath a tree, even if a sudden strike from the heavens would simultaneously solve her problem with offending vicars and having to wear puff sleeves.

'Come on,' Jed said, picking up her case. 'We'd better get inside.'

'But I'm already late . . .'

'A few more minutes to regroup won't hurt. And I'm late too, now.'

It took Tamsyn a couple of seconds to realise that he'd grabbed her freezing hand and was jogging to church with her in tow, only releasing her fingers once they were inside.

'That's marginally better,' he grinned, shaking his hair like a dog. 'Dry, at least. I turned the heating off in March; didn't plan on needing it again before November.'

'I don't suppose you did,' Tamsyn said, finding herself shivering now that she was out of the rain.

'Anyway, like I said, my verger is in charge of choir practice tonight, not that I can see anyone coming out in this weather. I'm going down to the pub, too, so once I've changed my shirt we can head down there together. I've probably got a raincoat or something that might keep you a bit drier. It's like a branch of M&S in the vestry, people always leaving things in the pews;

once I found a flask full of whisky – that one never got claimed . . .'

The second Tamsyn realised that Jed was hurriedly unbuttoning his shirt, she averted her eyes, but it was a second too late not to notice how the wet cotton of the shirt peeled off his firm chest. Was it possible to be struck by lightning inside a church, Tamsyn wondered, for noticing a vicar's wet chest? She braced herself, but the next time the lightning flashed, seemingly right overhead, it was still outside the window. A few seconds later a distant rumble of thunder followed, and Jed froze for a moment, looking up at the heavens.

'Not a fan of thunder?' Tamsyn asked him.

'Worried about the town,' Jed said. 'It's typical of Poldore people that everyone is hoping for the best and not preparing for the worst. They are all in the pub right now, as if they can simply drink through the worst storm we've seen here in years.'

'Well,' Tamsyn said, 'who knows, maybe they can? Probably do more good than praying, anyway.'

Jed grabbed a towel that was hanging over the back of a pew and dried himself, before pulling on a light grey shirt and a slightly darker sweater that was also waiting there.

'Well, of course you are entitled to your opinion,' he said. 'But so far I have yet to see evidence that getting drunk improves anything. Whereas prayer gives a great deal of people comfort and hope.'

'Hope,' Tamsyn said. 'I always think it's an overrated concept. Much better simply to expect that everything is going to hit the fan, and then be pleasantly surprised if things are less bad than you imagine.'

'Sorry,' Jed said, his brow furrowing briefly as he looked at her.

'For what?' Tamsyn asked him.

'That you feel that way, so pessimistic.'

'I'm not a pessimist,' Tamsyn said. 'I am a realist, and I just don't do the whole happy-clappy thing, that's all.'

'Shame,' Jed grinned. 'You are so going to feel awkward when everyone in the congregation stands on the pews and holds hands during the wedding . . .'

He stopped what he was doing to take in Tamsyn's naked expression of pure horror and then doubled up with laughter.

'Funny,' Tamsyn said. 'A funny vicar, how very modern. I bet you play guitar and rap the Lord's Prayer, don't you?'

'That's a pretty good idea,' Jed said, and Tamsyn found it was hard not to return his smile, although she did her best. She wasn't a fan of do-gooders. She'd met a lot of them, during her life. Always trying to understand her; always trying to work her out. She never wanted to be worked out; she just wanted to be left alone.

'I was just trying clear out the guttering when it

really started coming down. I was up a ladder when I saw you there in that long coat, but then I thought it had to be Catriona, the verger. Either way, good job you turned up when you did – if I'd still been up that ladder when the lightning struck, chances are it would be a small pile of ashes leading the service at your brother's wedding. God does move in mysterious ways. Towel? I'll get you a fresh one, of course.'

'I am, you know, sorry,' Tamsyn mumbled, rather half-heartedly, as he bent down between the pews and produced another towel, from where it seemed he kept an impromptu changing room. 'And not only because I'm dripping on your floor. I'm sorry I accused you of being a . . . pervert. You must think I am an idiot.'

'Not at all.' Jed smiled at her in exactly the way that one person who thought another person was an idiot would do, as he handed her the towel. Tamsyn made a vague effort at towelling her hair, which she let down knowing that the moment it approached anything near being dry it would snake into the same unruly, untamed curls that had blighted her teenage years. 'I'll just change these trousers, and then I can walk you down.'

'Mmm,' was all that Tamsyn could manage to say, waiting for Jed the vicar to strip off his kecks right in front of her, but it seemed that that was where his sense of propriety kicked in.

'Great, I'll be back in a second. I think there's an old golfing umbrella in the vestry too . . .'

'Take your time,' Tamsyn called after him, a little weakly. So, OK yes, she had made a fool of herself with the vicar, that was true. But on the bright side, her mother couldn't be cross with her lateness when it was the vicar's fault, because the vicar's lateness couldn't be misconstrued as sullen sulkiness, like Tamsyn's declining the offer to stay with Alex or Alex's mother had been. After she'd refused, Tamsyn's mother had asked her flat out if she was going to have a problem with Ruan getting married and she'd said no, of course she didn't disapprove of the wedding. She just didn't completely approve. Far away from Poldore, far away from this life of sexy vicars up ladders and torrential rain in June, sometimes Tamsyn forgot how everything had changed back here, and sometimes it slipped her mind that Merryn wasn't still here, living her life with her brother. So much so that it still felt as if the wedding she was about to attend would be featuring the wrong bride, although that didn't make any sense and she knew it.

It was odd, standing at the back of the church, so quiet and empty as it was now, only half of the lights switched on, filling the building with shadows that seemed to be watching her. The sound of the rain outside provided a sort of background static, but otherwise it was completely silent and still.

There had been a time, back in the days of the old vicar, the one they had so shamelessly baited, the one who was bald and fat and looked like a vicar should do, when she and Merryn had been in the choir. It had been her dad's idea. He thought if she'd joined something, she might have a sense of purpose, something that might then tip over into her school life, which she had avoided as much as possible. Every Sunday they'd giggled through the family service, singing like angels and telling each other silly jokes behind their hands through the sermon, until one reached Reverend East and he sent them out, the two of them sniggering all the way up the aisle like a pair of fallen angels.

Laura Thorne had despaired of her rebellious daughter back then, and Merryn's mum had even come round claiming that it was Tamsyn who was leading the other girl astray. Tamsyn remembered feeling especially proud of that claim, although it was not true. She and Merryn had just found everything so completely funny. There was no aspect of life they felt had to be taken that seriously, and that included school and church.

'Right, it's time to brave the elements!' Tamsyn spun round to see Jed pulling on a bright orange Superdry coat, just able to catch a glimpse of an actual dog collar, now tucked under the collar of his shirt, and what looked like dark blond hair as he pulled up his hood. 'If you promise not to attempt to have me arrested for harassment, I'll even let you come under my umbrella.'

He brandished the object at her, like a small boy

playing at swords, and Tamsyn wondered if he really was the vicar, or if she'd accidentally befriended a very attractively built delusional person, because that was normally the sort of thing that happened to her. Mad people on the Metro, angry people on aeroplanes, pretend hot vicars in rainstorms, egotistical but irresistible French fashion designers – that pretty much summed up her life.

'I don't think there's much point,' Tamsyn said, as he opened the door and they observed the sheets of water from the relative comfort of the porch. 'After all, it's only water.'

'That's what Noah said,' Jed said. 'And he had an ark.'

Chapter Two

There wasn't much small talk on the way down to the Silent Man. For one thing, the rain was coming down so hard and heavily that it was impossible to speak without having your words snatched away by the wind. Tamsyn had never known such a volume of water to come from the sky at such speed. Also, she knew that if she opened her mouth she would manage to say something unfortunate. Putting her foot in it was practically her hobby, and had been from the moment she could talk, according her mother. Like the time her Uncle Howard had come for Christmas and she had told him that he was too short to be a grown-up. She was eleven at the time.

Somehow in Paris it didn't matter; in actual fact it was almost a positive in her profession to say exactly the wrong thing to the wrong person at the wrong time. Within the design community she had developed quite the reputation for her cutting wit, ruthless efficiency and determination not to mince words. What no one, not even Bernard, had guessed about the Englishwoman who had somehow infiltrated the heart of the French fashion scene, was that none of it was by design. Tamsyn just had a habit of saying the first thing that came into her head and, as yet, at the age of twenty-nine, it wasn't a trait she had managed to grow out of. So, although she was always honest, often insightful, it was only Tamsyn who knew that her reputation as the '*Reine de Glace anglaise*', who must never be crossed, was entirely accidental.

As the rain ran down the back of her neck, she tucked her chin into the collar of her coat and allowed herself the briefest of moments to ponder on Bernard and what he would be up to now, right now, before deciding that it was probably best not to dwell on it. They had been 'together' for eleven months, since the night he had told her all her designs were '*épouvantable*' – dreadful – swept them off the pattern-cutting table and her into a passionate embrace. Tamsyn, who had been raised never to let any man assume such rights over her person, had punched him very hard on the nose and broken it. To his credit, in between howling in agony, Bernard had found it all very funny. He had apologised to Tamsyn as she'd taken him to a private hospital, to have his nose reset, without any fuss. He told her he wasn't in the habit of pouncing on women the way he had on her, and that he deserved her reaction. The flashing fury in her eyes had just been impossible to resist. Tamsyn had accepted his apology, because in that particular city it was impossible to keep a secret, and if Bernard had been a serial philanderer who preyed on the many much younger and more beautiful women he worked with on a daily basis, she would have known it. It seemed that his philandering was more sporadic and always consenting.

As Tamsyn had dropped him off at his apartment in the early hours of the morning, he'd asked her very sweetly if he might kiss her, and she had allowed it. And it turned out that Bernard, as challenging as he was as a boss, was an exceptionally good lover. So Tamsyn, whose love life up until that point could largely be summarised under the heading 'nothing special', had considered telling him where to go for about five seconds only. Another five seconds after that and she knew she was smitten.

Their affair could have been construed as inappropriate in the work place, of course, but Bernard had a talent for being beguiling at exactly the same moment that he was being infuriating. So despite the lack of any sort of courtship, Tamsyn had found herself very happy to be engaged in a romantic liaison with Bernard du Mont Père. The fact that Bernard insisted on keeping it a secret meant it had that extra frisson of excitement.

In the last eleven months, Tamsyn had learnt that the secret to sustaining her relationship with Bernard was never to let him see that she cared one bit about it, a trick she was rather good at as she had spent much of her life pretending not to care about anything.

And as for her success coming from her association with him, well, if anything the opposite was true. So far not one of her designs had made it to the catwalk, as it was mainly the business and PR side of things Bernard let her handle, although he did sometimes let her have a belt buckle, or a pocket, in one of his designs if he was feeling very generous. And Tamsyn didn't have a problem accepting that; it took a long time to get to the top in the fashion industry, and she'd rather pay her dues than think for even one second that her fondness for kissing Bernard had advanced her career before she had earned it.

'We made it,' Jed said eventually over the thunderous rain, pushing open the door of the pub for her, and for precisely one moment Tamsyn was glad to be out of the wet and in the steamy fug of beery warmth provided by the pub. And then she heard the cheers, and then she saw the banner 'WELCOME HOME TAMSYN!'

And then she wanted to throw herself into the swollen river and try and hitch a lift back to France on the next passing boat.

'Oh God,' she said to a room full of smiling, familiar faces, 'please tell me this isn't a party.'

'Tamsyn!' It was her mother who came and dragged her from the door, nodding politely to Reverend Jed as she hugged her rather wet daughter and unbuttoned her coat while she was at it.

'You're soaked through, you poor thing.' Tamsyn submitted as her mum dragged the sodden coat off her shoulders. 'You look like a drowned rat, and you're thinner. You are too thin, you know. I do hope that fashion isn't giving you body disorders.'

'What's a body disorder, if it isn't your mother always telling you that the body you were born with isn't too thin?' Tamsyn asked Laura, hugging her anyway.

'Mother, let the poor woman get in the door!' Her sister Keira grabbed her hand and pulled her over to a long table that had been made up from several separate ones, and was lined with people, most of whom Tamsyn recognised, such as professional busybody and local aristocrat Sue Montaigne and her husband, Rory, with their children. There was Vicky Carmichael, whom she'd known since childhood and who – she knew from her mother, who despite not living in Poldore for decades still had a hotline on whatever anyone was up to – was now a vet, and even old Jago and Mr Figg the chemist, still hanging in there, neither one of them looking older than the last time she'd seen them, almost as if they had been a hundred years old for all of her life. Of course, her sister Cordelia was there, knocking back shorts at the bar; and Eddie Godolphin, the town's mayor and landlord of the Silent Man, and his wife Rosie behind the bar. Despite the horrible weather outside the pub, inside it was warm, festive and friendly, almost as if they'd decided to hold the wedding breakfast a few days early, only with a great many packets of salt and vinegar crisps in place of canapés. Smiling and waving at everyone, Tamsyn took a seat, while at exactly the same time wondering if she'd be able to wriggle out of the window of the ladies' loo and sneak back up to the hotel in time to order room service.

'Boys! Look who's here!' Keira called to her sons.

Tamsyn braced herself for the onslaught of her nephews, twin four-year-olds, bundles of pure energy and noise, whom Tamsyn always secretly thought were a bit like cats, in that they seemed to seek out the people least fond of children and stick to them like glue. She had been there, at her sister's side, well, actually in the cafeteria a couple of floors down, when they had been born, and usually saw them just at Christmas and sometimes in the summer, if she popped over to Suffolk. The pair of them laboured cheerfully under the misapprehension that she liked them.

'Aunty Tam!' Jamie was the first to hit, closely followed by Joe, the force of the pair of them propelling her back into a chair.

'What?' Tamsyn asked as Jamie hung off her neck and Joe climbed onto her lap. 'What do you want from me? I've got no sweets, no toys, no money, nothing. I'm no good to you.'

'Say something in those funny gobbledygook words,' Joe asked.

'What, you mean French?' Tamsyn asked him,

amused despite herself. When Keira had brought them to visit her in Paris, she had taken them to the Louvre to see the art, and they had giggled a lot about the Venus de Milo's bottom. They had also found the French, speaking their native tongue, in their capital city, utterly hilarious and mimicked anyone they met with the bravado that only four-year-old boys can muster. Thank God they hadn't met Bernard, who was so French he was almost like a parody of himself, as they would have had a field day with him, and Bernard, for all his famous ego, was also rather sensitive.

'Are you coming to sleep with us tonight in the lighthouse?' Jamie asked her, his eyes big and round. 'The waves are so big they are coming almost to the top of the cliff! But Uncle Ruan says the lighthouse probably won't fall in the sea.'

'I said, if it falls in the sea we could say it was a submarine,' Joe said. 'Uncle Ruan says we have to keep a watch out for pirates!'

'You can share my sleeping bag if you like,' Jamie assured her, as if he were offering her the rarest of treats.

'To be honest,' Tamsyn told him, 'I'd rather wear something nylon and with an elasticated waist than go anywhere near your sleeping bag. You have the personal hygiene habits of, well, a four-year-old boy, to be fair.'

'Aunty Tam, we love you,' Jamie told her sweetly.

'And I can tolerate you in small bursts if I've had wine,' Tamsyn told him back, patting him on the head.

'Go and play with that dog,' Keira told them. 'Let Aunty Tam have a rest and get warm. I'm sure she'll play with you in a bit.'

'I won't,' Tamsyn assured the boys, but as ever they refused to believe that she didn't totally adore them. 'Definitely don't come back and expect me to play with you. I won't!'

'It's good to see you, sis.' Keira hugged her as their mother bustled about at the bar ordering Tamsyn food that she no doubt hoped would make her the proper weight for her height.

'You too,' Tamsyn whispered into her ear as they hugged. 'I wasn't exactly expecting this to be such a big deal, you know.'

'I think Mum thought that the more people there were here, the less we would actually have to talk to each other,' Keira whispered back. 'Ruan and Alex went out the back half an hour ago, and we haven't seen them since. Maybe they've done a runner.'

'I wouldn't blame them. Where's Pete?' Tamsyn looked around for her brother-in-law.

'Couldn't make it,' Keira said, the corners of her smile drooping just a little. 'Work. Again. Japan, this time. Couldn't get out of it. You know what it's like with futures.'

'I really don't,' Tamsyn said. Her brother-in-law's job had always been a mystery to her; she only knew it had something to do with making quite a lot of money.

'He couldn't rearrange, or find someone else to step in for a family wedding?' Tamsyn asked.

'He would have if he could,' Keira said, dropping her gaze for a moment, and she twisted the wedding band on her finger. 'He works so hard, and anyway, I don't mind. In a way it's more relaxing that he's not here. You know what he's like; always on email, hates wearing a suit when he's not at work, always telling the boys to keep the noise down to a dull roar . . . This way, we can relax and enjoy ourselves.'

'Enjoy . . . It's a subjective term,' Tamsyn said, returning the wink that Jago, Poldore's oldest, grumpiest and often drunkest working fisherman sent her down the table, and raising her glass to him. 'Anyway, you're here, and I'm here, and . . .'

'I'm here,' Cordelia appeared at her side.

'And we are in a pub, with alcohol, and we are all old enough to get served, so it will all be fine,' Tamsyn said, grinning at her little sister. 'Cordy, my, how you've grown. Which vampire bit you? Do you want me to stake him?'

'You're just jealous that I have my own sense of identity,' Cordy said, tossing her black glossy hair off her shoulders, and Tamsyn had to admit that she really did stand out in her black skinny jeans and black fishnet t-shirt over a scarlet vest, all topped off with what could only be described as a cape, mostly because it *was* an actual cape. During her teens Tamsyn had bleached her hair and then dyed it pink, had got a secret tattoo of a butterfly on her left shoulder blade and pierced her own belly button with a needle, until it went septic and she needed a course of antibiotics, but she had never had the courage to wear a cape in the town that fashion forgot. That was one thing Cordelia wasn't short of, courage . . . 'Mum's right,' Cordelia squinted at her. 'You are too thin – are you a size zero, or what?'

'I'm a ten!' Tamsyn exclaimed. 'I've been exactly the same size since I was nineteen. I'm just tall and leggy . . .'

'Rub it in,' Keira laughed. 'It's really not fair that you were the only one to get Dad's long legs. Well, you and Ruan, and he doesn't even need them.'

'I wouldn't say that. They do come in handy, especially for running away from all of my sisters.'

Somehow Tamsyn had forgotten for a few minutes that the reason she was in Poldore in the first place was because of Ruan, for his impending wedding, and now that he was here, standing next to her, she discovered she had nothing to say, caught as she was between an impulse to hug him and to hide.

'Sis,' Ruan nodded at her. 'Long time no see.'

'No,' Tamsyn nodded. 'Right, well, you know how it is.'

'Yep, five years fly by when you're making dresses,' Ruan said, that familiar storm brewing between his brows.

'Well, I haven't exactly noticed you beating down my door, asking to come and visit,' Tamsyn said. 'Mum did. Cordy, Keira and the kids did. Now I'm here, when have you ever been to Paris?'

'Why would I ever want to come to Paris?' Ruan asked her. 'It's full of French people.'

'Xenophobe,' Tamsyn said, her treacherously idiotic mouth betraying her before she could contain it. 'Although why I should expect more of my brother, the country bumpkin I don't know. Anyway, I see you found a replacement.'

'You—'

'—Are so kind for coming all this way.'

Tamsyn and Ruan broke their deadlock and turned to the newcomer. This had to be her, Alex, the woman that had got to Ruan. She was pretty, but not perhaps the siren that Tamsyn had been expecting. Lightly tanned fair skin, scrubbed clean of make-up, clear blue eyes and a thick mane of dark hair that looked enviably smooth and shiny. Pleasantly made, with hips and breasts, she was exactly the sort of woman who would never fit into one of Bernard's dresses, which, Tamsyn realised as she took in her outfit of a pair of comfortable jeans and a t-shirt, she probably wouldn't give two hoots about anyway. She knew Ruan had met Alex when she'd arrived to take on the job of Cornwall's first female harbour master, but from what Cordelia had told her, it had been their roles as Mary and Joseph in Sue Montaigne's

Christmas pageant that had thrown them together, and then quite a lot of toing and froing had ensued, including Alex saving her brother's life, before they finally got together. Alex looked like a real woman, an ordinary one, and despite certainly hearing Tamsyn refer to her as a 'replacement', she looked surprisingly friendly.

'Well, of course,' Tamsyn smiled. 'Mum said if I didn't come she'd kill me.'

A beat too late, she realised that what she said sounded incredibly rude, at exactly the same moment that Ruan looked like he'd quite like to tip the pint he was holding over her head.

'Mums are very convincing that way,' Alex laughed. 'You should meet mine. I didn't even know her for most of my life, then she turns up out of the blue, breaks into my home and now she's organising my wedding. Funny, isn't it, how just when you think there's no hope for something or someone, everything changes? I wouldn't be without her now.'

Alex's smile was sweet, open, genuine, kind. She wanted this to work, Tamsyn understood. She had asked Tamsyn to be part of her wedding to bring her and Ruan together again, to heal the rift that had opened up between them on the day Merryn went out to sea. Whether she thought it was the only way to banish the last remnants of the ghost of Merryn that still hung in the air, Tamsyn wasn't sure. But she was sure of one thing.

Alex Munro might know Ruan, but she didn't know what had happened between them all those years ago that meant they'd never be close again.

'Anyway, we're really pleased that you're here,' Alex said. 'And you've had a long journey, so have a drink, something to eat and relax. There will be plenty of time to catch up properly between now and the wedding.'

She gave Ruan a meaningful glance and, smiling once more at Tamsyn, she nodded in the direction of an older woman wearing tight white Capri pants and what looked suspiciously like a boob tube.

'Now, I need to go and talk to my mother about some final arrangements with the florists. I'm so looking forward to getting to know you, Tamsyn.'

Tamsyn nodded, and then, catching Keira's eye, said, 'Me too, I'm looking forward to getting to know me too, I mean you, I mean us. I mean, I'm really looking forward to the whole massive wedding thing and all that it entails. Brilliant.'

Ruan watched his departing bride before turning to look at his sister for a moment longer, and then, turning on his heel, he went to the bar.

'Nice work,' Cordelia said, downing a glass of wine that Tamsyn was fairly sure didn't belong to her. 'Way to have a reunion.'

'What?' Tamsyn looked at her and then at Keira. 'What?'

'I just wish you could be, well, like you are really. I

mean, you know, funny and kind and nice . . . Why can't you just come across that way to people that don't know you?'

'I don't even know what you are talking about,' Tamsyn said, though she did.

'It's not her fault,' Keira said. 'Remember Dad?'

The three women were silent for a moment, as they thought of him here in one of the places that had been his favourite, the Silent Man. Every Sunday Mum would send one of them down here to prise him away from the bar to come home for dinner, and there he'd be, always standing in the same spot, his hand wrapped around a pint, talking to his small group of friends. But if you were new in town, if you were perhaps asking for directions or the way to the gents', and it happened to be Alan Thorne that you approached, you could be certain that you'd quake and quiver under his monstrous, furious scowl that showed he absolutely didn't have time to be dealing with a fool like you.

No one, no one but his very close friends, his wife and his children knew that Alan Thorne was one of the kindest, gentlest men that had ever walked the earth, and was very much missed.

'We've all got a bit of Dad in us,' Cordelia agreed. 'Even Keira sulks like there's no tomorrow, but you, Tam, you and Ruan – you're the worst. And put the two of you together, and it's like . . .' Cordelia mimed something that Tamsyn supposed was an explosion. 'World War Three.'

'Well,' Keira said, 'now maybe, but once, the two of them, they were more like twins than the twins are.'

'Things happen,' Tamsyn said. 'People change, they grow up. It's not the law that you have to be best friends with your relatives.'

'Yes it is.' Laura Thorne sat down at the table. 'It is the law, it's my law and I want you and Ruan to get over this silly feud. He's getting married, Tamsyn, to a lovely girl. And I know you want him to be happy as much as the rest of us, so whatever disagreement it was that started this whole thing off, get over it. In two days' time you are going to be a bridesmaid at their wedding, and when you walk down the aisle I want to know that my children are united. Would you deny your mother that one happiness?'

'No, Mum,' Tamsyn said. 'Of course not.'

'So,' Laura said, 'you can forget this silly feud?'

'It's not a feud and it's not silly,' Tamsyn said.

'What is it then?'

Tamsyn shook her head. 'I'm going to the loo,' she said, getting up. 'I'd love a large gin and tonic if anyone is offering.'

How could she explain to her mother, to anyone, especially Ruan, that it was her fault? It was her fault that Merryn went out to sea and never came back.

Chapter Three

Tamsyn grimaced as she stood in front of the mirror in the chilly ladies' loo, and eyed the windows that had been so cruelly secured with iron bars. As she had made her way towards Poldore, she had had a vision of how things would be between her and Ruan. How they'd see each other and embrace, and he'd apologise (first) and she'd apologise and then everything would be the way it had been once before. Why couldn't she bring the poise and professionalism she carried off so well in Paris across the ocean to Cornwall? She blamed her hair; it was like it had a personality of its own. When it was straight and sleek she could keep the worst aspects of her personality in check, but when the frizz got out, it was like the stylistic version of the incredible hulk: there was no telling what would happen next, and before you knew it she'd be walking down a road to melancholy music, hitching a lift.

Because, unlike the vicar, the soaking-wet look did not suit her. Her hair had already begun its inevitable contraction into a frenzied mass about her blurred and pinched-looking face, that was smeared with diluted make-up.

Collecting a bunch of paper towels, she damped them down and scrubbed her face, rather painfully, until her cheeks glowed pink, and dragged her fingers through her hair, for all the good it did.

'You have to do better than this, Tamsyn,' she told her reflection sternly. 'You have to stop being accidentally bitchy, putting your foot in it with vicars and offending your brother's wife-to-be. You have to put your best foot forward, you have to be . . .' Tamsyn struggled to find a word that would fit her face. 'Well, you have to try and be nice. Like you know you are, deep down. A really, really stupid-haired nice person.'

'Only nice?' A young woman appeared in the mirror behind her. 'I always thought you were much more of a lovely.'

Tamsyn spun round and took in a familiar oval face.

'Luke Godolphin! I mean . . . Oh God, I'm so sorry . . . Lucy, wow!' Tamsyn couldn't stop staring at the woman who stood before her. 'I mean, wow. Mum told me you are a girl now. And you are gorgeous, you bitch, look at your hair! I always was jealous of your lovely smooth blond hair, even when you were a boy.'

Lucy laughed. 'I think I was always actually a girl. Now I've just made the outside fit the inside.'

It was true. Back in the old days, Luke/Lucy had been the quietest of their group of friends, always hanging back even then, her long hair falling in her eyes, covering her face, keeping secrets. The boy . . .

the human being she had known back then had worn black skinny jeans and pixie boots, used eyeliner and made friends with the girls instead of making out with them. Although there had been that one time, at a party, when Tamsyn had come across her friend hiding outside in the garden, silently crying. When Tamsyn had asked what was wrong, she had been grabbed and kissed with determination, if not exactly enjoyment. After the kiss had finished, the two of them had looked at each other for a moment, and then burst out laughing.

'Let's ditch this party,' Tamsyn had said. 'It's full of dicks.'

And they'd gone to the woods instead, got drunk, stared at the moon flitting between the trees and talked about how one day the whole world would know who they were. That person, that lost ghost boy who'd never really been there, was entirely gone now.

Tamsyn paused for a moment to take her old friend in. There was the familiar face, the delicate features, the blonde hair that was always long and fine, but the main difference was that now her friend dressed with very good taste, and there something else behind her eyes that Tamsyn had never noticed was missing when they were both kids. It was happiness.

'Yes,' she said, her smile spreading. 'Yes, you know what, it's really odd, but you look exactly like I remember you, or the way that I should remember you.

You do look like you! Oh Lucy, I'm so glad. I'm so glad it all fell into place for you.'

'That's what I'm talking about: lovely, so much better than nice. It's good to see you, Tam.' Lucy smiled and before Tamsyn knew it, the pair of them were enveloped in a hug. 'And things are pretty good now, at least in Poldore they are, but life can get pretty tricky sometimes, still. Some people never want to move on.'

'Who are they? Shall I beat them up?' Tamsyn offered.

'Too late, they've already run away,' Lucy smiled. 'And so, you're back, finally, back to be a bridesmaid at your brother's wedding.'

'I know.' Tamsyn turned to look at herself in the mirror. 'It doesn't seem real, somehow. I know I shouldn't, but I just keep thinking about her.'

'Merryn?' Tamsyn nodded and Lucy went on, 'You know she would have wanted Ruan to be happy, don't you? And boy, is he happy, I mean seriously. I haven't seen that sexy scowl of his in months. They make a good team, and if you give her a chance, you'll like Alex. She's become a good friend to me, the best kind, actually.'

'I'd sort of guessed that when you got the head bridesmaid gig.' Tamsyn bit her lip. 'I'm sure if I tried I could like her, but will she like me?'

'Of course she'll like you,' Lucy laughed. 'If you just stop . . . you know.'

'What?' Tamsyn asked her.

'Being you.'

Chapter Four

The first thing Tamsyn saw when she got back to the table was the rear end of a dog, its grey and white tail wagging furiously, and her heart leapt. 'Buoy! It's you.'

The dog ignored her and, bending down, she noticed that the other end – his head – was firmly buried in her handbag.

'Hey, mutt,' she said amiably. 'There's nothing in there that a little doggy would like.' At the sound of her voice, the dog turned around and Tamsyn realised she was wrong. This was not Buoy; the animal was far too young to be her sometime companion and cohort of her youth. This one was still mostly puppy and, it seemed, particularly partial to her very expensive lipstick, which was now liberally spread around his chops, giving him a sort of 'evil clown' look.

'Whose bloody dog is this?' Tamsyn asked, sticking her fingers into the young animal's mouth to retrieve the mangled lipstick barrel, and instead bringing out a handful of slime.

'Skipper! Naughty boy!' Alex came over from the bar, grimacing as she grabbed the animal by his collar and pulled him away. 'Oh God, I'm so sorry. I thought he was chewing Ruan's old boot out the back – it's his favourite, normally!'

'Sit!' she told the dog, who looked at her for a long moment as if he'd never seen her before, and then, noticing a packet of pork scratchings being opened at the other end of the pub, cheerfully trotted off without a backward glance, positioning himself in front of the unlucky snack owner and proceeding to menace him with his steely, doggy glare.

'You've got him well trained,' Tamsyn said, unable to stop herself from smiling.

'He takes after his father, I'm afraid,' Alex said. 'But with less of the redeeming qualities. His mother is a poodle of very fine breeding, but you'd never know it. He's basically a criminal.' She smiled tentatively. 'I don't know much about make-up, but I know that brand: that's about fifty quid I'll be clearing up in a pooper-scooper tomorrow, right?'

'Its fine,' Tamsyn said, looking at her gooey hand and wiping it on a napkin. 'Really. I work in the industry, and I got that free in a goody bag. It's so last season, anyway; your dog is very behind the times. When I get back to Paris I'll pop the latest shades in the post and he can snack in style.'

'Thank you,' Alex said, 'for being so good about it.'

'He is a very cute dog,' Tamsyn said, glancing over at Skipper, who was now drooling with intent on the owner of the pork scratchings' knee. 'Wait. You said he was like his dad. His dad is . . .' Tamsyn looked around. 'Buoy?'

'You know him?' Alex asked her.

'For a while, back in the day, I used to feel like he owned me. He took a shine to us Thorne kids, and he was always around. I heard about the accident. Mum told me how you saved Ruan, and how Buoy pulled you out of the water. I thought that might be the end of him, but he's still going?'

Alex nodded. 'See for yourself. By the fire.'

Tamsyn pushed through the crowd of people and there, curled up in ball by the open fire, was Buoy, his grey and white hair clean and brushed out, his nose buried in his paws. He looked just the same; well, except that now he seemed to be sporting a rather rakish eye patch.

Crouching down next to him, Tamsyn gently rested her hand on Buoy's head. He lifted it at once, growling, his one good eye menacing her, even though Tamsyn could see he was weary. She held her fingers under his nose for a moment, and wondered if he remembered when, as a younger animal, he used to tag along with her and Ruan, Lucy and Merryn too, sometimes even Cordelia if they couldn't get rid of her, trailing through the woods on long summer evenings, dropping him off at the harbour master's cottage on the way home, sneaking a bottle of beer from old Alf Waybridge as a thanks for wearing the young dog out for an hour or two. Buoy's nose wasn't as wet or as cold as Tamsyn remembered it, but he delicately examined her hand and then licked the tips of her fingers, hoisting himself up into a sitting position and nudging his head under her hand. Finally, someone she could be happy to see without fear of complications.

'He remembers you,' Alex said as she joined her by the fire, smiling. She bent down beside them both and ran her hand down the dog's back, as his tail thumped on the rug. 'Oh look, he's pleased to see you. That's a good sign. Buoy is only ever pleased to see nice people.'

'So, if you were going to accept a character reference from either this dog or my brother, whose would you trust the most?'

Alex laughed and kissed the top of Buoy's head. 'This dog has never been wrong about anything yet.'

The rain outside suddenly seemed to intensify, hammering against the window, and Buoy got to his paws, cocking his head to one side. Shrugging off the attentions of his female admirers, he trotted off towards the pub door.

'He's getting old,' Tamsyn said, as she watched him disappear on some unknown mission. 'I suppose that must mean that I'm getting old too.'

'How old are you now, Tamsyn?' Sue Montaigne asked her, appearing at her side. 'Forty?'

Tamsyn curled her mouth into a tight little smile. Sue Montaigne, descended from a long line of aristocrats, daughter of the family that had once owned Poldore and all who lived in it, and who now still owned what was essentially a castle, built right in the middle of the town. Her family name was such a part of the history of the town that her husband had been the one to change his name when they got married, which pretty much summed up the force of nature that was Sue Montaigne, and who was also very slightly her nemesis.

'Sue, if I'm forty, that would make you about seventy-eight, I think?' Tamsyn smiled and Sue narrowed her eyes. There had been very little love lost between them ever since Tamsyn had held a mini illegal rave one year on the set of the nativity, the day before the pageant took place, and had left Bethlehem looking like it could feature in an episode of *Road Wars*.

'There's barely ten years between us, and you know it. Although you did your best to age me prematurely in your short and terrifying career as a Brownie.'

'Now then.' A heavy arm fell around Sue's shoulder, and Tamsyn grinned as Eddie Godolphin shook himself like a big wet yeti all over Sue. 'You aren't still holding a grudge over that camp-fire incident, are you, Sue? Arson was never proved. All right Tamsyn, love?'

Tamsyn shrieked as he hugged her without any regard for his dampness.

'Eddie, you're soaking!'

'I just popped out to bring the window boxes in; it's

rough out there,' Eddie said. 'Big waves breaking over the harbour, high as houses. Rain's really coming down, never seen nothing like it; reckon we're in for a rocky ride tonight.'

'Sandbag-bad?' Sue asked him, concerned. 'We left Rory's mother looking after the children. I do hope they aren't too upset by it.'

'Might be heading that way; we'll keep an eye on it. Alex has already closed the harbour, so it's the people on dry land we need to keep an eye on tonight. That's if it stays dry land.' He grinned at Tamsyn. 'It's good to see you, girl, you haven't changed a bit!'

'Haven't I?' Tamsyn felt dismayed: she had worked quite hard to banish from her life the awkward, skinny, naughty frizzy-haired girl who had grown up in Poldore.

'Not a bit, still as thin as a rake, I see,' Eddie grinned. 'Hey, Rosie! Bring this girl some chips, would you. She's starving!'

'I'm fine, really, Mum's already ordered me some food . . .' Tamsyn said, but Eddie manoeuvred her away from Sue and sat her back down at the table where her sisters were deep in conversation with her mother. She could see Ruan was at the bar, his arm around Alex's waist, as she talked and laughed with Lucy.

'Now, you sit there,' Eddie said as a plate of sausage and chips was set in front of her, next to another plate of sausage and chips that she suspected also belonged to her, by Rosie who bent to kiss her briefly on the cheek. 'You tuck in, get some meat on your bones, love. And at least tonight I can serve you legally. I remember you and your mates, always hanging around outside, trying to get tourists to buy you alcopops.'

'I'm totally reformed,' Tamsyn told the room in general. 'I haven't been an underage drinker for years, not since I turned eighteen. And I eat like a horse. Although I draw the line at actual horses.'

No one seemed to be listening, and if this had been a welcome-home party just for her, it was certainly over now. Shrugging, she took a chip, scooped up a large dollop of ketchup and popped it in her mouth, closing her eyes for a moment as she revelled in the joys of saturated fat. French food was wonderful, but somehow nothing said 'home' like a really good chip.

Which was when Skipper appeared, positioned himself in front of her and fixed her with a gimlet stare. But Tamsyn didn't mind; she was happy to share. She had two dinners, after all.

'Aunty Tam, do you want to come and play with us now?' Joe asked her as he appeared, his brother behind.

'No,' Tamsyn said. 'I never play. I don't do playing, as you well know.'

'We'll hide,' Jamie said. 'You look for us, count to twenty-seven million and a hundred.'

'I'm not going to,' Tamsyn called after them. 'I never play. Ever!'

'So, still single?' Laura asked her, sliding along a seat so that she could interrogate her daughter.

Tamsyn had decided early on not even to attempt to explain her relationship with Bernard to anyone, but especially not to her mother. Laura Thorne had done that thing, that thing that only happens in films and books; she'd fallen in proper romantic love with Tamsyn's dad and they'd never stopped feeling the same way about each other in all the years they were married, and even after her dad had died. Tamsyn knew how much Laura still missed the one love of her life, even if she rarely talked about it any more. And she also knew that if there was one thing that Laura Thorne wanted for all her children, it was that they could find the same happiness she had. Well, Keira had been married for the best part of ten years, Ruan was about to be married and Cordelia had big plans and dreams, and seemed quite content to tell any potential suitors where to go in no uncertain terms. Tamsyn was the obvious target for her mother's matchmaking attentions. But she couldn't tell her about Bernard, because Laura would never understand why Tamsyn chose to be in a relationship with a man that was all business, except when it wasn't. She would never see what it was that Tamsyn got out of it, which was fair enough because a lot of the time Tamsyn wasn't that sure either. The only thing that she was sure of was that it seemed to work.

'What does that word even mean, if you really think about it?' Tamsyn said, feeding Skipper another chip.

'It means that you don't have another person in your life,' Laura said. 'That you don't have that companionship that can mean so much.'

'Well, that's not true,' Tamsyn said. 'I've got you, and my sisters, those horrible children who won't leave me alone . . .' She couldn't bring herself to mention her brother. 'There are loads of people in my life determined to keep me company whether I like it or not.'

'But not that special someone, someone you can fall in love with,' Laura pointed out. 'Share everything with.'

'I am sharing everything, all the time. Not just with one person at a time. Look, I'm sharing my dinner with this dog, right now.' Tamsyn pointed. 'Why is it so important to be in what you call love?'

'What do you think, Vicar?' Laura caught the eye of Jed, who'd been pretending not to listen in, half in conversation with Sue's husband, Rory Montaigne, who'd been doing his best to explain the very complicated plot of his as yet unfinished novel to the vicar, and by the look on his face Tamsyn guessed it wasn't the first time he'd heard it. The Reverend Jed Hayward seemed perfectly happy to get sucked into a tricky mother-and-daughter conversation if it saved him from Rory's epic fantasy. 'Do you think love is important?'

'Love,' Jed said thoughtfully. 'Love is putting the welfare of others ahead of all else. It's sacrifice, joy, contentment and fulfilment. Yes, I think love is what makes us human.'

'Well, yes,' Cordelia said, picking up another unattended glass, this time one that looked like lager, and downing it. 'And it's about meeting someone you want to snog the face off too, right?'

'Well,' Jed blushed, rather charmingly, Tamsyn noticed. 'I would say that was more of an animal instinct.'

'Even you must fancy someone, Vicar,' Cordelia said, and Tamsyn realised that her little sister was rather neatly diverting her mother's attention away from her and onto the poor, unsuspecting Reverend Jed. 'I mean, it's allowed isn't it, in the C of E, getting together with another person. A woman . . . Or a man?'

Jed raised a brow at Cordelia, who did her best to look innocent.

'I'm just saying, you've lived in Poldore for more than two years now, and we've never seen you on a date,' she grinned mischievously. 'And it's not like you haven't got options. How many ladies does the St Piran's sewing circle have, at the last count?'

'Forty-seven,' Jed conceded.

'That's one heck of a lot of hassocks,' Cordelia pressed him. 'And how many are currently single?'

'I don't actually know!' Jed laughed. 'Most of them are retired, and one of them is a man.'

'Thirty-eight, thirty-eight single women who are all secretly hoping that you need someone to help you manage that big old vicarage, but we've never seen you with a woman. Or otherwise.'

Tamsyn was reasonably sure that Cordelia had made up the figure, but she delivered it with such confidence that nobody questioned her knowledge of the marital status of the sewing circle.

'And there is a very good reason for that,' Jed said. Cordelia leant forward in her chair, as the vicar looked into her eyes with his silvery-blue gaze.

'I just haven't met anyone I want to snog the face off yet,' Jed replied, and this time it was Cordelia's turn to blush.

'Well, neither has Tamsyn,' Laura said. 'She's not what I'd call a churchgoer, but all my lot were christened . . .'

'I better go and look for the boys,' Tamsyn stood up abruptly before her mother could make an attempt to foist her onto a man of God. 'I must have had time to count up to twenty-seven million and a hundred by now – at least, it certainly feels like it!'

The boys were not hard to find.

In fact, they had forgotten to hide at all, and instead were standing one above the other on the stairs that led up to the pub's bedrooms, their noses pressed against the window as the storm raged outside, the lightning brightening the sky into blazing day for a few seconds each time it ignited, thunder seemingly rumbling in one continuous roll in the heavens.

'Monsters,' Jamie said, apropos of nothing, as he looked out at the sheets of rain driving against the window. 'Look, Aunty Tam, monsters!'

Tamsyn stood behind them, and saw the huge tree in a neighbouring garden swaying back and forth like a sapling, its thick green leaves trembling as it writhed against the storm. It did look a little bit as if the tree was doing its best to drag up its roots and run away. The wind wasn't so bad that it could bring down a tree that big, was it, Tamsyn wondered, guessing that if that particular tree came down, quite a considerable amount of it would end up crashing through the window and coming to rest on the spot where the boys were standing. How bad had it got out there? As she watched the weather tearing at the trees and roof tiles, a distinct feeling of unease settled in her stomach. Now she wished she'd paid attention to the weather forecasts on the radio in the taxi – and what was it the driver had said about a super-storm, what did that even mean?

'Come back into the bar,' Tamsyn said, taking her nephews' hands and leading them away from the window. 'I'll buy you both a fizzy pop full of sugar that will keep you up all night.'

'And then will you do some drawing with us?' Jamie asked. 'I've got my colouring pens.'

'No,' Tamsyn said. 'I never do drawing.'

'But Mummy said your job is drawing and colouring in,' Joe said.

'Did she now?' Tamsyn found that it was quite hard to argue that point. 'Well, fine, I will do one drawing. A small one, and then I want you never to bother me again, because you know I don't like playing with you.'

'Can it be a drawing of a very fat alien pirate with an orange head?' Jamie asked.

'What, you want me to draw a picture of you?' Tamsyn said, sending the boys into peals of laughter as they ran ahead of her into the bar.

'Looks like you're their new favourite aunt,' Ruan said. Had he been waiting for her to reappear, Tamsyn wondered?

'No, I am their favourite aunt to annoy, that's a completely different thing.' She hovered for a moment, wondering if he was going to say something else, or if she should. Or was he, like she was, thinking of the things they'd said to each other the last time they were together? Things that seemed to make it impossible to say anything now?

None of it seemed to make sense to her – to be back here, back in this place and time, to be standing opposite the person whom she had once felt closest to in all the world, and to be here for his wedding. His wedding to a woman that Tamsyn had only just met. She wasn't part of Ruan's life any more, that was the truth of it; she'd written herself out, out of Poldore's history, on the day that they had stood around Merryn's empty grave. And there was no way she could undo what had been done. Sue, Eddie, Lucy and the rest, they might still see her as that mischievous, skinny little girl who never stopped doodling, or that angry teenager, always getting into trouble, but that girl was long gone. They say that people never really change, but Tamsyn had transformed herself a long time ago into the sort of person who only ever looks forward, the sort of person who is happy having an affair with a man who will never own up to her in public, the sort of person who, when it comes to it, will always be able to manage alone. And she had begun that change the day after she told her brother it was his fault that Merryn had drowned, that he had driven her to her death. That day changed everything, including her, for ever. Because she'd hurt her brother, and damaged their relationship beyond repair, not because she believed what she said to him. Because of her guilt, guilt she still struggled with.

That was what made it so hard to look him in the eye now.

'Thank you,' Ruan said finally, 'for coming. Alex was pleased that you said yes.'

'And you?' Tamsyn asked him. 'Were you pleased?'

Ruan was silent, his eyes dropping to the floor. 'I want to put the past behind us, Tam. I'm starting a new life now. I want to be able to move on without any more . . . regrets. I will try if you will.'

Before Tamsyn could reply, Buoy appeared, soaking wet, leaving a trail of water behind him.

'Where have you been, Buoy?' Ruan asked as he shook himself, sending icy droplets cascading in a halo all around him.

Buoy danced, paddling his front paws for a moment, before running towards the exit and then back again, barking. It was a high-pitched, urgent bark, one that meant he wanted a human to pay attention to him.

'It looks like he's trying to tell us something,' Tamsyn said. 'Maybe some kids have fallen down a mine shaft.'

That wasn't entirely impossible, since there had been quite a tin-mining industry in the area in the past, and the old shaft had been left up on the moor behind the town.

'Although the last time he made this much fuss was because Alex and I hadn't given him any prawn crackers from the Chinese takeaway. He does love a prawn cracker.'

There was a silence between them as the conversation petered out, and the dog continued to run to the door and back again, yelping insistently.

'Well, I'm going anyway,' she said. 'So he can come out with me, and I'll see if there's anything he's trying to tell us. I'm staying at the hotel. Mum's got my number, so if there's a fitting or a rehearsal or something I have to be at, tell her and I'll be there.'

'Are you going?' Alex asked her, as she came to join her husband-to-be. 'And what's up with Buoy?'

'I'll check out whatever it is on my way to the hotel.'

Tamsyn pulled on her coat, which was still soaking. 'I'm . . . erm . . . looking forward to the dress-fitting. It will be so interesting to see what you've chosen.'

'Right, oh God, you will probably hate your dress,' Alex said, anxiously. 'I've got no idea what suits me. My mother chose everything. And you haven't met my mother yet. She would give Madonna a run for her money.'

Tamsyn hesitated, and then ever so briefly kissed Alex on the cheek.

'You would look lovely in sackcloth,' she told her. 'And as for the rest of us, it doesn't matter what we look like. We're only there to make you look good!'

Alex smiled and unexpectedly hugged her. 'Buoy was right about you,' she whispered in her ear.

'I'll see you tomorrow,' Tamsyn said. 'I'm now going to try and sneak out without my mother noticing, otherwise she is going to try and persuade me to stay with you all, and much as I love my nephews, I'd rather poke my own eyes out with a spoon.'

The door of the Silent Man threatened to fly off its hinges as Tamsyn opened it, Buoy shooting past her legs, though he waited for her on the cobbles, the wind lifting his ears and blowing them across his one good eye. For a moment Tamsyn felt that if she let go of the iron railings that stopped drunk people tumbling down the steep steps, she might very well be swept up in the maelstrom herself and end up somewhere that definitely wouldn't be Kansas. She could see Buoy barking at her, but couldn't hear him over the din of the storm. Grabbing her suitcase from the porch, she made her way down the steps and watched as he ran a few steps ahead of her and waited. He seemed to want to go in the same direction as her. Maybe he fancied a nice hotel room and room service too, Tamsyn thought.

Fifteen more minutes of discomfort, she told herself, and that was exactly where she would be. Except Buoy had very different ideas.

Chapter Five

The rain was still falling in a constant torrent, rather than in drops, and although it was almost the longest day of the year, and it should still be daylight as it was only just before nine o'clock, the sky was as dark as a starless midnight. Water rushed down the steep streets towards her, cascading down the steps that were the quickest way up to the hotel, flowing over Tamsyn's feet and around her ankles, its volume increasing with frightening speed.

As she followed Buoy she watched as a plastic recycling box was easily dislodged from its place on a doorstep and set on a new path that would no doubt involve a trip out to sea. She remembered the stream at the top of the hill, the one that ran through the meadows behind the hotel; normally it was barely more than a trickle, often even completely dry during a long summer, but it must have burst its banks by now, and the overflow was finding its own route towards the sea. Tamsyn had never seen anything like it, and she gasped as Buoy slipped into the freezing deluge, sliding down the street a few feet. Catching his collar, she dragged him upright, but he was determined to carry on up the hill. He really must want whatever it was that he'd found up here, near the top of the town.

Shuddering, Tamsyn drew her sopping coat around her for comfort more than the scant protection it offered, instinctively ducking as another flash of lightning briefly illuminated the sky, followed a moment later by the deep rumble of thunder so loud it sounded as if it were ricocheting off the walls of the houses. Ten more minutes, Tamsyn told herself, then a bath and wine, with possibly a soggy dog for a secret room guest.

The wind howled in her ears, tearing at her hair; it seemed to pinch at her cheeks, making her almost want to laugh. Right now she should be sipping something expensive in Club Silencio, dressed in something gorgeous and wearing a pair of shoes that were guaranteed to cripple her. Instead, she felt rather like she should be traversing the plains of Siberia, and that the major threat to her feet came from frostbite, and it was June! Tamsyn made herself smile, because although she didn't care to recognise the feeling, for the first time in her life she was frightened by the weather.

For the briefest of moments the wind dropped like a stone, and there was a fraction of deep silence, and then came a sound that made Tamsyn stop dead in her tracks and listen. She just caught a snatch of sound, a thin, high howl – no, more of a wail – a sound quite different from the roar of the wind that enveloped them once again. Was it an animal, or something human? Was this what Buoy had been fretting about? Had he heard something trapped and in distress?

Dropping her hood for a moment, so she could hear better, Tamsyn listened. Yes, it was still there, the noise – a cry? Perhaps it was a trapped cat, or a fox caught under a fallen tree. It was definitely the source of Buoy's distress, as he'd made his way to the gates of the churchyard and was barking at her, taking a few steps into the darkness of the churchyard and then back out again, as if he were as afraid of what he thought was there as much as he wanted Tamsyn to see it. Nevertheless, whatever it was, she found she couldn't walk away from it: Buoy wouldn't let her. She had no choice but to investigate.

Tamsyn left her suitcase parked by the wrought-iron gate and walked up the path towards the church. As she made her way into the churchyard, the water was ankle deep, sloshing between her toes. The old cedar that had stood sentinel over so much of her life creaked dangerously, looming towards her in the dark. It was so dark that the shapes of the ancient gravestones could only just be made out, and the steep grassy slopes that led up away from the path, now banks to the fast-flowing river running around her ankles. The lightning cracked against the steeple and, for a split second, Tamsyn saw it. The source of the wail, the reason that Buoy had been so insistent that she look in the churchyard.

Floating towards her on the inches of dirty water that now covered the path entirely was a Moses basket. It was a sight so incredible, and so unexpected, that Tamsyn thought at first that she must have been hallucinating, but then the lightning flared again, revealing the same image, and the dog barking at it, and at the tree that strained against its roots. In the seconds it was illuminated Tamsyn could see the basket was made of woven wicker, with a hood and lined with blankets, blankets that covered up . . . what? Her heart stopped for a second, her feet slipping from underneath her as she made her way towards the object, the crying now unmistakable. There was a baby, in a Moses basket, out in the cold in the middle of the worst storm that Tamsyn had ever seen, a real-life, actually *alive* baby. And it wasn't any hallucination; she wasn't safely tucked up in bed in her room at the hotel dreaming it all. This was real.

Then the creak of the tree became a groan, followed by deafening splintering sounds. Tamsyn just about had time to turn around to see one great branch crashing down towards her, and dived out of the way into the mud as it impacted with the path.

'Oh my God,' Tamsyn spoke, but she was unable to hear her own words. Kneeling down in the water, she dragged at a crushed blanket that was now caught under the fallen branch, but she could not free it. 'Oh my God, oh no.'

Then a damp head butted her, and she found Buoy next to her, a crumpled, sodden Moses basket at his side, and within, a bundle that was wailing inconsolably. Buoy must have snatched the basket out from under the tree just in the nick of time.

'Oh Buoy, oh God,' Tamsyn found herself trembling as she carefully took the bundle out of the basket, unwrapping the soaking blankets to find the relatively dry baby at their heart, still warm and yelling with enough gusto to reassure Tamsyn that it had not been out in the storm for very long. Carefully, although her fingers were now numb with cold, she discarded the wet blankets, feeling helpless as the baby's tiny face contorted in horror at the sudden cold that gripped it. She took the tiny but furious little person and did the only thing she could think of, which was to pull one arm free of her shirt and sweater, wriggle it inside her top and then take hold of the baby against her skin, tucking the child as safely as she could under her clothes. Once there, the baby stopped crying at once, making Tamsyn worry about whether it could breathe, but as she peered down the neck of her sweater she could just about make out the child turning its face towards her skin, perhaps hopeful it might find a source of food there.

But what now? Tamsyn looked around. The town seemed abandoned; there wasn't even a light on in any window. The mother had to be somewhere nearby;

surely there was no way that any mother would just leave such a tiny child to the mercy of the elements, was there?

'Hello!' she called out, shouting to try and make herself heard. 'Hello, are you there? Hello? Call out if you can. I can help you!'

What if she too was caught beneath the branches of the fallen tree? Switching her phone to flashlight, Tamsyn did her best to look into the branches, and could see nothing. Buoy wasn't bothered about the tree, either. He was standing at the gate waiting for her, his frame tiny and frail-looking because he was soaked to the skin.

The thought had struck Buoy before Tamsyn, it seemed – the baby had been abandoned. Wherever the baby's mother was, she was more than likely not to be found in the churchyard, and Tamsyn knew she couldn't stay there for very much longer before the rain would soak through her sweater and shirt too and the baby would get dangerously cold. She was about halfway between the pub and the hotel, and as there were people in the pub that she knew, people who would know what to do, Tamsyn make the snap decision to go back.

'I'm taking your baby and going to get help,' she shouted into the wind, just in case the mother was nearby. 'I'll take it to the Silent Man, where there are people who can help. I'm staying at the hotel. My name is Tamsyn Thorne! If you are there, if you can hear me,

I will make sure your baby is safe, I promise. But please, please get help! And please come and find me. I'm sure it's not as bad as you think it is!'

Tamsyn looked around her, at a scene that could have featured in some sort of disaster movie, and thought that perhaps it was just about as bad as it could possibly be, except that the baby was warm, dry-ish and wriggling in her arms. She had to move now.

'Right,' she said to the baby, reassured by Buoy's steadfast presence at her side. 'Now all we've got to do is get back to the pub, with only one free arm, and not get crushed like your Moses basket did . . .' As she said the words, a nickname for the baby popped into her head. 'Not a problem, little Mo, not a problem.'

Chapter Six

'I've got a baby!' Tamsyn cried out as she entered the pub. She'd expected to find it as she'd left it, but instead it was mostly empty now except for Jed, Sue Montaigne and her own family.

'Wow, you left terminally single and came back knocked up,' Cordelia said. 'Vicar, come quick, we've got a bona fide miracle!'

'No, no . . .' Tamsyn staggered in and sank down on a chair, Cordelia's face changing when she saw the state her sister was in. 'I m- m- mean, I found a baby, an actual baby in a Moses basket, in the churchyard.' Shrugging her coat off, Tamsyn used her free arm to lift the hem of her jumper and her gathering audience gasped as she revealed her precious cargo.

'I told you babies came from up jumpers,' Jamie whispered to Joe.

'It's a real baby,' Tamsyn repeated, just in case anyone was failing to believe their eyes. 'It might have died if Buoy hadn't heard it crying, and then, and then the tree came down and I thought it was crushed, but he saved it.' Buoy, shuddering himself from the cold, was sitting at Tamsyn's knee, continuing to protect her find.

'And this arm's gone numb, so could somebody please take it? It would be an awful shame if I dropped it now.'

'Of course.' It was her mother who broke the deadlock, stooping to scoop the infant into her arms, a fact that the baby didn't seem at all pleased about, mewling as Laura held it against her shoulder.

'Buoy, look at you,' Alex stripped off her jumper and rubbed at the dog's drenched fur. 'We need towels. Eddie? We've got to get them all warm and dry.'

Eddie nodded. 'I'm not sure how much longer we'll be dry here. I've never seen waves like these, and what with the storm coming from both fronts, it's looking bad out there.'

'I'll go out, see if anyone needs help with sandbags,' Ruan said, grabbing his coat. 'Are you OK, Tam?'

'I don't know. I found a baby, an actual baby,' she repeated as shock kicked in. 'In the rain.' Tamsyn shook her arm vigorously before realising that she still had her jumper rucked up just under her bra, which was when she noticed that a police officer in full uniform was standing at the bar.

'Oh, thank goodness,' she said. 'You need to call people, more police, doctors, ambulances, the coastguard. Mary Poppins. You need to call all of the people and get them right here, now. I found a baby!'

'Sorry, young lady,' the policeman said to her, not unkindly. 'It is very unlikely that any of that is going to happen now. I was just here to evacuate the pub. The rivers have burst their banks top and bottom; the high tide's swamping half the town and Poldore has been completely cut off. Me and the lads are down here to get everyone out from the harbour to the esplanade before it's too late.'

It was then that Tamsyn burst into uncontrollable tears.

'Moses basket.' Sergeant Jeff Dangerfield wrote down everything Tamsyn told him, as Eddie, Lucy and Rosie packed the pub up around them, carrying what they could to the first floor with the help of Jed, Alex and Cordelia. Alex's mum had left with Lucy's keys as well as her own, as they lived virtually next door to each other, in the hope of being able to move their most precious items to safety.

'Remember, save the dresses first,' Alex called after her as she headed into the night in a silver padded raincoat. 'Oh, and take care!'

'Any sign of the mother?' Sergeant Dangerfield looked around him, clearly nervous that it was taking so long to move these people on.

'No, I looked for as long as I could,' Tamsyn said, huddled in a blanket and now wearing two of Lucy's thickest jumpers and a pair of Lucy's jeans, which hung off her even when secured with a belt. The baby, also wrapped in a dry blanket, was back in the crook of her arm, the only place it seemed to be peaceful, its eyes closed resolutely as if it simply didn't want to know what was going on. Now Tamsyn had a chance to look at it properly, she could see that – young as it was – it had been cared for by someone. It was dressed in a tiny white vest under a white buttoned-up Babygro, and a little soft red cardigan and matching hat were keeping it warm under a sort of furry all-in-one affair that had ears like a teddy. Whoever had left the child had done their best to ensure that it was warm enough, which it would have been on any other June night. Perhaps they had left before the rain had really started to set in, or left the basket in a place of safety, unaware that the water was going to rise enough to flood the shelter of the church porch and wash the baby away. Whatever had happened, Tamsyn just had to look at the tiny teddy-shaped buttons to know that the person who had done them up could never mean this child any harm.

She watched the closed little face for a moment longer as everyone else bustled around them, preparing for what, she wasn't sure. What a way to meet the world! Soon the poor scrap would be getting hungry, if it wasn't already. And it couldn't stay in her arms for ever, even if, as far as it was concerned, that was the beginning and end of existence.

'We can't stay here much longer,' Sergeant Dangerfield told them, putting the notepad away. 'I'll radio St

Austell to tell them about the baby, but now we need to get everyone to safety. I've still got other houses to get to. I need to get people to higher ground . . . I was thinking, the hotel.'

'Castle House,' Sue Montaigne said. 'It's high enough and strong enough not to be washed away by a bit of water, and we have the empty moat, which should go a long way to making sure the flood doesn't breach our defences. And it's big enough to take in as many as we need to.'

Ruan came back inside from the storm. 'I'll help you round people up,' he told Sergeant Dangerfield. 'It's really bad out there. You're going to need help moving the elderly and the sick. We can collect dinghies, waterproofs.'

'I'll help too,' Alex said.

'No,' Ruan said. 'You'll be needed up at Castle House, and I think Buoy needs you too; look at him. He's made the trip once. I'm not sure his gammy leg can do it again.'

'Are you using my insane love for a dog to stop me from doing something that you consider to be too dangerous for a woman?' Alex asked him.

'No,' Ruan told her gently. 'I'm using it to stop the woman I love breaking her leg or worse in the days before our wedding.'

'On this one occasion I will concede,' Alex nodded, looking at Buoy, whose head was on Tamsyn's knee, as he felt duty-bound to stay close to his charge. 'Hopefully Skipper will pull me up the hill on his lead.'

'I can help you, Ruan,' Jed volunteered.

'Vicar, the thing is, we need someone to get this lot up to Castle House safely,' the sergeant said. 'And I know you are more than up to the job.'

A look passed between the two men that Tamsyn couldn't identify.

'Honestly,' Sue said. 'We're women, not poor helpless creatures that can't manage a bit of rain.'

'Ms Montaigne, I promise you that I have never in all my years of knowing you ever thought of you as a poor, helpless creature,' the sergeant said. 'However, that baby there is very vulnerable, and it's as bad out there as I've ever seen it. Worse. People get killed in storms like these. I think we'll be lucky if we don't lose someone tonight. Time is running out before the water is under the door, and I happen to know that the vicar here has the sort of training that is going to help you manage the trip.'

'Training?' Sue turned her gimlet eye on Jed. 'What haven't you told us, Vicar?'

'I used to be a boy scout,' Jed told her.

'Look, if we are going to go, can we go?' Tamsyn said. 'The baby needs food, a nappy and a place to lie down, like a bed. Can you put a baby in a bed, or maybe a drawer . . . a manger?'

Just at that moment, the lights snapped out.

'Right, that seals it.' The sergeant crossed to the window and peered out. 'The whole town is out. The storm must have bought the power lines down, which is dangerous in itself. I'd better get out there and, Vicar, I'm relying on you to keep these ladies – and the baby – safe.'

'Oh, for goodness' sake,' Sue said, and although Tamsyn couldn't see her, she thought she was most likely rolling her eyes. 'Castle House has its own petrol-run generator – it's as old as the hills but has never let us down yet, and we've plenty of firewood. I'm sure I've still got some newborn clothes somewhere. The only thing we will need to find is formula and nappies.' Sue thought for a moment. 'The Perkinses have just had a baby, and Elaine was poorly so couldn't breastfeed, so I'm sure they will have some we can borrow. I will go and collect some – no arguments, Sergeant, I think you'll find I can take care of myself. The Reverend can take this lot up to Castle House – the portcullis isn't locked. Rory, you get the urns out from the cellar, start tea – and there twenty loaves of bread in the freezer and a ton of jam in the pantry – we can feast like kings tonight!'

'Were you preparing for the apocalypse?' Cordelia, nanny to the Montaigne children, asked her boss.

'You clearly have no idea how much my children eat,' Sue said. 'Now, chop, chop – I think you'll find that's water seeping under the door. Toodle-pip!'

Sue clapped her hands together, her eyes glowing happily.

'Ms Montaigne . . .'

'No point in trying to stop her, Sergeant,' Rory said. 'She's got that look in her eye. I'll venture it's the same one her relative had during the Spanish Raid in 1595.'

'Oh, my pub,' Rosie said, looking at the water that was gradually seeping into the carpet. 'Oh Eddie, this is bad. It's really bad.'

'It's all right, love.' Eddie held his wife, kissing her. 'Come on. We can worry about the pub once we know we've got all our people safe, OK? Whatever happens here can be fixed, in time.'

'Right,' Jed said as the group began to don extra coats and jumpers. 'If everyone does exactly as I tell them, we will make it. I promise you.'

And Tamsyn didn't know why, but she believed him. She might not believe in God, but the vicar seemed like exactly the sort of person it was sensible to put your faith in.

Chapter Seven

'Stay close behind me,' Jed told them, as the shock of the cold and the rain that instantly drenched the small party made Tamsyn want to head back into the pub, even though she knew it was a bad idea. Her instinct was to hide away, to find a safe spot, a bed, maybe, and crawl under it, but that was the worst thing she could do, especially with a tiny life strapped to her chest by a scarf in a makeshift sling.

'Stick close to the buildings. There seems to be quite a current now. The water's really coming down.'

'And up,' Cordelia said, glancing over her shoulder. When Tamsyn followed her gaze, she could see that seawater now covered the square.

'Right,' Jed nodded briskly. 'We are going to do this as quickly as we can: no talking, no deviating. Keep your eyes peeled; there's bound to be debris, possibly falling tiles, trees, shop signs. You are each responsible for keeping an eye on the person ahead of and behind you. Keep a tight grip on the boys. Smaller ones don't do so well in fast currents. If you need help, shout out. Let's go.'

Tamsyn was surprised by the genuine fear that

coursed through her body as she began to follow Jed against the flow of the water that was tumbling down the narrow maze of steep streets, white-water rapids coursing through the town at devastating speed. It was as if the town she had grown up in had vanished entirely, lost in an alien nightmare version. Tree branches, plants and bits of fence tumbled past them at speed, and the downward drag of the water tugged at her legs, giving her the feeling that she could easily pitch backwards at any moment. Just as they neared the church, almost at the top of the hill, a terrifying metallic roar seared through the air and a car juddered into view at speed. Jed covered Tamsyn's body with his, pressing her and the baby back against the wall of a cottage, as the car veered dangerously close to the huddled group.

'Mummy, I'm scared,' Jamie said, clinging onto Keira, along with his brother. Keira did her best to look calm, although Tamsyn could see the anxiety wrought in her face.

'It's an adventure,' she told her boys, who were now both in tears. 'Just like in your storybooks!'

'And we are almost there,' Jed told the boys brightly, smiling for them. 'It'll be a walk in the park now. A piece of cake, made by the Poldore WI, which we can all have a big piece of once we are inside, OK?'

Tamsyn saw him glance just briefly at the churchyard, which was now entirely underwater. Merryn's headstone was probably lost in swirls of dark water, seeing as the cedar tree now lay crumpled across the path that led to the church.

'Come on,' he said grimly and they set off once again, veering right to take a narrow alley that cut off the corner and led to the gate to Castle House, water cascading down the steep steps like a waterfall. Tamsyn didn't think that in all her years living next door to the fanciful Victorian ideal of a castle, she'd even noticed that the bridge that led to the entrance went over a narrow but deep moat, probably because it was now filled to the brim with water for the first time in living memory, keeping the house and grounds that lay beyond the ramparts thankfully dry.

Fortunately Sue hadn't been mistaken when she said that the small, door-shaped gate that had been cut into the portcullis was open, and as they stepped through into the courtyard, it was as if the wind couldn't reach them behind the high walls, and finally the ground was dry beneath their feet. Tamsyn wasn't aware how much she had been holding her breath until she let out a long sigh of relief. They had made it.

'I'll get the generator going,' Rory said, heading off at once towards an outhouse.

'And I'll check on the children and Granny, and then I'll find some baby clothes and nappies,' Cordelia said.

'Come on, Buoy.' Alex set the old dog down, whom she'd carried for the last few yards after his legs gave way, bending over for a moment while she caught her breath. Tamsyn noticed how he leant against her legs, rubbing his muzzle against her knee as if in thanks, while Skipper, jumping around her feet, barked in excitement as Sue's dogs came out to greet them, yapping and baying, and suddenly the haven of the courtyard was filled with noise.

'Hey, Skipper, it's your mum,' Alex said as a regal-looking poodle led the doggy delegation. 'Come on, everyone, let's get inside. I'll put the kettle on.'

They had only been in the kitchen for a few minutes before the lights came on and Cordelia returned.

'The kids are up; they weren't scared by the storm – in fact, they're bouncing off the ceilings with all the excitement. Rory's mum was very pleased to see me; I think she was at the point of throwing herself from a turret. I'm going to take them some hot chocolate, maybe throw in a bit of brandy, see if I can get them settled. What about it, boys?' She grinned at Jamie and Joe, who were drenched through and clinging onto their mother. 'Fancy a hot bath, a warm drink and then a bed-bouncing competition?'

'I'm tired,' Jamie said, rubbing his fists into his eyes. 'And so is he.'

'You say that now, but you wait till I've given you a double espresso with ten sugars . . .'

'Wait a minute . . .' Keira said, as the boys, who were

always intrigued by the idea of getting something they shouldn't have, went to Cordelia.

'I am joking,' Cordelia said, as she began to lead her nephews away to get dry. 'Or am I?'

'Come here,' Laura said, unzipping Tamsyn's borrowed coat and slipping it off her. 'Let's have a look and see how that little one's doing.'

Tamsyn supported the child as her mother untied the makeshift sling from her back, taking its meagre weight in her arms.

She was surprised to find a pair of black eyes, wide open, watching her as she looked at the little face.

'Hello there,' Tamsyn said, feeling that she should probably say something. 'I am sorry, you've had a terrible first few hours, I know. But you are in a safe place now, and there will be lots of people to help you, I promise.'

'I've got formula!' Sue appeared, her hair dripping around her face, meaning it took a moment or two for Tamsyn to realise she was crying. 'It's awful out there, terrible.'

'It's OK, love,' Rory said. 'It's not that bad.'

'It is that bad.' Sue shook herself, straightening her shoulders and stiffening her upper lip. 'The ground floors of all the waterfront cottages are ruined, water's rushing in from the sea and down from the hill. It's awful. I saw your mum, Alex, she's on her way with Ruan. She told me to tell you she put the dresses upstairs, so they should be OK. She stopped to help with the sick people. Seems like half the town has come down with some sort of stomach flu, and they can barely walk. The lifeboat crew are bringing them up here. Oh, I can't bear it – my beautiful town being torn apart.'

'Suddenly the dresses don't seem important any more,' Alex said absently.

'But the town,' Sue continued, her voice quivering. 'My town . . . It's mayhem. Ruan and the lifeboat boys are doing their best, bringing people in. We are going to get very busy here tonight. Brace yourselves.'

'Here.' Lucy took a tin of formula and two bottles from Sue. 'I'll sort this out. You get dry, and get the kettle on.'

'There's a steam steriliser still in the pantry,' Sue said. 'Luckily I never got round to giving it away.'

Cordelia returned. 'Right, the boys are in the tub but they want you, Keira. I think they are still a bit shaken up by the trip up here,' she said, dropping a bundle of clothes onto Tamsyn's lap. 'And here are some fresh clothes and a nappy for the little one, Tamsyn. Better get back to my charges, and I'm taking a bottle of wine, Sue. Come on, Keira, you can come too. If there's two of us drunk in charge of children, there's much less likely to be an accident.'

'Me?' Tamsyn looked around. 'You want me to dress the baby? There must be someone else who can dress an actual baby. I've never done it before.' She held up the

Babygro, which seemed like an impossible maze of arms and legs that might have been made for an octopus rather than a human child. 'I mean, how do you get their arms in? Are babies' arms bendy?'

'Go through to the snug,' Sue told her. 'You remember where it is? I made a fire in there, and it should still be going. It's much cosier than in here. I'll bring you some tea and cake in a minute.'

'Yes, but how do you get this thing onto this thing?' Tamsyn asked her, lifting first the Babygro then the baby.

'I'm sure you can work it out,' Sue said. 'Aren't clothes your job?'

Tamsyn looked around, but everyone was busy with some sort of preparation, and even as she wondered about how a person was supposed to stand up while there was another very small person in her arms, the first set of refugees arrived through the door, shepherded by her brother, a gale blowing in after them.

'Catriona,' Jed rushed to support a woman in her forties, who stumbled against him. 'When did you come down with this?'

'I don't think she's that chatty,' Ruan said. 'We brought her up in one of the boats, lucky really. Her front door was open; she'd collapsed in the hallway. Loads of people have come down with it, so we'd better try and find a place for them away from everyone else so as not to spread it around.'

A young woman threw up noisily into a plastic bag that the man she was leaning on held for her.

'Yes, they need beds at once,' Sue said. 'Rory, Catriona looks like she can hardly walk. She can go in your study, onto the sofa bed. It's about time it was used as a force for good. Mabel, James, Dinah and the others can go in the old nursery suite. Fortunately I've been getting ready to move Meadow down there, now she's getting so grown up. That will take six of them at least, and if any more of the sick turn up, well, we'll cross that bridge when we come to it. Go on then, Rory!'

Tamsyn noticed the exchange between the husband and wife, but didn't really have time to think about it. Jed and Ruan helped the sick woman to Rory's study, and Rory led the others up the stairs.

'Do try not to throw up on the Axminster!' Sue called out after them.

Feeling a little queasy herself, Tamsyn got to her feet gingerly and went to find the snug.

It was a reassuringly warm little room, lined with books and piles of old board games. Family photos dating back at least fifty years crowded every surface, and best of all, the one tiny, vaulted window overlooked the courtyard, shielding the room from the worst of the weather. Tamsyn found that she was still terrified, even though they were now in relative safety. Then again, maybe it wasn't the storm that frightened her so much; maybe it was the baby itself that she seemed somehow to be in charge of, despite her lack of any sort of qualification in that area.

'I had a hamster once, you know,' she told Mo as she lay the baby down on a rug at what she judged to be a safe distance from the embers of the fire. 'It died.'

For several minutes she looked at the Babygro, turning it this way and that, trying to fathom out what was the back and what was the front, and then once she thought she'd worked that out, she looked at the tiny child lying before her and decided that it was simply impossible to dress its little body without breaking it.

'You could stay in those clothes,' she suggested, staring into the bottomless black eyes. 'Maybe when you get too big for them, you'll shed them and grow new ones, like a snake.'

The door opened and Jed popped his head round. The dog collar had gone again and his shirt was open at the neck. He had a very nice neck, smooth and kissable.

'Catriona looks like she needs to sleep, so I thought I'd come and see how you are doing.'

'Well,' Tamsyn said, 'on a scale of one to ten, I'd give myself a minus eleven. Who's that lady you were helping? I didn't recognise her from the last time I was here. Are you good friends?'

'She's my verger,' Jed said. 'Lay clergy. I couldn't run the church without her, and yes, we are close friends.

She and her mum moved here from St Austell a couple of years ago. She lost her mother a few months ago and it hit her hard; they'd always lived together, you see. I've been keeping an eye on her, making sure she is adjusting to life on her own, but I obviously failed her tonight. Poor woman is as sick as a dog.'

'Well, you did have one or two things on your plate,' Tamsyn said, nodding at the baby. 'I'm sure she'll understand. I was very grateful you were there when we were walking up the hill. And now I'm hoping you'll guide me through the minefield of baby clothes.'

Jed smiled, glancing at Tamsyn as he knelt on the rug beside her. 'You look like you could use a change of clothes, too; the bottoms of those jeans are soaking.'

'Oh . . . I . . . My suitcase! I left it at the church. It's probably halfway to America by now!' Tamsyn felt a moment of grief as she thought of her expensive case packed with clothes that she had carefully collected over several years, now probably all gone, swept out to sea. But they were only clothes, not people or animals. Although she did feel like she'd had one of the most meaningful relationships of her life with that vintage Dior tweed skirt and jacket.

'Ah,' Jed said. 'Well . . . maybe Cordelia could lend you something?'

'Oh, it doesn't matter.' Tamsyn kicked off the heavy boots she had borrowed and peeled off her wet socks.

'Now tell me, how do we change this baby's clothes without breaking it?'

Jed took the Babygro and arranged it into the shape of a baby on the floor.

'It's simple enough,' he said, reaching for the child and laying its body on top of the garment. 'First of all, we have to take these damp things off, don't we, little one? Yes we do! Yes we do!'

Tamsyn blinked at him, the hunky vicar, talking like a loon to the tiny child whose dark eyes were now firmly fixed on his face. Unlike most of the people she met in her day-to-day life, he was very difficult to categorise. He seemed much too young to be a vicar, although Tamsyn had to admit that there probably wasn't a lower age limit on the position, apart from being an actual adult. He was definitely too handsome, though. If there wasn't a rule about handsome vicars, there should be. The only light in the cosy little room came from the fire, which cast his high cheekbones in bronze, finding gold highlights in the long fringe that swept over what Tamsyn had now noted were silvery-blue eyes. And he didn't have the body of a vicar either: his shoulders were broad, his forearms, revealed as he pushed up his shirtsleeves to gently remove the layers of the baby's clothing, were strong, muscular. And the way he had led them up the hill, utterly calm and capable, it was almost as if it wasn't the first time he'd been caught in that sort of situation. Maybe he wasn't a vicar at all, Tamsyn mused; maybe he was an undercover cop posing as a vicar to unearth some sort of corruption in the WI, or maybe he was both a vicar and an MI5 operative, and spent his weekends jumping out of helicopters and then skiing down mountains to tackle super-villains ... And maybe she was a bit over-tired and emotional.

'Pull yourself together, Thorne,' she told herself silently. 'No time for bouts of mentalism in the middle of a crisis.'

'Tamsyn?' Tamsyn blinked, realising that that probably wasn't the first time he had said her name. 'See – if you pull the clothes off the limbs, rather than the limbs out of the clothes?'

'And what if it tries to escape, when you're dressing it? Climbs a curtain, or something. What then, a net? Mousetrap?'

'You're funny,' Jed chuckled, and Tamsyn didn't have the heart to tell him that she wasn't entirely joking. She really had no idea what babies were capable of doing at what point in their lives. She was fairly sure that newborns weren't that mobile, but that was about the extent of her knowledge. For example, it certainly felt like the twins had been talking non-stop since the day they were born. They were talking whenever she left them, and still talking whenever she saw them again, even if her visits to Suffolk to see her mum and sister were months apart. It was entirely possible that they were engaged in one long, mammoth conversation.

'No, this little thing is only a few hours old,' Jed told her. 'Won't be able to roll or move very much for a good few weeks yet.' He smiled down at the baby. 'Amazing, isn't it? All that is going on outside, and this tiny spark of life still manages to ignite. Now this is the tricky part, but they normally make the neck of these vest things nice and wide, so that you can just ease it over their little head, thus . . .'

'Oh God, what's that?' said Tamsyn, as Jed revealed the baby's tummy and a stump of something fleshy appeared above the nappy. 'Oh no, is it hurt, did I do that?'

'You don't know much about babies, do you?' Jed shook his head.

'I don't really see a lot of babies in my line of work,' Tamsyn said. 'I see quite a lot of small dogs in handbags, but it's not quite the same thing.'

'Well, anyway, that is the umbilical cord, or the end of it. The mother must have known enough to sever and tie it off, hopefully using sterile equipment. It looks like a pretty good job, but it needs to be checked by a doctor.'

'So that's normal, then?' Tamsyn asked him, wrinkling her nose. 'The stump?'

'Yes, and in a few days it will go black and drop off and leave a tummy button.'

'Ew,' Tamsyn looked appalled. 'How do you know so much about babies, anyway? Have you got a harem in the vicarage, and dozens of secret children living in Poldore?'

Jed laughed. 'No, no children yet. I'd like to be a father one day, if I meet the right person. Before I came to Poldore I worked abroad a lot. I spent some time in Rwanda, rebuilding an orphanage that had been destroyed. It was an all-hands-on-deck sort of thing; we were literally building around the children. I learnt a lot there about childcare.'

'That's an amazing thing to have done,' Tamsyn said.

'Not really,' Jed told her. 'It was my job. And now, the moment of truth. Which I think is an honour that should be down to you.'

'What?' Tamsyn asked.

'The nappy, if you can call it that. It seems to be more of a sort of tea towel . . .' Jed peered at the curious bundle that had been secured about the baby with a safety pin. 'This little one needs a fresh nappy, and I think it's only right that you are the first to find out if we have a little girl or boy on our hands.'

'Me?' Tamsyn stared down at Mo, who was sucking hard on a fist, and was clearly hungry.

'Yes, look at the poor little scrap. Come on, let's get him or her changed and dressed and then he or she can have a bottle.'

'Right,' Tamsyn said. 'I mean, it's only a nappy, right?

I've seen worse. I've seen purple and green polka dots in the Spring-slash-Summer season. This can't be worse than that.'

Steeling herself, she held her breath and opened the improvised nappy.

'A girl,' she smiled. 'I knew Mo was a girl.'

'You checked already, did you?' Jed asked her.

'No, I just . . . I just knew, I suppose,' Tamsyn said. 'I mean, look at her, she looks like a girl, doesn't she?' The two of them looked down at her red, wrinkled face, framed with fine, black, newborn hair, and Tamsyn did have to admit that her certainty must have been based on something other than aesthetics. Newborn babies were surprisingly unappealing to look at, especially considering their fragility, and even just looking at the tiny pink and red little person awakened something inside her that she had never felt before; a primeval urge to protect her. Jed handed her a baby wipe, and trying to look much more confident than she felt, Tamsyn dabbed the wipe on Mo's cheeks.

'Um,' Jed repressed a smile. 'It's for the other end. The other cheeks.'

'I knew that,' Tamsyn said, applying the same technique to Mo's bottom. Taking the new nappy, she carefully lifted Mo's chubby legs, and, sliding the nappy underneath, did it up with the sticky bits of tapes, sitting back on her heels to admire her handiwork.

'To think,' she said. 'I once sewed six thousand

crystals on a princess's wedding dress, and changing a nappy was a million times more nerve-racking that that, but I did it!' She beamed at Jed, who returned her smile. 'You can dress her, though. I don't want to break her now.'

She watched as Jed tucked Mo's little arms and legs into the Babygro, which was far too big, tying knots on the ends of the legs and rolling up the sleeves as much as possible.

'Here we are!' Lucy appeared in the doorway and handed Tamsyn a small bottle of formula, and put a plate with a large piece of coffee and walnut cake on it on a small table that was piled with thick novels. 'I tested it, it's the right temperature.'

'Well, what do I do with it?' Tamsyn asked her, getting to her feet and sitting back in the chair.

'You stick it in one end. I'll leave you to guess which one,' Lucy chuckled.

'But what about Mo?' Tamsyn asked. 'She's a beginner too, will she know what to do?'

'She'll know,' Jed smiled as he placed the dressed baby back in Tamsyn's arms.

Nervously Tamsyn took the bottle and rather gingerly placed the tip to the baby's lips. Amazingly, she seemed to know exactly what it was for, taking the teat between her lips and beginning to suckle.

'There you go, Mo,' Tamsyn found herself cooing. 'That's better, isn't it? Bet you were starving.'

'There, you're both naturals,' Lucy said.

'I'm not sure about that,' Tamsyn said. 'There must be about a dozen people in this building better qualified to take care of this poor child than me.'

'Nonsense,' Jed said. 'You're the one that found her, the one that saved her.'

'Well, you could argue that that was Buoy.'

'True, but he would be worse at nappy changing than you,' Jed said. 'And there is one really good reason why you are the best person to take care of Mo.'

Tamsyn waited.

'You're the only one that thought to name her.'

'Vicar!' Sue's unmistakable clarion call echoed down the hallway outside the door. 'Vicar, are you free to minister?'

'I'll check back on you two later,' Jed said. 'Right now I am being called to a higher purpose.'

'I'd better go too,' Lucy said. 'Sue's got me and Mum on sandwich duty. I'll let everyone know Mo's a girl!'

'Alone at last, hey, Mo?' said Tamsyn, watching as the baby's eyes closed while she sucked. 'Look, I'll be straight with you. I've got no idea what to do with a baby. I stayed away from the twins until they were potty-trained and could behave reasonably well in a restaurant. But I do get it, I do get that for whatever reason you are alone in the world and you need a person to be on your side. Well, I will be that person, OK?

Until we find your mum, until the water recedes and the roads are open again, I'll be your person and you'll be mine. And I will try really, really hard not to drop you.'

Just at that moment the door was pushed open and Buoy trotted in, looking the very definition of dog-tired. He took a moment to snuffle at Mo, checking that she was OK, and then settled at Tamsyn's feet, drifting quickly into a deep sleep. It seemed as if Tamsyn wasn't looking after Mo all alone after all, and she found the thought deeply comforting.

Mo was asleep, her rosebud lips parting as Tamsyn withdrew the empty bottle. Dimly remembering something about burping babies so that they didn't get colic, she carefully lifted the little girl onto her shoulder and rubbed her back, and was rewarded after a few seconds by a surprisingly sonorous burp that had Tamsyn feeling rather triumphant about her childcare skills. That was until she felt the warm trickle of a little regurgitated milk make its way down her back.

Chapter Eight

'Goodness, I've seen everything now,' her mother said as she opened the door to the snug.

Tamsyn started; she must have drifted off for a moment, the weight of a dozing baby on her chest soothing her to sleep in the warmth and comfort of the snug. Panicking a little, she looked down and found Mo still sleeping peacefully, her face turned towards Tamsyn's chest.

'A baby suits you. You should get one of your own.'

'Mum, really?' Tamsyn said wearily, sitting up a little. 'You're going to give me the "Why are you still single and childless" talk now? You do know that we live in the twenty-first century, right? A woman is not defined by the man in her life, but by her own achievements, and I've actually had quite a few of those.'

'I do know that, and I'm proud of you, and the life you've made for yourself in Paris,' Laura told her daughter. 'I just want you to be happy.'

'I am happy,' Tamsyn said, wondering if that was really true. She was busy, but her work never gave her a moment to pause and properly take in everything that she had achieved. She knew a great many people that she wouldn't exactly call friends, but with whom she spent a great deal of agreeable time, and then there was Bernard. And Bernard made her feel things that were probably best not to dwell on, not when her mother was in the room, and even though none of those things could exactly be called happiness, they were surely enough. If she thought about it, she was more than content with her life. Happiness, well, that was a negligible concept, a fleeting state of affairs that could only ever slip away. It was much better to have the kind of life that she had, one that was so much less likely to disappoint. One that was . . . satisfying.

'Well, it's mayhem out there! Sue and your brother have brought half the town here, by the looks of things, most of them sick with this horrible bug thing. Looks like we are bunking in with Cordelia. She's put the boys in with Sue's children. Apparently they are having some sort of sleepover, although there doesn't seem to be much sleeping going on. She's even found an old Moses basket for the little one.'

'Oh,' Tamsyn looked down at Mo. 'Given that her first experience of a Moses basket was a near-death one, I'm not sure she'll feel like giving it another go. And she really seems to like cuddles.'

'All babies like cuddles,' Laura said. 'You were the same, the worst out of all of you for not wanting to sleep on your own. Honestly, I think you'd have still been sharing my bed by the time you were sixteen if I hadn't put my foot down.'

'Sorry, am I interrupting?' Alex said, as she came in. 'Thought I'd see how you were holding up in here.'

'We're fine,' Laura said, keeping up the habit of a lifetime of answering for her children.

'Are you OK, dear?' Laura asked Alex. 'Not exactly the sort of drama a young bride-to-be needs.'

'Oh, I'll worry about that when the sun rises,' Alex said. 'Right now I'm just pleased that we've got most people who needed help to safety, and everyone seems pretty well, although Catriona is very poorly. The vet is looking at her now, and then she's coming to check on the baby.'

'The vet?' Tamsyn asked. 'Vicky the Vet?'

'Our GP is on holiday, so she's the nearest thing we have to a medical expert,' Alex explained. 'Sergeant Dangerfield wants a word too. And I'm glad to see Buoy is nicely ensconced in here with you. I think the younger dogs were starting to annoy him, and he does seem to be attached to the little one.'

'We're calling her Mo,' Tamsyn said. 'She's a girl baby.'

'That's nice,' Alex grinned. 'Not sure if I should congratulate you, or something.'

'Well, we are all set up upstairs for you when you are ready,' Laura told her. 'Cordy's prepared a few feeds for you and the bottle warmer is out in the kitchen.

Follow the sound of children refusing to sleep and you'll find us.'

Laura bent down and kissed Tamsyn on the cheek.

'I am proud of you, and everything you've done in Paris, but you know what? I don't think I have ever been more proud of you than I am tonight.'

'Well?' Sergeant Dangerfield asked Vicky Carmichael as she took the stethoscope away from Mo's chest. 'How's the little mite doing?'

'Well,' Vicky said. 'I'm obviously not a paediatrician, but I've delivered a lot of baby mammals in my time, and I'm a mum, so I know a healthy, content baby when I see one. Temp normal, colour good, she's feeding well, she's had a wet nappy. Her weight is good, too; a little over seven pounds according to these kitchen scales. I'd say she was less than a day old, probably, certainly very lucky that you found her when you did. I think that for now she's safe and well cared for, and in about as good a shape as she can be, considering what she's been through.'

'Right then, I'll just radio through to social services and see what's what,' Dangerfield said. 'Back in a mo, Mo.'

He chuckled to himself as he left. 'Mo, Mo.'

'You must feel a bit shell-shocked,' Vicky smiled at Tamsyn. 'It's not every day you find a baby floating down the road.'

'I haven't really had time to think about it,' Tamsyn said. 'I expect I'll be freaked out at some point; well, more freaked out, anyway . . .'

'Well,' Vicky knelt down next to Buoy and stroked his side. 'If you've got this old trooper keeping an eye on you, you'll be fine. I'd thought I'd lost him, you know, after he went into the water with Alex and your brother, but this is a dog that would not die.'

Vicky bent over Buoy and kissed the top of his head, before pressing her ear to his side for a moment and then kissing his ear.

'Now then, Buoy,' she whispered. 'You know that Alex wants you walking down the aisle with her, don't you? You hang in there, OK? Rest and stay well, you've got things to do.'

'Is he . . .?' Tamsyn couldn't say the rest of the sentence.

'He's in pretty good nick,' Vicky said. 'But I'd be happier if he'd slow down a tad in his old age. Not even a dodgy leg and one eye can stop him performing his heroics.'

'I am pretty sure the baby wouldn't have made it without him,' Tamsyn said.

'There's life in the old dog yet.' Vicky smiled. 'And lots of cake too, after all the treats he got in the kitchen.'

Sergeant Dangerfield returned. 'Tamsyn, I've spoken to a lady at social services, and she's running a background check on you as Mo's temporary carer.'

'Wait, what?' Tamsyn said.

'Well, someone needs to be officially in charge of her until we can get to the proper authorities. So I've named you, as you found her, and the Reverend Hayward, as she was found in the church, and he's a very capable man, pillar of the community and all that. I'm sorry, I assumed that you were willing to take care of her. Hopefully it will be just overnight.'

'Oh I am, but I thought of it more like babysitting,' Tamsyn said. 'I wasn't expecting a police check.'

'Got a criminal past to hide?' Sergeant Dangerfield asked her, and Tamsyn chuckled until she realised that the question was serious.

'No, of course not, well, not unless you count the lemon kick-flares I designed for my end-of-year show. And there was this one time I shoplifted some lipstick from Mr Figgs . . . Oh, and I got brought home by a policeman when I was sixteen for being drunk and . . . let's just say, singing Meatloaf a little bit too loud in a residential area at two in the morning, but I don't think any of that went on my record. Maybe the fire, the fire might have done. But it was mostly an accident, so probably not.'

Dangerfield's face did not crack. 'Right then, you and the Reverend are her official carers. I asked him and he was happy to be named. As such, it's procedure to run a police check. It looks likely your responsibility will only carry over until tomorrow, but we are endeavouring to have her in the hands of professionals at the earliest opportunity.' He looked up at the window. 'Things are bad out there now; no idea what the damage will be, especially now it's dark. But I'm glad she's in good hands. It means I can get back out there.'

'She shouldn't be in the hands of a professional though, should she?' Tamsyn asked, stopping him for a moment. 'Well, she should as a last resort, but really she should be in the hands of her mother. I mean, what are you doing to find her? She's probably a young girl, probably terrified, and who knows what sort of physical state she might be in . . . and in this weather. Has anyone searched the churchyard, or the church? What are you doing to find her?'

Sergeant Dangerfield pressed his lips into a thin line.

'It won't have escaped your notice that we have been dealing with something of a crisis here,' he said. 'We don't have a station in Poldore. It was pure good luck that me and two of my men were here, and it's been down to your brother and the other lifeboat volunteers that we've managed to bring so many of the elderly and vulnerable and sick up to Castle House . . .'

'I'm sure Tamsyn understands that, Jeff,' Jed said as he entered the room, which made Tamsyn feel sure he'd been standing outside listening through the crack in the door. 'She just has a very real concern for the child's mother. And she's right to. Things move quickly in these situations, you know that. In many ways, the storm, the flood, the delay in being able to get Mo to the hospital or social services, it's a blessing in disguise. It allows some time to try and bring her and her mother back together again. No one is saying that you aren't doing everything for the community; we know you are. But Tamsyn wouldn't be doing her job as Mo's carer if she wasn't concerned about reuniting her with her mother.'

'Maybe she is already here,' Tamsyn said, as Mo stirred in her arms. 'I mean, if so many people have arrived, maybe her mother is here and we might be able to work out who she is. Where is everyone?'

'Sue's filled up her guest rooms, but a lot of the younger ones are in the great hall,' the sergeant said. 'Sue seems to have a number of camp beds and sleeping bags left over from her days as Brown Owl. Bit of a festival atmosphere, if anything; you know what teenagers are like.'

'The chances are she is a teenager, or at least someone young and with no one to turn to.'

'Well, there's not much we can do at the moment,' the sergeant told her, not unkindly. 'We'll see what the situation is like at dawn, when hopefully the roads will be clear, and we might be able to get a call through to the local media, the radio stations. We will do our best to find her, Miss Thorne, I promise you.'

'OK,' Tamsyn said, smiling politely. 'Well, my sisters and mother are waiting for us in our allocated room. It's going to be quite the family reunion!'

Tamsyn got to her feet, realising that she had managed to stand while holding Mo and felt quite proud of herself. 'I'll look forward to getting an update from you in the morning.'

Sergeant Dangerfield nodded.

Jed waited for the door of the snug to close before turning to Tamsyn.

'What are you up to?'

'Who says I am up to anything?' Tamsyn asked him, offended, although as it turned out, she did have a plan.

'Your face,' Jed smiled as he looked at her. 'Your face has a textbook "I'm up to something" expression.'

'And that's why I always lose at poker,' Tamsyn said. 'I'm an open book.'

'Although I do like to think you don't get to do my job for the number of years I've done it and not learn to read people,' Jed said. 'Tell me, what's your plan?'

'My plan? Well, really,' Tamsyn said. 'I bid a good-night to you, kind sir.'

'"Kind Reverend", if you are going to go all Jane Austen on me,' Jed reminded her. 'And you seem to have forgotten that we are both responsible for Mo. If you have some sort of crazy idea to go out there and look for her mother yourself, then you need to tell me about it.'

'I wouldn't take her out in this!' Tamsyn said. 'That's not what I was planning. I was just thinking of taking her for a walk around Castle House, where there are people. In the great hall, the kitchen. I might not have lived in Poldore for a few years, but I know this town. Every single person here will have heard about Mo by now. They will know that I'm the one caring for her; they will know who she is. I just want to see if there is anyone here who reacts to her in a certain way, who could be . . . you know . . . her mum.'

'Not actually a bad idea,' Jed said, looking mildly surprised. Tamsyn wondered what it was about the first few hours of their meeting that had obviously led him to think of her as mostly bonkers: whether it was the hair, the weeping, or the inability to know how baby clothes work. Or perhaps he'd heard tales of her dissolute youth. But in any event, he seemed genuinely surprised that she had a good plan, which rankled with her a little, although she kept this to herself.

'That's what I thought,' she said, pulling Lucy's baggy jeans up around her hips, and wishing to God that Lucy hadn't found her a pink and fluffy top to wear with it. Smart women with good plans rarely wore pink fluffy tops, in her experience.

'Well, they've brought a lot of people in. The odds are still slim that she is here, but it's possible. God has a strange way of bringing together the people who need to be together, when it really matters.'

'Right,' Tamsyn said, suddenly feeling rather awkward. 'That's nice.'

'That makes you uncomfortable,' Jed noticed, tipping his head to one side as he appraised her sudden shift in body language. 'Me talking about God. Even given that I am a vicar and do my job in a church. It's probably the equivalent of getting freaked out when you start telling everyone that purple is the new black.'

'Purple will never be the new black,' Tamsyn assured him. 'And no, it doesn't make me uncomfortable, honestly.' Although secretly she had to admit that she found him easier to talk to when she was noticing his beautifully shaped upper lip, and the way his skin had a slightly golden hue to it. It had been a very long time since she had been so instantly attracted to a man. How typical of her life that when it did happen it would have to be a man who was so . . . well, just so different from her in every single way. 'It's just that . . . well, I don't think I believe in God.'

'Don't think you do?' Jed asked her. 'So there's room for doubt?'

'I don't know, maybe not, actually. I'm sorry. Do you have to attempt to convert me, or something? Is that in the handbook?'

'No,' Jed smiled. 'But I am not going to pretend that I don't have faith, or stop talking about it, or expressing my love for God. Is that OK?'

'Seems fair enough,' she said. 'Now, let's go out on operation Mo.'

*

Just as Sergeant Dangerfield had predicted, it seemed to be the younger dispossessed people of Poldore that had collected in Sue's great hall, some on Sue's strange collection of camp beds that she had had stowed away in one of the many old outbuildings, stables and sheds that made up the maze that was Castle House. Some had grabbed a duvet or a sleeping bag on their way out, while others were huddled under one of the many rough-looking pink and grey blankets that Sue had also produced. Unlike the older generations who were engaged in muted conversation in the kitchen, speculating on what bad news the dawn might bring, anxious about the damage that was being wrought right now on their own houses, and hoping for the best for the people they hadn't been able to contact, the teenagers were thoroughly enjoying the whole impromptu sleepover.

They'd grouped themselves in little circles, and there were a couple of guitars playing laboured covers of numbers that Tamsyn thought she might recognise as being by the latest rock band. There were some furtive-looking couples who jumped apart the moment Tamsyn and Jed entered the room, clearly up to a little more than holding hands under those prickly blankets, and that particular scent of hormones hung in the air, signalling that youth was present and very much incorrect.

'Looks like you're making the most of the circumstances,' Jed said cheerfully to a group of long-haired boys, who scowled at him from under their fringes, which made Tamsyn smile. He might be a handsome vicar, and popular within the town, but talking to teens was not his forte. Not like her; she worked in fashion. It was her job to be down with the kids.

'Great playing,' she told a girl with a guitar. 'Coldplay?'

'No,' the girl said, shaking her head and looking at her friend in disgust. 'They suck.'

'Oh, well . . .' Tamsyn shifted Mo from one arm to the other. 'Very derivative of Coldplay, if you ask me.'

'I didn't,' the girl said. 'I wrote it myself, actually. It's had thirty-seven views on YouTube.'

'Wow! Thirty-seven thousand?' Tamsyn asked.

'No. Thirty-seven.' The girl scowled and blushed, and Tamsyn remembered that when she was about the same age she would move heaven and earth not to have to exchange words with someone more than a couple of years older than her. There was no playing it cool with these girls, so she might as well stop trying.

'Is that the baby?' Another girl from another group spoke up. This one looked less frightening than the last, with lovely wavy blonde hair and the sort of complexion you only have when you are that young. 'The one that someone left at the church?'

'Yes,' Tamsyn said, eyeing her closely for signs of recently having given birth. 'We're very worried about her mother . . . She must be frightened and lonely and in need of medical attention . . .'

'Oh my God, she is *so* cute,' the girl stood up, and turned out to be wearing nothing more than an outsize t-shirt that was just long enough to cover her behind. Jed turned away at once, and started talking in earnest to a group of boys, who rather hastily hid what it was they had been looking at on their mobile phones under their sleeping bags as he crouched down next to them. 'I thought she'd be ugly or something, but she's not even!'

'Uh-huh,' Tamsyn blinked, searching the girls' open faces for any similarities to the baby, but she had to admit that unless Mo's mother turned out to be a red-faced, thin-haired tubby person who bore a striking resemblance to Buddha, it was very unlikely that she looked much like her daughter did at the moment. Besides, she had read somewhere that babies always looked like their fathers when they were first born, a primeval evolutionary development that stopped the male of the species feeding its young to a sabre-toothed tiger when they became too inconvenient.

'Poor little thing nearly didn't make it,' Tamsyn said to a chorus of oohs from the girls, as they clambered to their feet and crowded around the baby, cooing over Mo, who for the moment was oblivious to their attentions. If any one of these glossy-haired, creamy-skinned young women was her mother, then the baby didn't have a sixth sense about it, and besides, none of them looked like they had just given birth. They all looked as if they had just arrived from the sea in half a clam shell, every single one of them an Aphrodite in her own way. Tamsyn remembered how Keira had looked after the twins had entered the world. She resembled Wile E. Coyote, just after he'd been run over by a steamroller driven by the Road Runner. These girls, barely more than children themselves, all looked as fresh as daisies, despite the drama of the evening.

'I don't suppose you have any ideas, do you?' Tamsyn asked them, glancing over at Jed, who was resolutely engaging a young man in a deathly tedious conversation about the finer points of Minecraft, without raising his eyes towards the gaggle of half-dressed girls. 'I mean, anyone you know? Any friends at school, perhaps? Friends of friends, who might have got into trouble? Not known where to turn?'

'Oh, well,' the first girl said, cheerfully. 'Daisy Chambers got pregnant. Her dad said he'd kill her boyfriend. It was *hilarious*!'

'Did she?' Tamsyn asked her, looking around. 'Is she here?'

'No, they live up top,' the girl told her, 'on the other side of the river where the flooding isn't so bad. But she wouldn't have left her baby on a church doorstep. For starters he's, like, six months old, and secondly, she and her boyfriend moved in with her mum and dad, and she still gets to go out every other Friday.'

'Right,' Tamsyn said. 'So you don't know anyone who you think might have panicked, and abandoned a baby?'

'*No!*' Another girl, dark-haired this time, chimed in, incredulous. 'This isn't the twentieth century, you know! First of all, we all know how to use contraception, and second of all, there's no shame in having a baby any more. Why would anyone want to hide it? I don't know who left that baby, but it wasn't one of us.'

There was a chorus of agreement from the girls, and Tamsyn had to admit they had a point. The average young person was too clued up and sensible to fall pregnant by mistake, and even if they did, the chances of them leaving their baby somewhere were very small indeed.

Just then, another girl caught her eye, this one sitting on a camp bed on her own, her knees drawn under her chin, staring at a book that she was supposed to be reading but clearly wasn't. The book was upside down.

'You're missing the mark if you think Kirsten could be the baby's mum.' One of the pretty girls curled her lip. 'She'd have had to have sex with someone, and if she had a baby she'd probably sacrifice it to Satan, or something.'

The other girls giggled, and Tamsyn found herself moving Mo out of their grasp, feeling quite considerably less charmed by them than she had. The lone girl looked pale, lost. She certainly didn't fit in with the others, a state of affairs that Tamsyn had once been used to. There had been nothing about her at the same age that meant girls naturally wanted to befriend her, or boys were drawn to ask her out. She was awkward, gawky, skinny and sharp. It would have been so easy for her to be the girl that was always left out, like this one clearly was. Except that her brother, who was handsome and popular and loved by all, never left her behind. And her best friend, Merryn, the Queen of the May, made sure that Tamsyn was always part of everything. Besides, nobody knew how to half-inch four cans from the Spar like Tamsyn did.

The girls had already gone back to their chatter as Tamsyn strolled over to Kirsten.

'*Anna Karenina*, tough book to read, even when it is the right way up,' Tamsyn commented mildly, nodding at the thick novel. The girl looked at her and dropped it on the bed.

'You OK?' Tamsyn sat down. 'You look pale. Maybe you're coming down with this flu thing that's going round.'

The girl looked at her, and then at Mo.

'How is she?' she asked.

'I think she's OK,' Tamsyn said gently. Kirsten looked sad, tearful. 'She's probably missing her mum.'

'I'm glad she's safe,' Kirsten said.

'You're not hanging out with the others?' Tamsyn asked her.

'We don't have a lot in common,' Kirsten said. 'For starters, I like reading, they like being idiots.'

'So are you here with your family, then?'

Kirsten looked at her sharply, and Tamsyn sensed she had asked a few too many questions already.

'I live in the Swan Youth Project,' the girl told her. 'It used to be a pub? Then a few years back, the vicar and some others got it turned into a boarding house, for kids who were still in school but not living with their family.'

'Oh right,' Tamsyn nodded. 'Must be tough?'

'Not as tough as it was living at home,' Kirsten shrugged. 'Anyway, it's fine. I'm fine, so . . .'

She waited for Tamsyn to leave, but instead Tamsyn found herself reaching out and pressing the back of her hand against Kirsten's forehead. The girl flinched unthinkingly.

'Well, you don't feel hot,' Tamsyn said. 'But if you start to feel worse then let someone know, OK?'

'Yep.' Kirsten dropped her eyes.

'Is there no one else here, from the hostel, who you can hang with?'

'There's only two of us living there at the moment.' Kirsten's eyes slid over the group of boys that Jed was talking to, landing briefly on a tall lad with long hair, wrists covered in rubber bands and leather straps. 'And me and Chris aren't exactly talking.'

'I see,' Tamsyn said.

'You don't see,' Kirsten assured her, sharply. 'No one sees. He makes sure of that. All the girls like him, you see. He's cool. He doesn't want to have a girlfriend, but he does want to have me. Or at least he did, but he said I was getting too emotional.'

'Oh, Kirsten,' Tamsyn didn't know what else to say.

'It's fine.' Kirsten pulled her blanket up under her chin. 'I didn't really like him anyway. I was just bored, so . . .'

'Do you like babies?' Tamsyn asked her. 'You can hold her if you like.'

Kirsten slid down deeper into the bed.

'I've got a baby brother,' she said. 'He got taken into care, and now I'll probably never see him again.'

'Right.' Tamsyn sat there for a moment longer, listening as a chorus of something folksy struck up behind her. 'I do get it, feeling like crap, aged seventeen. I know you won't believe me, but I do. When I was seventeen I was a very angry person. My dad died, and I never felt like I fitted in much anywhere. I got drunk a lot, too much. I maybe hung around with a few more boys than I needed to, slept with them. If I could go back now, and talk to my seventeen-year-old self, I would say, you are so much more amazing than you know you are. You are so much more pretty and special than you think you are. And you are worth so much more than those thoughtless boys, who never think of how you feel, think you are.'

Kirsten screwed up her nose. 'I know I'm worth a hundred times more than that lot,' she said. 'Look, I'm not being funny, but I don't know who the fuck you are. Could you just leave me alone?'

'Fine.' Tamsyn stood, watching the young woman curl herself into a ball, shutting her eyes against the laughter and comradeship that filled the room.

'But look, if you want to talk about anything . . . well, it's never too late, you know. Just come and find me.'

Kirsten did not reply.

There was a lot about the young girl that seemed to make her an ideal candidate to be the baby's mother, but she was so detached from everything.

So who, then, who, in this day and age, would not be able to bear the shame of giving birth to a baby, who would leave it on the steps of the church, what did it mean, unless . . .?

Tamsyn looked around at Jed, as the girls scooted back under their duvets and sleeping bags and began discussing the merits of Ryan Gosling over Bradley Cooper. Unless the father of your secret baby also happened to be the town's handsome, single vicar.

Chapter Nine

Tamsyn almost walked into a woman, who was bent over double in the hallway, her hand stretched out, steadying herself against one of the dark, wood-panelled walls, and recognised her at once as Jed's poorly verger, Catriona.

'Are you OK?' Tamsyn asked her, although it was clear that she wasn't. The older woman was as white as a sheet and looked feverish, her greying hair clinging to her face.

'I was trying to find the bathroom,' the woman said. 'I've never really been up at Castle House before. I mean, I've been, but not further than the main hall or the reception rooms. Mother didn't really approve of it, Castle House, that is. She thought it was a great deal of stuff and nonsense, and that Ms Montaigne was just a silly little woman puffed up with hot air, although I always rather liked her.'

She held her hand over her stomach and groaned, closing her eyes. 'I'm afraid it's rather urgent.'

'Oh, there's one down the corridor here. Can you make it if I walk next to you? It's just the baby, you see . . .'

The woman looked up and saw the child in her arms, and smiled faintly, closing her eyes for a moment as a wave of something, nausea most likely, hit her.

'The lost baby,' she said. 'You must be Tamsyn Thorne. The woman who found her. Good job you did; it sounded like it was a close-run thing. I was supposed to be at the church; I should have been there, but I was coming down with this bug. I had no idea things had got so bad in the town until Ruan came to check on me. I was trying to get out to the church.'

'You look awful,' Tamsyn said. 'Here, let me help you, you look like you need a shoulder to lean on.'

'It's very good of you to offer, but I don't think you'd better touch me. Whatever this is I don't want to risk passing it on to that little one. The awful thing is, I was supposed to be at the church yesterday evening, getting it ready for choir practice, but then this bug laid me low, like it has so many. I should have been there, going about my business as usual, but I wasn't. Thank God you were passing.'

'Yes, you said,' Tamsyn reminded her as she walked next to the poor woman. Perhaps she was a little delirious, or confused from the sickness.

'I feel sorry for the mother. She must have been terribly desperate to leave her baby that way.'

'Foolish, more like,' Catriona said, closing her eyes. 'My mother always said that a person had no one to blame for the misfortune in their lives except themselves. You can't run away from your indiscretions and pretend they haven't happened. The stupid woman needs someone to sit her down and tell her that.' She stopped. 'Oh dear, I feel terrible. I don't suppose you might find someone to help me . . .'

'Of course, I'm so sorry. I'll find someone.'

What was interesting, Tamsyn thought as she turned around to find Jed, was that the mother of the baby had to be someone connected closely enough with the church to know about its regular routines. She had to be someone who would be fairly certain that under normal circumstances, Catriona or Jed would have been inside when they left Mo in the shelter of the porch, and that the baby would only be alone for a matter of minutes. The trouble was, unlike many other twenty-first-century towns, Poldore life still revolved very much around the church, which in one way or another touched the lives of most of those who lived near it. Whether they were true believers or not. And to be honest, if you were going to leave a baby on a doorstep, Tamsyn couldn't imagine anywhere else in Poldore that would seem like a suitable fit. The only other place that was frequented so often would be the pub.

'Jed!' she called, as she saw the vicar walking in the opposite direction. 'Can you help?'

'Catriona!' Jed jogged back, immediately putting his arm around his colleague's waist to support her. 'You look awful, what are you doing out of bed?'

'Oh, I'd . . . um,' Catriona said, lowering her eyes. A modest woman of a certain age, she probably didn't want to be talking about her urgent need for the bathroom with her vicar, her boss.

'Which way is the bathroom?' Tamsyn asked him, although she knew that to spare Catriona she would have to explain. 'Maybe you could just help Catriona down the corridor? She looks like she really needs to be in a room with an en suite.'

'I'll look after Catriona,' Jed told Tamsyn. 'Sue's in the kitchen. See if there's a better room for her, one nearer a bathroom, perhaps?'

'I don't want you making a fuss over me,' Catriona insisted as Jed helped her down the corridor. 'Mother always said that no one person's needs are any greater than another's, especially not mine. What do I have to lose but a few old sticks of furniture and some ancient carpet? It's the young families I feel sorry for.'

For a person who was so poorly, she certainly didn't have a problem with talking.

The large kitchen, with its long, ancient, well-scrubbed oak table, was bustling with people even now that it was well past midnight. Sue was still up, making what looked like a leaning tower of sandwiches, and Tamsyn saw her brother sitting at the table next to Alex, neither one speaking as they ate, just leaning against each other, shoulder to shoulder. It was an oddly affecting sight, the two of them like that. So quiet, so close, content just to be. Tamsyn remembered how Ruan always had been with Merryn, dear, bright, funny Merryn, who never seemed to be still for more than a moment. He'd once said that it felt like he always had to run to keep up with her. There was none of that between him and Alex; they were in exactly the right place at the right time. Together.

It suddenly struck Tamsyn what a miraculous and unlikely occurrence that must be for anyone, in any life. How fortunate they were to have found each other at exactly the right moment.

'Sue.' Tamsyn approached her host cautiously, in case she thought of something for her to do. Although the one thing to be said for discovering an abandoned child in a storm of biblical proportions, and all of the stress and anxiety that came with being responsible for it, did seem to be a good get-out clause when it came to doing chores. 'Catriona Merryweather, she's really quite poorly, don't suppose you have an en suite left that she can stay in, do you? I think she . . . might need to use the bathroom rather a lot.'

'Oh dear, poor Catriona.' Sue thought for moment. 'We don't have any; they hadn't been invented when the castle was built, you know. But hang on a minute – there's a commode in the Red Room upstairs, where I keep all of the things that I haven't got round to throwing away yet.'

'She calls it "haven't got round to throwing away",

I call it hoarding,' Rory told Tamsyn with a wink as he brought his wife another loaf of bread. 'And it's not just the Red Room that's full to the rafters, it's also the Chinese Room and the Solar, and don't get me started on that attic.'

'And isn't it a good job?' Sue said a little sharply. 'After all, if I had cleared out all of the so-called junk that you are so keen to be rid of, then we wouldn't be able to help poor Catriona out in her hour of need. Now go and fetch it down and put it in her room. You can be the one who makes sure it's emptied too.'

'Honestly,' Rory said bitterly. 'You talk to the dogs with more respect than you do to me.'

'There's a reason for that,' Sue said, slapping mustard onto ham with quite some venom. 'I *do* have more respect for the dogs. Loyal creatures, the lot of them.'

Tamsyn bit her lip and, just like everyone else in the room, pretended not to notice the fierce exchange between the couple. Alex was the only person who was openly watching them, a frown drawing her dark-winged brows together. Her sister-in-law-to-be looked like the sort of person who, if she had an opinion, found it difficult not to express it. Tamsyn watched as Ruan covered Alex's hand with his own and gently squeezed her fingers, telling her, ever so subtly, that it was none of their business.

'And while you are at it, you can show Tamsyn where

the rest of her family are. The baby will need another feed in about two hours, Tamsyn. Cordelia made up enough bottles to see you through the night. They are in the fridge, the bottle warmer is there, remember to test the temperature. It should be skin temperature, not too hot, not too cold, and . . .'

'Oh for God's sake, woman,' Rory said, 'she's not an idiot.'

'Well, I sort of am when it comes to babies,' Tamsyn said, but Rory had already left the room.

It had been a very long time since Tamsyn had visited Castle House, and even then she'd never been further than the ground-floor rooms for Christmas parties or the various committee meetings that her mother had been to, long ago. As children they had often roamed as far as they dared, playing games of hide-and-seek and sardines to amuse themselves while the grown-ups talked about Christmas pageants or Easter parades, or whatever occasion it was that Sue had been organising for what seemed like her whole life. But they had never strayed too far, in fear of the Blue Lady of Poldore who, legend had it, had thrown herself off one of the turrets over a lover, and was rumoured to roam about upstairs, screaming. It wasn't until much later that Tamsyn realised that most of the folly that was Castle House hadn't been built until the nineteenth century, and that the ghost was a tactic invented by Sue's mother to keep her children under control, a remarkably effective one as it turned out.

Upstairs, the interior of Castle House was like a world caught in aspic, almost a time capsule in itself, the echoes of lives long gone heard in every corner. The threadbare curtains that hung from the huge windows must have been very grand once, and the worn and well-trodden rugs that covered many of the polished oak floors would have been considered the height of fashion. Tamsyn wanted to stop and stare at the paintings that lined the walls, some of them hundreds of years old, dating back to the time of the buildings that had stood on this site long before Castle House, each of them fascinating, particularly the Regency lady in silver and blue silk, her jewels glittering on her shoulder, her hair powdered white. Tamsyn had to stop and look at her. Her beauty was very much of the age, but it was certainly there in those bright, sharp eyes, the shape of the nose and mouth. It could have been Sue with a wig and a corset on. What a strange life it must be, Tamsyn thought, to live amongst all of this grandeur knowing that it would never return again, and that all that could be done was to watch it slowly fade away. No wonder Sue never threw anything out. Tamsyn didn't think she would either if all this wonderful history belonged to her. What a wonderful setting for a fashion editorial this would make! She could see it now: Bernard's relentlessly modern and avant-garde garments against this aged and genteel backdrop. Perhaps she'd suggest it when she got back. Sue could almost certainly do with the money; it must cost a fortune to keep this place going.

A door closed somewhere in the distance and Tamsyn realised that by dawdling she had lost Rory, her guide, and she had no idea where she was supposed to be staying. Mum had told her to take the turret stairs, but she had not been specific about which ones – and there were six turrets on Castle House, not arranged nice and neatly at the corners of the walls, as a person might expect from a castle, but rising up from the main house at varying heights and angles. It was much more like a Disney idea of a castle than anything bearing a resemblance to historical fact. From this main upper gallery, spiral staircases seemed to peel off left, right and centre and her family could be at the top of any one of them. Tamsyn listened for the familiar shrieks of her nephews, but the house was eerily quiet, considering the number of people it was housing tonight, and for one fanciful moment Tamsyn wondered if she'd slipped into a long-ago, ghostly version of the building, one where ladies in silk dresses still powdered their hair. And then she told herself that she really needed to get some sleep and stop being ridiculous.

'Rory?' she called out, but her voice sounded too loud in the silent corridor. 'Well, Mo,' Tamsyn said to the baby, who stirred in her arms. 'We are lost in a faux Victorian castle. Still, it's not the worst thing that's happened to us. Rory must be around here somewhere; we're looking for the Red Room . . .'

As Tamsyn padded in her socked feet down the hallway, she was halted abruptly by a ghostly image in a very old and very foxed mirror. The blood drained from her face as she took in what she was looking at, something much scarier than the legend of the Blue Lady.

Her own reflection.

Tamsyn barely recognised herself; her dark hair frizzed wildly around her narrow, pale face, Lucy's borrowed – and certainly not best – pale pink fluffy jumper giving her a distinctly mumsy look that her sister Keira would have been proud of, and finally, in her arms the one accessory that she had never planned on sporting – a baby. Who was this wild woman staring back at her from the mirror? What had happened to the polished sophisticate who had stepped off the plane only yesterday? It was as if she'd gone feral and no one had thought to mention it.

'Oh, God, I need some moisturiser and a pair of straighteners, stat,' Tamsyn told her little charge, not that Mo seemed the slightest bit interested. 'If Bernard could see me now, he would certainly fire me, and throw up at exactly the same time!'

'Sue's got an iron,' Jed said, striding down the corridor towards her. 'If you're prepared to risk your ears you could try that, although I have to admit I prefer the natural look. You look sort of ethereal, like a wood nymph. I like it.'

'You do, do you?' Tamsyn eyed him suspiciously, remembering her new theory that he had to be the father of the baby.

'What does that mean?' Jed asked her, surprised.

'What do you mean, "What does that mean?"?' Tamsyn narrowed her eyes at him.

'I *think* it means that you are overtired and rambling,' Jed said. 'And that maybe you need to get some sleep. Mo's been pretty good until now, but who knows when she might decide to wake up and stay up for the foreseeable? Babies do have a habit of doing that.'

'Well, we are joint carers, aren't we?' Tamsyn said, scrutinising his face and then the baby's for any shared genetic traits. Mo had her own particular kind of charm, but she didn't have the vicar's hair – or much hair at all, to be fair – or indeed high cheekbones (or any cheekbones that Tamsyn could identify), and while her mouth was a sweet little pursed ruby rosebud, it bore no resemblance to the generous curves of the vicar's firm lips. Maybe there could have been something about the eyes that looked a bit like Jed, but that might be because both Jed and Mo were watching her with a distinct air of scepticism at that very moment.

'Of course,' Jed offered, holding out his arms. 'I had a good scrub down after getting Catriona back to her room, so I should be all right to take her. Would you mind helping Rory with the commode?'

'Well . . .' Tamsyn glanced back at herself in the mirror and made eye contact with the woman who looked like she'd been raised by wolves in a branch of Primark. The idea of shifting about a primeval Portaloo was even less appealing, 'No, it's OK. I'll take her. You help Rory with the toilet.'

There was an awkward silence for a moment, the two of them really not sure what should happen next after that groundbreaking sentence in the world of small talk.

'So you didn't find any possible secret mothers when you talked to the girls in the hall?' Jed asked her after a moment.

'No,' Tamsyn said. 'If anything, they were at great pains to point out to me that they would never be so silly as to get pregnant, and that if they did, they certainly wouldn't be leaving their offspring on church doorsteps. Although there was one girl, a bit of loner . . . but I don't know, she didn't seem to care about anything.'

'Kirsten.' Jed recognised the description at once.

'Yes, she said you had something to do with the hostel she lived in?'

'A very little. I got the diocese to buy the pub, when it was about to be turned into flats, but the rest is about fundraising. It has its own committee now. Catriona is on it, and I help where I can. There are four self-contained bedsits, one occupied at all times by a youth worker. And downstairs there is a non-alcoholic bar, where the kids go for discos and such. It's a good little fundraiser.'

'So this seventeen-year-old girl lives there on her own with two men?' Tamsyn asked.

'No, the youth worker is a woman, and the other tenant, he's a young man. I was just talking to him. He's a nice boy, transformed from the kid that got excluded from every school he went to. Kirsten, though, she had a hard time when her mum got a new boyfriend, had a baby. Went off the rails a bit. She couldn't stay at home, and then soon after she left, the mother got into drugs, the brother went into care. It's no wonder she seems a little distant. I suppose she's lost all of the people she loves.'

'Hmmm,' Tamsyn wondered. Would it be possible for a child who'd been through so much just to detach herself from something like having a secret baby? It could happen. But then there were those little teddy buttons. Buttons that seemed to tell much more about Mo's mother than she could imagine.

'Well, there were no likely candidates amongst the boys I spoke to, either,' Jed said. 'Although a lot of them were extremely good at World of Warcraft. Well, it was worth a try; tomorrow is another day, and all that.'

Whatever her thoughts were about Kirsten, Tamsyn

decided to keep them to herself for now. If she was Mo's mother, she seemed in good health, she wasn't harmed or in danger. Much better just to see how things went over the next few hours than charge in like a bull in a china shop, as the worst possible thing that could happen would be to scare the girl away.

'Do you think it means something that they left Mo at your church?' Tamsyn asked him. 'I mean, the teens had a point. Who leaves a baby at a church these days? Almost no one thinks it wrong to be a single mother any more, and while it might be a tad old-fashioned, Poldore is one of the most tolerant places on earth. A baby out of wedlock, well – it would have to be a certain sort of person to be ashamed enough of it to leave their child in a church porch.'

Jed thought for a moment, and Tamsyn could see a look of concern cloud his face.

'So you think it's someone who comes to church regularly?' he said thoughtfully. 'Someone very . . .'

'Religious,' Tamsyn prompted him.

'Traditional, with traditional values,' Jed said. 'But then, that sort of person wouldn't be running around and getting pregnant, especially as the first four or five names of my most dedicated parishioners are all members of the over-sixties club.'

'Well, perhaps the mother is the daughter or grand-daughter of someone who attends your church. Or someone with something to hide, maybe,' Tamsyn added. 'Someone who thinks that if anyone finds out they have had a baby it will lead to a scandal, or disaster, the like of which Poldore has never seen!'

Jed smiled at her. 'You certainly have a talent for the dramatic, Tamsyn.'

'Well, I work in fashion, darling. We tend to get giddy even about zip positions.' Tamsyn blushed a little; somehow calling the vicar 'darling' seemed a bit more daring than she'd anticipated.

'So, who?' Jed asked. 'Who would think that the world would come crashing down around them if they were discovered to have had a baby out of wedlock?'

'There is one obvious candidate,' Tamsyn said, lowering her gaze to Mo, who looked like she was taking her sleep very seriously indeed.

'Is there?' Jed looked troubled. 'Who? Cordelia?'

'No, you idiot. I think it's you! Or at least, someone who got pregnant by you, the vicar!' Tamsyn said, before she had even had a chance to think about what she was saying, or if it was an awfully good idea to say the words out loud. The trouble was that Jed was so unusually easy to talk to that she seemed to have trouble *not* talking to him, even when it was about him, and not particularly flattering at that. Now she had gone and done it.

Jed was silent for a long moment, and then something unexpected happened. He started laughing – not just a chuckle or a giggle, but actual guffaws

– breath-stealing, side-splitting guffaws that made him bend over and grab his knees.

'Me?' He managed to splutter the word out between ragged breaths.

'It's not funny.' Tamsyn felt indignant. 'Abusing your position as a moral compass to seduce some poor young woman is not cause for hilarity!'

'I am not Mo's father,' Jed managed to say eventually, shaking his head as he looked at her, laughter still shaking his shoulders. 'If I was, I'd be so incredibly proud, I'd be shouting it from the rooftops. I certainly wouldn't ever put myself in a situation where a child of mine ended up being left in the porch of a church. Sadly, I am not Mo's father.'

'How can you be sure?' Tamsyn said, her confidence wavering as she looked into Jed's cool, clear eyes.

'Because, Tamsyn Thorne,' he said. 'I haven't been with a woman that way in a very long time. Several years, in fact, if you are so determined to know. And despite my job, I consider pregnancies that aren't preceded by sex something of a rarity.'

'Oh,' Tamsyn said, her voice now ever so tiny and small. 'Well. OK, then.'

'Not that it is any of your business,' Jed reminded her gently. 'But for the record, I would only have sex with someone that I really loved, and it would only happen after we were married.'

'Because you're a vicar?' Tamsyn asked him.

'Because I believe in the sanctity of marriage.' Jed nodded.

'But you said . . . you implied that you have "been" with a woman before,' Tamsyn stumbled on, aware that she was being incredibly crass, and utterly uncertain as to why she couldn't simply withdraw from the conversation with what little tatters of dignity she had left, except that the information still seemed to be vitally pertinent to her.

'I wasn't always a vicar,' Jed said. 'I wasn't ordained until I was twenty-four. Now, is there anything else you'd like to know about my personal life? Times and dates, telephone numbers of old girlfriends, maybe a DNA sample?'

'I'm sorry,' Tamsyn said. 'You must think me very rude.'

'Not rude,' Jed said. 'Not that. It's just that you don't seem to understand that what I do is not just my job, that happens to come with a nice house, outdated uniform and a great big ancient shed I need to keep raising funds for to have the roof fixed. This is my life, Tamsyn. My life, that I have dedicated to God. I take my faith seriously, and I would never, *ever* leave a woman in a situation where she had to abandon a child of mine on a doorstep. I'm not that man, and I have to say, given that our acquaintance is only a few hours old, for you to even hazard a guess at what sort of man I am is actually rather insulting.'

'But I wasn't . . . It's not that . . .'

'I don't suppose . . .' Rory's head appeared around a door at the end of the corridor. 'Ah Vicar, good. It's a great big lump of furniture, this; any chance you could give me a hand?'

'Of course,' Jed said, nodding politely at Tamsyn. 'Your family is at the top of the tall turret,' he said curtly. 'The central spiral staircase to the left of the Blue Lady.'

'Thank you,' Tamsyn said. 'And, Jed, I'm . . .'

She had been about to say sorry, but he had already disappeared after Rory, into the depths of the Red Room.

Chapter Ten

'There you are,' Laura said, as Tamsyn shouldered open the vaulted turret door. The room that the Thorne women had been allocated was semicircular, with four single beds, three of which were camp beds, forming a sort of star in the middle of the room. This was usually Cordelia's room when she was sleeping over at Castle House on nanny duty, as it was at the top of the tallest turret where Sue Montaigne housed her children, for maximum noise-containment purposes – one floor above Meadow and opposite the boys. Sue had been known to joke that she'd have put the nursery in the dungeon if only she'd had one.

'Any noise coming from the pit?' Cordelia nodded at the boys' bedroom. 'I looked in twenty minutes ago and it was like a CBeebies production of Armageddon.'

'No, completely quiet,' Tamsyn said.

'Ominous,' Cordelia said. 'The only time they are ever completely quiet is if there is some sort of arson-related activity going on. I'd better go and take a peek. There's wine; you'd better not have too much, though. Don't want you getting drunk in charge of a baby.'

'Again,' Keira said pointedly.

'I wasn't drunk, and I wasn't in charge of them and they were *three*,' Tamsyn said, referring to the one time she had been left to babysit the twins, on a rare visit to Suffolk. 'And I told you not to go out and leave me with them; I warned you.'

'I just didn't expect you to actually let them glue their Lego to the sofa,' Keira said. 'And then draw a city all around it in permanent marker.'

'They were being creative!' Tamsyn used the same defence every time the Lego sofa/permanent marker incident came up. 'And anyway, I bought you a new sofa, and to be frank it was much nicer than the old one. Not to mention more washable.'

'Now, now, girls,' Laura said to her daughters. 'It really is about time you let that incident go, Keira. Tamsyn, let me have a look at that little darling there. Come on, stop hogging the baby.'

'You do know we can't keep her, don't you, Mum?' Tamsyn said as Laura hungrily took hold of Mo, cooing at the poor child and pressing several kisses on her forehead, which Tamsyn thought belatedly was a nice thing to do. She didn't suppose that Mo had been kissed as much as a baby should be in her first hours of life. Even so, this would be the prelude to some inevitable variation of the 'I don't think you're happy in life' discussion that her mother seemed to try to have with her whenever they were in the same room.

'She's not a stray kitten. At some point someone in charge will come and take her away, you know.'

The baby, sensing the change in her situation, opened one dark eye and flushed a deep red.

'Oh, someone's having a poo,' Laura said cheerfully. 'Are you having a poo? Are you having a little baby poo? Shall Aunty Tamsyn change your little botty-bots? *Shall* she? *Shall* she?'

'Mum, she's a baby, not an idiot,' Tamsyn said. 'And anyway, I've already changed her.'

'You do know you have to do it more than once, right?' Laura asked her.

'Well, you were the one who was so keen to get hold of her. Surely there's a rule that whoever it is who's holding her when she poos has to be the one to change her. Isn't that a rule? That should be a rule. Like the last person to use the bath always has to clean it. Or whoever smelt it, dealt it. That one.'

'Oh, for goodness sake, I'll change her,' Keira said, taking a nappy from the packet that Cordelia had brought up with her and holding her arms out for Mo. 'Oh, look how tiny she is; it makes me feel broody. Doesn't she make you feel broody, Tamsyn?'

'I don't know,' Tamsyn said. 'Is broody like a sort of low-level sensation of exhaustion, anxiety and grief over your long-lost suitcase? If so, then yes.'

'They are asleep,' Cordelia said when she came back. 'And amazingly all in a bed, although not the beds they

started out in, but still, I'm counting that as a victory.'
She looked Tamsyn up and down. 'Have you seen
yourself, Tam? You look like you just escaped from a
trailer park.'

'A rude but accurate assessment,' Tamsyn was forced
to concede. 'These belonged to Lucy, apparently, but
I've seen her taste in clothes and it's definitely not
this. I think this came out of the lost-property box in
the pub. These are the sort of clothes that a person
has to be drunk to wear. Have you got something I
can borrow, sis?'

'Well, what do you give a bedraggled fashion designer,
who smells faintly of baby sick, to wear at nearly two
in the morning?' Cordelia mused cheerfully.

'Literally anything but this,' Tamsyn pleaded. 'And
I forgot about the baby sick. She's going to need a feed
in a minute and . . . oh God, I had a go at the vicar,
smelling of baby sick!'

'You had a go at Jed?' Cordelia said. 'What did you
say to him? What could you possibly have a go at Jed
about? He is, like, the goodest person I know. He's like,
one step down from Jesus, really.'

'I may have slightly accused him of secretly being
Mo's father,' Tamsyn mumbled, cringing as she remembered that she had genuinely made the ridiculous
accusation, and out loud, too.

'Oh my God, Tamsyn!' Laura gasped. 'I've raised you
better than that. Only just, I know, but still.'

'I know, but it all made sense to me at the time.' Tamsyn sat on the edge of her bed and pulled her cloud of candyfloss hair over her face, just like she had when she was a little girl in maths class and was doing her best to avoid getting noticed by the teacher. 'And then he was all noble and heartfelt and "How could you even think such a thing" and I felt awful. And I must have smelt of sick and looked like I'd escaped from an eighties Australian soap . . .'

'He wouldn't care what you looked like,' Cordelia said primly. '*He's* not that shallow.'

'But why would you even think like that?' Keira said. 'You should have talked to Cordelia first. Cordelia thinks the vicar might even be gay. Although her evidence for that fact is mainly that he doesn't seem to fancy her.'

'That's not what I said, what I said was, he didn't look at me in the way that most men do, which is from the chest up.'

'He's not gay,' Tamsyn said, perhaps a little too quickly.

'How do you know, and why do you care?' Keira raised an eyebrow.

'I don't know,' Tamsyn said. 'I just . . . I don't think he is, that's all. He talked about wanting to get married someday, to a woman. And he's had intimate relations in the past, before he was a vicar.'

'Anything else you covered during this conversation?'

Cordelia asked her. 'Like what sort of underwear he wears, favourite cheese, that sort of thing?'

'Look, it's been a very strange day and I am very tired,' Tamsyn said. 'You know, I came here for my brother's – who I am not really talking to – wedding, not to get caught up in a hurricane and find a baby and meet a s . . .s . . .erious vicar.'

Keira and Cordelia exchanged a look that Tamsyn knew only too well, and her heart sank like a lead balloon.

'You were going to say "sexy", weren't you?' Cordelia said.

'No.' Tamsyn crossed her arms and her sisters shrieked with glee.

'Girls, we've just got the boys off to sleep, and this little one doesn't need you lot shouting in her ears – settle down,' Laura told her daughters, although the look on her face showed she'd been here a million times before and knew exactly how it was about to play out, and settling down wasn't going to have anything to do with it.

'You were,' Cordelia pointed at Tamsyn. 'You were going to say I met a sexy vicar and I fancy him, you love the sexy vicar, *you love the sexy vicar*! Tamsyn and Jed, sitting in a tree . . .'

'I do *not* love him!' Tamsyn protested. 'But you have to admit, he is quite attractive. I mean, it's his fault, really, that I accused him of fathering an illicit love child. If he looked like a vicar was supposed to look, then it never would have occurred to me.'

'Tamsyn Isobel Thorne,' Laura said. 'I thought I'd brought you up not to judge a book by its cover.'

'She doesn't want to judge his cover, Mum,' Cordelia smirked.

'No, she wants to rip it off,' Keira added, and her sisters cackled like a pair of little fiends.

'Girls!' Laura shushed, tutting loudly. 'Well, you are going to have to go and apologise,' she told Tamsyn. 'Reverend Hayward is officiating at your brother's wedding in a couple of days. We can't have you standing at the front in your bridesmaid's dress with this accusation hanging between you.'

'It's not an accusation she wishes was hanging between them,' Keira said, making Cordelia stuff a pillow into her mouth to stop her howls of laughter.

'Oh, shut up!' Tamsyn told her sisters. 'And, fine, I will apologise to him. In the morning. Or maybe when I'm back in Paris, by letter. Everyone likes to get a letter.'

'You will go and do it now,' Laura said. 'I brought you up properly. You may have ignored me, most of the time, but I still did it. Go and say sorry.'

'I smell of baby sick!' Tamsyn pleaded.

'She can't go and tell him she loves him smelling of baby sick,' Keira said.

'Fine, go and have a shower, and then come back

and Cordelia will sort you out some fresh clothes, and then it will be time for Mo's feed and you can go downstairs and get the bottle and say sorry at the same time. You have ten minutes.'

'Can I straighten my . . .?'

'Now!' Recognising her mother's don't-mess-with-me tone, Tamsyn grabbed a towel from the hook on the back of the door and hurried down a level of twisting stairs to the bathroom opposite Meadow's bedroom. She shut the door and stood there for several seconds, getting the distinct feeling that she had forgotten something. And then she realised. It was the weight of Mo in her arms that she was missing.

Tamsyn stood outside the kitchen a little after two a.m. and listened to the sound of voices. There were fewer now; she could only hear her brother and Alex. And Jed. Just the three of them in there, only two of whom she had mortally offended. Which was pretty good for her: most of the times she walked into a room she could be reasonably sure that at least seventy-five per cent of the people in there hated her. Actually, now she came to think of it, she realised that two out of three was almost seventy-five per cent. This wasn't fair; Ruan had his reasons, but Jed, he was supposed to be all about forgiveness and love and . . . not that sort of love. Nice love, sensible love. Love that could take a wild accusation of loose morals and move on, no big deal.

It would have been better if she wasn't preparing to make her entrance in a black and white onesie in a cat design – complete with a hood that had little pointy ears. There was also a tail.

Her sisters had been unable to contain their delight when she'd returned from her shower to find Mo fretting on her mother's shoulder as she paced up and down on the limited floor space. Then they'd showed her the outfit they had found for her.

'Tell me that's not all you have for me to wear,' Tamsyn said. 'Mum, tell me that you're not going to let them do this to me.'

'It's all I can find,' Cordelia said. 'I mean, it's two in the morning nearly, and I've got three extra beds in my room, in front of the wardrobe. What do you want from me? A Tamsyn Thorne original?'

'Well, we did also find you this,' Keira said, producing a red, lace-edged basque from under her pillow. 'But we thought that, given the sexy vicar's horror at your accusations, you'd better wait for the second date to wear it.'

'Oh my God, Mu-um!' Tamsyn wailed, but Laura only looked resigned, busy as she was comforting the increasingly fed-up baby, jiggling her up and down.

'Go on,' Keira said. 'Put on your jammies and then go and find your new boyfriend. Tell him you're purrrrrrfect for him.'

Cordelia snorted with unbridled and undignified joy.

'He's not my boyfriend,' Tamsyn had said. 'I already have a boyfriend, actually! We've been together for nearly a year.'

The bombshell had worked to a certain extent, in that it had made her two sisters stop tormenting her and stare at each other, open-mouthed. Only now she knew that when she got back from apologising to Jed, she would have to explain to her family why she had kept Bernard a secret for so long, which was going to be hard to do, because all the reasons that seemed to make perfect sense to her when she was with him made her feel distinctly uncomfortable now.

Still, one humiliating, self-abasing thing at a time, Tamsyn told herself, although her feet still refused to move. It was Mo who, fed up of waiting for her next feed, made her mind up for her and howled, a cry that was answered at once by Buoy on the other side of the door.

'What are you doing out here?' her brother asked her, opening the kitchen door.

'Um, coming to get a feed for Mo,' Tamsyn said, shuffling past him, hoping that he wouldn't notice that her pyjamas had cat feet.

'Why are you wearing a massive Babygro? Are you trying to make sure that Mo doesn't feel like the odd one out?'

'Ha, ha, very funny,' Tamsyn said, although she smiled at him. It was good to hear that old familiar warmth in his voice, albeit sarcastic, older-brother warmth. He looked surprisingly bright-eyed and bushy-tailed, despite it being two in the morning and after all he and the other lifeboat volunteers had been through already. That must be what love does for you.

'Just watch yourself around Buoy,' Ruan warned her. 'He does like to terrorise cats. The bigger the better, in his opinion.'

'Evening,' Tamsyn said to Alex, who was sitting on the old armchair in the corner, or at least Tamsyn was fairly sure she was there. It was hard to tell because at some point during the evening Buoy had transferred himself from in front of the fire in the snug to curled up on Alex's lap. Except, because he was a dog of considerable size, it was more than her lap he was covering, and his head was resting on her shoulder. Skipper was sitting at Alex's feet chewing cheerfully on the toe of her Timberland boot. Alex smiled at her through Buoy's fur.

'How's Mo doing?'

'Well, her lungs are healthy,' Tamsyn said, having to speak up to be heard over them as she hastily retrieved a bottle from the fridge. She went purposefully over to the bottle warmer and looked at it. It wasn't rocket science, she told herself. She'd organised runway shows that involved choreographing thirty models, so she should certainly be able to work out a bottle warmer. But the more she looked at it, and the simple dial, and the numbers, and the friendly baby-blue and white plastic, the less of a clue she had about how to make it work.

'You need to put water in it,' Jed said. 'But not too much, otherwise it will flood over the top when you put the bottle in. Here . . .' Tamsyn watched while he filled a mug from the tap and poured a little into the bottom of the warmer, taking the bottle out of her hand while Mo wailed in abject misery in her ear.

'God certainly made sure babies knew how to tell everyone they were hungry,' Tamsyn said, smiling hopefully. Jed smiled in return, but it wasn't the same smile, the one he'd greeted her with in the graveyard, or the one he'd treated her to when he'd been showing her how to button up a Babygro (which had come in useful when she'd been forced into the crime against fashion that she was currently wearing). It was a polite smile – it was a vicar-shaking-hands-after-the-Sunday-service smile. No, it wasn't even that, because Tamsyn had no doubt that Jed smiled at his parishioners with a good deal more warmth than this.

'Let me take her for a moment,' Jed said, holding his arms out for the squalling infant.

'There's no need.' Tamsyn found herself swaying from side to side as if she were aboard a boat on a rough sea. 'I'm not totally useless, you know.'

'I didn't say you were,' Jed replied, his tone calm and soothing.

'Don't talk to me like I'm a toddler,' Tamsyn said, realising belatedly that she'd stamped a fluffy foot as she said it. Taking a deep breath, she tried a new manoeuvre, a sort of side-to-side jiggle, which seemed to calm the baby for a few moments.

'I'm sorry,' she said. 'I thought I was good at coping under pressure and taking life as it comes. After all, I've had to re-sew fifteen ballgowns after the models got drunk and went on a KFC binge. Fifteen, in an hour! But this . . . I think it's driven me a little bit . . . I lost perspective.'

Jed nodded, smiled that same 'nice' smile, used that same calm tone. 'It's bound to have.'

'Look,' Tamsyn said, 'I'm trying to apologise for accusing you of being a dog-collared Lothario, so please don't give me that vicar shtick.'

'I beg your pardon?' Jed said.

'You know what,' Ruan said to Alex, 'I think it's about time we went to bed, before Buoy smothers you.'

'Shtick, I said shtick not shi . . . Not that word!' Tamsyn said, just as the light went out on the bottle warmer.

Ruan lifted Buoy off Alex and carried the old dog in his arms like a baby. ''Night, sis,' he said to Tamsyn. 'It's been . . . memorable.'

'Ruan,' Alex hissed at him as she grabbed Skipper's collar, detaching him with some force from the table leg he'd clamped his teeth around, in a bid to stay up later.

''Night, Tamsyn,' she said. 'I'm so pleased that you're here. And I'm so sorry it's been so dramatic!'

'Not your fault,' Tamsyn said. 'It's nice to meet you, Alex. You seem far too good for my brother.'

Mo was quietened at once by the bottle in her mouth, although for several seconds she continued to make angry little noises, just to emphasise that she didn't expect to be kept waiting in future, and really the service could be improved around here.

Tamsyn couldn't help but smile as she looked down at the angry little face, scrunched up around a nub of a nose. She looked furious, and Tamsyn supposed she had good reason. Did she know, Tamsyn wondered, could she sense what had happened to her? Was she feeling lonely and lost and sad, and wondering where her special person was? Tamsyn hoped not. She hoped that Mo knew nothing about it at all, that the expression on her face was all about having to wait for a feed, and nothing about feeling abandoned, amongst strangers.

She glanced up at Jed, who had his sleeves rolled up as he tackled the washing-up.

'I'm sorry if I offended you,' she said to his back. 'I was just trying to work it out; to find out who on earth would leave a baby in a churchyard in this day and age. It seemed plausible to my weary, sleep- and wine-deprived brain.'

Jed pushed his hair out of his eyes, leaving a little garland of bubbles on his forehead which Tamsyn found rather endearing.

'Only if you think that what I do, what I believe and the way that I try and live my life is a joke,' he said.

'I don't, truly I don't,' Tamsyn assured him, sitting down carefully on one of Sue's rickety kitchen chairs. 'I suppose I just don't often meet people who believe, well, in anything. Unless you count the belief that carbs are the root of all evil and horizontal stripes are the devil incarnate. It's rare to meet a person who has faith. I am truly sorry, and really, you should be accepting my apology about now. Otherwise you start to lose the moral high ground and just come across as a bit sulky.'

Jed almost smiled as he picked up a tea towel – a glimmer of a proper smile – and dried his hands.

'Apology accepted,' he said, sitting down at the table. He watched her for a moment with those beguiling eyes. 'I am sorry, too. I think I probably could have seen the funny side for a bit longer. I do get a bit humourless when it comes to things that I am passionate about. And, well, if I'm honest, I wish I had met the person I felt I could share my life with completely. I look at Ruan and Alex, and I see . . . wonderment. I get lonely. I'd love to be a father, to have that sense of joy whenever I look at the person I love. I pray that someday it comes to me, just as it has to your brother.'

'But, I mean,' Tamsyn hesitated, trying really hard not to say the wrong thing. 'Do you think you can *know* that a person is that person when you don't "know" them in the, you know, biblical sense?'

'Yes,' Jed nodded. 'Yes. I think if a person is the right person, then your hearts and minds will connect long before your bodies do. For me, a conversation with the right person can be just as thrilling as a kiss, and a kiss just as erotic as sex.'

'Mmmm,' Tamsyn said, pressing her lips together and wondering what it was about what Jed had just said that made her heart beat a little faster. 'So as a vicar, you are allowed to say "erotic" and "sex", then.'

'Yes, I can say those words,' Jed said. 'I can feel those feelings, feel desire for a woman. It's not an alien concept to me, although it's been a very long time since I felt it last.'

Tamsyn listened to the ticking of the clock on the kitchen wall and wondered how many seconds had passed while they said nothing, and just looked at each other. It was the strangest sensation, and one she was almost certain was making her weary brain hallucinate.

'Well,' she said, trying to sound sensible and not at all beguiled by a Man of God. 'That still leaves us with a little girl with no family, and no clue as to who might have left her in the porch.'

'I think you're right that it must be someone familiar with the church,' Jed said. 'Someone who thinks of it as a safe haven. The trouble is, we have a healthy congregation in Poldore. It's a very community-led parish. We are involved in all sorts of ways: youth groups, supporting our elderly, working in the schools, visiting the sick . . . And all sorts of people use the parish rooms. The sewing circle, the WI; there are life-drawing classes; Rory leads a creative-writing class. We have a project that helps young, unemployed people gain skills and qualifications. I don't think you can categorise the people that are involved with the church; they come from all walks of life, all age groups, all backgrounds.'

'Oh, Mo,' Tamsyn said to the little girl. 'If only you could talk. If only you could tell us who your mummy is.'

'You must be tired,' Jed said, gently. 'She should sleep for a few hours now. Do you want me to take her while you get your head down?'

Tamsyn hesitated. There was a large part of her that really wanted to curl up alone in a cool bed, close her eyes and fall instantly to sleep, which she knew was exactly what would happen. And yet to her surprise, she wasn't biting Jed's hand off to accept his offer.

'It's just, she's had so much upheaval already,' she said, not quite believing her own words. 'I don't want her to have any more that isn't completely necessary.

I'm exhausted and my arm feels like it's about to drop off, but it's only for a few hours, isn't it? And then one way or another she'll be out of my life. I just want these first few hours of hers to feel as secure and as safe as they can.'

'You sound a little surprised to be feeling that way,' Jed said, but he wasn't mocking her.

'I suppose I am,' Tamsyn said. 'Must be jet lag. And sobriety.'

For a few moments they listened to the roar of the wind outside, and the rain occasionally blowing against the window, sounding like handfuls of pebbles.

'You should sleep,' Tamsyn said, finally. 'You've been all over the place being all vicary. Did you get a bed when Sue was allocating bunks?'

'I did,' Jed said. 'But I don't sleep very well. Insomnia; I've had it for a few years now.'

'You can't count sheep, or angels, or something?' Tamsyn asked him. 'I can't imagine not being able to sleep; it would be the worst feeling in the world.'

'I get enough sleep, somehow,' he said. 'I just don't try to go to sleep. I wait until my brain can't take any more and switches off, and then I usually have a few good hours. But that's a long way off yet.'

'I love sleeping,' Tamsyn told him. 'Sleeping is one of the best things in the world.'

'It's not the sleeping I have issues with,' Jed hesitated. 'I suppose I am just one of those annoying people whose brains won't stop ticking and thinking. I always write my sermons in the early hours of the morning.'

'What made you become a vicar?' Tamsyn said, her brain, almost asleep, articulating the words that had been knocking around in her head almost since she'd first met Jed in the rain under the cedar tree. 'Did, erm, God talk to you or give you a sign, or something?'

'If only,' Jed said. He leant back in his chair, stretched his arms out wide and revealed his throat, which Tamsyn discovered she wanted to press her lips to in a series of little butterfly kisses. 'Wouldn't it be so easy and simple if faith was something so certain? But then I suppose it wouldn't be called faith.'

'So you didn't grow up in a religious home, then?' Tamsyn asked him. 'I mean, Mum and Dad always said when we were filling in forms that we were C of E, you know. And Dad had a proper funeral, with hymns and everything, and we were all christened, and Ruan's having a church wedding. But, I don't know, I wouldn't say any of us are what you'd call *religious*. What is it that makes you so good at believing?'

Jed rubbed his hands over his face; he had a little smattering of golden stubble around his jaw that glistened in the lamplight.

'There's no certainty,' he said. 'Only hope. And faith and love of my fellow man, and love of God. I believe because I feel it, in here.' He tapped his chest. 'In my heart and soul. I believe because, to me, not to believe seems impossible. I'm sorry, I don't suppose that explains it very well.'

'Well enough,' Tamsyn said, 'considering the late hour, or early hour, whichever one it is now.'

'And what do you believe in?' Jed asked her.

'Would it sound awfully shallow if I said the thing I had the greatest faith in the world in is Prada?'

'Yes,' Jed said.

'That's what I thought.'

Chapter Eleven

Something woke Tamsyn with a start, and she realised with quiet horror that it was the sound of her own snoring. Sitting upright, she looked around at the unfamiliar surroundings and waited while the events of yesterday gradually came back, the most tangible reminder being the tiny, open-mouthed baby that slept soundly on her shoulder. Blinking, she winced as she straightened up and realised that what she had been leaning on was not a cushion or a firmly padded chair back, but a vicar.

'Oh.' Tamsyn formed the word with her mouth, but she did not say it out loud because Jed was still asleep, a state of affairs that she now knew didn't come easily to him. He was a very neat sleeper, Tamsyn couldn't help noticing. No slack-jawed dribble, no rattling snores; he slept with his mouth very slightly open, his golden lashes brushing the tops of his cheeks, his hair in his eyes making him look much younger than he was, and innocent.

They had come into the snug at about four a.m., when it had grown chilly in the kitchen, to see if the fire was still lit. Tamsyn had sunk down onto the battered old dog-hair-covered sofa, still warm from its last occupier, a very fat pug called Wash, and Jed had stoked up the embers of the fire again. She didn't really remember much after that, except that she'd been in a curious state of deep but conscious sleep, so that even when she was dreaming she hadn't forgotten the baby in her arms, and she'd been constantly aware of the sound of her breathing, the crackling of the fire.

Mo stirred, screwing her face up in what was fast becoming one of her characteristic looks of displeasure, and from the delightful scent that pervaded the tiny room, Tamsyn guessed that she probably needed yet another nappy change. Besides, the clock on the wall told her that Mo would be hungry soon, at a little after six a.m. Grimacing as she remembered her outfit, Tamsyn crept out of the room, taking one more look at Jed as he slept. He was extraordinarily restful to look at, after all.

The long corridor that ran through the house was all but silent; even the great hall seemed quiet, and Tamsyn didn't care to guess what was going on upstairs, though she was certain that of all the refugees who had taken shelter in Castle House overnight, her twin nephews would be up by now and probably jumping on her sister's head. She was well out of it down here.

'That's the trouble with children,' she whispered to the baby as she crept into the kitchen with Mo snug in her arms. 'They have no idea of the concept of lying in. Remember that, as you get older; remember lying in. It's a wonderful thing.'

It took Tamsyn a second or two to realise that the huge kitchen wasn't entirely empty, because sitting at the other end of it, almost blending in with the grey and white kitchen in the gaunt light of the dawn, was Catriona Merryweather, her hands wrapped around a mug of steaming tea.

'Did you sleep?' Tamsyn asked Catriona, who looked worse than she had done yesterday. Her greying hair, which Tamsyn guessed she usually wore in a bob, was ratted and tangled and she had a waxy sort of complexion and an expression that spoke of prolonged pain and the exhaustion that came with it.

'A little,' Catriona said. 'I have to admit, I still feel rotten. But there is so much to do, so many people who need help . . . I thought I'd be back on my feet by now.'

'You can never predict this sort of illness,' Tamsyn said. 'I had a bug in the winter that knocked me out for a week. I tried to go back to work but I kept throwing up, and it's amazing how much supermodels don't enjoy you throwing up on them.'

Catriona smiled weakly. 'How is the little one?'

'Doing well, I think,' Tamsyn said. 'She's had two feeds and I'm about to do her third, right after I've changed a nappy. I don't suppose you'd mind holding her while I go and hunt one down?'

'I don't think I'd better.' Catriona shrank back in her chair. 'I think I'm probably still very infectious.'

'Of course,' Tamsyn nodded. 'Well, you should go back to bed. Can I get you anything?'

'Perhaps some paracetamol?' Catriona asked her. 'I don't usually take painkillers, but this time I think I am defeated.'

'Yes, I'll find some at the same time as the nappies,' Tamsyn said.

'But don't you bring them,' the older woman warned her, nodding at Mo. 'If you see Jed, perhaps he might? I could do with a word with him, in any case.'

'Oh yes, I've just left him,' Tamsyn said. 'We slept together.' Tamsyn put her hand over her mouth, horrified by what she'd said. 'Only, not like that,' she added hastily. 'On the sofa, with all of our clothes on. I was wearing this, which you have to unbutton all of even just to go to the loo, so it's definitely not good for sex . . . Anyway, I'll get him to come and see you.'

'Thank you.' Fortunately for Tamsyn, the poor woman seemed too overwhelmed by her illness to be listening to Tamsyn's rambling, bending over double in agony as she tried to stand.

'Actually, I'll get that nice vet lady to pop in and have a look at you if she's still around,' Tamsyn said. 'You look pretty terrible.'

'Thank you,' Catriona said, straightening with some effort. 'But I am quite all right, really. It's just this horrible bug; loads of us have got it. I've had worse. Mother always used to say that ninety-eight per cent of all illness was in the mind, and she never had a day of it in her life. Not until the cancer. I do sometimes think if she hadn't ignored the symptoms for quite so long we might have had her around for a bit longer, but as she always said, when it's your time it's your time, no point in crying about it.'

'Your mum sounds like quite a lady,' Tamsyn said, tactfully. 'You must miss her terribly.'

Catriona's face seemed to crumple inwards as she struggled not to let her emotions get the better of her.

'I do,' she said. 'I do. Mum told me that the grief would pass, that I'd find new interests. People always thought she made me live with her, made me look after her. They always thought I'd sacrificed my youth to run around after a silly, selfish old woman, but it wasn't like that at all. I loved her, I loved our life together. I never really wanted a husband or anything, outside of the church. I'm a quiet person; I only want a quiet life. If anything, Mother put up with me. She could have had another life altogether after Father died. She could have had another husband, more children. She gave all that up for me. So yes, yes I do miss her. You must think I am a very silly fool to talk so.'

'I don't,' Tamsyn said gently. 'I don't know what I'd do without my mum, even though she is actually the most annoying person I know. I don't think there is ever an age when you're ready to lose your mum, no matter what sort of person you are. Everyone always needs their mum. I hope Mo's mum realises that and comes back for her.'

Catriona shuddered, despite the beads of sweat on her forehead. 'Silly girl, probably not got enough sense to take care of her child. The baby is most certainly better off without her.' She rose from her chair, taking a breather about halfway up to gather her strength. 'Now I'm off back to quarantine. I think I'd better take this mug with me.'

'Well, Mo,' Tamsyn said, as soon as they were alone again. 'Nappy-change time. Cover me, I'm going in. But preferably not in poo.'

Chapter Twelve

'Dirty stop-out,' Cordelia opened one eye, still smeared in yesterday's make-up, as Tamsyn crept in. She'd had no luck at all in finding nappies anywhere else on the ground floor, and had been forced to bring Mo back upstairs for her feed. 'Honestly, only you could pull, in the middle of a national crisis, in a castle, while holding a baby. It's like that time when the whole of your class got kept in detention and you made out with Danny Harvey under a desk, and everyone thought you were the coolest, and then Danny Harvey's girlfriend walloped you with her geography book.'

'Is it just me whose past indiscretions you love to bring up at every available opportunity, or is everyone else in our family fair game?' Tamsyn asked her in a whisper. 'I was going to come back up, but I didn't want to wake you all.' Keira's bed was empty; she had probably been dragged in to play with the boys already, but their mother lay prone on her back, her candlewick bedspread pulled right over her face.

'You didn't want to answer the questions about the secret boyfriend, more like,' Cordelia yawned, forcing herself into a seated position. Tamsyn gently put Mo down on the bed in front of Cordelia, shaking out her arms for a few moments before she reached for a nappy and the wipes.

'Imagine leaving this gorgeous little thing like she's a bag of rubbish,' Cordelia said, as she looked down at the face that returned her gaze with an air of gravitas.

'Someone must have been desperate, I suppose. I hope they find her today, whoever she is,' Tamsyn replied.

'Getting bored of babysitting?'

'No, just worried for the poor mother. I may work in fashion, but it's not compulsory that I have to be evil, you know. It's just that the industry happens to attract a lot of people from the dark side. They like the capes, you see. And the plucked eyebrows.'

She took a deep breath as she swiftly changed the nappy, and Cordelia covered her nose with a pillow. Tamsyn bagged up the offending article and before she could decide what to do with it, Cordelia grabbed it from her and threw it out of the open diamond-paned window.

'You can't do that!' Tamsyn cried, going to the window and peering out. 'That's littering! At altitude!'

At least it had stopped raining, and the air seemed to have a particularly clean quality to it, as if every atom had been washed. Puddles laced the courtyard below, which was strewn with debris that had been blown high enough to find its way over the ramparts.

'It's fine. I'm not going to leave it there. I'll go and collect it when I'm up, and put it in the appropriate bin,' Cordelia told her. 'I've had the same system since Petal was this big. That's what happens when you insist on putting your nanny seventeen flights up. Can I feed her? It's been ages since I fed a baby.'

'OK,' Tamsyn said. 'Might give me a chance to get some feeling back in my fingers.'

'So, what gives with the secret French lover, then?' Cordelia asked her. 'Is he married?'

'No!' Tamsyn sat down on the edge of her bed and flexed her fingers. 'Well, except to his job, and also maybe his reflection.'

'Right, so he's really into you then?' Cordelia looked sceptical.

'We understand each other,' Tamsyn said. 'We both take what we want from the arrangement and we don't expect it to be more than it is. It's modern, it's simple, it works.'

'What is it that works so well?' Cordelia asked her.

'Really, really great sex,' Tamsyn said, quite honestly.

'Oh my God, wash your mouth out! Laura sat up suddenly, making Tamsyn jump.

'Mother, I thought you were asleep!' Tamsyn was horrified.

'Strumpet!' Laura said.

'Bit unfair, Mother,' Cordelia said. 'And I hate to burst your bubble, but none of us are virgins any more, Mum. We've all done it.'

'I am sadly aware of that,' Laura said. 'But as your mother, I don't want to have to think about it, and as for you, Tamsyn Thorne, I thought you knew better, thought you'd learnt your lesson.'

'Learnt what lesson?' Tamsyn asked her.

'Not to treat yourself so cheaply,' Laura said. 'You deserve so much more; a real relationship with a man who will care for you.'

'I can't think of anything worse! I'm enjoying my independence, my career and a very fulfilling physical relationship. There's nothing wrong with that, Mum.'

'Not if it comes with love and respect,' Laura told her. 'You father and I had amazing sex.'

'Oh, God!' Cordelia covered Mo's ears and then her own. 'Now who's the strumpet?'

'Too much information!' Tamsyn said at the same time.

'Well, we did; our bodies were in perfect harmony,' Laura assured her two younger daughters, gesturing to illustrate her point. 'Rub us together and we made sparks fly.'

'Seriously, stop it,' Cordelia told her. 'I'm on nanny wages, I can't afford therapy.'

'But the reason it was good,' Laura ploughed on in the face of Tamsyn pretending to throw up into a pillowcase, 'was because we loved and respected each other. Because we cared. And all the technique in the world can't make up for that, Tamsyn. You might think the sex is really, really great, but that's because you haven't had sex yet with a man who truly loves you. You're wasting yourself on this man, whoever he is.'

'I am not!' Tamsyn insisted. 'Honestly, he's really great – funny and clever. I see Bernard every day and he does care about me, he cares about my reputation and my career, which is why we've kept it a secret.'

'Oh my God, you are shagging your boss,' Cordelia said, horrified. 'That Bernard bloke!' She pronounced Bernard's name in the English way, as if he were a darts professional and not a member of the French fashion aristocracy.

'Well,' Tamsyn said, 'what if I am? It's got nothing to do with my work. I keep it completely separate.'

'Oh Tamsyn, darling!' Laura said. 'What mess are you getting yourself into over there?'

'No mess at all,' Tamsyn said. 'My life is very neat, ordered, stylish and happy. I love my life in Paris, I love my job and I love . . .'

'Bernard?' Cordelia finished the sentence that Tamsyn had just about managed to hold back from completing.

'I love my arrangement with him,' Tamsyn said, although the hard-won certainty that their relationship was completely equal and respectful seemed suddenly rather naive. When she thought about Bernard there was an ache around her heart, a sort of longing for something she couldn't quite put her finger on. He was kind to her. He treated her with his own sort of respect, other than insisting on keeping their relationship on the down low. Really, there was only one thing missing. Bernard might like her very much, but he certainly did not love her. Tamsyn had always thought she didn't care about that, that love was an outmoded concept in the twenty-first century, but sometime last night – or was it this morning – she'd seen the way that Alex had leant against Ruan, and realised it was that simple certainty of affection that was missing. And knowing that had hurt, like a sharp, sudden blow to the ribs. She had gone and done exactly the thing she had promised herself would never happen to her. That had to be the explanation for the way she was feeling. She had fallen for Bernard, knowing he would never feel the same way about her. And it *hurt*.

A knock at the door punctuated the moment of revelation, and Tamsyn was glad when Alex's head appeared.

'Hey,' she said. 'We're going down to help with breakfast and then Mum, Jed, Lucy and I are going to check on the dresses and the church. I don't suppose any of you would like to come along, would you? Ruan's gone off already to see what the lower half of the town is like. See if they can start cleaning up, and making things safe. I've heard it's pretty bad out there; a lot of people have lost a lot.'

'I'll come,' Tamsyn said unexpectedly. Alex looked just as surprised as she was by the offer. 'Well, Mo could do with a bit of fresh air, and I think I can see a tiny bit of blue sky out there. We won't go anywhere that's not safe and besides, I need to get out. It's suddenly stifling in here.'

Chapter Thirteen

Her departure from the house out into a surprisingly benign, blue-skied and warm June morning was significantly delayed by Sue producing a contraption she claimed was called a baby sling, but which, Tamsyn decided as she patiently waited for Sue to strap her into it, most resembled a sort of baby-shaped bullet-proof vest. Tamsyn watched Alex, who was leaning against the door waiting for her, and couldn't help but admire her long, strong-looking thighs and the way her hips tapered into a waist. She was the very definition of hourglass, whereas Tamsyn was and always had been more or less straight up and down, whatever way you looked at her. In Paris, or in fashion in general, this was positively a very good thing, but when confronted with such a glowing example of womanly health, she had to admit that she felt rather meagre and inadequate. Besides, it was always boring designing clothes for the same shape of woman again and again, and that size-zero ideal rarely existed in real life.

Sometimes Bernard would let her help him with his couture work, which every now and then involved crowbarring a normal-shaped woman into one of his creations and promising her that she didn't look terrible, but even then, there was no pleasure in it. Tamsyn would look at the client and imagine the dress that would bring out all of her best features, and then have to measure her for something that would make her resemble an air-conditioning unit. And yet that was how the fashion business was, the way it had always been and always would be, labouring under the conviction that clothes were meant for hangers rather than people.

'Then we pop Mo in here, thusly,' Sue said, producing the baby and sliding her legs into two holes at the bottom of the sling thing. 'Do this button up here, and hey presto, you can walk around with her all snug as a bug and keep your hands free for . . . well, whatever it is you want them for.'

'Thank you, I think,' Tamsyn said, looking down at her new appendage. 'I feel a bit like I'm in one of those sci-fi movies when something evil bursts out of your stomach.'

'Welcome to motherhood, darling,' Sue said.

'I'd forgotten it was June,' Tamsyn said to Lucy as they stood at the top of the hill looking down into the town. 'It's actually warm. Look at the sea; it looks so beautiful, sparkling, like it's full of crystals.'

'And strangely quiet,' Lucy added. 'I think the storm must have scared away all the birds. It was just a storm, wasn't it? We didn't miss the official end of the world, did we?'

'I'd hope I'd get some sort of notice if that was the case,' Jed said as he listened to the ominous quiet. 'Four horsemen, maybe some sort of plague.'

'Come on then,' Gloria hooked her arm through Alex's. 'Let's go and see what the damage is. And remember, everything always looks worse than it actually is.'

'Well, except for those safety-pin leggings of Cordelia's that you are wearing,' Lucy told Tamsyn. 'They really are that bad.'

The damage was considerable, and as the extent of it gradually revealed itself the further they descended into the town, Tamsyn was surprised by how deeply it affected her, liked someone had taken her childhood glitter-globe memory of the town and smashed it, hard, onto the floor.

They had only had to take a few steps down the steep incline to see that the road was strewn with debris, not all of it the sort of thing you would imagine coming in the aftermath of a British storm. Smashed roof tiles scattered the cobbles, yes, and the muck and mud that had been dragged through the town by the deluge from the swollen stream at the top of the hill silted every inch of the road, making it dangerously slippy. But there was also a selection of smashed photo frames that had fallen out of a broken window, and Buoy was investigating someone's laptop, sitting open in the middle of the road, its screen dark and cracked. Tamsyn rested her palm gently on the top of Mo's head. Somehow, in the daylight, after the storm had cleared, the true extent of exactly how lucky Mo had been not to be badly hurt, or worse, was even more terrifying.

'Oh my God,' Alex said as they turned a sharp bend that revealed, or should have revealed, the harbour and the square below. The tidal surge that had invaded the town during the night had receded, but had left in its wake lakes of water that still pooled in every slight indentation or dip, the water mirroring the freshly washed blue sky, shining silver amongst the wreckage.

'Oh no,' Lucy pressed her hands over her mouth. 'My cottage, your cottage, Gloria. They'll have been badly hit.'

'Everyone's place down there has serious water damage.' Eddie greeted them, out of breath as he walked up the hill. His expression was grim, and anxious. 'Nothing below the esplanade got away with it. I'm sorry, love, sorry, Gloria.'

'Oh Dad, the pub?' Lucy put her arms around Eddie's middle.

'It will be some time before we can open again,' Eddie said. 'At least we were insured, and at least we are all safe. I was talking to everyone in the town; there don't seem to have been any major injuries, although Frankie Wassell got knocked out by a stray brick.

Luckily his missus was with him, and he's not looking too bad. They're waiting for the roads to open so they can take him for an MRI. Helicopter job, if it's not in the next couple of hours. Though Frankie always wanted to go in a helicopter. I told him, hell of a way to wangle a ride, Wassell.'

'I should go and see them,' Jed said. 'Get down into the town and see what I can do.'

'To be honest, Vicar, at the moment you'd mostly be in the way,' Eddie said. 'People are just trying to get their heads around it. I reckon there'll be a few who need help sorting out insurance claims in a day or two, and quite a few who didn't have any insurance at all. They'll be the ones that need the most help.' He grimaced at Alex. 'I'm afraid the florist's has taken it bad, Alex. Maisey told me to tell you she's not sure she can do the flowers for your wedding any more. She said there's a woman in St Austell who might able to, but it could be tricky ordering in the exact kind you wanted.'

'Oh right, well, flowers,' Alex said. 'Overrated, especially at weddings.'

'At least the dresses were laid out in my spare room,' Gloria said, linking her arm through her daughter's. 'They should be fine on the first floor. My lovely new sheepskin rug won't have been so lucky. Brian and I did so enjoy it . . .'

'Shall we go and see the church?' Alex said hastily,

before Gloria could add any details of just how her mum and her rocker boyfriend had enjoyed the rug. And Tamsyn held Mo a little tighter as they approached the churchyard, the fallen cedar still barring their way into the grounds.

'Well, at least the church is still standing,' Jed said. The cedar that had stood watch over the town, and Merryn's headstone, had been half ripped from its roots and toppled across the pathway, the remnants of the trapped blanket still visible beneath it. At some point, before becoming impaled on the spiked railings that surrounded St Piran's, the tree had taken down a large chunk of the rectory roof with it.

'Thank goodness Mo wasn't still in that basket,' Jed said, reaching unconsciously for Tamsyn, his hand resting reassuringly on her shoulder for a moment. She found she could not look him in the eye for fear of weeping, the shock and drama of what had happened only just hitting her. Trembling hit her body in waves, and for a moment she was afraid that her knees would give way.

'Tam, are you OK?' Lucy asked, as she buckled, and suddenly Jed's arm was around her waist supporting her, and she shook her head, cradling Mo against her, closing her eyes until the world would stop shifting around her.

'I'm fine,' she said, allowing herself to lean for just a moment into Jed's strong frame and regroup. 'It's just

. . . Looking at that blanket; everything could have easily gone so badly wrong.'

Tamsyn steeled herself and broke away from the far too tempting shelter of Jed's shoulder. She was a strong person and she could cope with this; after all, a lot of people had a lot worse to deal with.

'The rectory looks pretty bad,' she said, rebooting her composure. 'Can't really see how the church fared, past the tree.'

'Let's hope it escaped the worst of it,' Jed said. He walked up to the great trunk of the cedar, patting it fondly. 'Well, we can't go in this way today. Follow me; there's another way in.'

Taking a moment to peep under the outsize sunhat that Sue had found for Mo, to find her peacefully oblivious, Tamsyn followed the small group around the side of the graveyard, down a narrow path and into Kissing Alley, which ran behind the church. Halfway down the alley there was another gate, which led to a tiny, Gothic-looking oak-panelled door, which would not have been out of place in *Alice in Wonderland*. Tamsyn smiled as she saw it, amazed that during all the time she had spent down here, she had never noticed it before. A fact made all the more surprising when she considered what very bad and boring kissers most teenage boys were, back then. As Jed found a huge bunch of keys in his jeans and commenced jiggling and rattling them, looking for a particular key, she allowed herself a moment to wonder what she'd be able to notice, or not, if it had been him she was kissing in Kissing Alley. Did kissing fall into his 'not before marriage' rule, she wondered, before catching herself and stopping that particular train of thought dead.

'You OK?' Gloria asked her. 'You look a bit flushed.'

'Do I?' Tamsyn looked surprised. 'Must be the portable heater I've got strapped to my front.'

Finally Jed located the right key and with some effort turned it in the lock, pushing the fiercely squeaky gate open, repeating the process on the secret-looking door in turn, which it turned out was not made for very small Cornish pixies at all, but in fact led down two steep steps directly into the vestry. The interior of the small room was oddly quiet and cool, and smelt of must and dust, but it looked untouched by water damage or the storm's fierce gales.

'So far, so good,' Jed said, opening the door that led out into the church.

The scene that greeted them wasn't nearly as comforting.

The first thing they saw was one of the Victorian oak doors hanging from a broken hinge, leaning against the font. Soon after the door was either blown or forced in, it looked as if the church had become a temporary reservoir for the fast-flowing water that had gushed down the hillside; its tiled floor, still glazed with dirty river water, was silted in mud debris and bits of branches. The force of the water must have been quite strong, because some of the pews had been shoved into one another and lay zigzagged at jagged angles across the aisle that in just two days Alex was due to walk up as a bride. A tidemark could clearly be seen against the whitewashed walls, the hangings and artworks. It all looked as if it had been dipped in mud, and everywhere there were little sodden islands of hassocks that had been sewn and embroidered by families for generations, some to commemorate town events, some to remember loved ones. Tamsyn recalled her granny working so hard on her prayer cushion, after Tamsyn's father had died. One of these bedraggled and sorry lumps had his name on it.

'The window, too,' Jed said, pointing to a beam of golden sunlight that flooded in through a jagged break in one of the church's three stained-glass windows. 'There must have been quite an impact to shatter it completely.'

'Oh,' Alex said, simply pressing her hands over mouth, her eyes filling with tears. 'Oh no.'

'Oh, darling.' Tamsyn watched as Gloria wrapped her arms around her daughter, kissing her cheek. 'There, there.'

'It's OK,' Alex sniffed, wriggling free of her mum's embrace and brushing away her tears. 'It's fine. I mean, it's not fine; the poor, poor church. But really, it's just a wedding. It's just a day, it can be any day, we can rearrange it, it's fine . . . Maybe we'll have an autumn wedding, or a Christmas one. It's not important, really, when it happens, just that it happens. I'm fine, I really am. I am not the sort of silly woman who's going to have a meltdown about postponing her . . .'

But anything else Alex might have said was lost between sobs, as she furiously attempted to brush away the tears that would not stop coming.

'What's wrong with me?' she hiccuped. 'I'm not this shallow!'

Tamsyn felt a sudden rush of warmth towards the girl who was trying so hard to pretend that the idea of not marrying Tamsyn's brother in two days' time wasn't breaking her heart. She really loves him, Tamsyn thought. What a lucky man Ruan is to have loved, and been loved in turn, twice in his life. Perhaps the idea of romantic love that her mother kept banging on about wasn't quite so old-fashioned or outmoded as she pretended to think it was. Bernard wasn't made that way; he would never cry over a wedding being postponed, well, perhaps if it meant he didn't get to wear his favourite pair of duck-egg-green breeches that had a strange sort of crotch that started just above the knee . . . that might make his eyes smart a bit.

'You know what,' Jed walked down into the church and looked around, pushing a few pews back into position, his boots squelching in the silt. 'We don't have to cancel the wedding, not really. Not as long as the weather is going to hold, which the weather forecaster said it is going to do. The church is filthy and it stinks, and the window's broken, yes. And sure, right now the outside is a bit like a bog, but all it needs is to be spruced up a bit. A good scrub down, some flowers, some ribbons and, before you know it, it will be absolutely ready for a wedding. A nice, airy wedding, too, with half a door and most of a window gone.'

'But . . . really?' Alex snuffled loudly as she surveyed the scene. 'You think it's possible?'

'I do,' Jed said. 'We just need to get all hands on deck, that's all. Let everyone know what's happened and what needs doing, and I bet you we'll have twenty or thirty people here by lunchtime, ready to help clean up and get the church ready again.'

'There, you see, love?' Gloria said. 'You see, it will be OK. I can help with decorations. I'm thinking maybe a few glitter balls, and oh, Vicar, maybe we could paint it? You know, liven it up a bit. Have you ever thought about a nice gold on the walls, Vicar?'

'Yes, but so many houses have been flooded, homes destroyed. What makes our wedding more important than anything else?' Alex shook her head. 'No, it's not right. We need to sort out people's homes first. The wedding will have to wait. I'll get over it. No one tell Ruan I was this upset, I don't want him to think that I've been hiding the crazy all this time.'

'I don't think anyone could accuse you of hiding the

crazy,' Lucy teased her gently, soliciting a small, watery smile from Alex.

'Well, of course you're right,' Jed nodded. 'Of course we need to reach out and help everyone in need, but that's what's special about Poldore, Alex. Community. There are many pairs of helping hands here, more than enough to go round, and the top half of the town was barely damaged at all. And I truly think that doing something that helps bring about a joyous occasion will lift everyone's spirits, especially when it's something for you and Ruan.'

'And,' Tamsyn mused as she looked around the space, her designer's eyes seeing past the dirt and damage, 'as much as I love the idea of gold paint, Gloria, what we could do, after we've cleaned it up, is just embrace the broken door and the shattered window. We can bring Cornwall into the church, fill it not only with flowers, but garlands of the fallen branches. Most of them are still laden with blossom. We can save a lot of the stuff that has been torn down and blown about. We could put ivy up the pillars, wild flowers along the pews. I think with the warm air blowing through the hole in the window and the broken door, it will be almost like a woodland wedding and a church wedding all at once. It can be stunning, *better* than you imagined. And it sorts out the problem of the flowers in one fell swoop. You could even have a wild-flower bouquet.'

'You think so?' Alex asked her.

'I do, actually. We can get Keira on to it. She did half a degree in theatre design before she got whisked off her feet into marriage, and she hardly ever puts her talents to good use.' Tamsyn nodded, smiling, as she saw her vision unfold before her. She caught Jed's eye and saw a look of appreciation, which gave her a curious little fizz of happiness. She liked it when he approved of her.

'I suppose we could ask,' Alex said, her tone brightening just a little. 'But only if people don't mind, and only if . . .'

'Oh, shut up,' Lucy said. 'Seriously, if you were any more noble we'd have to borrow the halo off that saint over there and stick it on your head. When are you going to pull a Bridezilla on me, stamp your feet and demand stuff? I've been waiting for a hissy fit for months now, and there's been nothing. You can't really be that nice.'

'I'm saving that up in case anything has happened to the dresses,' Alex said. 'Honestly, all my life I never thought I'd care about wearing a dress. It's funny what getting married does to you.'

'Come on then,' Gloria said. 'I've got my galoshes on, so let's get out there and rescue those dresses.'

'Are you coming, Tam?' Lucy asked.

'Um, no. I think any further down might not be a good idea for Mo, not if the streets are still underwater.

Good luck, though, with the dresses. I can't wait to try mine on.'

'I just know the lilac puff sleeve is so going to suit you,' Lucy grinned.

Out of nowhere, Alex came over and hugged Tamsyn and Mo all at once, and kissed Tamsyn on the cheek.

'You know, there are no puff sleeves,' she told Tamsyn. 'It's all just a joke those three cooked up to torment you with. But I can't let it go on. You are too nice to be threatened with outdated sleeves and bad colour choices.'

'What did I do?' Tamsyn shifted uncomfortably. 'I didn't do anything. I just stood here. With a baby. And talked about indoor trees.'

'You came here,' Alex said. 'You don't know how much it means to Ruan that you came. He might not have said anything, but I know it means a lot. And I'm so glad you did. I feel like you're a lucky charm.'

'Lucky?' Tamsyn laughed. 'I turn up, there's the worst storm in recorded history, the church and town are wrecked and someone abandons a baby who barely escapes with her life!'

'Yes,' Alex said. 'But think how much worse it could have been.'

'Are you OK?' Tamsyn asked Jed, once Alex and the others had left. He had seemed remarkably calm, considering the amount of wreckage to his beloved church. Tamsyn didn't know how she knew that it was beloved to him, only that it most certainly was. He ran his hands along the fallen pews as he righted them as if they were old friends, and pressed his palms against the walls, looking for all the world as if he were offering them a gesture of reassurance. Every line and angle of his body told her how much this building, and what it symbolised, meant to him.

'It's just bricks and mortar, glass and a door,' he said. 'And a lot of really smelly river mud, but it's not so bad, and besides, wherever there are two or more people coming together in the name of God, then you have your church, no matter where it may be. This is just a building, although I will admit to it being one that I have grown to love. No one has been badly injured or killed, and you were in the right place at the right time to make sure that little girl wasn't under that tree. I can only be grateful for that.'

Tamsyn nodded, 'You know,' she said, 'you are allowed to be upset by what's happened, the unfairness and stupidness of it all, aren't you?'

'Of course I am,' Jed looked at her. 'It's just that I've witnessed a great deal worse in my life. This' – he made a gesture all around him at the ruins of his church – 'is just inconvenience. Isn't Mo due a feed?'

'Well, yes, I suppose so,' said Tamsyn.

'Come with me, then. I can pick a few things up from the rectory, maybe make you a cup of tea, see how big the hole is and hopefully be able to make some calls, if I can get a signal. I'll need a tree surgeon to sort the tree out, a builder, a stained-glass expert – but obviously, as this is Poldore, we've got about five of those.'

Tamsyn couldn't help but smart a little at the way he'd brushed off her good-natured concern, but she followed him back through Kissing Alley and next door to the rectory. He paused for a moment, looking up at the damage caused by the cedar. 'Looks like it's more of a graze than anything. The building still looks structurally sound, so that's a blessing.'

'Engineer too, are you?' Tamsyn muttered under her breath as he opened the front door of the rectory.

'Yes, actually,' Jed told her. 'I did a degree in it before I became a priest.'

That shut her up as he led the way down a cool, tiled hallway and into a surprisingly light and airy kitchen at the back of the house. It was nicely fitted with everything that a family house needed, centred around a small, oddly orange, ancient-looking table with round corners and legs that splayed outwards. It must have been the height of fashion once, back in the 1950s Tamsyn guessed, and would cost a lot of money if it ever found itself on sale on the Portobello Road.

'Right, the kettle's there,' Jed said. 'And here's a jug, to warm the bottle in, teabags, milk in the fridge, obviously. I'll be back in a second. I just want to see how the upstairs is holding up, make a call or two.'

And he was gone, leaving Tamsyn and Mo, who was still sleeping peacefully on her chest, without showing even the slightest sign of wanting to wake up, standing alone in the kitchen. Tamsyn went to the cupboard above the kettle and opened it, but it was empty. And then she went to the next one, and the one after that. All empty. The smallest cupboard right at the end of the row offered up six mismatched mugs, a jar of instant coffee and a Tupperware box full of what Tamsyn hoped were teabags. She opened the fridge to look for milk, and realised when the light didn't come on that the power must still be out. They'd been spoilt up at Castle House with the backup generator, but here in the town there would be no cups of tea made in the traditional way. Or bottle warmers, for that matter. The hob was electric too, not gas, so she couldn't even attempt to light one of the rings.

Wondering how to break the news of the lack of power to Jed, Tamsyn looked around the kitchen again. What she had taken to be a minimalist style statement was actually just a room bare of any of its occupier's personality. There were no pictures, no photos, not even a pot plant. And yet Jed had been in Poldore for over two years now, he'd said. Curious, she wandered back out into the hallway. She could hear Jed's voice somewhere upstairs, which she hoped meant he'd got through to someone on the phone, and not that he was chatting to someone he'd once murdered and stuffed like a dead dog in this strange, empty house. Hesitantly, she pushed open a door at the front of the building, thinking it should lead to a sitting room or a study. The room was empty, whitewashed, clean. It was furnished with nothing but a small model of a wooden boat, which Tamsyn was fairly certain had always been in the rectory window, even when she was a little girl. Closing the door softly behind her, she checked the room opposite and the other room to the left of the stairs. They were all the same: absent of any sign that anyone lived here. Tamsyn stood for a moment at the foot of the stairs, gazing upward. Maybe Jed wasn't the vicar; maybe he turned up two years ago, murdered the old vicar and now he was pretending he was the vicar and had sucked the whole of Poldore into his dastardly scheme to . . . be really nice and take care of people. Nope, it didn't quite fit into the psychotic, evil genius pigeonhole.

'Jed?' Tamsyn called up the stairs, as Jed had stopped talking. Well, she told herself, she could always just pretend that she was looking for a bathroom. She climbed the stairs as noisily as possible, humming as she went, and when she got to the landing called his name again.

'In here!' he called her from the front bedroom. Tamsyn was quietly relieved to see that this room looked like a normal person actually lived in it. It was lined with photographs, had a bookshelf full of books and a desk in the corner, where Tamsyn supposed he

wrote sermons, perhaps in his pyjamas, gazing thoughtfully out of the windows, an image that gave her cause
to remind herself that she was not a character in *The
Thorn Birds*.

'Oh good,' she said out loud, looking around the
room.

'"Oh good" what?' Jed asked. He was standing by
the window peering into a small notebook. The strong
sunlight picked up the gold in his smooth, straight hair,
and Tamsyn was sure that if she happened to run her
fingers through it, it would be silky-soft to the touch.
'I left my bedroom window open and can you believe
that the only thing to get soaked was my address book?'

'You still have an address book?' Tamsyn said. 'And
it was an "Oh good you do have at least one furnished
room in your house, so maybe you aren't a crazed
psychopath after all".'

'Oh that,' Jed said. 'I always forget that people find
that weird, but I don't know why. I'm one man; why
would I want to fill up empty rooms with things that
I have no need for? Truly this house is too big for me.
I asked them to let me have a cottage, and to rent this
out to a local family at an affordable price, but there's
some sort of covenant in the deeds that means it has
to be the vicar of St Piran's that lives here. It's such a
waste. I really want to use the rooms for something
purposeful. I've been on at the bishop about it since I
arrived, and I'm making progress, slowly.'

'But you don't even have a living room?' Tamsyn asked him, looking around. 'Not even a telly?'

'I've got a laptop, if I want to watch a movie,' Jed smiled. 'No, this is the first house I've ever lived in as an adult. I don't think I will ever get used to it.'

'Where did you live before?' Tamsyn exclaimed. 'Institutions? Prison?'

Jed grinned. 'I did flat shares at university, and then . . . well, in the army I was in barracks.'

'The army?' Tamsyn repeated to herself. Jed gestured towards a photo on the wall of a group of young men in dress uniform. 'That's me, and some of the guys. I joined up as a padre; they make you an officer at the same time. It seemed like the logical thing for me to do. I'd just been ordained, and I was full of fiery passion. I wanted to be somewhere where I felt I could really be of use and help people. Iraq was my first post.' He paused for a moment as he looked at the photo. 'Then Sierra Leone and Rwanda, and finally Afghanistan.'

Tamsyn didn't really know what to say, so she didn't say anything. Instead she stared for a long time at the faces of the young men in the photograph. Jed was still exceptionally good-looking, back then, his hair as golden as his tan, but there was something entirely different about him. In the photo he was laughing, and there was this light in his eyes. He looked at ease with the world, and there was a kind of surety about him that wasn't there now, despite the quiet strength he seemed to exude. Perhaps he missed his life of adventure; rattling around in a house that was too big for him in sleepy Poldore was about as far from anything interesting as any person could be, unless a person was very interested in crocheting.

'So, how did you end up here?' she asked him.

'I left the army, and the church thought this was a good spot for me.' Jed shrugged, peering at his address book. 'I wonder if that's an eight or a zero . . .'

'You didn't want to work in an inner city, or a prison or something?' Tamsyn asked him. 'After the things you've seen, isn't all this . . . "niceness" a bit boring?'

Jed looked thoughtful, bowing his head.

'It's not boring,' he said after a while. 'It's just as real a life as any.'

'But does it fulfil you, I mean?' Tamsyn asked him.

Jed looked back at his soggy address book, and Tamsyn noticed how his grip on the object tightened slightly, along with the muscles in his jaw. What had she said to elicit that response, she wondered? She was fairly sure she hadn't said anything that offensive.

'You know what? I think I'll ask Sue. Sue has the name, address and, more often than not, front-door key to almost every house in the town. She'll be bound to help me get sorted.'

'OK,' Tamsyn said, taking the hint. 'I just came to tell you, the power is still out, so I'll take Mo back to Castle House to feed her there.'

'Oh, OK,' Jed said. 'I need to sort a few things, so . . .'

'Right, well, bye then,' Tamsyn said.

'Bye.' Jed turned back to look out of the window, though when Tamsyn looked up as she passed the house on her way back, he was no longer there.

There was no time to reflect on the abrupt change of mood of the vicar when Tamsyn got back to Castle House, as there was an official-looking reception committee waiting for her in the kitchen. Sergeant Dangerfield was sitting at the table with a mug of tea and a large plate of sandwiches in front of him. Another woman, who Tamsyn guessed straight away was the social worker, was sitting next to him, but as Mo had now decided in earnest that she was hungry, they both had to wait as Tamsyn made up her bottle, conscious all the time that she was being watched and judged. She warmed the bottle, performing what now seemed like a regular ritual of wafting Mo from side to side at the same time as jiggling her up and down, while she did it.

'So,' Tamsyn sat down with Mo in her arms, 'any news?'

'About the mother? Not yet,' Sergeant Dangerfield said, regretfully. 'But the team in St Austell have been on to the local news, and there's a film crew hoping to get here today, as the main roads through are already improving. So they'll do a little film of you, and appeal for the mother to come forward and get help. And the recording will go out on the radio too.'

'Good,' Tamsyn said. 'Except the power is still out, so I'm not sure how anyone will be able to listen in.'

'They're working to get the power back on today,' Sergeant Dangerfield told her. 'Oh, and this is . . .'

'I'm Tess Jameson.' The woman, who had a pleasant, kind face, stretched her hand out across the table, and then, seeing that Tamsyn had her own hands full, withdrew it again. 'Nice to meet you. I've heard a lot about you from Ms Montaigne.' She blinked. 'A lot.'

'Ah, Sue,' Tamsyn smiled. 'I hope at least some of it was good?'

'Oh, she's very impressed with you,' Tess assured her. 'So first of all, thank you for taking Baby on. I know it must have been quite a responsibility for you, to be landed with her like that.'

'Well, it was a shock,' Tamsyn admitted. 'But what else was I going to do?'

'Why are you here?' Tamsyn looked up and saw Kirsten in the doorway. She didn't look as if she had slept a wink last night, but it was Tess she was focused on. 'Are you here about me?'

'Hello, Kirsten.' Tess obviously knew the girl. 'No, love, we're not due a meeting for another couple of weeks, are we?'

'Well, why are you there then?' Kirsten advanced another step into the room, glancing briefly at Tamsyn. 'Is it about Chris?'

'No, the baby.' Tess nodded at Mo.

'You met her last night, remember?' Tamsyn asked Kirsten.

'You're going to take it away?' Kirsten asked. 'Into care?'

'Well . . .' Tess looked uneasy. Obviously she didn't really feel like she could continue the conversation with Kirsten there, but she didn't have a reason to send her away. Tamsyn watched the teenager closely, the way her shoulders were turned ever so slightly away from her, the way she couldn't bring herself to look at Mo. Last night she hadn't had any reaction at all to the baby, but today, she seemed both interested and frightened at the same time.

'Well,' Tess focused her attention back on Tamsyn. 'The good news is that the roads are clear, although we don't have any suitable foster-carers available to take Baby right away . . .'

'Mo. She's a she and her nickname is Mo,' Tamsyn said, feeling herself unexpectedly bristle with irritation. Kirsten took a few more steps into the room and opened the fridge.

'That's sweet,' Tess's smile was warm and kind and Tamsyn had no doubt that the sentiment was genuine, yet she found herself rapidly cooling to the other woman, her hold on Mo tightening just a little. Tess continued, 'So anyway, to cut a long story short, I will be able to take Mo off your hands today. Now, actually.'

'Now?' Tamsyn asked. 'Like, right now?'

'We'll wait till she's finished her feed,' Tess chuckled. 'Oh, can you make a note of what brand of formula you've been giving her, so we can make sure we use the same one?'

'Where will you take her?' Tamsyn asked her. 'If there aren't any foster-parents?'

'Are you taking her to a home?' Kirsten asked, holding a carton of orange juice. 'Already? But it's too soon.'

Tess glanced irritably at the girl, and Tamsyn wondered if she really could spot the very large red flags that were popping up all around the room. Kirsten's interest in the baby had to mean more than she was letting on.

'To a hospital for a few more days, so her health can be monitored, and then, if we still haven't had any luck with foster-carers, there are care homes. But it probably won't come to that, and after all the paperwork's done we'll be able to find her a permanent adoptive family easily. There are always people who want to adopt babies.'

'Whoa, hold on.' Tamsyn pushed her chair back a little, increasing the distance between Mo and Tess by a few inches, and glancing at Kirsten. 'We still don't know that her mother is out of the picture. I know I feel like I've been up for a decade, but actually this only happened yesterday. You're moving too fast. We need to give the mum a chance to think about what's happened, to realise that things might not be as bad as she thinks they are. We need to give her a chance to come forward and get some help. And what about the TV crew? They'll want to film Mo, so you can't take her now.'

'Of course, we're still doing all we can to find the mother, and help her if and when she comes forward,' Tess said. 'That remains one of our top priorities, but we have to think of all eventualities for Baby.'

'Mo,' Tamsyn said firmly. 'Her name is Mo, and I don't want you to take her today. I'm not going to let you.'

Tamsyn saw the faintest ghost of a smile on Kirsten's face as she poured herself a glass of juice. It seemed like this castle was full of young girls who needed someone in their corner. And Tamsyn had been that girl, once; God only knows what would have happened to her if her family and friends had given up on her when she was making terrible choices and getting into all sorts of trouble. Who was doing that job for Kirsten?

There was a pause, and Tess and Sergeant Dangerfield exchanged looks, looks that very much said Tamsyn was getting overemotional. And perhaps she was, but what else was one human being supposed to do when it came to the welfare of another – just shrug and look away? Tamsyn straightened her back and remembered the time that she had to march an internationally renowned supermodel out of the building because she'd threatened one of their dressers with a pair of serrated-edged scissors. She could take down Tess Jameson, no trouble, she told herself.

'I see you've become attached to Baby,' Tess said, ever so kindly. 'And that's lovely, but I have to remind you that you don't actually have any say over what happens to her.' Tamsyn felt a cold drench of fury just as Sue walked into the room and leant against the counter, for once remaining silent as she assessed the situation. 'We temporarily authorised you to care for Baby under exceptional circumstances, but now those circumstances have passed and we are able to take her into our care.'

'But that makes no sense,' Tamsyn said. 'I've been looking after Mo for the first twenty-four hours of her life, during which time I've pretty much never put her down, and I've got the backache to prove it. She knows me. I'm the one that makes her feel safe. I know it's not my job, I know it can't be my job for ever, I don't having any hopes of keeping her. But what I will do, if it is the very last thing I do, is make sure that she feels safe and secure until there is a proper and certain future for her, whenever that may be. Everyone deserves at least that, especially her. And she won't get it in some plastic crib on a ward in a hospital, no matter how kind the nurses are. And she won't get that in a children's home or with foster-carers, who she'll just start to get to know before you take her away again.' Tamsyn shook her head resolutely. 'I'm not letting you take her until you can demonstrate to me that you have a safe, caring and as good as permanent home for her. And that's after you've done everything you can to make sure, first, that there isn't any hope of her being reunited with her mother.' She looked at Sergeant Dangerfield. 'You can arrest me if you like.'

Tamsyn glanced at Sue, who nodded in approval.

'You see,' Sergeant Dangerfield said rather gingerly, 'you don't actually have any legal right to . . .'

'Oh, don't be so ridiculous, Jeff,' Sue stepped in. 'And you, Mrs Jameson. I know you have a difficult job to do, and there are rules and regulations. But look at that baby! She is a little person. A human being, not just a statistic. And more than that, she is a Poldore baby, and I don't know about you St Austell lot, but in this town we look after our own, including her mother, whoever that may be. You know full well that, if you want to, you can let the baby stay here until either you find her mother or proper arrangements have been made. You just need to extend the temporary care order that was issued for Tamsyn and Jed. It's easy enough.'

'We can't just bend the rules like that,' Tess insisted. 'Not even for you, Ms Montaigne. Not for anyone.'

'It's always got to be all by the book,' Kirsten said. 'Even if the book is full of crap.'

'Kirsten, I really don't think you are helping . . .'

'She's right, though. Of course you can bend the rules,' Sue said briskly. 'All you have to do is decide to be decent about it. Decide what is really and truly best for the child and act on it. It's awfully simple if you think about it.'

'Well, even if that were a possibility,' Tess argued, 'I don't know how long this is going to take. 'Miss Thorne has been very good about caring for Baby . . .'

'Her name is Mo,' Sue said.

'Thus far,' Tess continued, her feathers almost visibly ruffled and puffed out. 'But I understand that you live and work in Paris, Miss Thorne? Will you still be here next week, or the week after that? Or in a month, if, heaven forbid, it takes that long?'

Tamsyn hesitated, thinking of next year's Fall collection that needed pulling together, and all the work they had to do to get ready for fashion week in October. Bernard hadn't even wanted her to come to the wedding at all; he'd been horrified at the idea of her taking a few days' holiday, especially when he was on the brink of agreeing a highly lucrative deal with a high-street chain to mass-produce a very watered-down range of his clothing. He had only relented because she promised to be constantly at his beck and call when she got back for at least a solid year, including Christmas and New Year. Her life, her exciting, busy, glamorous, cosmopolitan life that she had worked for almost every moment since she was an adult, was in a state of suspended animation, just waiting for her to come back again and step right into the middle of its whirling, wonderful vortex. Annoyingly, Tess Jameson did have a point. How long was she prepared to make this stand?

She hesitated, looking down at Mo, who, having drained the bottle, had pushed the teat out of her mouth and was now sleeping, her tiny profile turned towards Tamsyn, as if she needed reassurance that she was still there. Really, they were nothing at all to do with each other; there was no blood relation, no sense of being beholden or responsibility. Yes, Mo was a Poldore baby, but Tamsyn hadn't thought of herself as a Poldore woman for a very long time, for quite a long time before she'd actually left if she wanted to be specific, and yet . . . Every day a great many people knowingly placed their trust in her to do what was right, to get the collections in on time, to make sure the right fabrics were on order, in exactly the right amount, to book models that would show the clothes off in exactly the way Bernard had envisioned them. Hundreds of people made conscious decisions to depend on her. Mo hadn't had that choice; she hadn't ever had a moment where she was able to decide to rely on Tamsyn. She simply did, and Tamsyn knew that the baby trusted her, with the simple certainty of a brand-new human. And Tamsyn realised with a sudden and terrifying jolt that, based on their very short acquaintance, she would never betray that trust. She would not let Mo down, no matter what or how long it took, or what it cost her. And she wouldn't let Kirsten see her walking away from someone who needed her.

'I'll be here for her,' she said. 'For as long as it takes for you to settle her properly. I won't go back to Paris until she is taken proper care of.'

'Come on, Tess,' Sue said, sitting down and smiling in that frighteningly predatory way she had when she had her target in her sights. 'Don't tell me you can't do a bit of jiggery-pokery and extend that temporary care order? It's not like Tamsyn is alone, either. You have our vicar here backing her up, and she's welcome to stay here with us for as long as she needs to. Her sister is a nanny with an NVQ3 in childcare, and I'm a mother of three. Look at Mo, look at her. What do you honestly believe in your heart is the best thing to do for that baby?'

Tess pressed her lips together and squirmed in her seat, Jeff Dangerfield studying the back of his hand with great care, as she thought.

'Very well,' Tess said. 'I'll extend the temporary care order on a rolling basis with weekly reviews. But she will have to be seen by a GP, not a vet, *today*, in my presence, and I need to see where she is sleeping, go through her feeding regime and make sure you know what you are doing.'

Tamsyn blanched, as she clearly had no idea what she was doing, and they didn't really have a place to sleep at present, apart from the sofa in the snug, which she suspected wouldn't qualify.

'Wonderful,' Sue said, setting down a huge, thickly

filled Victoria sponge in front of Tess. 'Well, you have a piece of that, and a nice cup of tea, and I'll just see if Dr Morris can get over from St A's. He owes me a favour, you know. I lent him one of our cats when his surgery was overrun with rats. You sit tight, and I'll sort it.'

Sue winked at Tamsyn so dramatically that Tamsyn was sure that Tess, Dangerfield, Kirsten and all of the various dogs at their feet must have noticed it.

'And while you're at it, you think about your act for tonight.'

'My act?' Tamsyn blinked.

'Yes, I'm putting on a show, right here,' Sue said, 'in the great hall, to cheer everyone up. And also to match people in need with people who can help them. I'm hoping for a bit of a skill swap: carpenters, painters and decorators, that sort of thing.'

'That's a good idea,' Tamsyn conceded. 'Jed's looking for a stained-glass expert.'

'Oh well, darling, this *is* Poldore. There's about ten of those,' Sue said.

'And you couldn't do that without the singing and dancing element?' Tamsyn asked her, imagining that her mother would insist on doing something from the burlesque-ercise class that she went to for her 'turn'!

'Well, I could, Tamsyn,' Sue said. 'But seriously, where would be the fun in that?'

Chapter Fourteen

'And that's where they're sleeping,' Sue said, leading Tess and Alex out of her and Mo's new room, which had materialised quite suddenly in another turret. Comfortably furnished with a double bed, with a little crib next to it, it was situated opposite a bathroom, which Sue assured the social worker would only be used by Tamsyn and Mo. And Tamsyn had to admit, she loved the room, though its velvet curtains were worn and its carpets threadbare in places. If the scent of frenzied Febreze'd vacuuming in the air was anything to go by, it had recently been full of some of Sue's treasures, but it still had enough glamour about it to make Tamsyn smile.

'Very nice,' Tess said, nodding her approval. 'And even a little fridge and a bottle warmer so you don't have to go up and down the stairs.'

'Yes, that's courtesy of my daughter, Meadow,' Sue said. 'She's very kindly donated you the drinks fridge she has in her room, not that she knows it yet.'

'And a changing station. You know you mustn't leave B . . . Mo unattended on it, don't you, Tamsyn? Even at a few days old there's a chance she could wriggle off and hurt herself.'

'Of course,' Tamsyn said, although she had known no such thing. As far as she was concerned, Mo might stay just as she was for the next year or so, or start walking any time next Tuesday, the developmental milestones of children and what they should do having so far passed her by, even when she *was* a child.

'Good,' Tess said, 'and the GP's happy, so I'm happy to go ahead and extend the temporary care order, subject to police checks.' She paused for a moment, and then rested her hand gently on Tamsyn's upper arm. 'I know you want the best for Mo, Tamsyn. But, well, you know you will still have to say goodbye to her at some point. Don't get too attached.'

'Excellent,' Sue said, hooking her arm through the social worker's and leading her back downstairs. 'Now tell me, Tess, do you tap-dance?'

Tamsyn waited for them to go, and then sat down on the edge of the once-gilt-framed bed and looked out of the window. A wave of exhaustion engulfed her, and she barely noticed that the pale blue sky was beginning to fill at its edges with dark purple bruises of clouds yet again.

'Well, Mo,' she said, placing the slumbering child in the crib and leaning back. 'We might as well rest our eyes for a minute.'

'Sis! You're needed urgently,' Cordelia burst in through the door, startling Mo and causing her to scream furiously. 'Oh my God, you've got your own room, and it's much nicer than mine, you bitch!'

'I'm needed for you to urgently complain to?' Tamsyn asked her, scooping Mo up in her arms. 'Nothing changes.'

'No, not about the room, although, frankly, yes about the room. But there's a massive emergency going on downstairs, more massive than abandoned babies, historical storms and wrecked churches!'

'What is it?' Tamsyn said, concern shaking her awake, and thinking first for some reason about Jed.

'Alex's wedding dress? And all the bridesmaids' dresses?' Cordelia paused for dramatic effect. 'Totally ruined!'

Alex was sitting in the old battered armchair in the nook, with Buoy at her side. Sensing her mood, he had rested his head on her thigh as a sign of solidarity, a demonstration that he, a dog who did his level best to avoid a bath more than once every two to three years, totally understood what despondency a set of ruined bridal garments could inspire in a human woman. She wasn't wailing or crying, nor were there tears, as there had been earlier in St Piran's. She was just sitting there, slumped, her arm dangling to one side, letting Skipper gently nibble her fingers as if they might be food.

'I'm sure we can do something,' Gloria was saying as she gingerly picked through a heap of soaking-wet, muddy satin on the table. Tamsyn surmised that this was the remains of one wedding and five bridesmaids' dresses. 'Ah, here's the expert.'

'I design dresses,' Tamsyn said. 'I have never yet resurrected any from the dead.'

Alex's laugh was dry, mirthless.

'Look, it doesn't matter,' she said. 'I don't care if I'm wearing jeans and a jumper. If I get to marry Ruan the day after tomorrow, surrounded by my friends, then what does it matter if I'm wearing the only wedding dress that I could find that I loved, and that took months and months to choose, and which made me feel graceful and beautiful and special? What does it matter at all, really? After all, it's not as if I am the sort of person to get superstitious about all the bad omens, or start to think that the whole thing is doomed, is it?'

Her voice rose with each word, finishing in a sort of strangulated shout of restrained misery. If this was her Bridezilla act, she needed to work on it a bit. Bernard had once designed a wedding gown for a countess who ripped out a large handful of the dresser's hair after she accidentally stuck a pin in her. There had been a court case and a large payment made to the dresser, who gave up dressing and went to live on a yacht in Capri, but the countess was not the least bit repentant. Now *that* was Bridezilla.

'Do you have a nice frock you can wear instead?' Gloria said, gently, going to her daughter and sitting on the arm of the chair to embrace her. 'OK, well, you don't have any frocks, but I've got loads. You could wear one of those, perhaps. What about that nice little number with the leopard print?'

'Yes, yes, Mum, I really want to get married in my mother's cast-offs,' Alex said unhappily.

'Or the boutique,' Lucy said. 'What about Purple Hearts? They always have the most beautiful dresses in the window, although I have literally no idea who buys them or why anyone would need a full designer ballgown in a seaside town, but still. One of those?'

'They don't make designer dresses for women with breasts or hips,' Alex said, taking a moment to narrow her eyes at Tamsyn, who had to admit that this was true.

She picked up what would have been a bridesmaid's dress, the oyster-grey satin utterly ruined, and then looked at Alex's dress, which was in an even sorrier state. It had been a plain ivory organza over satin, light, simply cut to make the most of her figure. It would have suited Alex, Tamsyn thought, but there was no way that any sort of cleaning would get the stains out now.

'What's going on?' Jed appeared, and seeing Mo reposing in a baby rocker that Cordelia had brought down from the attic, picked her up and cradled her, kissing the tip of her nose.

'Well,' Sue said, 'I was organising a little mood-raiser talent show for tonight, but then the girls returned from Gloria's having found that a tree has left a whacking great hole in Gloria's roof on its way through, and although the dresses were in her bedroom, they are totally ruined.'

'So, oh dress designer of greatness,' Keira said, keeping an eye on her boys as they chased a crazed Skipper around the courtyard, along with Sue's children and a huge poodle. 'Any ideas? Any miracle fixes?'

'Well,' she hesitated, not sure how to deliver the final death blow to all hope. 'There are a few patches here and there that I could cut out, but even then I don't think I'd have enough material to make one wedding dress. I'm so sorry, Alex, there's not much I can do for these.'

'It's fine.' Alex shrugged, the tears rolling down her face, so that Buoy heaved himself up onto his back paws and began licking her cheeks. 'They're only clothes, after all. I don't even know why I care. Everyone knows I don't care about things like dresses.'

'You are allowed to care about your wedding dress,' Gloria said gently.

'Of course you are,' Keira said. 'Tamsyn, perhaps you could have a look at what we have got, dresses and things, and put something together, like a stylist.'

'Maybe,' Tamsyn said. 'But Alex is right; to really look her best she needs something bespoke: she's tall and curvy. She's maybe a twelve on the bottom and, what, a sixteen on top? Her legs are long, and her arms . . . It's unlikely that a borrowed dress is going to make her feel any better than she does in her favourite pair of jeans.'

'Harsh,' Cordelia said.

'I'm sorry. I don't mean to be harsh,' Tamsyn said. 'I just wouldn't want you to feel uncomfortable on your big day.'

'Could you make her something?' Jed said suddenly. 'I mean, I know you're a designer, but can you sew too? We have a sewing circle in Poldore, and about eight machines, a whole host of embroiderers and seam-stresses that I'm sure could help.'

Tamsyn looked at Mo, whose care she had just promised to commit to, and wondered if she could in all conscience take on a last-minute wedding-dress commission, even if she had the materials, which she didn't.

'You could do it with Mo at your side,' Jed said. 'And I can do feeds, and change nappies . . .?'

'In between cleaning up the church?' Tamsyn asked him.

'I've got twenty volunteers on that already. They're doing the first clean and then are coming up here for the show,' Jed said. 'And Keira's already been down to have look at the church and made some drawings about what she is going to do with it.'

'It's going to be wonderful,' Keira said, her eyes alight in a way that Tamsyn rarely saw these days.

'But even if I could make six dresses in a day and a half, I don't have the material, or any beads or crystals, or even a pen or a tape measure.'

'I know exactly what you need,' Sue said, triumphantly. 'Follow me. For once again, I, Sue Montaigne, have the means to save the day.' She positively smirked at Rory, who Tamsyn hadn't even noticed was lurking in the corner, looking decidedly green around the gills, probably coming down with the Poldore bug too. 'Hoarding, my arse,' she said.

Tamsyn, Alex and Gloria followed Sue into the depths, or more accurately the heights, of Castle House once again, leaving Keira and Cordelia to attempt to wrangle the children, while supervising the roasting of several meats for an after-show party.

'Rory might moan about it,' Sue said. 'But I'm glad I just can't throw anything away. I think it must be a Montaigne trait dating back generations. Up here.' At the end of the first landing there was a door secreted in the panelling, which opened on to a narrow, dark staircase that had to lead into some attic space, Tamsyn supposed.

'I was only twenty-two when I officially inherited the old girl. Funny, I grew up in this house, but there were so many locked doors that even I'd never seen behind. Father was a dear, dear man, but he never could cope with the size of the place. He used to pretend he lived in a four-bedroom semi. Shut off rooms, whole wings even, covered stuff with sheets, it was terribly sad. Although a good deal cheaper. Anyway,' she paused at the stop of the stairs looking down on her followers with a typical Sue-style sense of drama, 'the first thing I did when I got the keys was to open every single locked door I could find. This room was the room I discovered last.' She pushed the door open. 'I think Mother must have been up here quite a lot; the latest period seems to be from the sixties.'

Tamsyn gasped as she walked into the dark, vaulted space, lit only by a few weak light bulbs and dirty windows, but she didn't need to see better to know that she was in a room filled with clothes. There were racks and racks of clothes, and chests, too: old-fashioned ocean liner-style chests, as well as older-looking oak and leather chests that dated back even earlier, most of them emblazoned with the Montaigne crest, piled one on top of the other from floor to ceiling. This had to be how Howard Carter had felt when he'd opened Tutankhamen's tomb, Tamsyn thought.

'Oh my goodness,' she exclaimed in sheer delight. 'Oh, I've died and gone to fashion heaven.'

'Well, I've spent a few happy hours up here,' Sue said. 'I think the earliest garment I've uncovered is perhaps Regency, but there is so much. Surely in here you'd find something you could update, adapt, customise, cut up even, to make the dresses?'

Tamsyn ran her hand down a rail of garments that looked as if they were from the 1950s. 'It would be a sin to cut some of these up. Were these your mother's? She had beautiful taste. I can see Dior, Chanel . . . simply stunning.'

'Oh, they're only old clothes!' Sue said casually. 'You can do what you like with them: take them in, let them out?' she suggested.

'No, that wouldn't work. Women of that era were just smaller than us. But there's so much here. I'm sure I can find some garments to work with, bring them new life.' Tamsyn's eyes glowed as she looked around the room. She felt her heart pumping, and even in her state of exhaustion discovered that she was filled with the most overwhelming joy.

'I'll need a big table,' she said.

'Dining-room table seats forty,' Sue told her.

'Very sharp scissors, and a pencil, 4B, sewing machines, helpers – lots of helpers, people who know their way around a pattern. But only the best ones, the ones that really care; I don't want do-gooders, or amateurs. They will have to submit a sample of their work for me to OK.'

'Good.' Sue nodded approvingly. 'Good.'

'I need Alex and all the bridesmaids' measurements, their actual ones. Not to the nearest centimetre, but to the last millimetre.'

'I'll do it,' Sue said, with grim determination.

'And I need some time alone in this room, to see what there is,' Tamsyn added finally, although what she really meant by that was she needed time alone to dance around like a little girl who'd just been given the keys to a toyshop.

'Right, come on, girls.' Sue bustled Gloria and Alex towards the door.

'Wait.' Alex stopped and turned round. 'Tamsyn, what's happening?'

'Alex,' Tamsyn's smile could have lit up the whole town, never mind the attic. 'I'm going to make you a Tamsyn Thorne original. I'm going to make you the wedding dress of your dreams, and the first time you are going to see it will be on your wedding day.'

Chapter Fifteen

Tamsyn was sitting amid a whirlpool of fabric, having selected a half-dozen likely candidates for recycling during her initial rummage through the treasure trove of fashion, when Ruan opened the attic door, ducking to come in, and stood there in silence for a moment, taking it all in.

'It's like the mother of all jumble sales,' he said.

'Oh, it's so much more than that,' Tamsyn smiled, lifting a length of teal-coloured silk to her face and rubbing it against her cheek.

'You look different,' Ruan said, smiling a little.

'It's the hair, the revenge part two, and this time it's beyond help. I think it's taking its vengeance on me for so many years of straightening. This hair does not want to go back in the closet.'

'I like it,' Ruan said. 'But it's not that. You're happy here, aren't you? In your element. I've never seen you doing what you really love to do before.'

'Although strictly speaking, rolling around on the floor in vintage dresses isn't exactly what I do in Paris,' Tamsyn said. No, Paris wasn't nearly so much fun as this.

It was nice to have this conversation with him, as cautious and careful as it was, although the room soon fell into silence again, and Tamsyn wondered if now was the right time to say what she had to say. Did she have the courage? Was that why he'd sought her out, to try and lay their ghosts to rest?

'Ruan, I've . . .'

'The thing is . . .' he interrupted her. 'The reason that I came is that Mo's missing you a bit. Jed must have walked her about forty-five laps of the kitchen table, but every time he sits down she starts wailing again. He won't let anyone come and get you.'

'Oh,' said Tamsyn. 'Well, I think I'm nearly done.'

'Already?' Ruan asked her.

'No, God no. Choosing dresses and fabric to make into gowns . . . There's so much here, Ruan. I could live up here; it's just like when we used to play dressing up as kids. Do you remember when Keira and I dressed you up as a princess, and Lucy did your make-up? You were such a pretty girl!'

Ruan grinned. 'Yeah, Dad was horrified.'

'Oh, he wasn't really,' Tamsyn said. 'I think Dad was a bit of a glam rocker in his day.'

'Are you OK?' Ruan asked her. 'I heard about what you told the social worker about Mo. That you're staying in Poldore with her until she's properly settled.'

'Yes,' Tamsyn said as she began to fold the dresses she had chosen to work with into a neat pile. 'I must admit, it took me a bit by surprise too. But it might not be for that long. I'm still hoping that her mum is going to turn up soon.'

'You've wanted to leave Poldore for so long; you were always telling our friends not to get stuck here. I can't imagine you wanting to be here a second longer than you have to be.'

'Well, I won't be,' Tamsyn said, smoothing her hands over the pile to hide the unexpected hurt the comment had caused her. 'What do you think of this blue? Isn't it the exact shade of Alex's eyes?'

Ruan crouched down beside her, touching the fabric. 'It is,' he said. 'You are being very kind.'

'No need to sound quite so surprised,' Tamsyn said, a little sharply. 'Just because a person is dedicated to her career, it doesn't make her a monster. The sort of person who'd let her brother's bride get married in jeans, or send a baby off to a faceless hospital ward without a second thought.'

'I didn't say that.' Ruan stood up again, his demeanour cooling slightly.

'So, what are you saying?' Tamsyn asked him. 'You're about to get married to a woman who, as far as I can tell, is deeply in love with you. So if there is something you have to get off your chest, tell me. Tell me now.'

'Did she talk to you?' Ruan asked her, and Tamsyn knew who he was talking about at once.

'Who?' she replied, even so.

'Merryn, did she talk to you before the accident?'

Tamsyn looked away, her brow furrowed. Now wasn't the time to go back to that point, to that terrible day, not now. Not when he was about to get married, and everything in his life was going forward so perfectly. And if he knew, well, what good would it do, except to make Tamsyn feel better? And yet, she had always promised herself that if he asked her directly she would tell him the truth.

'Yes,' she said, finally. 'She spoke to me.'

'Before she spoke to me, before she told me she was leaving?' he said.

'Yes,' Tamsyn nodded. 'A long time before. She had been thinking about leaving for ages. She loved you, Ruan, but she loved life, and she wanted so much of it. More of it than you could give her in Poldore. That was how she felt back then, on that day. She knew she had to tell you.'

Ruan was silent for a long moment, his fists clenched at his side, and Tamsyn felt something small and painful tearing inside her. She'd thought, she'd hoped that the pain of what had happened had faded for him now, that it wouldn't matter so much, but obviously it did.

'Look, now isn't the time to think about Merryn,' she said. 'It won't change anything.'

She stood, gathering up armfuls of dresses.

'Don't do this now,' she said. 'Alex loves you, so much. I barely know her, but it's written all over her. And you didn't love Merryn the way you love Alex. I see you two together and it makes me think . . . well, it makes me have faith. You two together, you make me believe.'

Tamsyn thought of Jed as she said the words, and the thought was followed by the strangest sensation, one that was almost like sadness and almost like joy and a sudden longing to be in the same room as him.

'I know how much I love Alex,' Ruan said. 'I don't need you to tell me that. I'd tear the world apart for her, and put it back together again, but . . . don't you see, Tamsyn, in all the years since Merryn went, I've never known. I've never really understood what happened, and I know you know, otherwise . . . you wouldn't have said what you said to me at her funeral; you wouldn't have been so cruel. I'm begging you to tell me everything because I have to know. I have to know why I lost Merryn, because . . .'

'Um.' There was a cough, and Alex stood in the doorway. 'I heard you were back, and I . . . well, I'd missed you.'

'Alex,' Ruan said. 'That didn't sound like – I wasn't—'

'OK. Well, I'll be . . . somewhere else.' She turned on her heel and fled, running down the narrow flight of stairs.

Ruan buried his head in his hands, and made a noise that was something between a growl and a groan and consisted of pure anguish. She had to tell him, Tamsyn knew.

'She's going to think I don't love her,' Ruan said. 'She's going to think she's second best!'

'And is she?' Tamsyn asked him.

'No, no, not at all. The way I feel about her, it's the real thing. I thought I loved Merryn, I *did* love her. But not enough to want to let her go, to want her to be truly happy. I thought we were sorted for good: business, house and each other. That's what I thought. I thought that we had each other, and that was enough. I loved her, but it was nothing compared to what I feel for Alex. But I have to know what went wrong so I don't make the same mistake again, not with Alex.'

'Then you need to go and make her believe that now,' Tamsyn said. 'Because if she's calling off the wedding, then I don't have to start dress designing and I might even get some sleep tonight.'

'She's not calling off the wedding,' Ruan said.

'Are you sure about that?' Tamsyn asked him.

He thought for a moment, and then ran down the stairs after Alex.

Chapter Sixteen

Tamsyn bowed her head, pressing her lips against the top of Mo's head and inhaling at the same time. It was funny how babies had this scent that made you feel as if everything in the world was worth the trouble of getting up in the morning, or in the middle of the night, or not actually going to sleep at all.

Castle House's long dining room, with its impressive sixteenth-century windows that looked out over the town and then to the sea beyond, was one of the few original parts of the building, and a peaceful place. As Tamsyn stood there, waiting for Mo to do the decent thing and bring up some wind, she had a wonderful sensation of anticipation, the way that she always felt just before she was about to embark on creating something. It was a fleeting moment of perfect happiness, those rare few seconds of certainty that she had found her vocation in life. That was, of course, unless the bride told the groom where to shove his explanations, and then her vocation could be shelved again for the time being.

It was still light outside, but the threat of rain hung in a fully charged sky. The weather forecast had said there would be no more deluges, at least not for the foreseeable future, but it had warned of electrical storms, a sort of aftermath of the rain that had preceded it. And on the horizon Tamsyn could see lightning crackle with sudden flares and flashes over the ocean. She hoped it wasn't a sign. Tamsyn had never normally been the sort of person who believed in signs; she believed that everything happened as a result of a random chain of events, but there was something about her stay in Poldore that felt, well, fateful.

It had been a busy couple of hours since Ruan had unwittingly put his foot in it with Alex, and Tamsyn hadn't had a moment to catch up with either of them. The second she had come down to the dining room with her armfuls of old dresses, Jeff Dangerfield had been waiting for her to talk to the TV crew. A very orange young woman, with bright pink lipstick, had greeted her as she walked into the room, after Jed had taken Mo, whom Tess insisted wasn't to make an appearance on TV.

'Here she is, the hero of the hour,' the woman smiled, offering Tamsyn a surprisingly limp handshake. 'I'm Natalie Nixon.'

'I'm not really a hero,' Tamsyn said.

'Yes you are, and just before we start, I wanted to let you know that the national news has picked this story up. It's got that feel-good factor amid all the terrible doom and gloom, so you'll be on the *News at Ten*!'

'The feel-good factor?' The phrase made Tamsyn feel deeply uncomfortable. 'I thought this was about making an appeal to a mother who's just given up her baby? I don't suppose she feels very good.'

'Well, it's the coverage that might just reunite her with her child,' Natalie said happily. 'So we'll just do a little bit about how and when you found her, and about the dog, if you don't mind. We tried to get the dog to come and be in shot, but he seems a bit grumpy.' She pulled the corners of her mouth down into an exaggerated pout, and then laughed. 'Maybe we should have talked to his agent first! Anyway, people love an animal-hero story, so we'll take some shots of him when he's not looking and cut them in later. And if you could say how, if you'd been a moment later, she would probably have been horribly crushed to death, and then you can tell me any message you've got for the mother, got it?'

Tamsyn had wanted to turn around and run back out of the room, and go and join Buoy in his silent protest against a manipulative media, but this would probably be her only chance to try and reach out to Mo's mother, even if she did happen to be the young girl who was hovering in the corridor outside, peering at what was going on from within the small group of strays who'd gathered to watch. Besides, it seemed like Natalie Nixon was in a hurry to get to her next appointment, where she would be interviewing an old lady who'd found a World War Two mine washed up in her garden. She answered Natalie's rapid-fire questions as best she could, all the time thinking that she should probably have changed out of Cordelia's little chiffon dress printed with a skull-and-crossbones pattern, and the safety-pin leggings, although into what she had no idea, and wondering if, on her debut appearance on national television, she would look mostly like an ageing and exhausted goth. Before she knew it, Natalie was nodding very seriously at her and saying, 'And what message do you want give to little Mo's missing – feared dead – mother?'

Tamsyn looked at Natalie, and then rather warily at the camera, and then back again at Natalie, and realised she didn't know what to say. So she looked at the camera again and imagined Mo's cross, crumpled little face and thought of the angry young woman she had been once, the girl who'd just lost her dad and didn't understand why, the girl who just wanted to run away and forget. And she tried to talk to her. 'Please, please get in touch,' she said into the lens. 'You probably think that life is just too difficult and that you can't cope, and that it's too late to go back. But I promise you, there are so many people who want to help you. Who want to make sure that you are well, and give you any care you might need. Most of all we want you and Mo together. Mo is just the nickname I gave her; she's waiting for you to come and tell her what she is really called. Because only you know . . . and it's never too late. It's never too late to start again and make things right.' Tamsyn hesitated for a moment and then looked back at Natalie.

'Is that OK?'

'That was amazing,' Natalie said, with heartfelt sincerity. 'But could you just do it again? Kevin said the sound was off.'

Tamsyn had been very glad to see the back of Natalie Nixon and her film crew. And after receiving word that the wedding wasn't off, she found that working alone, or almost alone, in Sue's dining room was the happiest and most content she had felt in a long time, a really long time, in fact. Even before she came to Poldore for the wedding. It had been an age since she had been the mistress of her own creative urges. Bernard guarded the creative control of his label so carefully, that during the time she'd spent working for him she had become adept in knowing exactly what he wanted a finished design to look like, which wasn't something she begrudged. It was always the way of the apprentice. You had to learn from the master, pay your dues, wait for it to be your moment to spread your wings and fly free. Although it did rather feel like she'd been waiting a long time.

'Hello.' Alex appeared in the doorway, Buoy at her side. 'Sue said you needed to see me?'

'I do,' Tamsyn said. 'At least, I hope I do. My brother

has explained himself to you, I understand?'

'He . . .' Alex faltered. 'Well, he tried, and I want to understand, it's just . . .'

'It's your time, and you thought that all he should be thinking about is you,' Tamsyn finished for her matter-of-factly.

'Yes, but that sounds awfully selfish, doesn't it?' Alex said unhappily, sitting down. 'I think I've turned into a total "me, me, me" merchant, since I got engaged.'

Tamsyn's laughter was genuine. 'Oh darling, you have to come and visit me in Paris. You are positively Mother Teresa in comparison to some of the people I know.'

'You think so?' Alex looked dubious.

'I do, and the thing is, he was only asking me about Merryn for your sake. Merryn was my best friend, you see. I knew more about her and what she was thinking than he did, especially at the end. You know how it is, women talk to each other, really talk. I think he's just trying to understand what happened, and . . .' Tamsyn hesitated, 'the day we stood around her empty grave, I blamed him. I told him it was all his fault that she drowned. That he smothered her, trapped her, cornered her, and that she had no option but to run away from him, that he drove her to head out to sea in a boat that was too small, without any safety gears. I told him, in front of everyone, that he sent Merryn to her death, that it was his fault that he had lost her, that I had lost her.'

'Oh my God,' Alex said quietly, not in anger but as if she finally understood. 'He said you two had fallen out, but he never said why. Not even Cordelia or your mum said anything. I suppose I thought he'd tell me when he was ready.'

'I was hurt and sad and . . .' Tamsyn couldn't express the other words that crowded against the roof of her mouth, fighting to be spoken. 'I lashed out at him, and because Ruan is Ruan, he took it to heart. It's not an excuse, it's not even a reason – it was just the way it happened. And I owe him an apology. More than that: an explanation. I've been putting it off, hiding from it, because I suppose so much of my life is so far away from here, and so far away from Merryn. When I think about her, it isn't as if she is some lost soul. I think of her living the life she dreamt of, seeing the world, kissing all the boys, having the time of her life. Facing up to that day means I have to face up to having lost her, and . . . I've been too much of a coward to want to do that. I will talk to Ruan, I will make things right between us, I promise. But until I do, please know that that man loves you, with all of his heart and soul.'

Alex nodded. 'I know you're right. But it still hurts. I don't want him to have loved anyone else. Even someone he loved before he ever met me, and that's so stupid, isn't it?'

Tamsyn thought for a moment, rubbing her cheek against Mo's.

'I don't know,' she said finally. 'I don't really understand love.'

She thought of Bernard, whom she hadn't thought of for days. Was that love? What did it mean to fall in love with someone. How did you know? She knew when she was near him: her heart raced, her body tingled, every moment they were working together was full of expectation and anticipation about the moments when they would not be working. But she also knew that as soon as she wasn't in a room with Bernard, he didn't think about her, unless it was to give her an order. Yes, the phone lines had been down and her mobile didn't have a signal, but she knew that if she were able to miraculously check her voicemail, there would be no messages from him, or at least none that weren't work-related. When they were together, it seemed like the whole universe was centred round the two of them, but when they were apart, those feelings didn't linger. Could that be love? Was love the same for everyone?

'I thought I was in love, before Ruan,' Alex said. 'With this guy Marcus. I thought I loved him for years and years, and I did, but in a brotherly sort of way, as it turned out. I just didn't know enough to know what it was I was feeling. He's married now. I'm a little bit scared of his wife, but they're good together. Anyway, they're supposed to be arriving with my dad and his partner tomorrow. Marcus is going to be an usher. I'm worried about him being an usher. He thinks it's funny to rugby-tackle people he has never met. What if he rugby-tackles Ruan's mum, or Jed? Oh my God, what if he rugby-tackles Jed? He would so do that. I need to phone his scary wife and make sure she terrifies him into behaving. I think I can get her to do that if I promise to sit her next to Riley Rivers at the reception.'

'Alex . . . Alex?' Tamsyn interrupted her. 'I think you are slightly digressing.'

'Am I? What was I talking about?'

'The "how you know that you are in love" thing.' Tamsyn reminded her, because she really wanted to know.

'Right, well, when I thought I was in love with Marcus, I felt like you. I couldn't understand why the person I thought I wanted made me feel so unhappy so much of the time. And then there was Ruan, and I loved him. And he loved me, and I didn't have to wonder if he loved me because, because I felt it, I *knew*. It was such a relief. Life is complicated and difficult, but I wouldn't walk away from him because of his life before me. It's his life before me that has made him the man I love.'

Tamsyn nodded. 'You are quite smart. And you know that just before you came in he was explaining to me exactly how much he loved you. You should marry him, and not just because I am going to make you the most beautiful dress you have ever seen, although that could be considered a good enough reason.'

'So, do you have sketches?'

'Not yet,' Tamsyn said, carefully placing Mo in the baby chair that Cordelia had found for her. 'I want to talk to you about what you want and like, and then we'll take it from there. Sketches and patterns sorted by ten tonight, and then I start cutting and sewing. Make the most of this insight, because you won't be seeing your dress before you put it on to wear it down the aisle. It's going to be a surprise – my gift to you.'

Sue found her, with Mo asleep in the chair by her feet, as she was carefully drawing out the patterns for the new dresses on sheets of baking paper. It was almost midnight, and taking much longer than she thought, as she was having to tape sheets of paper together to make big enough pieces.

'Anything I can do?' Sue asked her.

'Not yet,' Tamsyn said. 'First of all, I need to get the patterns sorted and the fabric cut, and then we can get the sewing army on the case, hopefully first thing in the morning. Normally I'd make a calico toile – a kind of mock-up dress – but we don't have time for that, so we're just going to have to hope that the Poldore sewing circle pulls it out of the bag.'

'You are doing marvellous things,' Sue said. 'I'll bring you some food in a little while. It seems wrong that we are having so much fun in the great hall while you are in here all alone. No chance that I can tempt you through for a quick sausage roll, and perhaps a turn at singing? We have the best Poldore band you can imagine, you know: Brian Rogers, our very own seventies rock legend on guitar, and your sister on backing vocals. And former boy-band heart-throb Riley Rivers keeps trying to do breakdancing, but his back has gone. Now there's a man who doesn't know how to age gracefully, bless him and his trousers that he persists on wearing hanging halfway down his behind.'

'Has my mum done her burlesque-ercise thing yet?' Tamsyn asked.

'Not yet . . .'

'Then I'll stay here for now.' Tamsyn smiled. 'My sisters can bear witness to that particular marvel. Listen, Sue, I haven't had a chance to thank you for supporting me with the social worker, and sorting out a room for me and Mo, not that we are going to see much of it tonight.'

'I was glad to,' Sue said. 'I always thought you were a funny little girl, not as, erm, strong as the other Thornes. Always looked like a good breeze would blow you out to sea. And as for the tearaway you became as you got older, well, I've never had to expel anyone from Brownies except for you. I think you managed to offend everyone in the town before you were eighteen. When you left, I didn't expect to see you again, and, if I'm honest, I didn't really want to. And yet here you are, actually being quite extraordinary.'

'Thank you, I *think*,' Tamsyn said, her pencil hovering while she tried to work out exactly what it was Sue had just said. 'You know that girl, Kirsten? She reminds me of me, the me I used to be, only she has a much better reason to be that way than I do. I was angry at a world that had never done anything that terrible to me.'

'Ah yes, Kirsten,' Sue looked thoughtful. 'She does OK, living at the hostel. Very bright, just needs a bit of direction in life. Bit of a loner, though. You know how cruel girls can be.'

'Have you seen her . . . I mean, she seems quite interested in Mo,' Tamsyn said hesitantly, never sure what sort of whirlwind of activity she might be releasing in Sue. 'I might just be imagining it.'

'You think she might be the mother?' Sue asked. 'It's possible. She always looks so lonely, and so sad. They just couldn't find anyone to foster her, you know. She ran away from everywhere, hated everyone. Tried to run away with her little brother at one point. The hostel was the only place for her, but she seemed more settled there, more at peace, even if she didn't have much of a social life.'

'I get the impression there was something of a romance, and that it's over now,' Tamsyn said. 'I might be wrong, but, well, will you help me keep an eye on her? Either way, she looks like she needs a friend.'

'You are quite the caring, sharing person these days, aren't you?' Sue said, cocking her head as she watched Tamsyn work.

'I'm really not,' Tamsyn said. 'I'm utterly heartless, in fact, famous for it.'

'Well, I will keep an eye on Kirsten, but for now I'd better get back to the party. Rory's been flirting with one of Cordelia's friends. I'd better go and put a stop to it before he makes a fool of himself *again*.'

'Sue.' Tamsyn stopped her from leaving. 'You and Rory, you've been married quite a while now, ten years or so?'

'Or so,' Sue said.

'Do you love him as much as you did on your wedding day?' Tamsyn asked her. 'Look, don't answer if you don't want to. I'm just trying to get my head round some feelings of my own. I look at Alex and Ruan, and I think they will surely love each other for all of their lives, but I see you and Rory, and the way you were talking the other day in the kitchen, and it's almost as if . . . Well, does the love part always turn into annoyance, bitterness and regret?'

The look on Sue's face was quite unexpected, and Tamsyn realised she hadn't thought of Sue's feelings, but she was so used to her being as tough as the castle walls, she hadn't thought her bluntness would affect her. The last person to upset a Montaigne had been beheaded, so Tamsyn was devastated to see Sue's face crumple and her hands fly to her mouth to stifle a sob. She realised that she'd caused injury where none was intended.

'Oh, Sue,' she said, as her host crumpled onto a dining chair. 'Oh God, I'm so sorry. I was being crass and rude. I've got no right to pry. I'm sure you and Rory love each other just as much as you always did. What would I possibly know about it?'

Sue shook her head, furiously blinking back tears as she took a moment to compose herself.

'There's a difference between the relationship that I have with Rory, and Alex and Ruan's,' she said, finally, composing herself. 'I'm not what you would call a classic beauty. Even when I was young. Short, red curls, beaky nose. Bossy, loud, strident, opinionated. Not exactly the girl boys go for. I'd never had a boyfriend, not one who lasted more than a few weeks anyway, before I met Rory. I never thought that anyone would ever want to spend their life with me. When he said he did, well, I loved him just for saying it. I was grateful to him. We worked well together for a while, and we love each other still, from time to time, but . . . he has hurt me more than once, and I just treat him like a dogsbody most of the time, which makes him want to hurt me even more. We both know that we will never have the same sort of deep companionship that Alex and Ruan have, or that your mum and dad did, and that makes us angry with each other. And yet I would never leave him, and although he thinks he might leave me, he never will. He doesn't have the strength. So we muddle on, and sometimes it's even quite nice. And at least the children are happy. That is one thing that we do very well; we make happy children.'

Tamsyn nodded. 'Well, I mean, that's what life is like. Nothing is perfect, is it? No marriage is a fairy tale. I only have to look at Keira to see that. She barely ever sees her husband. He rarely comes to any family get-togethers; it's almost like she made him up. Might as well have, considering the support he gives her, which is none, aside from money. The fairy tale, the thing they all con us into believing, that's the problem, isn't it? It's because we all expect so much, but life just isn't like that.'

'You should talk to your mother about love,' Sue smiled. 'Your mum and dad were happy in the way that Ruan and Alex are. I don't know if a love like that is possible for every single one of us; if you have to be somehow more lucky or more brave to find that kind of love, or if it's just the luck of the draw. But it does happen. Sometimes. Just not to me.'

'Anyway,' she stood up abruptly, briskly wiping the heels of her hands across her eyes, 'I'd better get back. Do come through in a little while, perhaps when Mo needs her next feed? Everyone is missing you.'

'I will,' Tamsyn nodded. 'But only if Mum's already done her nipple-tassel thing, even if she does put them on over a jumper. Mo isn't ready to see that yet. And Sue . . . I'm sorry.'

'Don't be,' Sue straightened her shoulders. 'Does one good to let it all out now and again. A constant stiff upper lip can be awfully tiring, you know.'

Chapter Seventeen

It was a little while later, when the first pattern was almost finished, that the thunder started rolling in over the town and the window frames began to rattle as the wind rose. Mo started to mewl as the lightning whipped ever closer, and Tamsyn had to admit that the sheer power of the storm that she could see marching towards her through the gallery window unnerved her. Scooping Mo into her arms, she went to visit the party, suddenly feeling like she could do with some company. How Sue had arranged such a raucous event in the space of a few hours, particularly when most of the shops in the town were closed for business, and at least half the guests here were temporarily homeless, she would never know, but it occurred to her that Sue Montaigne would make the most wonderful manager of a fashion house; it could actually be her calling. Sad, really, that there weren't any Poldore-based designer labels.

Sue had set her brood, and all the teens, to decorating the hall all day, and they'd done a good job of it, too; there were even coloured lights, and Gloria's disco ball to top off the party atmosphere. Brian Rogers and his pub band The Poldore All Stars, which featured Cordelia's vocals, were in full swing on a little stage, currently backing Eddie Godolphin's explosive rendition of 'Bat Out of Hell'.

'Kill me now,' Lucy said, pushing through the dancers to get to Tamsyn's side. 'Just kill me.'

'He's pretty good,' Tamsyn said as she watched Eddie wobble his stomach in time to the music. 'I think he's pretty hot.'

'Oh my God!' Lucy looked appalled. 'If you weren't holding a baby . . .'

'Ear defenders!' Sue appeared, gently positioning something that looked like massive purple headphones over Mo's head, which she didn't seem to mind even though they were far too big for her.

'Hello, darling!' Laura danced up to her in that embarrassing way that only mothers can, a sort of combined conga-come-seizure style. 'How's the dressmaking going?'

'Well, I think,' Tamsyn said. 'How's the alcohol consumption going?'

'Getting there,' Laura giggled, launching herself back into the fray and then shimmying against Mr Figg the chemist, who had to be nearly ninety if he was a day. Children ran in and out of the adults, screaming for no apparent reason; the teenage boys stood in one corner, huddled around mobile phones, as if they'd just discovered the secret of making fire; and the teenage girls lounged against whatever they could find to lounge against in another corner, eyeing the boys and giggling. Scanning the room, Tamsyn couldn't see Kirsten anywhere, and she wasn't surprised; this sort of party would have been her own idea of hell at the same age. If Kirsten was anything like Tamsyn, she had stolen some beer and was sitting outside now, hopefully not smoking. When she got a chance, Tamsyn would see if she could track her down; maybe all Kirsten needed was someone to trust.

Around her – those brave or drunk enough to take to the makeshift dance floor – stood a good cross section of the Poldore community, all of them making the most of a moment of levity amongst the serious consequences of the storm. Tamsyn silently hoped that they weren't about to be given a repeat performance of the destruction it had wrought, for if the church suffered yet another drenching it would be impossible to get it ready for the wedding in time. Lightning flashed outside the window, followed at once by a deep roar of thunder that could even be heard over the music.

'Another storm is bad news,' Tamsyn said. 'I'm not sure the town can take any more rain.'

'Well, this one is supposed to be mainly thunder and lightning, something to do with thermals,' Lucy said. 'Not too much rain, so hopefully it will be OK, if quite scary. As long as nothing gets burnt to the ground – we couldn't be that unlucky, could we?'

'I really hope not,' Tamsyn said.

'And at least we are all together. It's nice, isn't it? I bet you don't get such community spirit in Paris.'

'I have certainly never been to a party like this.' Tamsyn smiled as she watched the knitting circle get up on stage to perform a cancan.

'Just before the ladies of the knitting circle start their turn . . .' Sue grabbed the microphone from Cordelia.

'Or have a turn,' some bright spark at the back shouted.

'I've asked Reverend Hayward to share a few words with us,' Sue smiled and nodded, and Tamsyn realised she hadn't really seen Jed today, not properly, not since she'd left his house feeling like she'd somehow upset him. They'd handed Mo to each other once or twice, smiled and nodded, exchanged a few words, but that was it. And it was curious, because given that she'd only met him yesterday, Tamsyn realised that she had actually missed him being around.

'Friends,' Jed said into the microphone, 'it's so good to see so many of you here, pulling together during this time of need. It what humans are best at doing, and it's funny how we go along, day to day, grumbling about each other under our breath. Moaning because so-and-so's parked in your space, or her next door's left her wheelie bin in the road again. And then something like this happens. Homes are ruined, important mementos lost, months of discomfort and difficulty lie ahead. But instead of turning on each other, we turn *to* each other and offer a shoulder to lean on, even when our troubles are as great as our neighbours'. We remember we are part of a community, and that no man is an island – although we came pretty close to Poldore becoming one last night.' Jed's smile was shy, and there was a polite ripple of laughter. 'I feel privileged to be part of this community, to know our people as friends, who would set aside their own troubles to get the church ready for Alex and Ruan's wedding.' The crowd cheered, and looking around, Tamsyn saw Alex, her arms around Ruan's neck, her head on his shoulder. 'And to help Tamsyn rescue the wedding outfits!' There was a rowdy and very drunken cheer for the sewing circle, who seemed to be engaged in some sort of drink-off with the knitters that made Tamsyn fear for her hems. 'And to Sue, who has not only housed and fed many of us, but has also thrown this party to lift our spirits.' There was a round of applause that went on for several seconds. 'Jesus told us to love our neighbour as ourselves, and I am proud of every single one of my neighbours tonight, who embody that commandment and make this town the very special place it is. Thanks be to . . .' A huge crack of thunder crashed so loudly that it almost felt as if it was in the room, and Tamsyn was sure she felt the floor vibrate beneath her feet as the group of people screamed and laughed and held onto each other. Tamsyn and Tamsyn alone saw Jed flinch briefly, his eyes closed against the noise.

Tamsyn looked at him, surprised. Most of the crowd rushed to the window to look at the storm, small children crying, the teenagers suddenly thinking of reasons to hug each other. The chatter gradually turned to nervous laughter, and by the time they returned their gazes to the vicar, the moment was past and Jed looked utterly in control again. 'That was just the Lord, giving us a round of applause,' he told the congregation. 'Thanks be to God, amen.'

Handing the microphone back to Sue, Tamsyn saw Jed hurry out of the hall, and she followed him, watching him as he stood, pressing a palm against the wood panelling in the corridor outside, seemingly to try to steady himself. Was it talking in front of people that had thrown him? It couldn't be the thunder, not after he'd been so brave and stoical in the storm when he'd brought them up here. Whatever it was that had happened, she could sense that he was unsettled, shaken.

'Jed?' She said his name so quietly that it couldn't be heard over the din of the party, now back in full swing, or the storm that competed with it outside the rattling windows. Jed did not hear her, or see her standing in the shadows, with Mo cradled in her arms, oblivious to everything, safely cocooned from the noise. Pushing himself off the wall, he pulled down at the hem on his shirt and then, taking a few more steps, knocked on the door of the room where Catriona was staying.

'Catriona, it's Jed, are you in?' Tamsyn watched him wait for a reply, and then knock again, and this time his tone more concerned. 'Catriona?'

'Everything OK?' Tamsyn announced herself, and saw how weary Jed looked when he glanced up at her, as if the last few minutes had exhausted him, his golden skin drained of colour.

'If I take Mo, would you go in and see if she's OK?' Jed asked. 'I was hoping she'd feel a bit better today, but the tray I left her is still outside the door.'

Tamsyn kissed Mo's ear as she handed her over, and knocked on the door again before pushing it open.

The room was in darkness, warm and musty, a sure sign that its occupier hadn't left her bed in several hours. The town was in chaos, and everyone was so busy trying to set things straight and pull together that it looked as if no one – including herself – had thought to check on Catriona Merryweather for quite some time.

Switching on a lamp, Tamsyn was relieved to see that she was sleeping, although fitfully. Her brow was shiny with sweat, her hair darkened, damp and matted. Sitting on the edge of the bed, Tamsyn gently touched her arm.

'Catriona? It's Tamsyn. Catriona?'

Catriona grumbled and turned her head away, waving

her arm limply, as if making a half-hearted attempt to swat a fly.

'Catriona . . .'

'Oh Mother, how many times? I don't like broccoli,' Catriona replied.

Tamsyn pressed the back of her hand to Catriona's forehead, which was blazing hot. She pulled off the heavy quilt and opened the window, for all the good it did. It seemed like the great crash of thunder that had rattled Jed had heralded the crescendo of the storm, which was now fading into the distance, leaving hot, still air behind.

Tamsyn opened the door and gestured for Jed to stay where he was.

'She's in a bad way,' Tamsyn said. 'She seems to have got it much worse than anyone else; they are all mostly on the mend now. Maybe it's something else, like her appendix . . . Do you know if the doctor that looked at Mo is still here?'

'I think he stayed for the party, yes,' Jed said.

'Can you see if Mum or Keira will take Mo for a while, and bring the doctor? On second thoughts, don't give her to them, they're too drunk.' She thought for a moment. 'Give her to Alex. I trust Alex.'

Jed nodded and Tamsyn stood watching him recede up the dark hallway to find the doctor. There was no time to wonder why exactly a man who had led them to Castle House in a storm had flinched at a little lightning, but Tamsyn sensed he was keeping a secret, not just from her – but from everyone.

Sue had put an old-fashioned ceramic wash bowl and a jug full of water on the dressing table, and a flannel, which Tamsyn soaked in the thankfully cool water and pressed to Catriona's head. There was an unopened packet of paracetamol on the top of the chest of drawers next to bed.

'What?' Catriona turned her head, her eyes taking a moment to focus.

'Is it still raining?' Catriona asked Tamsyn. 'I can hear rain coming down, so hard. It's not right, it's not right, you know.'

'You've got a fever, a really bad one,' Tamsyn told her, not sure if Catriona knew who she was, or if it mattered. 'You didn't take any paracetamol?'

'I don't believe in it,' Catriona said, coming back to herself a little. 'I've never believed in masking symptoms. You should always be able to listen to what your body is trying to tell you. Tamsyn? How is the little one?'

'Fine,' Tamsyn said. 'Considering. But how are you?'

'You shouldn't be here,' Catriona dragged herself up a little. 'I don't want you here.'

'Don't worry,' Tamsyn said. 'I'll shower and change my clothes before I pick up Mo again. And Cordelia's got this antiviral hand stuff she buys in bulk. She says children are essentially disgusting and should be considered a potential biohazard at all times.'

'It shouldn't be you who's here,' Catriona insisted. 'Where's Jed?'

'Coming; he's bringing the doctor.'

'I don't need a doctor,' Catriona told her. 'There's nothing wrong with me. A touch of flu, that's all. I'm forty-four, and the only time I've ever needed a doctor was the time I broke a wrist leading a rambling expedition over Bodmin Moor, and that was all a lot of fuss and bother. It's not as if I couldn't have walked back home. I didn't break my leg.'

Tamsyn smiled. 'You're very stoic, Catriona.'

'Nothing wrong with that,' Catriona nodded. 'That's the trouble with the modern generation. They think that everything is a drama, every little hiccup that happens makes them the centre of the universe and that everyone has to look at them. God wants us to take our trouble on ourselves; he wants us to be strong, to endure. To accept the consequences of our actions, and then he will forgive us. If he knows we have repented, he will forgive us.'

'There's no harm in asking for help,' Tamsyn said, thinking of Jed's mini-sermon. 'Love thy neighbour as you love yourself.'

'That's all very well and good,' Catriona said. 'But what if you hate yourself?'

'Here we are,' Jed said. 'Sorry it took so long. I was

just getting Dr Parsons a very strong coffee.'

'Right then, Catriona, how are we?' Dr Parsons, a very affable man, especially after a cider or two, sat down on the chair next to the bed.

'Well, you look a little the worse for wear,' Catriona told him. 'I am fine. It will pass. All this too will pass, Mother used to say.'

'It would pass a lot quicker if you'd take paracetamol to bring down this fever, and keep up your fluids,' Dr Parsons told her. 'You need to help yourself, Catriona.'

'Fever is nature's remedy,' Catriona insisted.

'To a point,' Dr Parsons agreed. 'But there's no need to feel as bad as you do. Take the paracetamol every four hours. Jed tells me you came down with this yesterday evening, so hopefully in the morning you should start to feel better. But we need to drink plenty, don't we?'

'Well, it seems that you're taking care of that side of things for us,' Catriona said, turning her face away.

'Isn't there anything else we can do?' Jed asked. 'Antibiotics maybe?'

'You know as well as I do that antibiotics won't do a thing for a virus. She needs rest and fluids. She'll be on the mend again soon enough, Jed.'

Remembering the commode, Tamsyn opened the lid, but found that the ceramic bowl it contained was bright, clean and unused.

'You haven't needed the loo?' Tamsyn asked her,

concerned, because although the extent of her medical knowledge mostly came from watching *Grey's Anatomy* dubbed into French, she had a good idea that it might mean something was wrong with Catriona's kidneys.

'None of your business,' Catriona snapped, sighing when all three of the intruders in her room continued to wait for an answer. 'Look, I'm not so sick that I can't walk to the toilet. And I am not so old that I am ready to let other people clean up my . . . business.'

'I think she'll be fine,' Dr Parsons said. 'I think you just need to check in on her. It looks to me like it's the same bug that everyone's got. Some people just get it worse than others, that's all. It's horrible but not life threatening. Perhaps arrange a rota, but be careful of the children, babies and the elderly. Anyone with asthma who hasn't had a flu jab should stay away. It can be very nasty.'

'I don't need anyone to check on me,' Catriona said.

'Well, a full packet of paracetamol and an undrunk glass of water would say otherwise,' Dr Parsons said. 'Come on, take two while I'm here. It's just gone eleven, so you should take some more after five.'

Tamsyn waited for Jed and the doctor to leave.

'Catriona, is there anything you can tell me that you don't want to say to a man?' she asked. 'I mean, you seemed to be in quite a lot of abdominal pain yesterday. Are you passing urine OK?'

'Of course I am,' Catriona said, affronted. 'I'm fine,

really.'

'OK,' Tamsyn said. 'Well, I'd better get back; got a lot to do and I've barely started. I'm making new dresses for Alex and the bridesmaids. Her old ones got trashed in the flood.'

'And the baby?' Catriona asked her. 'What's happening to the baby?'

'We're still hoping the mother will come forward,' Tamsyn said. 'If not, they will start looking to find her a more permanent home. But Sue made the social worker let her stay with me until that time comes.'

'There will be a couple out there,' Catriona said, 'who will cherish her. Who will see her as a gift from God, and she will have a wonderful life.'

'Perhaps,' Tamsyn said. 'Perhaps, but perhaps there is still a chance for Mo and her mum. I hope so.'

But Catriona had turned her face to the wall again, and after a few more moments of silence Tamsyn supposed she was sleeping again.

Just as she was leaving she caught sight of someone moving outside, and taking her moment, Tamsyn let herself out of the front door and into the courtyard. The wind howled around her and the air crackled and crashed in fury, and sitting on the steps next to a very bedraggled bay tree, was Kirsten.

'I'm not sure you should be out here,' Tamsyn said, having to shout to make herself heard.

'Why not? I'm not sitting under a tree or anything,'

Kirsten said. 'It's beautiful, isn't it?'

'It's amazing, yes,' Tamsyn agreed, 'but come inside. Please. I feel nervous, leaving you out here.'

Reluctantly Kirsten got to her feet and followed Tamsyn inside, another crescendo of thunder unleashing just as Tamsyn managed to push the door shut against the wind.

'You don't fancy the party?' Tamsyn asked, having to catch her breath a little.

'No one in there likes me,' Kirsten said, matter-of-factly.

'Or is it just that you push them away?' Tamsyn asked her.

'No. They don't like me. They think I'm a skank. And you know my mum chose my stepdad over me and my brother . . . It does kind of undermine your self-esteem. That's what Tess says, but she doesn't know that I'm glad to be rid of her. It's better to have no mum than one who hates you.'

'Oh, Kirsten,' Tamsyn looked down the corridor, past the noise and laughter of the party, and wondered where Mo was; suddenly she wanted to hold her close. 'Your mum doesn't hate you. She might not be very good at being a mum, but she doesn't hate you.'

'And how do you know that?' Kirsten asked her. 'You weren't there when she told me . . . oh, what was it now? Oh yeah, that she hates me.'

'You feel quite crappy, don't you?' Tamsyn said.

'But you know, you are not alone. There are loads of people who . . .'

'Care about me?' Kirsten's laugh was mirthless. 'Like you, you care about me, do you? You turn up out of the blue and decide to care about everyone you bump into? Look, you might have bunked off school a bit when you were a kid and had one too many ciders in the park, but that is nothing like what's happening to me. And the thing you people really don't get is that I don't care. I would rather be on my own than at home with that bitch, or in there with those fake cows. I'm not pretending not to care – I actually don't. Now please, just go and take an interest in someone else. I don't want to be your holiday project.'

'But what about . . .?' Tamsyn stopped herself just in time from asking about Mo outright. Kirsten was angry, hurt. But at least she was here. The last thing she wanted to do was chase her away. 'How about you come and help me out with the dresses? I'll need someone to help me organise my threads, my beads, sort out materials, maybe even do some cutting. I'll need a dogsbody. What about that?'

'Sounds like shit,' Kirsten said, turning her back on Tamsyn and walking up the hallway, past the party and into the darkness.

'So you'll think about it then, yes?' Tamsyn said.

Chapter Eighteen

It was almost three in the morning when Tamsyn could take a step back and know that everything was ready for sewing. At the far end of the tables was Alex's dress, the pieces all cut and laid out, next to the pattern and ready to go. In an idea world Tamsyn would have made a calico toile first, to make sure that the pattern fitted, but there was no time; it was an almost impossible task as it was. All she could do was hope that the Poldore sewing and embroidering circle was as good as Jed and Sue claimed it was. The trick was going to be to work out what was best to do first, as the sewing, embroidering and beading all needed to happen at the same time. Panels would have to be embroidered and sewn in a particular order, that meant the dresses could be assembled at the same time as being embellished. Tamsyn was sure there would be a solution but her head hurt, and her brain was clouded from being so focused on her task and Mo, currently sleeping in her carrycot, was due a feed in three hours. It was time to get some sleep, perhaps make a cup of tea and go and find their room. After her shower, Tamsyn had raided Cordelia's closet once again, found several pairs of her sister's staple black leggings and a fine-knit grey sweater. It was really more like two squares sewn together, and was happily loose, because Tamsyn wasn't as blessed as her little sister in the chest department, so it made more sense to go braless rather than put something on that would look like two deflated balloons under her clothes, unless she packed it with tissues, something she had vowed never to do again after the terrible date disaster of 2003.

The kitchen was lit only by lamps dotted around and about, and the odd flash of lightning, the last remnants of the storm that Mo somehow seemed to sleep happily through, although it had still taken Tamsyn about eighteen goes to put her into the carrycot without her noticing at once and protesting, vociferously.

By two in the morning, the last of the partygoers had left and the motley crew of remaining house guests were quiet at last, most of them trying to come and take a peek at what Tamsyn was up to on their way to bed, including her mother and sisters. She'd chased her sisters away with threats of making them look fat and frumpy in their dresses, if they crossed her. At last she had the means to control them.

Putting the carrycot down, Tamsyn found a mug and a camomile teabag and waited for the kettle to boil. Which was when she saw the figure lurking below the table. She stifled her scream back into her mouth with her fingers as she realised what she was looking at. It was Jed: Jed was under the table.

Crouching down, Tamsyn couldn't quite believe what she was seeing. His eyes were wide open and unseeing, his arms clenched tightly around his legs.

'Jed?' Glancing at Mo, who still slept, Tamsyn pulled aside a chair and knelt on the floor in front of him. Whatever he was seeing, it wasn't her, and wherever he thought he was, it wasn't under a kitchen table. He looked terrified, his teeth were chattering and he seemed to be caught in an endless moment of fear, and it was agonising to watch. Tamsyn dithered, uncertain what to do. Perhaps there was something she could do to soothe him, without shocking him.

Sliding herself under the table, Tamsyn managed to arrange her long limbs so that she was opposite him. Reaching out, she touched his shoulder, withdrawing it when he flinched.

'Go away,' he said. 'Please, Tamsyn, go away. I don't want you to be here.'

'No,' Tamsyn said calmly, this time talking as she touched him, keeping her voice low and soft. 'No, I'm not going to go away. I don't understand what's happening, but I do know when someone needs a friend. So I'm staying.'

Jed buried his face in his knees, his shoulders shaking with dry sobs. What was this?

'When I was a little girl,' Tamsyn said, 'my friend

Merryn and I, we used to make camp under tables and pretend we were pirates. Once we tied Cordelia up and put her in the broom cupboard, which might be where her love-of-bondage thing comes from.' The lightning came again, but this time there were seconds, perhaps as many as ten, before the rumble of thunder. The storm was passing, hopefully for good this time.

'It's OK,' Tamsyn said, running her hand down his arm and repeating the gesture at once. 'It's OK, you're safe. You are safe, and everything is OK.'

Jed looked up at her as she repeated herself over and over again; she saw the fear in his eyes recede a little, his breathing gradually eased and the tension in his muscles slowly dissipated, until finally he rested his forehead on his knees once again and closed his eyes. They stayed like that for a minute or two until she heard his breathing deepen and she guessed he had fallen into a restful sleep. Tamsyn watched what little she could make out of his face in the low light; the straight nose, the precision-cut jaw. He looked so certain, so strong, yet Tamsyn didn't think she'd ever seen anyone, man, woman or child, as genuinely frightened as Jed had been just then. What had happened to him? What was it that he had come to Poldore to hide from?

'Jed,' she said, a little louder. 'Jed, what's happening?'

'Tamsyn,' He looked at her. 'I'm so sorry.'

'I . . .' But before Tamsyn could say anything more,

Jed had taken her hand from his shoulder and pulled her forward into his arms, virtually onto his lap, put his arms around her waist and held her close to him. Sensing that he needed to know she was real, Tamsyn returned the embrace, winding her arms around his neck, burying her face in his shoulder. It was by no means comfortable; her legs were cramped, her body was twisted at all the wrong angles and yet she didn't try to move; she didn't want to. It was impossible to know for how many minutes they stayed like that, wordlessly holding each other under the table in the kitchen of Castle House, and it wasn't important. All that was important was, as each second passed, Tamsyn could feel Jed's body relax around hers, and she became aware of the strength in his arms, the muscles under his shirt flexing under her fingertips. Neither one of them moved their hands or touched each other, except for the places where their bodies met, and yet Tamsyn had the overwhelming emotion that this was the most truly intimate moment of her life.

'Thank you,' Jed said eventually, making no attempt to release her. 'I'm so glad it was you who saw me like this, and no one else.'

'What happened?' Tamsyn asked him, whispering. 'You looked so . . .'

'Frightened,' Jed finished the sentence for her. 'I'm glad it was you, but I also wish it wasn't you. You are the last person I wanted to see me this way.'

'What way?' Tamsyn shifted herself back a little, touching the palm of her hand to his cheek.

'I thought, I believed that it was over, that I was . . . They said that there might still be flashbacks, but it's been so long, I thought they were gone for good. I was wrong.'

'Jed, what are you trying to hide, because you know, whatever it is, your friends and the people who respect you will feel just the same. Well, unless it turns out you are a licensed to kill, secret MI5 agent. That might change things a little bit.'

Jed managed a small smile, and Tamsyn was so relieved to see it she found herself leaning forward, pressing her lips to his cheek and feeling for one delicious moment the graze of his stubble against her skin.

'It was my last tour with the army before I left,' Jed said. 'In Afghanistan. Us padres, they went to great lengths to keep us out of harm's way, to keep us safe. I spent most of my time on the base ministering to the troops, and security was tight. Checkpoints, double checkpoints. It was a base near Camp Bastion: the unit I was with were training the local police to take over when the army pulled out. It was a good day. Morale was high, a lot of the lads were about to go home. I was about to go home. I'd enjoyed it. Not many of them were particularly religious, but they liked having me around. They thought of me as their lucky mascot. The bomb-disposal boys would all come and put their hands on the top of my head before they went out. 'Get a bit of God off the padre,' they'd say. I always said prayers for them, each one of them, as they rubbed the top of my head . . .'

He faltered, and Tamsyn found herself entwining her fingers in his, holding his trembling hands steady as she waited for him to continue.

'One of the guys they'd been training came on duty as usual, and nothing seemed out of the ordinary. There were no signs, none at all, that he'd turned up that day seeking to become a martyr.'

'He was a suicide bomber?' Tamsyn asked, her voice barely audible.

Jed nodded. 'He killed three soldiers. There were five injured, life-altering injuries, they call them. And the noise, you think you know what a bomb is going to sound like from TV or films or news reports, but really you have no idea how very loud it's going to be, or that the smoke will get so deep in your eyes and your lungs that sometimes you think you can still taste it.' Jed swallowed.

'Was it the thunder?'

'I don't know, or at least, not only the thunder. You never know what it's going to be, what's going to trigger an attack. A smell, a sound. Something you can identify. They say it's at times of stress and upheaval that you become more sensitive, but I . . . I thought I was stronger than this. It's my job to be the strong one.'

'Oh, Jed,' Tamsyn gripped his hands a little tighter. 'Were you injured too?'

'Some shrapnel, in my legs and back, which meant a few weeks lying on my stomach while I healed, but on the whole I got off lightly, except . . . Post-traumatic stress disorder they call it, you've probably heard of it. I have been luckier than most; I had the support of the church and the army. I did the therapy, took every sort of help they offered, and of course I've had my faith, but . . .'

'What?' Tamsyn asked. 'You can tell me anything.'

'I looked into the bomber's eyes, in the seconds before it happened,' Jed said. 'I don't know why, what made me do it, but I did. Our eyes met. And he . . . all I saw was fear and confusion. And now, if I close my eyes, any time I close my eyes, it's his face I see, and I don't understand it, Tamsyn. Never before in my life have I had to question my faith in this way, and what it can do. If it can drive a frightened young man to the worst possible act, then . . . well, it's made me question everything. Everything that I believe in. The church sent me to Poldore to recover; they found me a parish that they thought needed some fresh, young energy to shake it up a bit, but somewhere that would be a safe haven for me. They've never said so, but they don't think I've got what it takes to go into inner-city parishes any more, or on mission in Africa. They told me to come to Poldore and liven up the congregation, but they knew before I did that the congregation here has always been really strong. It's one of the few places in the country where that is true. It wasn't me that saved the people of Poldore. It's been the people of Poldore that have saved me.'

'But no one here knows?' Tamsyn said. 'About the PTSD?'

'No,' Jed said with a look of horror on his face at the very thought, 'no one except for you and Jeff Dangerfield. He came round for a cup of tea after he and his wife separated and he saw my photos, we got talking. He's a good man; he's kept my military past to himself.'

'But why are you keeping it a secret? It's nothing to be ashamed of,' Tamsyn told him. 'It doesn't mean you're weak, or any less good at being a vicar. If anything it makes you more qualified to do the job, because you've lived life. You really know about loss. I'm no expert, but I think that probably matters in your job.'

Jed shook his head. 'I am supposed to be certain, Tamsyn, and strong and steady. I don't want anyone to know my weakness, how much I dread closing my eyes and seeing it all again. That I spend long, long nights trying to rectify what I feel in my heart with what I know about the world. I'm not the man I should be, the man I want to be. I'm weak. I don't deserve this town, and the belief and generosity that its people have shown me. I'm broken.'

'Jed,' Tamsyn said quietly. 'You are only a man.'

They looked into each other's eyes, two bright points of light in the darkness, for a long moment, and Tamsyn wondered what it was that was passing between them, flowing back and forth like a tidal wave of emotion, building in intensity and force with each breath that she took.

Jed reached out to touch her face, and Tamsyn found herself holding completely still as he traced the contours of her jaw with his fingertips, her eyes roaming over the planes and valleys of his mouth, such a very kissable-looking mouth.

Without really knowing what she was doing, she leant forward, pressing her lips to his, just because the longing to feel them under hers was impossible to resist, and because in that moment she felt so close to him that it seemed perfectly natural to want to feel closer still. Tamsyn waited for him to pull away, to resist, for the moment of heat to turn into one of awkward rejection, but her heat beat once, twice and a third time and the moment never came. Instead, Jed looped his fingers into her mass of hair and kissed her, pushing her lips open with his tongue. It was a kiss that Tamsyn realised she was dying to respond to, pressing her body closer against his, under the table. His hands left her hair and she felt the soft planes of his palms soar up her bare back, and her own hands tugged at his shirt to find his warm, golden skin beneath. She began unbuttoning his shirt, pausing only to allow him to lift the grey jumper over her head, and suddenly they were skin to skin, her breasts pressed against his chest, their kisses becoming hungrier and hungrier, and Tamsyn knew that there had never been an embrace like this before in the whole of history, she was certain; that this was a kiss that made sense of the world and everything in it, and that whatever was to follow next would be nothing short of a revelation.

And then Mo's wail pierced the silence, filling the room with noise, and all of the everyday life of Poldore and reality came crashing back in.

It was Jed who broke the kiss, and at the same time the spell they had both been under, turning his eyes away from her nudity and handing her Cordelia's jumper as he buttoned his shirt.

'I need to go,' he said, pushing the chair out from under the other side of the table and scrambling to his feet, presumably so that he didn't have to slide past her.

'Jed?' Tamsyn called after him, caught in a complex vortex of horror and need. 'There's a slight problem. My leg has gone to sleep. I can't actually move.'

But Jed had gone, rushing off and leaving her stranded, her skin singing from his touch even as it dawned on her how horrified he had been by their encounter, which she guessed was about the same amount as she had been thrilled by it. Feeling deep discomfort in the pit of her stomach, Tamsyn dragged herself and her duff leg out from under the table, as there was some feeling coming back in her toes, and got to the carrycot. At the sight of her, Mo's cries quietened a little.

'Oh, Mo,' Tamsyn said, as she vigorously rubbed at her feet. 'I know how you feel, darling. I feel like crying too.'

Chapter Nineteen

Screams, followed by peals of giggles from the children's turret, echoed down the corridor. Weary as she was, Tamsyn suddenly felt that she didn't want to be alone to think about what just had and hadn't happened, so she climbed the cold stone stairs. She quickly realised that Meadow and the boys' bedrooms were empty, and she pushed opened Cordelia's door, which elicited another round of shrieks, through all of which, now full of milk, Mo slept soundly. 'What's going on in here?' Tamsyn asked her. 'It's loud enough to wake the dead and it's nearly four in the morning!'

'The children were scared of the storm,' Cordelia told her. 'So I employed my age-old technique of taking their minds off things that scare them by telling them really, really frightening ghost stories.'

'It's brilliant!' Joe said, his eyes wide and wired, and Tamsyn couldn't imagine him sleeping at all for the rest of the night, if ever.

'Not exactly whiskers on kittens, is it?' Tamsyn said, amused, despite herself.

'You wait and see,' Cordelia said, catching Tamsyn's sceptical look. 'Fear is a very exhausting emotion. Once all that adrenaline has drained away they'll sleep for hours.'

'Well.' Tamsyn looked at the room, wishing there was a corner free that would fit her and Mo. 'I guess I'd better go and get some rest before the sew-a-thon in a few hours.'

'Are you OK, sweetheart?' Laura asked her, smothering a yawn. 'Have you taken on too much, what with Mo and the dresses? You looked flushed; I do hope you haven't picked up that lurgy that's going round.'

Well, Tamsyn thought to herself, she had come down with something, but it wasn't anything as easy to get over as the flu. Was there a scientific name for the fever brought about by kissing a man who quite clearly felt the whole thing had been a terrible mistake – no, worse than that – possibly even a sin?

'Are you missing your Bernard?' her mum said, insisting once again on pronouncing his name the English way, as if he were some Northern comic. So far, Tamsyn had escaped a thorough grilling from her mother on the subject of her French lover. Clearly her mum had just been biding her time.

Tamsyn thought of Bernard: sexy, self-centred, unpredictable and yet so basically uncomplicated. Bernard, who always kissed her exactly when he meant to, and meant it whenever he did. He never wondered about the consequences of his actions, because the concept of self-doubt was entirely alien to him. Yes, actually, she thought that she did miss him and the easy feelings she enjoyed whenever she was with him, which were nothing at all like the muddle and mixed-up feelings that the embrace with Jed had stirred up in her.

'I suppose I do,' Tamsyn said. And ignoring the questioning, concerned look in her mother's eyes, she pulled herself together long enough to say, 'Well now, I need to sleep before this little one decides she wants a chat again, otherwise I might accidentally sew a massive bow onto the back of Cordelia's dress.'

'Sleep,' Cordelia commanded, gesturing at five children who were now dozing off peacefully amongst the adults. 'And if you are having any trouble, I'll come down and tell this tale I know about the Blue Lady of Poldore, who once stayed in the very room you are staying in . . . until she jumped to her death! Mwah-ha-ha!'

'Hmmm,' Tamsyn said, 'I don't think she'd have had much worse than a very nasty broken ankle if she'd jumped from my window. But still, thanks for trying. Goodnight all.'

As Tamsyn eased herself between the cool, clean sheets, her hand still on the carrycot, because Mo seemed to sense it at once if she dared remove it, she closed her eyes and thought of Bernard, and the playful way he would look at her when the urge to take her to bed would suddenly grab him; his dark eyes, the sensuous mouth, the expertise with which he despatched with her clothes, the polite passion that ensured she was always satisfied before he was, the friendly embrace afterwards, that Tamsyn was sure always lasted the exact same amount of minutes every time, before he was up making an espresso and smoking out of the window, whatever time of the day or night it was. Theirs was an affair with order and routine, albeit with some laughter and passion. She wanted the deep, yearning pain that seemed to have formed in the pit of her stomach to be about missing Bernard, she really did. And yet she had this strange, sneaking suspicion that she was longing for a man who was probably right this minute not sleeping on a sofa in the room that was almost directly below hers, a man who'd found what they had done tonight deeply troubling and difficult. A man who, when all was said and done, would probably never even consider a relationship with a woman – a heathen, even – like her. After all, what did she and Jed have in common, apart from Mo and the ability to create the best kissing that history has ever known?

Chapter Twenty

Of course it had been Sue Montaigne who had worked out the complicated sewing and embellishing rota for the dresses. In no time at all she had the volunteer seamstresses sitting around the great table, their sections of material carefully labelled and numbered, their instructions taped to the polished surface of the table, their faces looking expectantly at Tamsyn as the very early morning sunshine swept in through the gallery windows.

Tamsyn realised they were waiting for her to say something, which was a shame because she didn't think she had the power of speech any more. In fact, she was fairly sure that her brain had switched talking off as non-essential power drainage, because she was running almost on empty on energy.

'Ladies,' she said, testing her tongue on the word. 'And gentleman . . .'

She nodded at a man in his sixties who was sitting at the furthest corner of the long table, flirting outrageously with the woman sitting next to him. Sue had told her that Kenneth had joined the sewing circle after his wife left him for another woman and that he hadn't looked back since.

'Thank you so much for giving up your time to come together and make this happen for Alex and Ruan. I know that you all know them really well, and that they mean a lot to you – if they didn't, you would be mopping out your own houses instead of being here. And I'm very grateful that you have all given your time – not to mention your independently verified expertise – to make their day special.' She was rewarded by a little Mexican wave of smiles and nods. 'Now, if you follow the design and the schedule as detailed in your personalised set of instructions produced by the logistical genius that is Sue here, then there will be no problems. As soon as you've finished your job on your piece of fabric, pass it to the next person on the list and by the end of today we will have four stunning bridesmaids' dresses and one wonderful bridal gown fully assembled and waiting for a final fit. I will be constructing, boning and embellishing the bodice of the bridal gown myself, so I will be in the Solar.' Tamsyn had learnt from Sue that this was a posh person's name for the conservatory. 'And that's where you need to bring the skirt panels to me for assembling once they are complete. I trust you to finish the bridesmaids' dresses yourselves. Thank you again for your help. Sue tells me there is unlimited tea, coffee and cake available, but no food or drink items in the workroom please. Um, so that's it, thank you.'

Tamsyn blushed as the force of volunteers applauded

her, and hurried off before she did something silly like cry, or ask them what they would feel like if they'd done half-naked kissing with a vicar under the kitchen table.

The Solar, an aged and dilapidated moss-covered construction off the courtyard, was pleasingly cool on this hot June day. It was shaded further by long-neglected rubber and cheese plants that seemed to be its only organic occupants and that had reached Triffid-like proportions. Best of all, she was able to open a door out on to a small walled area that had once been a kitchen garden, but that was now overrun with wild flowers and butterflies.

Sadly, in amongst the rails and rails of clothes that Sue had locked away in the attic, there had been no tailor's dummy, so Sue had had Rory bring in a neo-classical nude statue from the overgrown secret garden, and although her proportions bore no resemblance to Alex's, at least the smooth white complexion gave Tamsyn a guide for her colour scheme.

'Well, then.' Tamsyn started as Kirsten walked into the Solar, looking very much like she wanted to leave it again.

'Well then, what?' Tamsyn asked her.

'You said you wanted me to help you,' Kirsten reminded her. 'Sort out beads, or some shit.'

'Oh,'Tamsyn blinked. 'It's just that you weren't overly enthusiastic when I mentioned it. But oh, good, good that you are here. Go up to the attic – here's the key – there's all these skeins of ribbon up there, can you bring some down? Here, take these swatches to colour-match, white, blue or ivory. And while you are there, have a look at the hats – you'll see piles and piles of hatboxes in the corner. They are so cool. I have half an idea about little hats, but I haven't seen what's there yet, so you can find some good ones for me.'

'Really?' Kirsten took the key with a distinct look of mistrust in her eye. 'You want me to go and pick out hats, like, choose hats? The ones I think are the best?'

'Yes. Does that seem really lame?' Tamsyn asked her.

'Yeah,' Kirsten said, but she was smiling as she rolled the key between her fingers. 'Lamest thing ever.'

Tamsyn was smiling to herself when Kirsten paused in the doorway.

'Where's the kid?' she asked. 'Is she OK?'

'She's fine, she's with Jed,' Tamsyn told her, adding carefully, 'You seem very interested in her well-being.'

'I just know what it feels like to be left by your mum, that's all,' Kirsten said. 'I feel sorry for her.'

'Well, maybe her mum will come forward,' Tamsyn said, trying her best not to sound too pointed, but Kirsten had already gone.

'Tamsyn, are you in there?' Tamsyn had only been alone a few minutes when a voice called from the other side of the internal door. 'Can I come in?'

'Er, no,' Tamsyn said. 'I'm making you a surprise wedding dress, remember?' Tamsyn had already covered the glass windows nearest the courtyard in dust sheets to keep out prying eyes.

'Yes, but I was thinking, I always thought the bride got to oversee the creation of her dress,' Alex said. 'And decide what she liked?'

'Darling, this isn't Debenhams,' Tamsyn called back. 'My job as your designer is to create the dream dress you didn't even know that you dreamt of. Trust me.'

'Well . . . can I send Buoy in to a have a look?'

'Are you serious?' Tamsyn laughed, supposing that knowing Alex's bond with the dog, she probably was. 'Hold on a minute, you nutter.'

Selecting an offcut of thick black satin that she'd been toying with but discarded, she went out into the hallway and, seeing the look of concern on Alex's face, smiled as she tied the makeshift blindfold around her.

'This has all gone a bit *Fifty Shades of Grey*,' Alex joked as Tamsyn guided her back into the conservatory.

Tamsyn smiled down at Buoy, who seemed clean and dry, and at least – unlike his offspring, Skipper – was past the stage of wanting to chew everything that moved, and everything that didn't, just to be on the safe side. Buoy, it seemed, was much more interested in the little garden, full of fascinating things to sniff at and apparently not claimed by any other alpha dogs in decades.

'I'm not sure why you're letting me in, if I can't see it,' Alex said.

'Because you are the closest thing I have to a tailor's dummy, dummy, and I need to do some fitting. Stretch your arms out. No – to the side.'

Before the sewing circle had arrived, Tamsyn had made Cordelia donate her best black satin gothic rock-star bodice, the one that had come from Agent Provocateur, to the cause. It was very well made, so Tamsyn had taken it to pieces, in order that she could use its innards to structure and bone Alex's bridal corset. Now she had Alex, she was able to place the support rods in exactly the right place and check the various bits of underwire that she had collected from some of Alex's bras that Gloria had sneaked out to her first thing.

'That tickles,' Alex said, as Tamsyn worked out her strategy.

'It will be worth it, won't it, Buoy?' Tamsyn said to the dog, who, having returned from claiming the garden as his sovereign right, sat leaning against an old Lloyd Loom chair, eyeing her with what looked like a healthy dose of disdain.

'You think you can get away with just sitting there, being all doggy,' Tamsyn told him, pausing to plant a kiss on his head and whispering in his long ear. 'But what you don't know is that Mo and I have got plans for you, oh yes we have.'

'Did you get any sleep at all last night?' Alex said.

'I feel like me and my wedding have rather taken over your life.'

'I didn't get much sleep,'Tamsyn confessed. 'Sue told me that babies start waking up after the first few hours when they find out how boring sleeping is, and she was right. But it's a good thing, really. It's stopped me thinking.'

'Thinking about what?' Alex asked her, turning her head.

Tamsyn wondered for a moment about what she should say, if anything. It had been a very long time since she'd truly had a confidante, a best friend that she could say anything to. She was close to her sisters, at least as close as a person could be when they lived on the other side of the Channel, but it was a closeness born out of years of proximity. The last person she had really been able to talk to about anything without fear of judgement was Merryn. Would it be a betrayal to confide in Alex, Tamsyn wondered briefly? And then she decided Merryn would have been pleased that Ruan had found the right woman in the end. She would have liked Alex a lot; it was hard not to. Tamsyn bit her lip, unable to stop herself from wondering what an amazing, incredible life Merryn would have gone on to have, if only she hadn't taken the boat out that morning.

'I kissed the vicar last night, mostly naked,'Tamsyn said, at last. 'Well, earlier this morning, to be precise.'

'Pardon?' Alex looked, even blindfolded, in the

direction of Buoy, who, raised his shaggy brows in reply. 'Did you just say that . . .?'

'Yep, me and Jed did topless kissing.' Saying the words out loud made her feel unbelievably foolish and indiscreet. But she couldn't tell Alex where or how the kiss came about, she wouldn't do that. It was just that she couldn't bear not to tell someone about it. It was as if she just had to say Jed's name out loud, so that she could hear it, feel the texture of it on her tongue. Remind herself that it had actually happened.

'Flip!' Alex said.

'I know,' Tamsyn said. 'And other, much worse swearwords than that.'

'I mean, don't get me wrong, Ruan is the only man for me, but Jed is hot,' Alex emphasised the last word. 'What was it like?'

'Amazing,' Tamsyn said miserably. 'Like the best and most amazing kiss that I have ever had in my life.'

'Are you saying you have feelings for Jed?' Alex said, her hands flying to the blindfold, and Tamsyn batted them away at once.

'I can't have feelings for Jed, not really,' she said. 'I only met him the day before yesterday, I think. We've spent a total of about three hours together. And we are the two most different people there can possibly be. So, no, I don't have feelings for him. Not unless you count this gut-churning, heart-wrenching, clothes-ripping-off longing that I'm feeling in my chest.'

'Oh my God,' Alex smiled. 'My mum says love doesn't work on schedule. You just don't know when it's going to hit you, like a bolt out of the blue.'

'Did you fall for Ruan at first sight?' Tamsyn asked her, intrigued.

'No,' Alex laughed. 'I thought he was rude and stupid. It was more like second or third sight, and even then that was more lust-based.'

'OK, this is my brother we are talking about.' Tamsyn pulled a face at Buoy, who seemed to mirror her disgust.

'But you might have fallen in love with the vicar at first kiss?' Alex asked. 'Is that what you are saying?'

'No, no, of course I am not,' Tamsyn replied, between teeth gritted around pins. 'How can I be? I mean, just because a person happens to be strikingly handsome, looks awfully good soaked through to the skin, is amazing with babies, and generous and kind and resilient and funny and human in ways that you never might have guessed, it doesn't mean that anyone would fall in love with them after one very long, intense, firm-bodied, deeply erotic kiss. I'm not in love with him. I just can't stop thinking about him, and I don't understand why. I really want to see him, and I also never, ever want to see him again. What's that about?'

'It does sound an awful lot like you are in love with him,' Alex suggested mischievously. 'Because when you think about people they get together and they spend weeks playing it cool before they feel like they can say "I am in love with you", but if you press them on it, if you really try hard to get them to remember when exactly the moment of love occurred, more often than not they will say, I knew right away, or within hours or days, and despite what I just said, when I think about it, the second I looked at Ruan, when we first met and he was so angry with me, there was this connection that flowed between us. Like someone had just thrown on a switch which I couldn't turn off, even though I tried. I think sometimes love happens that way, all at once. It doesn't mean it's any less real.'

Tamsyn had stopped, her scissors in mid-air, and she tried to fathom the consequences of what Alex had said. She couldn't be right about that, could she? Her head was just in a very romantic place because she was getting married, against the odds, and to her everything seemed covered in roses and love hearts. That wasn't what had happened earlier that morning, was it? It hadn't been love that had happened under the kitchen table, surely?

'Well, I'm not sure it actually matters how I feel,' Tamsyn said. 'Not when he literally ran away from me in horror. And if he hadn't, I don't really see how a very sceptical agnostic who lives in Paris and whose world revolves around vanity and superficiality, could possibly fall in love with a man of God who lives in Cornwall and actively embraces the WI.'

'Oooh, I wonder if the ladies of the WI go funny too when he actively embraces them,' Alex teased.

'You know, all it takes is a couple of stitches from me to cut off the circulation in your arms,' Tamsyn threatened mildly. 'No, it's craziness. It's the Thorn Birds syndrome. I've met a man so diametrically opposed to me and my life that I've just got in a bit of a muddle about him and his gold hair and his cool, silver-blue eyes, and that skin and his arms and the way he smiles with just one corner of his . . .'

'Am I interrupting?' Jed asked, as he arrived with a fitful and fed-up Mo on his shoulder.

Tamsyn, who had somehow managed to avoid having anything to do with him directly since the table incident, burst into a fit of hysterical laughter, which swiftly turned into a yelp as she got stuck with a pin in her bottom lip, making it bleed.

'And then the barman said, "Why the long face?"' Alex said randomly, to try and cover for Tamsyn's manic behaviour.

'Oh hello, Jed,' Alex said. 'We were just telling jokes.'

'Right.' Jed looked distinctly uncomfortable, although at some time since he'd pressed Tamsyn's naked breasts against his chest and kissed her silly, he'd clearly showered and had a shave, maybe to try and cleanse himself after their encounter. 'Mo's had a feed, a burp and a change,' he said, 'but she won't settle, and I don't seem to be doing the trick. I thought maybe she wants a cuddle from you.'

'I've missed her, too. Here,' Tamsyn put down the scissors, patted herself for pins and took the tiny little person into her arms. At once Mo quietened and seemed content, and Tamsyn felt her own sense of unease dissipate.

'Um,' Alex said, after a moment or two, 'I would leave, but I don't know which way the door is.'

'Here.' Jed escorted her out, before returning with the blindfold. 'I can take her again, if she's settled.'

'Have you got the carrycot?' Tamsyn asked him, and he brought it in from outside. 'I'll hold her for a moment more and see if she'll go down in it, but if not then I'm afraid I'll have to bring her to you. How's it going at the church?'

She thought it was best to press on as if nothing had changed between them; that was her favourite way of dealing with troubling issues, especially kissing-related ones, and she didn't see any reason why that should change now.

'Very well,' Jed said. 'It's almost back to its old self, apart from the window, and the door still needs to be hung. That probably won't happen in time, but I don't suppose that matters. And the hassocks and wall hangings will be keeping the sewing circle in jobs for decades to come.'

'Good,' Tamsyn said, avoiding meeting his eye.

'Great.' Jed continued to stand there and Tamsyn waited, discovering that whatever it was he was about to say filled her simultaneously with hope and dread.

'I wanted to thank you,' he said finally, 'for last night, for . . . your kindness.'

'Oh, it was nothing,' Tamsyn said. 'Anyone would have done the same. Well, maybe not the taking off their clothes bit, but the rest of it.'

'But I'm glad it wasn't anyone,' Jed told her, looking at her with his silver eyes. 'I'm glad it was you, glad and . . . sorry.'

'Sorry?' Tamsyn asked him.

'I lost control a little,' he said. 'We both know you didn't take your top off; it was me.'

'Oh right, so we are going to talk about that bit then, the bit where we made out and then you ran away,' Tamsyn asked him, her brow furrowed.

'It shouldn't have happened,' Jed said.

'Why?' Tamsyn asked him. 'Am I that repulsive?'

'Oh no, is that what you think I think?' Jed asked her, aghast. 'Tamsyn, you are beautiful, gorgeous, desirable. And I do desire you, and I do want you, as much as I wanted you last night, but it can't happen.'

'Because of God, and all that?' Tamsyn asked him, confused. 'Because I know you said no sex before marriage, but you didn't say anything about kissing.'

'Because you are a kind, decent, honourable woman, who deserves a great deal more respect and care than

I afforded you last night. I treated you like an object of desire.'

'I didn't really mind, though,'Tamsyn offered rather weakly. 'I mean, I was treating you in the same sort of way, I seem to remember.'

Jed blushed. 'You deserve more, better than me. I'm damaged, broken. I'm not ready to be in another person's life yet, not without dragging them down. And yes, because of God. Because my life is so different to yours. I don't see how they could ever fit together.'

'We only snogged,' Tamsyn said, rather crossly. 'I wasn't proposing marriage to you.'

Jed sighed, running his fingers through his smooth blond hair.

'We barely know each other, and that's why you don't understand what I'm trying to say. I can't kiss you again, because kissing you again would mean that I would never want to stop kissing you, because it wouldn't take me any effort at all to fall in love with you, and I don't want that. I don't want to fall in love with a woman who will never want what I have to offer her.'

'Why, because I am such an awful ungodly prospect?' Tamsyn asked him, bewildered by the feelings that were racing around in her chest.

'Because before I kiss you again, I want to be the man that you deserve. The man that can make it through a thunderstorm without losing it, the man who stands by his conviction and his faith with a clear and strong conscience. The man you deserve.'

'And don't I get any say in this?' Tamsyn asked him. 'Because I'm not saying that I do want you just the way you are, but . . . what if I want you just the way you are? What if I think the way you are right now is incredibly lovely and sexy and great? Even if you do believe things that I don't, couldn't we just agree to disagree about that part?'

'But . . . I mean, really?' Jed paused a moment, to take in what she'd said. 'You really feel like that?'

'I'm not saying that I do feel like that,' Tamsyn said carefully. 'Not unless you want me to say that, in which case, I am.'

And then there was that moment, the moment that comes just before the one you see in the movies and read about in the books, when the hero sweeps the heroine (after carefully popping the baby in the carrycot) into the romantic embrace to top all romantic embraces, and the credits roll and the last page is turned. That pre-moment happened.

But the moment that followed wasn't the one that Tamsyn was expecting at all.

'Tamsyn!'

The world shifted under Tamsyn's feet, and two realities collided so violently that it took more than a moment or two to understand exactly what she was looking at. It was Bernard. Not just a vision of him, some weird kind of hallucination created by her fevered and exhausted brain, it actually *was* Bernard, standing there in the Solar, next to Jed, his arms outstretched. And in the seconds that it took for her to process what was happening, he crossed the room, circumnavigated Mo's carrycot without giving her so much as a second glance, and kissed Tamsyn on the mouth, a kiss which Tamsyn surrendered to as much out of shock as anything. All she could think was that this was the wrong moment.

'I've missed you,' Bernard told her, with barely a trace of an accent, as, like everything he embarked on, he had learnt English to perfection.

'What are you doing here?' Tamsyn said, feeling her face alight with embarrassment.

'I've come for you, of course,' Bernard told her, grinning at Jed with a sort of 'Women, what are they like?' expression. 'To be your date at the wedding, just as you wanted me to.'

Chapter Twenty-one

'Mo and I will get out of your way,' Jed said, reaching out for Mo.

'Nice baby,' Bernard said. 'Something you want to tell me?'

'No,' Tamsyn said. 'Jed, you don't have to go, or take Mo.'

'I think you've probably got a lot of explaining . . . I mean catching up to do,' Jed said.

'I'm sorry. I am Bernard du Mont Père.' Bernard offered a hand to Jed. 'I'm Tamsyn's boss, and also her lover.'

Tamsyn knew perfectly well that Bernard's English was good enough not to use that particular word without fully knowing what impact it would have on the conversation.

'Jed Hayward,' Jed shook his hand. 'Tamsyn and I hardly know each other, it seems.'

Tamsyn watched dismayed as Jed and Mo left the room, and turned to see Bernard casting a critical eye over the pieces of Alex's dress.

'What's this?' he said. 'It looks like a giant silkworm has thrown up in here.' He laughed, but Tamsyn didn't.

'Why are you here?' Tamsyn asked him.

'Aren't you pleased to see me?' Bernard said, wrapping his arms around her waist and pulling her against him. It was funny; whenever she thought about Bernard, she imagined him quite differently from the man he really was. In her mind's eye he was tall, muscular and deeply charismatic, which was the one thing about him that was incontrovertible. The truth was that Bernard had a knack for transmitting a personality into a room that was much bigger than he really was. In the cold light of day, he was actually maybe half an inch shorter than her, and though his eyes were as black as night, his mouth was sensuous and his beard was carefully trimmed, his build was slight, wiry, his hands delicate – artistic. What couldn't be denied about him was the way he filled any atmosphere, overwhelming any space as if he was the sun, in all its blazing glory, demanding that the worlds and their moons revolve around him. And usually she was caught in the pull of his magnetic gravity.

Just not today; today, she found his presence deeply annoying. No, not his presence, his existence. It was his existence that riled her. Which, of course, she knew was completely unfair. Jed was right to run away from her; a man should run away from a woman who could fall in and out of love within a matter of hours. It wasn't Jed who was the hot mess, it was her.

'Of course I'm pleased to see you,' she said, taking

a breath and trying her best to remember the life that she had worked so long and hard to build up. 'Of course I am. It's just so unexpected. You're planning a show, we're in the middle of Autumn/Winter, you very nearly didn't let me leave, so how on earth can you possibly be here?'

'I saw you on Twitter,' Bernard told her. 'A friend called me to tell me about it, about you finding the baby. There are photos all over the internet and you looked terrible, and I thought perhaps you might need me to come and help you.'

'Help me with the baby?' Tamsyn was deeply confused.

'Help you with your hair, darling. You look like you've put your finger in the socket and stood in a puddle.'

Tamsyn laughed, and suddenly she was quite glad to see him.

'No, really, I thought you might need me, by your side.'

She was struggling to understand this gesture; it meant something, but she was unable to decipher what it was just yet.

'Bernard . . . Thank you for coming, but honestly, you don't have to be here. I'm really busy with the baby and the dresses.'

'Ah yes,' Bernard picked up the hem of the dress and examined it. 'Charmingly naive and rustic, darling. Of course, not your best work, but I don't suppose the yokels will know or mind; just please make sure no one associates "this" with my label and your work there.'

Tamsyn blinked. 'That's not why you are here, is it? To tell me off for running up wedding dresses for my brother's wedding?'

'Well, darling, strictly speaking it does contravene the contract of exclusivity that you signed with me when you came to work at Du Mont Père, but no, of course that's not why I am here. I am here because you were gone, and then I saw your face on the internet and it hit me in the chest; I missed you. I wanted to be with you, and I suddenly had this impulse, this strange impulse to make it happen. So I came.' He shrugged, and Tamsyn couldn't help but smile. It was so unlike Bernard, so unlike him to admit to any kind of dependency on another human being, that it touched her.

'So, we go now, to your hotel where your suite is still waiting for you to arrive, and we will have the most wonderful reunion. And then dinner.'

Tamsyn laughed as Bernard kissed her neck, his hands running over her buttocks.

'I can't,' she said, finding herself peeling his hands off her. 'I have to finish these dresses. I'm already really behind schedule and soon, my pensioners' sweatshop out there is going to expect me to oversee them assembling the bridesmaids' dresses. Actually Bernard, as you are here, it would be so wonderful if you could help me. Imagine what a gift that would be, to present my sister-in-law-to-be with a Bernard du Mont Père wedding dress?'

'Come with me to the hotel,' Bernard said, kissing her ear in a way that usually made Tamsyn squirm. 'I need to be alone with you, right now.'

Perhaps it was the exhaustion, the excitement or Jed, but either way Tamsyn looked at Bernard and realised she had never felt less enthusiastic about a sexual encounter in her entire life, and that included the time she got Julian 'Dribble' Bentley in a game of spin the bottle. She'd just have to find a way to tell her boss that the romantic part of their arrangement was over, she realised now. Even if she had managed to ruin Jed's opinion of her in one fell swoop by having a secret boyfriend, at least what had happened between them had made her realise that everything outside of her professional life with Bernard wasn't working for her at all.

'Perhaps half an hour,' she said, 'just for a break. We need to talk.'

Outside of the castle's portcullis a local minicab was waiting, his meter still running, even though the hotel was a short walk away. Bernard had been so certain she would come with him he had kept a taxi waiting.

'Another beautiful building,' Bernard said as he swept her into the foyer of The Poldore Hall Hotel. 'You have to check in, for us to get a key.'

'Right.' Tamsyn apologised to the girl behind the desk for not showing up for the first two nights of her prepaid stay and accepted a key in return, which Bernard at once took out of her hand, leading her up the grand staircase to where the suite was situated. Unlocking the door, he picked her up, which was no mean feat considering his stature and her protests, and carried her inside, finding the bedroom and flinging her on the bed.

'We're not getting married,' Tamsyn said, irritably.

'Not yet,' Bernard said, kneeling on the bed and looking at her. 'Oh my God, what are you wearing? It is a testament to my desire for you that I can still want you even though you wear this jumper that hurts my eyes!'

'It's not that bad!' Tamsyn said as Bernard dragged if off over her head and threw it on the floor, revealing the tight black vest top she wore underneath in place of a bra.

'Yes,' he said, 'yes, it is, but the view is improving. Now . . . these Lycra and elastic in the waist! I should sack you for these.'

'Bernard,' she said, stopping him as he tried to drag her leggings off her, 'stop. No, I don't want to.'

'You don't?' Bernard looked surprised. 'You are tired. You feel better later on.'

'Why are you here, really?' Tamsyn said, reaching for her jumper again. 'I mean, if you saw me on the internet and realised that you had to be with me, why not a phone call or a text, anything at all to say that you were coming?'

Bernard sighed and flopped down onto the bed next to her.

'Really?' he said. 'You want to talk about this now?'

'Well, I don't know.' Tamsyn sat on the edge of the bed. 'It's just, I am sort of right in the middle of something here, in my own time, on holiday, and you've just turned up and dragged me out of my life. A bit like you think you own me.'

'I haven't dragged you out of your life,' Bernard said. 'This place, this baby you have found, these funny costumes you are making, they are the distractions. It's me, the business, your work that is your real life. This, this is all a nonsense.' He waved his arms around him, and Tamsyn had to suppose that he meant Poldore and everyone and everything in it. 'There is no time for you to be here, playing at being a mother, and pretending you are in some bad musical. I need you, Tamsyn. I need you at my side. I want you to come back to Paris with me tonight. We have much to do. I came because you are not answering your phone, and it is very irritating.'

'What?' Tamsyn said. 'So that stuff about being my wedding date? Being by my side? What was that?'

'I meant them. I will be your date if you want, but how much better would it be for me to be by your side in Paris? Working on the job we love?'

'But Ruan and Alex's wedding is tomorrow. I haven't finished the dresses, and there's Mo – can't you see that I've a few things going on at the moment?' Tamsyn looked at him, a suspicion forming. 'Bernard. What is this about?'

'You remember you brought me those drawings, a few months ago, before I started the new collection? The coats?'

'Yes,' Tamsyn said. 'You said they were too much of me and not enough of you. You said they didn't fit in with your vision, or your look, and that I had a lot more to learn about your philosophy before I could design a whole garment for Bernard du Mont Père!'

Tamsyn remembered the conversation so clearly because she had repeated it in her head, over and over again, for weeks after it had occurred. Bernard hadn't said those things; he'd shouted them, before tossing her drawings back in her face. It had been right at the start of her career, before their relationship had developed, and she'd been so excited by her new job, in a new city, with a chance to really make her mark. At the time it had felt as if, having seen her enthusiasm, Bernard had felt compelled to stamp it all out, to crush her ego before it had any chance of matching his own. And then she'd got to know him better, especially after their affair had begun, and she'd decided that she had misjudged him, that really he was only showing her the way it must be done. You work your way up, you pay your dues. You don't expect any express routes. It was so unlike Bernard to bring up anything from the past, let alone acknowledge that a good deal of it had actually happened, that she got a deeply uneasy feeling in her gut.

'Your designs, darling. I had to go to a meeting with the retail chain, remember? Well, it seems that somehow your drawings made their way into that presentation.'

'And?' Tamsyn's eyes widened. 'Did they ruin the whole thing?'

'They loved them, darling,' Bernard said, and Tamsyn squealed. 'And, best of all, they really want them. They want a whole collection based around them.'

'Oh Bernard, that's amazing,' Tamsyn leapt into his lap, wrapping her arms around his neck and kissing him on the cheek. 'Well, of course, of *course* I'll design more for them. I'll have to make sure Mo is sorted, but I can start drawing, after the wedding dresses are done, and if you help me with them it will happen at twice the pace and . . . I can't believe this is happening! Oh, Bernard, thank you. Thank you so much for believing in me this way. In showing your faith in my work. You don't know what it means to me.'

'Darling,' Bernard patted her knee. 'Darling, I took your drawings to the meetings . . . and, well, really what matters is that they loved them and they are bringing their business to du Mont Père, and you achieved that.'

'But they will have my name on?' Tamsyn said, a

little uncertainly. 'They are my designs, so they will say "Tamsyn Thorne at du Mont Père"?'

'Darling, darling Tamsyn,' Bernard picked up her hand and kissed each one of her fingers individually. 'My darling girl, I took your designs to the meeting. But I said that they were mine.'

'What?' Tamsyn asked him, too shocked to move, even to remove her arms from his.

'It was never my intention that this should happen. I took them merely as padding, to show I had alternatives. I was sure that they would find something right in my own creations, and they should have. They were works of genius, but my vision is too brilliant for normal women, apparently. Your drawings were safe, commercial,' he waved his hand dismissively, as if the very words he was coming out with disgusted him. 'Didn't challenge their little minds too much.'

'And yet you are still happy enough to put your name to them, and take the money and the glory,' Tamsyn said, standing up. 'And that's why you're here, being kind and sweet, to make sure that I play along with you?'

'Of course.' Bernard seemed genuinely confused by her ire. 'Of course I did that, it's what is best for both of us, don't you see? The money will feed the business and keep my staff employed, it will allow me to concentrate on creating the works of art that I am truly born to bring into this world, and you can take over the retail side, build it up from scratch. It will be your baby, and one that you can be proud of owning, not some stray that no one else wanted.'

Tamsyn discovered that she was very good at slapping Bernard hard in the face, although she wasn't aware of what she had done until just after the moment had passed. Horrified, she clamped her hand over her mouth, watching as a five-fingered flower blossomed bright red on his cheek. It hadn't been the way he'd misappropriated her work in such a cavalier way that had moved her to violence, or even his idea that she'd be happy to work twice as hard in his name, without getting any credit, although that told Tamsyn a lot more about what Bernard thought of their relationship than anything else he had ever said or done, that made her want to hit him. No: it was his casual dismissal of Mo that had brought out the tigress in her. It was a simultaneously shocking and thrilling revelation to know that she could get so angry. And yet above and beyond the fury, there was something else. The blood was drumming in her ears, her chest felt full of passion and she felt alive.

'I'm sorry I slapped you,' she said.

'It's fine. A little passion in a woman is a good thing. You are an artist, a creative,' Bernard said as he rubbed his cheek.

'You can have my designs,' Tamsyn told him. 'Those coats, you can say they are yours. But you can also have my resignation.'

'What?' Bernard stood up. 'Tamsyn, you don't mean that, darling. You are angry and you are punishing me, and perhaps I deserve it, but you don't want to throw everything away – your career, your name – over something so trivial.'

'I'm resigning,' Tamsyn said, 'effective immediately. Even if this wasn't love, I thought you were, my friend, I thought you cared about me. Despite all of your vanity and immaturity and selfishness, I thought that there was something between us that was real. But I see now that I wrong.' She paused to look at him. 'I'm not even sure that you like me. Although I am sure that I don't like you.'

'But I do like you,' Bernard said, following her as she left the room, collecting her things on the way. 'Tamsyn, I like you very much, you are one of my most favourite people. The top five at least, top three, perhaps!'

'Oh, go away,' Tamsyn said as she walked down the stairs. 'I'm done with you.'

'You will never work in fashion again,' Bernard chased her out into the corridor, shaking his fist at her. 'No one will work with you again after this . . . this unprofessionalism. I will make sure your name is blacklisted!'

Tamsyn stopped at the bottom of the stairs and looked up at him, and it was suddenly as if she were seeing him in a whole new light, this small, insecure man whose charisma and talent were simply a construct made of smoke and mirrors.

'I don't think you will do that, will you, Bernard?' she said, perfectly calmly. 'You see, I have copies of every drawing I have made, dated and signed, on my laptop. I don't think you'd want those drawings to find their way into the public eye, would you? No, I think that what you are going to do is issue a press release, with wording approved by me, stating how sad you are to lose one of the most talented designers you have worked with in years, and wishing me luck in my future venture, launching my own label in Cornwall.'

'What?' Bernard shouted after her as she strode out of the hotel. 'Are you crazy?'

And as she headed back to town, Tamsyn had to admit that the answer to that question was probably yes.

Chapter Twenty-two

The enormity, not to mention the mind-numbing insanity, of what she had just done, had yet to sink in as Tamsyn marched purposefully back to Castle House feeling positively empowered. Yes, she had thrown in her dream job, not to mention her entire life, including the means to pay for her Parisian apartment, and come up with a hare-brained notion to start her own business at the literal arse end of the world, where no one came except to paddle and eat fish and chips. She'd offended one of the most powerful men in her profession, with whom, until today, she had been on French-kissing terms, and alienated Jed, the first man she had met, perhaps ever, who seemed to truly move her, and yet – she did feel awfully good about it. Like she had done something positive with her life at last. It had to be sleep deprivation, or perhaps she was coming down with Catriona's bug, or maybe she had lost her grip on reality and was just going cheerfully mad. In any case, her own personal Armageddon felt surprisingly upbeat.

As soon as Sue's dogs spotted her they clamoured around her shins, joined by Skipper, who greeted her with twists and jumps, expressing his pleasure at seeing her by nipping at the tips of her fingers. Buoy ambled out after them, his tongue lolling in the heat of the afternoon, which made him look as if he was smiling indulgently at the noisier, younger dogs. Although, knowing Buoy, he was probably planning ways to herd the tiresome rabble into the moat that was still brimming with rainwater.

Leaving the pack chasing each other, baying loudly, she followed Buoy back inside, kneeling down to put her arms around him. He licked her ear.

'Buoy,' she said. 'I'm not altogether sure what I've done. Any ideas?'

Buoy threw her a baleful look, and then glanced meaningfully at the kitchen worktop, where the sandwiches that had been laid out for the sewing circle were sitting under pretty mesh domes, no doubt the only thing that had prevented him from making off with a few of them already.

'OK, fair enough: you're only going to give me the benefit of your wisdom if I cross your paw with food, I get it,' Tamsyn said, grabbing a couple of sandwiches of the roast beef variety and throwing them under the table. 'But don't tell anyone.'

Buoy batted at the back door with his paw.

'Good point,' Tamsyn said, closing it just before any of the rest of the animals got a whiff of the treasure within and robbed the old dog of his bounty. Tamsyn ruffled his ears until he shook her off and turned his back on her, in a clear signal that their conversation was over and it was the sandwiches he was giving his full attention to now.

Buoy was right, she decided, as she went to check on the progress of the bridesmaids' dresses. The thing to do, she told herself, was not to worry about the catastrophe that was her life right now. No, it was time to focus on the things that mattered: Mo, and Ruan's wedding. And Ruan.

She had barely seen her brother since she'd arrived, and there was still so much for them to say to each other, especially if, as it turned out, they might be about to become neighbours again. Tamsyn laughed out loud at the absurdity of it, rolling her eyes at a suit of armour as she passed. For most of her life she had done every- thing she could to get away from Poldore. She'd been back for just a few days and now she found herself not wanting to leave again. There were many people she needed to see, to talk to and many feelings and impulses that she had to at least attempt to understand. But not now: now was all about making dresses. That was one thing that she knew how to do.

'Oh there you are, thank goodness. Come with me,' Sue said, grabbing her and dragging her through the great hall and towards Rory's office, where a collection of the people still staying at Castle House had gathered outside the door.

'What's happened?' Tamsyn broke into a trot as she followed Sue. 'Is Mo OK?'

'She's fine. Except that Tess wants to take her away.'

'What? But I thought we agreed?' Tamsyn looked at the social worker, who was standing in Rory's office with Mo in her arms. Jed was standing by the fireplace, his face turned away from her and towards the window. Jeff Dangerfield was there too, unable to meet her eye.

'What's happened?' Tamsyn asked. 'Have you found Mo's mum?'

Tess shook her head. 'As you know, when I agreed that you and Reverend Hayward be authorised as temporary carers for Baby, I had to run checks on both of you for suitability,' Tess said. 'It has come to light that Reverend Hayward is not a suitable guardian for a minor. He was discharged from the army, with certain issues pending that mean he requires further investigation. And in the best interests of Baby's safety, I feel that I have to rescind my original decision and take her into the custody of social services.'

'Wait, what?' Tamsyn shook her head in disbelief. 'What are you talking about? You've got this wrong.'

She turned to Jed, but he avoided her gaze, the brief connection they had shared seeming to have evaporated into thin air.

'Wait, you don't mean him,' she said. 'You mean me. I got picked up for shoplifting lipstick when I fifteen, kicked the security guard in the shins and tried to do a runner, but it was only a warning and I was just a kid, that's what you mean, isn't it? Or something like that, right? You've got him mixed up with me.'

'I'm afraid not,' Jeff Dangerfield said. 'I knew about Reverend Hayward's problem, that he is doing his utmost to conquer, prior to recent events, and I should have declared them. However, I have to admit to not feeling that they were pertinent.'

'Which is a serious oversight on your part,' Tess said. 'We don't make up these rules for fun, you know; we are trying to protect the vulnerable.'

'But he hasn't done anything wrong,' Tamsyn insisted. 'He's been a victim of circumstance, but that doesn't mean he can't look after a child.'

'Tamsyn, it's fine,' Jed said. 'Tess is only trying to do what's best for Mo. She has to be sure about me, and she can't be . . .' He paused, and Tamsyn, unable to see him looking so vulnerable for a moment longer, went to him, taking his hand in hers. Their eyes met, his hand tugging slightly away before it relaxed and his fingers gripped hers. 'PTSD and its effects can be unpredictable, as we realised last night. I'm sorry. I've let you and Mo down.'

Jed let go of Tamsyn's hand and walked out into the hall to face his parishioners, who had gathered outside the door. 'I'm sorry,' he told them. 'I should have told you everything about me when I arrived in Poldore.

I've failed you, I've kept things from you, I haven't been honest. I'm not the person you think I am and, in this job, there is no excuse for that. I'll officiate over the wedding tomorrow, and then I will ask the Diocese to find a replacement for me.'

'Jed, wait . . .' Tamsyn watched as the crowd parted and Jed walked away, leaving them all silent and shocked.

'No, this isn't right.' She turned back to Tess. 'He's not dangerous. He's suffering from post-traumatic stress disorder. Because he was working as a padre in Afghanistan and witnessed something terrible, and he's going through stuff. But he's getting help, he's dealing with it, and it doesn't mean he isn't a suitable carer for Mo. She loves him, and he's great with children, much more experienced than me. He taught me how to dress and change her. He's a good man, a strong man.' She looked at the concerned group of Poldore residents outside the door. 'We don't condemn a person for having lived a difficult life, do we? We don't abandon them because they've been through things that change them, do we? He is still the person we all think of him as. He's still at the heart of your community. He's still one of the finest men I've ever met!'

''Course he is.' Heads turned towards the sound of Eddie's voice. 'Jed Hayward cares about this town, and us, even the heathens. And the people, including the heathens, care about him.' He looked at his fellow townsfolk. 'We're not going to let him leave thinking he's let us down, are we?'

He was answered with nods and murmurs of agreement.

'In fact,' Eddie continued, 'we're not going to let him leave at all. We need to show him that he has the support of each and every one of us. I'm going down to the church to tell him that right now. Who's with me?'

The murmurs became something of a cheer, and Eddie left, his people, or perhaps more accurately, his regulars, in his wake.

Tamsyn turned back to Tess, who was still holding Mo in her arms.

'You're holding her all wrong,' Tamsyn said. 'She likes to be able to see, and it's better on her tummy if you hold her more upright. Here, let me have her.'

'I'm sorry,' Tess moved a step away from Tamsyn's open arms. 'But there are some rules that I cannot bend. It's the sort of issue that takes time to clarify. We'd need to assess Jed for suitability, and I had no choice but to step in.'

'Fine, I get it, you've got a job to do, and I think the choice you've made is the wrong one, but perhaps you have to make it, because perhaps the next time in a similar situation it would be the right one. I understand that. But it's done now. Let me take her. I've got a lot to do.'

Tamsyn stretched out her arms, but still Tess did not budge.

'You don't understand. I can't leave her with you if Reverend Hayward is also going to be in the building.'

'But . . . of course he's going to be in the building,' Tamsyn looked at Jeff Dangerfield, who looked at his feet. 'He's officiating at my brother's wedding tomorrow, not to mention that there's a massive great big hole in the ceiling of his house.'

Sue put a calming arm on Tamsyn's shoulder. 'He's not here now, is he?' she said to Tess. 'Look, it gives me no pleasure to say this about a man I admire, but if I have a word with Jed, I know he will willingly stay away from Castle House and from Mo, if that's what is best for the baby. She will be safe here with us at Castle House. We have ramparts; we even have a cannon that still works, if things get really bad.'

Tess looked at Mo, who had begun to squirm in her arms, her face twisting as she built up to a cry of protest about something, and this time Tamsyn did not wait for the baby to be passed to her, she simply took her, holding her so that Mo's eyes peered over her shoulder, a vantage point that seemed to soothe her at once.

'It was Jed who found out how she likes to be carried,' she told Tess. 'Don't take her, I don't agree with it, but Sue is right. What's best for Mo now is the same as what was best for her yesterday, and that's to be with people she knows until you find either her mother or a proper home for her.'

Tess sighed and looked at Jeff Dangerfield.

'She's right,' he said. 'Sometimes, Tess, you've got to trust your gut.'

'And Jeff's got a lot of gut to trust,' Sue pointed out.

'Twenty-four more hours,' Tess said. 'I might be able to stretch out this highly irregular situation for that much longer, and I will be doing everything I can during that time to find a place for Mo where you can be reassured she will be happy. That's the best I can do, Tamsyn, I'm sorry. I wanted to be able to bend the rules for you and for Mo, but I need to put that baby first, which is what I am doing, even if you don't feel like that is the case.'

Tamsyn nodded, resting her cheek against Mo's. Exhaustion dragged at her, as if filling her limbs with lead, and in an instant the adrenaline that had kept her on such an artificial high for so long was gone.

'Well, you know your way out,' Sue said to Tess, her tone brisk. 'Through the kitchen's quicker, although I can't promise you won't get mauled by animals or children. Or both. You remember the raptors in *Jurassic Park*? Very similar scenario to that happened to the postman last week.'

Sue waited until Tess had gone and the sound of dogs baying could be heard in the courtyard.

'Go after Jed, Tamsyn,' she said. 'I know Eddie and the others have gone down to the church, but he won't be there. Before Tess arrived he told me he was worried that Catriona still wasn't improving like the others. He'll probably be with her, trying to persuade her to go to A&E before he leaves here.'

'But . . . me? Why me?' Tamsyn said. 'And the dresses . . .'

'The dresses are wonderful,' Sue said. 'They are perfectly on schedule. I know, I'm overseeing them myself. And why you? Because he's the finest man you have ever met, Tamsyn, and you are in danger of letting him walk out of your life.'

'I don't know what to say to him.' Tamsyn held Mo a little closer. 'I feel like he was having a perfectly nice, ordered life until I turned up and dragged him into a world of chaos.'

'You'll think of something better than that,' Sue said, nodding at the doorway.

How strange it was, Tamsyn thought, as she began what seemed like the longest walk of her life, with Mo resting against her shoulder, how easy and simple it had seemed to throw her life away in an instant, only recently. How she'd made a commitment to a new life before she was even certain of what that commitment might be. But now the simple act of walking down a corridor to say hello to a friend seemed terrifying. Which should not be surprising, she supposed. After all, falling in love was a rather terrifying thing to do.

'There you are.' Kirsten appeared in the corridor. 'I found hats, but you weren't there, no one was, and no one knew where you were.'

'Kirsten,' Tamsyn stopped, suddenly realising exactly how to make everything better. 'You are the answer to all of this. you know.'

'Answer to all of what?' Kirsten looked perplexed. 'What are you talking about? I went to get hats for you.'

'I know it's scary, and so massive, and you are so young and you haven't had a chance to think it through, and I've tried, I really have tried, not to force the issue, but don't you see. It's going to be too late soon. They want to take her away, and you are the only one who can stop it. So you have to come forward, face it, face what you did and speak up. I'll help you, I promise I will.'

'Wait, what?' Kirsten's face clouded. 'What exactly is it you think I've done?'

'You . . . you have to tell someone that you are Mo's mother,' Tamsyn said. 'Now, before they take her away from you! Look at her, Kirsten, really look at her. She needs you so much; don't pretend you don't see her.'

'What?' Whatever traces of a smile had been left on the young woman's face vanished in an instant. 'Oh my God,' she said quietly. 'I thought you were actually interested in *me*, I thought you liked *me*. But all this,

this has just been about the baby. You think I'm the one who left her out there in that storm?'

'But . . . well, yes,' Tamsyn said. 'You said you'd been having a secret thing with that boy from the hostel, and you looked so upset, so . . .'

'Sad,' Kirsten said. 'I'm very, very fucking sad, because my life is very, very fucking sad, and lonely and loveless and hard, much harder than life should be for someone my age. But you . . . I was starting to like you. Shit, I told you about my mum leaving me. I would never, ever do that to a child of mine, not ever. She's not my baby, and you . . .' Tears filled Kirsten's eyes. 'You are just the same as the rest of them. I thought you were my friend.'

'Kirsten, wait!' Tamsyn watched dismayed as the girl ran out of the front door. How could she have got that so wrong, so very wrong on all levels, pushing away a fragile friendship in the blink of an eye? And if Kirsten wasn't Mo's mother, then who was?

Hurrying after Kirsten, she walked out into the courtyard and found the girl sitting on the stone steps, sobbing angrily into her hands.

'You didn't run away very far,' Tamsyn said, sitting down next to her.

'That's the most depressing thing about my life,' Kirsten told her bitterly. 'I've run out of places to run away to.'

'I'm sorry,' Tamsyn said, holding Mo against her. 'I

really am. I put two and two together and made a hundred. But it's not because I think you are a bad person, it's the opposite. It's because I was hoping for the best, for Mo. I honestly thought that if you were her mum, then you would be the best for her. Don't you see? I wanted it to be true because I actually do have faith in you.'

Kirsten sniffed, wiping her sleeve under her nose, looking sideways at Tamsyn. 'Really?'

'Really,' Tamsyn said. 'You know about life; you'll be a great mum one day.'

'Well, she is a cute baby, but I'm not going to get pregnant, not before I'm ready. Not until I've got something to offer another person.'

'Well, that's sensible,' Tamsyn said. 'You're smart, and I'm sorry I didn't give you enough credit for that. But for what it's worth, I do like you. And as it looks like I've just moved back into town, I could do with a friend, so how about it?'

'You're a bit too old to be my friend, to be honest,' Kirsten said.

'Well, beggars can't be choosers,' Tamsyn retorted gently. 'You've got a year left at school, right?' Kirsten nodded. 'Well, it's too soon for me to make any promises, way too soon. But if I get premises, if I get a business off the ground, well, how about I mentor you? Help you get through your exams, teach you a little bit about starting up a business. Fashion might not be your thing, but perhaps together we can find out what is.'

'You mean that?' Kirsten looked suspicious. 'Even though I'm not Mo's mum?'

'I'm sad for Mo that you are not her mum,' Tamsyn said. 'But not for you. And the next time someone who thinks they are much smarter than they are says "There are a lot of people that care about you", I want you to be able to think to yourself that actually, yes, there is one. Me. Deal?'

Tamsyn offered her hand, feeling the formal approach was the best, and Kirsten took it in hers and shook it once.

'Deal.' They sat in silence for a few moments.

'Shall we go and look at hats then?' Kirsten asked her.

'Not quite yet. I've got one more thing to do first,' Tamsyn said. 'I've got to go and tell the vicar I love him.'

Stopping in her tracks outside Catriona's room, Tamsyn held Mo against her thundering heart as the revelation hit her again and again, a repeating wave of something like joy and something like dread.

What was she was planning to tell Jed when he came through the door? Was she planning to tell him that she loved him?

'Dear God, Mo, I'm not sure I can,' she whispered into the baby's ear, just as the door opened.

'I just wish you'd let me take you to get checked out, Catriona,' Jed was saying, his back to her. 'I think you should be past the worst now, really. If anything, you look worse.'

Tamsyn couldn't quite hear what Catriona replied, but if there was such a thing as shrift, then this was it and it was very short. She braced herself to face him.

'Fine,' Jed said. 'I'll call you later.'

'Oh, Tamsyn.' The sound of activity somewhere deep in the house punctuated the silence. 'I'm not sure you should be here with Mo.'

'I'm sorry,' Tamsyn rushed the words out, because it seemed like the most appropriate thing to say. 'I'm so sorry about your house, and the church, and you getting dragged into looking after Mo. And I'm sorry that you were put in a position where someone found out something that is only your business and used it to stop you doing something kind and wonderful. And I'm sorry that while we were talking before, my ex-boss and ex-boyfriend turned up and . . . I'm really sorry, Jed, that I didn't tell you about him before. I'm sorry I kissed you when I wasn't free to kiss you, and I'm sorry . . . I'm sorry. I'm so sorry, that's all. Before I arrived in Poldore, your life was much better.'

Jed shook his head, the afternoon sunlight that found its way in through the stained-glass panels in the great door dappling the side of his face with jewel-like colours.

'You are a force of nature, Tamsyn,' he said, 'but I

am fairly certain you aren't responsible for the storm, or for the reasons that Mo's mum felt unable to take care of her.' He lowered his gaze. 'I wonder, if I had been more willing to show my weaknesses to my community, then perhaps Mo's mother would have been more willing to share her predicament with me.'

'You're not weak,' Tamsyn resisted the urge to step closer to him. 'I think you're one of the strongest people I have ever met. You certainly make me want to lean on you, and I have always thought that I didn't need anybody.'

'You don't need anybody.' Jed looked up, his silver eyes pinning her to the spot. 'You many want them, but that is another thing entirely.'

'Well, I do,' Tamsyn said. 'I do want you in my life, Jed. Which is, at least for the time being, going to be in Poldore, due to a series of unforeseen events that led to me chucking my job in earlier today and dumping my boss.'

Jed's silvery eyes widened.

'Yes, I know what you are thinking. It does perhaps indicate a borderline personality disorder, but it was a choice that was made, if not exactly out of logic, then out of integrity. It's a choice I made for myself, and not just because I want you in my life. I'd been pursuing a dream I've had all of my life, so relentlessly that I forgot what it was, and the more I tried to make it come true, the further away I got from it. And it's been in here, in Castle House, that I've remembered that dream again, and how much it thrilled me. I want to design and make dresses for all women, dresses that make them feel wonderful about themselves, whatever their shape or size, and I want to make things that are beautiful, not modern, or avant-garde. I want to make people feel pretty. Which probably sounds a bit shallow, given that you want to save people's souls. But anyway, I can't help thinking it would be an awful shame if you moved away just now . . . I mean, I know you are a vicar and I am a heathen, but does that really mean we couldn't just . . . see how we get on with some kissing and hand holding? Because the way I feel about you, the way that the feelings I am having around you make me feel, as if . . . well, maybe we could, you know, fall in love . . . sort of thing.'

After the first several seconds of silence, Tamsyn turned her face away from him, looking towards the sunlight transformed on its journey through the coloured glass.

'So anyway,' she forced the words out, determined to exit the situation with as much of her dignity intact as was possible, 'I'd better get going – lots to do.'

A crash sounded on the other side of Catriona's door, followed by a cry.

'Let me,' Tamsyn said, putting Mo in Jed's arms before he could refuse her. 'It might be that she doesn't want a man in there.'

Catriona lay on the floor, a pool of blood forming beneath her hips, her eyes closed, her skin almost grey.

'Call an ambulance!' Tamsyn called to Jed, 'Now!'

The thin, mewling cry of the baby answered her. Jed, who stood in the doorway, didn't hesitate.

'Catriona, what's happened?' Tamsyn took her hand; it was freezing. 'Can you hear me? I need you to stay with me, OK? Tell me what happened.'

'Where is she?' Catriona opened her eyes, focusing them briefly on Tamsyn. 'Where is the baby, is she safe? I heard her crying. Is she safe?'

It was then that all the pieces finally fell into place, and Tamsyn understood. Catriona was Mo's mother.

'Ambulance will be here soon,' Jed told her, stopping at the threshold of the door.

'Give me Mo,' Tamsyn reached up for her.

'Are you sure . . . if Catriona's that ill?' Jed said.

'What she's got isn't catching,' Tamsyn said. 'Catriona has recently given birth to a baby, a baby that she hasn't told anyone about. And she's in a bad way. Quickly.'

Looking shocked, Jed transferred Mo into Tamsyn's arms as he knelt on the floor beside his friend, taking her hand.

'It wasn't raining when I left her,' Catriona's voice was barely more than a whisper. 'It was warm, and the rain had passed. I thought that someone would be there, for evensong. I would never . . . I didn't mean . . . I didn't want . . .'

'Here she is.' Tamsyn held Mo as close to her face as she could. 'See? She's well, and beautiful, and so full of personality, even at two days old. Your little girl is perfect.'

'She doesn't deserve a mother like me,' Catriona wept, turning her face away. 'She deserves so much better than a silly old woman like me.'

'I can hear the sirens,' Jed said. 'They'll be here any second, Catriona, hold on.'

'Look at her,' Tamsyn said. 'Please, just look at her face.'

Slowly, Catriona turned her head, and mother and daughter looked into each other's eyes. Mo mewled, one thick, chubby hand batting against Catriona's cheek.

'See how she knows you,' Tamsyn smiled. 'She's saying hello.'

'I love you,' Catriona told her daughter just as the room filled with paramedics and Tamsyn was ushered out of the way, into the hall, where she waited with Sue.

'I'll go with her,' Jed said as they wheeled Catriona out on a gurney. 'I'll ring you from the hospital. I didn't see; how did I not see this?'

'You weren't alone,' Sue said. 'None of us saw this.'

Chapter Twenty-three

The bridesmaids' dresses were almost done, and Tamsyn was thrilled with the skills that the sewing circle had displayed; each stitch was perfection, each bead that had been carefully harvested from a selection of costume jewellery placed exactly as Tamsyn had instructed.

Now it was only Alex's dress that was far behind schedule, and that was Tamsyn's fault entirely. There was no time to think or fret or worry, and that was a good thing; the only thing she could do was take care of Mo, make the most beautiful wedding dress she could muster and wait.

Setting a smaller group onto finishing and fitting the bridesmaids' dresses, she brought the still incomplete bodice of the bridal gown into the dining room.

'Well, ladies and gentleman,' she said. 'Time is running out. It's been a very eventful day, and we need to press on to make this dress the most wonderful garment that Alex has ever laid eyes on. She's trusted me entirely with this project and I can't get it wrong, so it's all hands on deck. Are we in?'

'Damn straight we're in,' cheered a tiny lady who

looked around ninety, pumping her fist in the air.

Tamsyn scanned the room, looking for someone of a suitable height and build, and found Cordelia hovering in the doorway. There was a lost sort of quality about her, the way she was lingering on the edges of the action, that reminded Tamsyn of when her baby sister had been a little girl; always a bit too young to join in with what the rest of her siblings got up to, she had been forced to find her own way in the world from the start.

'Cordy,' Tamsyn called her over. 'You're the nearest I've got to Alex in terms of height and hips and waist, although she's bigger on top, but that's OK – that part of the bodice is finished, at least. You're our model.'

'Wait, what does that mean?' Cordelia protested as Tamsyn caught her hand and led her into the centre of the room, pointing at a rather rickety-looking foot-stool that she had pilfered from the library.

'It means you are going to stand here, on this stool, and we are going to construct the dress around you. If we all work together, it shouldn't take more than an hour or two, and then I can finish the beadwork and embroidery on the bodice once it's a whole piece. Kirsten, pass me the pins, please.'

Kirsten, who had been at her side since she began to work on the dress again in earnest, obliged.

Tamsyn had to admit that the way the sewing circle gathered around Cordelia as she teetered on the stool was a little bit intimidating, as if there was a small chance they might be about to pop her into something wicker and set fire to her.

'You want me to stand on this thing for an hour?' Cordelia asked her. 'I'm not sure I can take it. I'm not sure it can take me. I'm a girl who eats pies, you know.'

'I know, and we love you for it. The stool is, like, two hundred years old, so I'm sure it can last another hour or so. Woman up: this is for your brother's wedding tomorrow.'

'You know how much I hate being altruistic,' Cordelia complained.

'Yes,' Tamsyn agreed. 'You really are the most unpleasant person I have ever met, and yet, I don't know . . . I seem to quite love you.'

'Jesus, what's happened to you – early menopause?' Cordelia wrinkled up her nose.

'An epiphany,' Tamsyn told her. 'The realisation that sometimes the things you already have can be more than enough. Now, if you move, I will stick a pin in you on purpose.'

The group worked in near silence for a long time, Tamsyn only looking up every now and then to check on Mo, who was lying on the floor on a brightly coloured padded mat that someone from the town had produced. She seemed to like it better than her carrycot, her black eyes seeming to look around and take in the beautiful plaster ceiling. Tamsyn smiled as she paused for a moment to watch her. It had been only two days, and yet she'd become so used to having the little girl in her life that she had started to feel like a permanent fixture. She supposed that some silent part of her fevered brain had even begun to entertain the idea of becoming her permanent foster-mother, and even perhaps one day adopting her. It wasn't something that Tamsyn had thought or even felt consciously, but now that Mo wasn't a lost baby any more, now that they at least knew who her mother was, if nothing else about the circumstances of her birth, the time that she would be in Tamsyn's care would now be whittled down to hours. And yet, as much as she would miss her, the best that she could hope for Mo would be to return her to her mother. Closing her eyes for just one second, she thought of Catriona and wished her better, as if perhaps wishing might be enough to make it so.

It was strange how you could know a child for so short a time, a child so tiny, so barely there in many ways, and feel so attached to them so completely. For a person so small, Mo had ensnared Tamsyn with the force of her personality, her charm and sweetness, and yes, it had happened in the space of just two days: Tamsyn had fallen in love with the little girl. And if she could fall in love with her after only two days' acquaintance, then did that mean she could fall in love with someone else too, someone who sometimes wore a dog collar and looked awfully good wet?

Don't think about it, Tamsyn, she told herself. Don't think about anything except Alex's dress. The dress is all that matters.

Gradually, as they worked, the room filled up with more and more people coming to watch, although Alex was not one of them. Lucy and Gloria had taken her out for something approaching a hen night. Although the town was still mainly closed, they had salvaged a couple of bottles of champagne from the pub cellar and had hired a cab to take them to a disco in nearby St Austell. As for Ruan, Laura said he was at the lighthouse, busy making it ready for when he brought his new bride home. Rory came in, followed by Rosie and Eddie. Brian Rogers arrived carrying a battered old acoustic guitar, which he began to play, perched on the edge of the table. Skipper and the rowdy dogs had been shut away somewhere, probably with the children, but Buoy walked into the room, with statesmanlike dignity, and after turning around three times placed himself next to Mo, his nose pointed at her head, appointing himself her protector. Tamsyn was sure that the tiny child smiled when she saw him.

Tamsyn was certain that by now everybody had heard the news about Catriona, but nobody mentioned it. The crowd that gathered wasn't there to gossip or speculate; even Sue, who came in and set up a tea urn at the far end of the room, away from the dresses, was quiet, thoughtful. As the group sewed on, carefully placing each stitch with the sort of care and attention that Tamsyn rarely saw, Mo began to fret, causing Buoy to cock his head to one side and whimper in return. It was Keira who picked her up from the mat and, cradling her in her arms, began to sing to her. Just a soft, tuneless murmuring at first, which gradually became a hum, which slowly turned into a song Tamsyn recognised. It was 'Somewhere Over the Rainbow', and it only took a moment or two for Brian to pick up the tune and accompany her. Before long, the group of seamstresses began to join in and hum along, a few picking up the lyrics and crooning them under their breath, and then even Kirsten, followed by the bystanders, all gently singing as Keira rocked the baby, until finally Cordelia, her beautiful voice soaring over the group, joined in, smiling at Mo as she sang. Tears pricked behind Tamsyn's eyes at the outpouring of love and care that was being directed at one tiny, lost little person, and her equally lost mother. Everyone who had come into the room tonight hadn't come to sneak a peek at the dresses, or even just to socialise. They had come because they wanted to be near each other. It was an impulse that came out of instinct more than anything, to come together and keep watch over baby Mo for her mother's sake. It was a vigil.

The song was repeated once more, and Mo settled

into one of her deep baby sleeps, from which nothing would rouse her. Keira didn't put her back in her carrycot, but held her close against her chest, kissing the top of her head as the people in the room fell back into companionable silence.

'There.' Tamsyn stood back as she secured the last panel of the skirt into place and looked at the dress, complete except for the final beadwork and embroidery that had yet to be done on the bodice. 'You have been truly amazing, Poldore sewing circle: look what you have made.'

A rash of smiles broke out as everyone looked at the dress, and gradually a ripple of applause went around the room, gaining in momentum as it travelled, until finally it snowballed into cheers and whoops, and Tamsyn laughed as the ladies of the sewing circle (and the one gentleman) hugged each other and punched the air as if they had just won the World Cup or landed a spaceship on the moon. It was the sound of Sue's phone ringing that stilled the celebration. The whole room turned to look at her.

'Jed,' Sue told them. She held the phone to her ear. 'Hello?'

The room waited, and Tamsyn was sure that everyone was holding their breath, just as she was.

'Yes, yes, of course. He's asked for you.' She held the phone out to Tamsyn, who put her scissors back in her pocket and took the phone, and, aware of dozens of pairs of eyes on her back, walked out of the room into the dark, shadowy hallway.

'Jed?' she said.

'I thought you should know first,' Jed said, the sound of his voice in her ear comforting her at once. 'Catriona's in a bad way. Not all of the placenta was delivered after the birth, it seems. She obviously wasn't aware of that. I don't suppose she knew what to expect after giving birth by herself. Having kept the pregnancy a secret for so long, she was determined it should stay that way.'

'Oh my God, the poor woman,' Tamsyn breathed. 'Have you found out why?'

'She hasn't been coherent since they put her in the ambulance, but the doctors say she must have delivered Mo on her own, left her at the church and then tried to go back to life as it was before. She developed an infection and then, when the placenta worked its way loose, she lost a lot of blood. They took her straight into theatre the moment we got here, and she's hooked up to all sorts of antibiotics now. Can't really get much sense out of her, but the doctors think they've caught the infection before septicaemia has had a chance to set in. They're confident she's going to make a full recovery, in time.'

'Oh, thank God,' Tamsyn breathed, finding herself sitting down on the top stair of the grand staircase, as her legs felt less than reliable. 'I mean, thank goodness. That's good news. I'll tell Mo.'

'There's still a lot to try and understand,' Jed said. 'Like how I can work with a person every single day and not know or notice what she was going through. Let alone the fact that she was pregnant. And who's the father – where he is now? And why Catriona thought she couldn't ask me for help. I spent a lot of time with her shortly after her mother died, which was around the same time that this must have happened. I talked to her a lot, and she to me. I let her down.'

'You didn't,' Tamsyn said. 'I think she couldn't bear to talk about something she couldn't even bear to think about. It happens. People try to hide from the things they are thinking and feeling all the time. There are things that both you and I have kept to ourselves, aren't there? Even though they might be really, really obvious to others. People still feel afraid, and try not to notice the feelings.' There was a pointed silence between them. 'Anyway,' Tamsyn ploughed on, 'if you think about it, it was you that she had the most faith in.'

'How do you work that out?' Jed's tone was weary, but warm, Tamsyn thought. She leant her ear towards him.

'Well, it looks as if she was planning on entrusting Mo to you. She left her at the church, expecting you to find her. And that is exactly the way it would have worked if it hadn't been for the storm, and for me and Buoy. You would have found her. Catriona trusted you with her.'

There was silence on the other end of the line, and even though she couldn't see his face, somehow Tamsyn could feel the sadness in Jed, the exhaustion and the worry. She wished she could put her arms around him and hug him, the way she had under the kitchen table, only perhaps without the cramp and the numb bottom, the inappropriate topless kissing and the awkward aftermath.

'Where are you going to go now?' she asked him. 'Not back to that draughty old vicarage to be alone?'

'No,' Jed said. 'I'm going to stay here, at the hospital, in case she wakes up and wants to talk. I'm not really supposed to stay the night, but the nurses seem very friendly, and they've said I can sleep on the sofa in the family room if I promise not to bother anyone.'

'Ah, those friendly nurses,' Tamsyn smiled, imagining what an impact the handsome, caring, distraught young vicar would have on the nursing staff. 'But you won't forget to come and marry Ruan?' Tamsyn asked him. 'I've nearly finished the dress; the sewing circle has been so amazing.'

'I'll be there,' Jed said. 'Funny to think how much has happened since I found you under that tree. I feel a little bit like I met you, and my whole life changed in an instant.'

'I'm so sorry,' Tamsyn said unhappily.

'Don't be sorry,' Jed said. 'I'm not. Tamsyn, you know what you said about how people try not to know things that they know . . .?'

There was a series of beeps and the call ended. When Tamsyn tried to return the call and it went straight to Jed's voicemail, she guessed that his battery must have died. She listened to the sound of his voice on the answerphone, but didn't leave a message. She had no idea what to say.

Everyone was waiting as she went back into the dining room.

'They think she's going to be fine,' Tamsyn told them, taking Mo from Keira's arms and kissing her on the tip of her nose. 'Did you hear that, my little one? Your mummy is going to be fine.'

Chapter Twenty-four

Tamsyn woke up on a chaise longue in the dining room, her eyes snapping open as the first light of the June dawn flooded in through the huge windows. She had meant to go to her room after Mo's last feed at about three, and had just closed her eyes for a moment, but clearly things hadn't worked out quite the way she planned them. It took a moment or two for the events of yesterday to come flooding back to her and she sat up in a panic, wondering if she had also forgotten to finish the dress, but there it was, in all its splendour, hanging from a chandelier. And truth be told, it really was a little bit wonderful.

Picking Mo up, who, it seemed, had been guarded all night by Buoy, who was stretched out at the side of her carrycot, Tamsyn looked at the gown, sparkling like the sea in the morning sunshine, and felt a rush of happiness surge through her. She had made this; she had created this dress from scratch and it was hers – well, it was Alex's, but hers too. The last twenty-four hours of frenzied designing and sewing had created something that would always be special to its recipient, not just for a day or a season, but for ever. And it was the most wonderful feeling.

'Do you know what, Mo?' Tamsyn said. 'I think I might have found my vocation.'

There was a cough behind her, and Tamsyn turned to see Alex, wide-eyed and white as a sheet, her dark hair tousled and tangled, looking like she hadn't had a wink of sleep.

'I'm sorry,' she said, 'but I am getting married today and I thought it was a bit odd that everyone at the wedding has seen the dress except for me, the bride, in person.'

'Or the groom,' Tamsyn said, beckoning her in. 'Here,' she stood aside to reveal the dress. 'What do you think?'

As Alex took in the gown, her eyes filled with tears and her mouth dropped open.

'Oh God, do you hate it?' Tamsyn asked her. 'Did I get it wrong? I really thought I'd got it right. That's my design strength, you know, sensing what a client really wants. Or at least, I thought it was. Well, if the worst comes to the worst I can get a job as a waitress.'

'No . . . it's perfect.' Alex's voice was thick with emotion. 'It's beautiful. It's so much better than the one I chose for myself. And yet, it *is* the dress I would have chosen for myself. How did you know?'

'I was inspired by the Lady in Blue in the portrait in the hallway,' Tamsyn said. 'I know everyone wants to be married in white, but I don't know why. Your eyes are so stunning, and this pale blue colour matches them perfectly. Those panels come from a nineteen fifties evening gown that I found in the attic. I beaded and corseted the bodice to fit you exactly, so that you shouldn't need any underwear. Want to put it on?'

'Yes!' Alex said.

Laughing, Tamsyn laid Mo down on her mat next to Buoy and helped Alex step into the dress, lacing it up at the back. She was relieved to see that it fitted like a glove, pulling Alex's waist in and making the most of her generous curves. With her dark hair flowing around her bare shoulders, the colour of the gown matched her eyes, just as Tamsyn imagined.

'You look like a mermaid,' Alex said, 'or Aphrodite. You look beautiful.'

Leading Alex over to a huge mirror that hung at one end of the room, Tamsyn helped her up onto the footstool so she could check the length of the gown and make sure that everything was perfect. Tamsyn was pleased and impressed that the sewing circle had followed her instructions to the letter and there was nothing that needed to be altered. Alex stared at herself in the mirror.

'Oh Tamsyn,' she whispered. 'Thank you.'

'Well, thank *you*, actually,' Tamsyn said. 'Yesterday I had this crazy moment where I finished with my boyfriend and changed track on my career, and I wasn't sure why I did, or if I did it for the right reasons. But now I think I know. I think I'm going to come back to Cornwall to start my own couture wedding-gowns label. Because that's what I want to do, and I want to do it here, where there are craftswomen and a craftsman who can make garments more beautiful than any I've seen for a long time, and I have the perfect business manager in waiting, even though Sue doesn't know it yet. I'm going to turn Poldore into a cottage industry.'

'Really?' Alex might not have been listening quite as attentively as Tamsyn could have hoped for, but that was because she was twisting and turning in her gown, admiring herself from every angle. 'I'd hug you, but I'm slightly afraid I'll trip up over this skirt. And are you going to make sure that Jed doesn't go through with this stupid idea of his to get out of Dodge. Are you going to tell him he has to stay here, and go out on dates with you because you went and fell for him and his general loveliness?'

'Really?' Tamsyn was stricken. 'Am I that obvious?'

'I think whatever it is that is happening between you and Jed is obvious to everyone. Even Buoy was talking about it the other day.'

Tamsyn laughed. 'I know you're joking, but I wouldn't be surprised. That dog seems to know everything.'

'Oh darling,' Gloria gasped, as she walked in through the door with Laura, Keira and Cordelia, all of them in a selection of nighties and dressing gowns. 'Oh my beautiful girl, you are stunning. The finest bride I've ever seen. I think there's even a good chance you might move your father to tears when he arrives.'

Alex's smile was radiant, and as her mother embraced her, Tamsyn's mother smiled proudly at her daughter-in-law-to-be and at Tamsyn. 'Oh, Tam, you are clever,' she exclaimed. 'And you know what they say: marry in blue, your lover is true!' she added.

'I should hope so,' said Gloria, as Tamsyn leant her head on Laura's shoulder. There they all were, Ruan's women, brought together in this moment, and suddenly Tamsyn felt the force of how much she had missed her close bond with her brother more strongly than ever. As soon as there was a moment during this wonderful day, she had to find him and make things right between them.

'Put some clothes on and pop Mo in a sling,' Keira whispered to Tamsyn as Gloria helped Alex take the dress off. 'We're going out on a ramble to pick some wild flowers for Alex's bouquet and the headdress. I saw some lovely Sheep's Bit and Spring Squill, stunning Sea Carrot and, best of all, some Kidney Vetch.'

'We're talking about a bridal bouquet here, aren't we?' Tamsyn asked her. 'Not some sort of stew?'

'I've been doing my research,' Keira told her happily. 'It's been wonderful, and I even got the boys in on the fun. We'd find a plant or flower and then search for it in our book. My absolute most favourite is Sea

Campion. It's so pretty and delicate, it will look wonderful against Alex's hair.'

'I want to come,' Tamsyn said. 'But Mo's due a feed.'

'You girls go. I'll feed her,' Laura offered. 'Such a darling little poppet, and I've hardly had a chance to know her.'

'You know you have your own flesh-and-blood grandchildren, right?' Keira said. 'Two of them.'

'Yes, and I love them very much,' Laura said, cooing at the baby, 'but little Mo here doesn't talk back or make constant jokes about poo.'

'This may be the last feed I give her,' Tamsyn said, sitting down rather suddenly. 'Oh, do you know, I think I'm going to cry.'

Her shoulders shaking, she held Mo close to her, kissing away her own tears from the baby, pouring as much love as she possibly could into one moment, so that perhaps even years from now, just a small trace of the days she had spent with Mo might remain hidden away somewhere in Mo's memory.

'I'll fetch her bottle,' Keira said. 'We can wait for you, and then you can bring Mo out with you in the sling. She'll love the Rock Sea Spurrey.'

'Can I just say, in a hackneyed attempt to cheer you up,' Cordelia said, looking at her bridesmaid dress, 'you've not done half bad with these dresses either. They aren't too hideous, they will suit each of us and I like the way that they all go together but that none of them is the same. You are fairly talented, as it turns out.'

'Affirmation from my family at last,'Tamsyn laughed, wiping the tears from her eyes. She'd made the brides-maids' dresses out of a variety of ballgowns in the attic, all in complementary hues of deep blue. Each dress was slightly different to flatter the different figures of Lucy, herself and her sisters, but they were clearly a set. 'Well, it's a good job you think I am not too bad at this stuff.'

'And why's that?' Laura asked her.

'Because I'm coming back to Poldore for good,' Tamsyn said, before her mother engulfed her in a hug.

It was beautiful on the hill above the meadow, the day was warm, the sky a bright, clear blue that exactly matched the colour of Alex's dress.

'So tell me what was it about the handsome, sexy vicar, with the enormous free house, that made you decide you wanted to hand your notice in, dump that French bloke and come back to Poldore?'

'This isn't about Jed,' Tamsyn said, and that was mostly true. Her heart was talking to her, telling her what it needed to be happy, and although Jed could be a vital part of that, he wasn't essential. The essential part was the heart-pounding, nerve-shredding joy she had experienced in every stage of making Alex's dress, of doing what she simply loved. 'I think I needed to get out of Paris and away from Bernard to get some perspective on what my life was really like there. I thought I was going places both in my job and with Bernard. But I was never going to be the sort of designer who fits into that world. I wanted to be, but it's just not where my heart is. And you have to be where your heart is, don't you?'

'But you hated it here when we were growing up,' Keira said, as she collected some long-stemmed purple flowers which she assured them were called Thrift to the growing bunch of bright, optimistic daisies. 'Ever since you got hormones, you wanted to leave. I don't know why. I didn't want to leave, not ever.'

'You did, though,' Tamsyn reminded her. 'You got married and left.'

'Yes,' Keira sighed, tucking a little yellow buttercup behind her ear, shading her eyes as she watched her boys racing into the distance, their sights set on a hill they planned to roll down. 'I fell in love and followed my heart, and now here I am, attending my brother's wedding alone, while my husband works on the other side of the world.'

'I can understand why you wanted to leave,' Cordelia said. 'You had to go out there and see the world, and get experience and stuff. I need to do that too, I know I do. Once Brian and I have finished my album, that's it. I'm packing up and going to London, or LA maybe. It's not wrong to want to follow your dreams, and see the world, and have a million lovers if you feel like it.'

'I don't know about a million,' Keira said thoughtfully, pausing to look out to sea, where the clear blue horizon was punctuated only by the sails of a little white boat. 'Sounds awfully tiring. One; I could do with one lover.'

'Keira!' Tamsyn exclaimed. 'And you a married woman.'

'It wouldn't be so bad if I actually spent time with my husband,' Keira said. 'I don't suppose I want a lover, just quality time alone with the man I married.'

'Well, I don't really want any lovers,' Cordelia said. 'Not until I've made my mark on the music industry, then I shall have many and they shall all be incredibly cool, talented people, and I shall discard them, like they are so much . . . stuff.'

'Do you think that it's the right decision to come back here and launch a business?' Keira asked Tamsyn. 'Because, you know, Cornwall is pretty far to come for a fitting.'

'Don't you worry,' Tamsyn said, tapping the side of her nose. 'I've got plans. I've got plans that are going to make them come from far and wide.'

'And if a certain sexy vicar *does* seem like he might be on the menu . . .?' Cordelia asked with a cheeky wink.

Tamsyn wavered; there was so much uncertainty about what was or was not happening between her and

Jed, it was probably much simpler not to even think about it. After all, they had time now; if he still wanted it, if he listened to all the people that cared about him and stayed in Poldore. They had all the time in the world to get to know each other and work out if a man of God and a woman of . . . shoes could really find enough common ground to have a relationship.

'Oh no, is that rain?' said Tamsyn, and even as she held out her hand to check, one of the little purple clouds that had billowed on the horizon was now drifting over them, showering them with cool, gentle rain, even though the sunshine was still strong and warm.

'It's going to rain on my wedding day, isn't it?' Alex exclaimed gloomily.

'No, look!' Keira pointed at St Piran's, nestling amongst the houses, and arcing over the spire was a perfect rainbow that seemed to begin at the tip of the spire and finish somewhere over Castle House.

'It's beautiful,' Tamsyn said.

'It's a sign, I think,' Cordelia said to Alex. 'And I totally don't believe in all that bull.'

And as Tamsyn thought about last night, and the song they had sung to Mo while they had been waiting for news of her mother, she knew suddenly what she had to do, and it was something that couldn't wait.

'Here,' she put her armfuls of flowers into Cordelia's arms. 'I've got to go.'

'Go where? We've got to get dressed and get ready for a wedding!' Keira shouted after her.

'Yes, but not yet. We've got a couple of hours, right?' Tamsyn turned round, taking a few backward steps.

'Two hours, maximum!' Alex insisted.

Tamsyn waved in reply, and broke into as fast a walk as she could manage with Mo in the sling, as she headed back down to Castle House, knowing that there wasn't a moment to lose. This was a union that had to happen sooner rather than later, or it might never happen at all.

Chapter Twenty-five

It hadn't taken Tamsyn too long to persuade Sue to lend her the keys to her battered old Volvo and find a car seat that would fit Mo. After Rory had fitted it for her, she strapped the little girl in and drove to the hospital, much slower than she would have normally have driven anywhere, particularly in the free-for-all that was Paris. But she was suddenly gripped by the weight of responsibility of having another human life to take care of.

The ward Catriona was on was easy enough to find, but before Tamsyn got to her, she saw Tess.

'You've brought her,' Tess said, looking at Mo, who was securely strapped to her chest.

'Yes,' Tamsyn said. 'I don't think there's any more time to waste, do you? I think that if Catriona's up to it, we should get mum and baby together. They've already been apart too long. The sooner they are together, the sooner they can bond.'

'There's a lot to determine first,' Tess said. 'We haven't had a proper chance to assess Catriona's physical and mental health, to see her living conditions, to make sure that she is capable of taking care of a baby. She left her out in the middle of that storm, Tamsyn. It's not as simple as "Never mind, here's your baby, off you go".'

'I understand that,' Tamsyn said. 'But it's not like Catriona is a drug addict or a drunk. She's a woman of faith, who's recently lost her mother. And something happened to her that she hasn't been able to face. She was desperate and low, frightened and confused. That doesn't mean she doesn't deserve a chance to be a mum, does it?'

'No,' Tess said, 'of course not. But you can't go in there and tell her you've brought her baby back and that's that. There are steps, there are procedures. I promise you, I want them reunited as much as you do, but this time you have to understand that it will be me who is overseeing this process.'

'But I can take Mo in to see her?'

'Well, what kind of person would I be if I said no?'

Jed was sitting next to Catriona, his hand over hers, their eyes both closed in prayer. A thick growth of stubble now coated his chin, giving him a rougher quality, which, with his dark-golden hair falling over his eyes, did rather suit him. From where she was standing, Tamsyn couldn't hear the words he was gently murmuring, but she felt like she should close her eyes too, and so she did, finding a moment or two to think back on the last few days. It seemed like years ago that she was accusing him of being Mo's father, and now, Tamsyn couldn't imagine how she had ever thought that. Somehow she had come to know the man in the span of those few days, and he was a man she wanted to know better. It was Mo who decided it was time to make her presence felt, announcing herself with a yowl.

'Tamsyn.' Jed's smile was so sweetly warm when he opened his eyes, that she wondered how inappropriate it would be to simply rush over and hug him right now. What would he say, she wondered, if she mentioned that the very thing she wanted to do most in the whole wide world was to lie down on a big bed with him, rest her head on his chest and go to sleep?

'I've brought Mo,' Tamsyn said, rather stating the obvious, 'for a visit. I thought you might like to see her, Catriona. To hold her for a while.'

Catriona pulled herself up a little in the bed, gripping at the sheets and drawing them towards her.

'I'm not sure,' she said uncertainly.

'Well, you don't have to,' Tamsyn said breezily, sitting down on the other visitor's chair, her eyes meeting Jed's for a moment. 'We can just talk, catch up for a bit. I'm glad to see you're looking better,' she told Catriona. 'You've been through a lot.'

'I've been stupid,' the older woman said, being careful not to look at the baby. 'Mother would be turning in her grave if we hadn't had her cremated. She said to me, "Catriona, I want to be cremated. I don't want to spend the rest of my life turning in my grave".'

'Well, Mo is doing fine,' Tamsyn said. 'She feeds really well, has settled into a routine quite quickly, which my mum keeps telling me is more than any of us ever did. She likes to look around, and she really likes dogs and people singing to her. Yesterday lots of us sang to her, at least half the town. She liked that a lot. She loves cuddles, and I think she smiles, although my mum and my elder sister say she's too young to actually smile. She certainly smiles with her eyes.' Tamsyn looked down at Mo, who, freed from the sling, was propped up in the crook of her arm, her dark eyes focused on Catriona as if she were thinking, 'I know you from somewhere . . .'

Catriona shook her head, turning her face away.

'Cat,' Jed's hand remained in Catriona's. 'Can you tell us what happened? When it happened, why you didn't come to me, talk to me? You know I would have helped you.'

'Mother died,' Catriona said. 'You were there when she died, Jed. You know what a very long time it took, how ill she was. I know that everybody felt sorry for me, like she was a burden. "Poor old Catriona Merryweather, she's nearly fifty and she's never had a life." I know that's what they all thought, that I was sad and pathetic still living with Mother, and she could be difficult. We all know that she could be difficult.'

'She was a character.' Jed smiled. 'But she was also one of the kindest people I have had the pleasure of knowing.'

'It was hard for her, losing Dad so young, but she never talked about him. It was always just us. She used to try and get me to go out into the world, to meet more people. She never forced me to stay at home with her, to be her carer. I told her I had enough to be happy. I was happy to live with her, to work with you, Jed. I had my faith, my work, my friends. I had everything I needed.'

'It must have been very hard losing her,' Tamsyn said.

'I was lost.' Catriona turned to face Tamsyn, still keeping her eyes away from the baby. 'And so lonely. I know it was her time to go. She was ill; she'd had a good life. And yet I felt angry, bitter. I couldn't understand why she'd been taken from me.' Catriona frowned. 'I loved her so much. I made her too much a part of my life. I didn't know how to be on my own.'

'So you found some solace,' Jed said. 'There's no sin in that.'

Catriona looked at him. 'You know very well that's not what either of us believes, Jed Hayward. Shortly after Mother's funeral, I went to a special retreat. A place for people of faith to gather, to think, to meditate. I enjoyed it. There was plenty of time to be alone, but time together with people too. Time to pray and talk and eat and discuss. That's where I met him.' Catriona lowered her eyes. 'We had a lot in common. Same sort of age, both alone, both lost. I . . . I am not completely ignorant about intimacy. I've had a couple of boyfriends in my time. And Ben and I were both far away from home, and I felt that I had to grab hold of my life, and somehow it didn't feel wrong. We said goodbye. We didn't make any promises . . .' She looked at Jed, her cheeks colouring. 'I didn't want to. I felt that I should feel worse about it than I did, but I didn't. I didn't feel sad, or guilty, I felt happy. It had been a good experience. But I felt guilty about not feeling guilty.'

Jed smiled as Catriona continued: 'I didn't even consider I might be pregnant, not at my age. I thought I was more likely to be going through the change than anything.' She whispered to Tamsyn, 'I've never been regular. When I started to feel sick, and my stomach began to swell, I was certain it was the same thing that took Mum, the cancer. I suppose it was stupid to stick my head in the sand about it. If only I'd gone to a doctor when I first started having symptoms. And I planned to, I did. It was just that there was always so much to do. And then on the day that she came, I can barely remember it. It's like I blocked it out – I remember the pain, and the sudden knowing, understanding what was happening to me. I remember that.' She shook her head. 'And then she was there, crying and large as life. And I think I went into some sort of shock. I was so calm. I cut the cord. I found some old clothes, which had been collected for the jumble sale. I dressed her, wrapped her up. There was this doll-sized Moses basket. She was so little, she fit in it. I wrote her a note. I don't even know what it said. It was early evening. I went out and it was raining a little, but I don't think I noticed. The pain, you see, and the shock. I put her in the porch, where she was safe and dry. It was ten minutes until evensong. I knew Jed would be there soon. I knew he would take care of her. I never thought of keeping her, of phoning for help, or going to hospital. It never even occurred to me. I don't remember going home. I managed it somehow. I think I must have passed out. I woke up and there was a storm outside, a terrible storm. And I wondered how I could find out if Jed had discovered her, and then I reached for my diary, because that's where I keep his number written down, and that's when I remembered it was my turn to lead choir practice. I was the one who was supposed to be opening the door. I didn't know what to do. I tried to get to the church again; I was so frightened, and then I realised exactly what I'd done. I'd put a brand-new baby out in a storm, the worst storm in living memory. My baby, and all I wanted was to get to her . . . The next thing I knew I woke up at Castle House. Sue told me straight away that a baby had been found, and I thought, well, it must be the way it should be. She was found, so she would be cared for. It had been decided. I thought I would be OK after a few days' rest. I thought I would get up and get back to normal, but I can't . . . I can't stop thinking about her.'

'It hasn't been decided,' Tamsyn said, trying to be careful not to promise too much, like the social worker had said. 'There's still time for you and Mo to be together. Especially if you want to love her, and want her in your life, which I think you do.'

Catriona shook her head. 'No, I can't. How can I? I've let everyone down. I let my mother down, Jed. I've let God down. And the baby, I've let the baby down. I left her. I left, and there is no way back from that. I can't be a mother, not at my age. Not when I am all alone. I can't.'

'You can,' Jed said. 'Sometimes what you think of as the wrong thing is the one thing you can't stop happening. You were blessed with a child, a child who will be as loved by God as she is by you. And you are not alone. You have me, and the whole town behind you. And you have your faith, the same faith that you have shown me is strong enough to heal any wound, in time. And I know, I just know, what a brilliant mother you will be, if you give yourself a chance.'

'How can you possibly know that?' Catriona asked him sharply.

'Well, I know how good you've been at mothering me since I arrived in Poldore,' Jed smiled at her. 'And you can start today by meeting your daughter. Just say hello to her, that's all.'

Catriona looked towards Tamsyn, her gaze falling on the baby for the first time. 'I don't even know how to hold her,' she said at last.

'I didn't either,' Tamsyn said, standing carefully and lowering Mo into Catriona's arms. 'But funnily enough, you first seem to realise the right way, without anyone having to tell you.'

Mo settled into the crook of her mother's arm, and the woman and the baby looked at each other. After a moment or two of contemplation, Mo's face crumpled and she began to cry, and Tamsyn felt the most curious tug in the centre of her chest. She had to stop herself from reaching out and taking Mo back. After a moment's thought, Catriona lifted the baby onto her shoulder, easing her into her favourite position.

'She loves to be sung to,' Tamsyn encouraged her. 'It's one of her best things, even when it's me, or Buoy, although Buoy is a slightly better singer than I am.'

'I don't know many children's songs,' Catriona said, but after a moment she began to hum something that sounded familiar, perhaps a hymn or a folk song, Tamsyn thought, and Mo seemed perfectly content, perched on her mother's shoulder.

'I've had a word with the nurses and with Tess,' Tamsyn said. 'They said if you'd like to keep Mo with you while I'm at my brother's wedding today, then that would be OK. Tess will come and have a chat with you about what happens next, and the nurses can bring in a crib and help you out, any time you need a rest or aren't sure what to do.'

'I'm not sure,' Catriona said. 'I'm not sure about anything.'

'I don't agree.' Tamsyn leant forward, brushing the backs of her fingers against Mo's cheek. 'You're sure that you love her, aren't you?'

Catriona nodded. 'She looks like Mum,' she said.

'Oh, there you go then,' Tamsyn said. 'Perhaps you can name her after your mum. What was her name?'

'Gladys,' Catriona said. Tamsyn's eyes widened, the laughter bubbling up before she could stop it, relieved to see that Catriona was smiling too.

'Yes,' she agreed. 'Perhaps not. Anyway, she's already been named, and it suits her,' she said, kissing the little girl on the ear. 'I think we'll stick to that. Mo, short for Morwenna. I always liked that name. Morwenna Gladys.'

'It's a nice name,' Tess said, as she walked into the room. Tamsyn wondered how much she had heard. 'I wonder if you have time for a little chat with me now?'

'Well, I'm not going anywhere,' Catriona said.

'Unlike me,' Tamsyn said. 'I really have to go and get ready for a wedding.'

'And I need to go and get ready to marry two people,' Jed said.

'So, if you like I could . . . I have Sue's car. I think there's an eighty per cent chance that it will make it back in time for the wedding. I'll take you.'

'Thank you,' Jed said, politely. About as politely as any man has ever said anything who's ever kissed a girl under a kitchen table and then changed his mind, and Tamsyn understood that Jed wasn't going to be part of her crazy new life, but she couldn't let that slow her down. Right now, there were several far more important things that were happening to her, and the first of those was that she had to say goodbye to Mo.

'Well, little Mo.' She rested the palm of her hand gently on top of the baby's head. 'We've had some adventures, haven't we? And you won't remember them when you grow up, but I will. For someone so small and so frequently smelly, you've changed me, you odd little person. I will never forget you, Mo.'

Catriona caught her hand before she could leave. 'You won't get a chance to,' she said. 'Tamsyn, you don't know me very well yet if you think I would let the person who saved my daughter's life, and so my life, get away without being pestered by the pair of us for ever and ever. And besides, I expect it might be a while before they let me take care of Mo by myself. We still need you. We both do, if you are willing to help.'

And Tamsyn Thorne, who had arrived in Poldore with hair smoothed into a chignon, in her designer clothes, with her perfect look and her dream life, stood there in a pair of leggings with an elasticated waist and a vest that had tiny coffins printed on it, her toes crammed into her sister's Converse trainers, her hair proving that it was possible to defy gravity without going into space, and, well, she felt the most important and the most special that she ever had in her whole life.

'You can count on me,' she said to both mother and child. 'See you later, guys.'

An almost physical pull brought her to a near stop before she crossed the threshold of the hospital room.

'Hello you,' she heard Catriona say, her voice as soft as a summer breeze. 'It's me, your mummy.'

Chapter Twenty-six

It was a short drive from the hospital back to Castle House as the crow flies, except that the crow didn't have to stop and wait for the car ferry to trundle back across the river and pick them up, and the crow certainly didn't have to deal with a series of awkward silences, relieved only by comments about a passing cow, or how green the trees looked for, um, June. But somehow the long silences seemed louder than anything, a jumble of unspoken words surging between them.

'That must have been hard for you,' Jed said eventually as they waited for the ferry to travel inch by inch across the river. 'To leave Mo there. I know you'd only had her for a short time, but you'd bonded.'

Tamsyn nodded. 'It was harder than I expected, although I don't have any right to feel that way, not really. I know Catriona's her mother, and seeing her looking at Mo that way, I knew it was the right thing to do. And she's going to be around in my life for a while yet, her and Kirsten. I'm going to keep an eye on her, help her out when I can.'

'That's good of you,' Jed said.

'Is it good, or just . . . the right thing to do?' Tamsyn asked him.

'It's both.' Jed nodded. 'And now, the wedding day. I hear the church is looking amazing; that Keira did an incredible job.'

'I don't doubt it,' Tamsyn said, slowly pulling Sue's rickety old car onto the ferry, reasonably sure that the brakes would kick in again before it drove off the other side. 'My sister is much more talented and creative than she gives herself credit for. I'm looking forward to seeing the finished product.' She smoothed the fabric of her leggings down her thighs as if it were the finest tailored skirt.

'And then, pastures new,' Jed said. 'For both of us, though I suppose technically your pastures are more like recycled, if that's a thing.'

Tamsyn pulled the car over into a lay-by and turned to look at him. The action must have alarmed him a little because he sat back in his seat, his hand on the door handle, perhaps in case he felt like he might need to make a quick exit.

'You know that kiss, under the table? The one where you took my top off.'

Jed looked away from her, keeping his eyes fixed on the road ahead. 'Tamsyn, we've got to get to a wedding. Do you think now is the time?'

'I just need to know, Jed. What did it mean? What did it mean to you, did you feel anything?'

'Of course I did.' Jed still would not look at her. 'You are a beautiful woman. I'm a man of flesh and blood. Of course I felt things, a lot of things. But they are feelings that disrespected you, and me. And what I believe.'

'Why did they disrespect me?' Tamsyn asked him. 'I quite liked them.'

'Because you deserve more than a man's lust, Tamsyn, a confused and damaged man's lust. Surely you realise that you are worth more than that? A million times more than that. You deserve to be cherished, adored, worshipped, admired and loved.'

'I see,' Tamsyn said, because it couldn't really be any more obvious. It was the hot vicar equivalent of telling her that she was a great girl, just not the girl for him. After all, Jed could have his pick of the good Christian women of Poldore; why would he settle for a heathen like her? Though she wanted to argue with him, instead she settled for agreeing. 'Of course I know I'm worth a lot more than that, that's why I ended things with Bernard. Well, I'm glad we talked about it. Cleared the air. Now, haven't we got a wedding to get to?'

It was clear that something was very wrong the second she caught sight of Cordelia and her mother's faces as they stood outside Castle House. Laura was on the phone, her face etched with concern, and Cordelia, whom Tamsyn had always thought would take everything up to and including a zombie apocalypse in her stride, rubbed her hands repeatedly across her face, her loosely braided hair threaded with wild flowers, even though she was still wearing a pair of shorts and a t-shirt.

'What's going on?' Tamsyn asked, as soon as she got out of the car.

'Oh Tamsyn,' Laura shook her head. 'It's Ruan. He's not at the lighthouse, he's not at the hotel, he's not answering his phone. No one knows where he is.'

'To put it bluntly,' Cordelia added, her tone darkly serious, 'our brother has done a runner.'

Chapter Twenty-seven

'I know where he is,' Tamsyn said, looking up at the clock that stood over the portcullis of Castle House. 'I'll get him.'

'Well, where?' Laura asked her. 'There's less than an hour to the wedding. Alex is up there now, having her hair and make-up done, and she looks so lovely, all happy and dewy and excited. Her dad, Marcus and the others have arrived. Champagne corks are popping – we can't have word getting round that Ruan has gone AWOL. Even Buoy's pacing back and forth, growling. If we're not careful she'll find out what's going on.'

'She'll have to find out sooner or later,' Cordelia shrugged. 'Maybe better now than at the altar, you know? Tam, maybe you should go up there now and tell her, like, straight out. Treat it like you are whipping off a Band-Aid.'

'No.' Tamsyn shook her head. 'This is not happening. I haven't made all of these dresses for no one to wear them. Ruan doesn't want this. He wants to marry Alex, he loves her. He's just being stupid. And I'm not having it. Because, quite frankly, I've had enough of stupid men to last me a lifetime.' At this, she couldn't help but cast a pointed look at Jed. 'I'll go and find Ruan. I'll bring him to the church. Anyone tells Alex, and they'll have me to deal with, got it?'

'Oooh, big sis is on the rampage, *yes!*' Cordelia punched the air.

'But you need to put a dress on too,' Laura exclaimed. 'Alex will wonder where you are.'

'Take my dress to the church and leave it in the vestry. I'll put it on when I get back.' Tamsyn looked down at the Converse trainers she was wearing. 'And some shoes, lip gloss, eyeliner, tweezers and a hair brush. Actually, strike the hairbrush; it just looks worse if I brush it. It will be fine. I'm on the case.'

And Tamsyn had to admit that the mud she splattered all over Jed, as she spun the Volvo's wheels pulling away at speed, did give her a very small amount of pleasure.

It didn't take long to find him. There was an outcrop of rock that burst up from the ground not far into the woods behind Poldore. It was where they had always gone as teenagers – to talk, build campfires, listen to music and make out. It was where Ruan and Merryn had spent a lot of time alone together, and where, etched into the rock somewhere under the mould and the caked mud, there was a heart with their initials in it. The ground was still soft, and wet underfoot, her feet squelching in the canvas Converse, her toes already filled with ooze.

Ruan was standing with his back to her, his hand resting on the rock, his head bowed.

'Your trouble was, you always tended towards the melodramatic,' Tamsyn said, crossing her arms. 'You're getting married in about half an hour. What the hell are you doing?'

At least Ruan was dressed for the church in a brand-new suit that he had chosen himself, a white shirt, open at the neck, and a waistcoat of blue silk that Tamsyn had run up for him from offcuts of his bride's dress. He'd also had the foresight to pull on a pair of Wellingtons, which the legs of his trousers were neatly tucked into, and that gave Tamsyn hope. If he was trying to keep his wedding suit mud-free, then surely he planned to turn up, at least.

'Am I doing the right thing, Tamsyn?' he asked her. 'I need to know.'

'Are you crazy?' Tamsyn said. 'Of course you are. You love Alex, she loves you. I have never known two people more right for each other. It's a no-brainer; of course you are doing the right thing. Now come on, I've spent the last few days looking like crap, twenty-four hours a day, I feel like my heart's been trampled by a troupe of country dancers, so all I ask is that you get me to the church in time to put mascara on.'

'I loved Merryn,' Ruan said, looking around him as

if he might see her there, laughing amongst the trees. 'I loved her and I hurt her. I tried to change her, to make her into someone she wasn't. If I hadn't loved her, or tried to keep on loving her, if I'd been brave enough to let her go, I might not have driven her away. What if I do the same thing to Alex?'

Tamsyn closed her eyes. This was her fault. It was all her fault that he was standing here, pacing up and down, instead of greeting his guests as he waited for the bride. She should have told him sooner; she should have told him years ago. No matter how much he might hate her for it, she had to tell him now.

'It's not your fault,' Tamsyn said. 'It's not your fault that Merryn died that day. It's mine.'

Ruan shook his head. 'What do you mean?'

'I never thought that Merry should stay in Poldore and marry you. I never believed she would be happy, or you, for that matter. You were always so different, and yet neither of you saw it. But I did; I knew you both. Better than you knew each other. I didn't say anything to her, not until she called me one day. I was working for that department store, remember? She told me she wasn't sure if she could stay in Poldore with you, she wasn't sure if she loved you enough. She said everybody expected you to get married, wanted it. Everybody but her.'

'How does that make it your fault?' Ruan asked her.

'Because I talked her into leaving you,' Tamsyn

said simply. 'I gave her a place to stay, found her a job, and told her the best possible thing she could do for you and for her would be to leave. I spoke to her the morning before you had your row. And even then she was in two minds about what we had planned; maybe she should wait a few weeks, maybe her feelings could change, if she only tried harder. She almost called the whole thing off. I talked her into going through with it. I talked her into that argument with you, and I might as well have talked her into that boat.' Tamsyn took a step closer to her brother. 'Ruan, she was always going to leave you, sooner or later, but it didn't have to be that day. It was only that day because of me.'

'You told me, you told everyone that it was *my* fault, that I as good as killed her,' Ruan said. 'It was bad enough that I felt that way myself, but when you said it, then it was real. Why would you say that?'

'Because I was angry, hurt, guilty, stupid, messed up.' Tamsyn shook her head. 'I tried to blame you because I blamed myself so much. I meant to put it right, but the days went by, the weeks, the years. I'm sorry, Ruan. I'm so sorry. I was going to tell you after the wedding; I sort of thought that running up five dresses in a day and a half for your bride might soften you up a bit . . . Be angry at me, hate me, don't speak to me for five more years, I can take that. I can take rejection, I've had a lot of practice. But please, I am begging you:

don't mess up your future with this wonderful woman. I know that you two are meant to be together, and even if you hate me, you know I am right.'

The slightest of breezes snaked through the trees above their heads, and he watched her for the longest time, and Tamsyn waited, feeling each second fall away with agonising speed.

'You'd better drive,' he said, fishing a carrier bag from behind a rock. 'I've got to change my shoes.'

'And we're OK?' Tamsyn asked him, as they trotted back to the car.

'Get me to the church on time, Tam, so that Alex never knows that I was this stupid. Do that and we're even, because, well, I've missed you. And now you've admitted you were in the wrong, I don't see any reason to miss you again.'

'Spoken like a true Thorne,' Tamsyn said, slotting the key into the ignition. 'Now, pray that this damn thing starts.'

Tamsyn was shimmying into her bridesmaid's dress and struggling with the zip at the back, when she heard a polite cough behind her. It was Jed in his full vicar's uniform – cassock and everything.

'You really are a vicar, aren't you?' Tamsyn said. 'It's not an optical illusion, is it?'

'I really am. Do you need a hand? Everyone is out there; Alex is seconds away.'

'Would you mind?' She gestured at the strip of bare flesh that showed between the panels of the dress. Turning back to look at the old stone wall, Tamsyn closed her eyes as she felt Jed standing behind her, felt the pull of the zip fastening shut.

'That's you sorted,' Jed said. He sounded a little hoarse. 'You'd better run round the side and meet the bride.'

'Good luck,' Tamsyn said, turning to catch his eye before he left.

'And you,' he nodded. 'And you.'

And then it was time for a wedding.

'Where the hell have you been?' Lucy demanded, looking lovely in the deep sea-blue, knee-length dress Tamsyn had designed for her, its hem sparkling with beads that were just a shade lighter than the dress.

'Snogging the vicar, I reckon,' Cordelia said.

'Well that's where you would be very, very wrong. The vicar is not interested in me, not in the slightest,' Tamsyn said, 'and that is fine by me, as it happens.'

'You haven't straightened your hair!' Keira said, aghast. 'It's all wild and curly and lovely, and crazy. And a bit tangled at the back, a bit like you've been snogging a vicar.'

'I have not been snogging,' Tamsyn repeated. 'I have been up for two days in a row, saving the day on an hourly basis, and something had to give.'

'Well, in any case,' Alex said, her smile radiant, as she hooked her arm through that of her proud-looking and straight-backed father, who seemed to be doing his best not to shed a tear. 'It's time to do this thing. Let's go and get married.'

'How are you feeling?' Tamsyn whispered as they waited in the porch for the music to start.

'Nervous as hell,' Alex breathed.

'Well, there is one more person, waiting in the church for you, who might calm your nerves a bit,' Tamsyn said. 'I sorted you a page boy.'

'Oh.' Alex carefully maintained a smile, although her voice faltered. 'One of the twins?'

'Or should I say, a page *B–U–O–Y*?' Tamsyn grinned, as Alex's friend Marcus pulled open the door to reveal that Buoy was sitting, waiting patiently for his human, wearing a blue satin bow around his neck, with remarkable good grace for a dog who considered soap to be a serious violation of his dog rights.

'Oh *Buoy*!' Alex bent to hug him. 'You look amazing.'

He rolled his one eye at her, thumping his tail on the tiles, and somehow Tamsyn knew that Alex was the only human that Buoy would go through such a horror for, and that right after the ceremony he was certainly going to chew the stupid bow to a pulp.

The organ had been quite badly water-damaged, but they needn't have worried as Brian Rogers led a full rock band in the choir stalls, striking up the bridal march as Alex and her father began to walk down the aisle. Tamsyn didn't need to see the bride's face to know how delighted she would be with the interior of the church, because she herself was completely enchanted, gasping in wonder as she looked around. Keira had indeed brought the Cornish countryside into the church, making bowers of broken branches, still heavily laden with blossom, and garlanded it with cowslips, buttercups and daisies. At the end of each pew there were posies of pansies and daffodils. Keira hadn't even tried for a colour scheme; instead she'd simply filled the church with all the colours of a meadow in full bloom, and the ancient place of worship, with its broken door and shattered window, was filled with the scent and warmth of a summer day, with even the occasional butterfly flitting from pew to pew.

Tamsyn watched as her brother's eyes met Alex's, and saw the slow, certain smile spread over his face, which she just knew was returned by his bride. As Alex reached him, he took her hand and pressed it to his lips, as he looked into her eyes.

Tamsyn took her place to the side of the aisle next to her sisters and Lucy, and looked at the smiling faces of the congregation, who had all turned out to support their friends despite everything they had been dealing with themselves, and the strangest thing happened: she fell in love in that very moment. Not with a person, or even the wedding, but with the place that had proved to her something she was never really certain she believed until now.

People were good. People were good, and kind, and brave. People wanted the best not just for themselves but for each other, and that was what defined them, what made them human. And somehow, although out in the wider world, where often those basic truths had been forgotten or pushed aside, here they still mattered. And that was enough for Tamsyn to realise that regardless of what had happened between her and Jed, being here, starting her life here again, was exactly the right thing for her to do. Here she could be the person that she wanted to be, she could be herself.

It was impossible not to let one or two tears fall, as Jed conducted the service with such sweetness and sincerity that did nothing at all to help Tamsyn curb the feelings she had for him. And when she saw the tears of joy in Ruan's eyes as he made his vows, she actually had to grab a tissue from Gloria sitting in the front row and blow her nose, loudly enough for her mother to give her that 'only you, Tamsyn Thorne' look.

When Cordelia sang, unaccompanied, her own version of 'Amazed', the whole church was charged with an upswell of emotion that was almost palpable, and Tamsyn thought it quite likely that soon the whole of Poldore would be weeping uncontrollably. That was until Buoy lifted his head and decided to join in with a heartfelt howl, turning any threat of tears into gales of fond laughter. With delightful good grace, Cordelia stepped down from where she had been singing and crouched next to Buoy, winding her arms around his neck, as nose to nose they howled the last chorus together in a curious sort of harmony that seemed to work, despite itself.

Finally, when Jed declared that Ruan and Alex were man and wife, everyone stood up, cheered and applauded, and Tamsyn laughed and hugged her sisters, which was when Brian and his supergroup struck up once again, playing the bride and groom back down the aisle with a cover of 'Don't Stop Me Now', because Queen were Ruan's favourite band.

The congregation poured out into the small church-yard, and then onto the street, and there were colours and confetti everywhere, the air fully charged with joy as photos were snapped under a sky that was as warm and benevolent as it had ever been. Tamsyn stood on the church step, a sanguine, bow-less Buoy at her side, content to watch the happiness unfurl around her. Jed had been right: everyone wanted to be happy, to push their cares and worries to one side and have a reason to celebrate, and this was the best reason that she could think of. Jed was annoyingly right about a lot of things, which meant she supposed that she had to believe him when he said that he wasn't right for her, even if looking at him made her feel so differently.

'Tamsyn, come on!' Cordelia bellowed at her from

a little further up the hill. 'It's reception time! No baby to take care of, no dresses to make, *finally* we can get properly ratted!'

'I'm coming!' Tamsyn called back, hesitating for a second or two longer before making her way down the path. The old cedar that had failed to withstand the storm had been taken away by tree surgeons the day before, and until now Tamsyn hadn't had a chance to discover what had become of Merryn's gravestone. She was relieved to see that it was still there, standing proud, washed clean by someone, shining in its newly sunny spot.

'Well,' she said, to a stray raven that was sitting uncomfortably on the iron railings, looking as if it was wondering where its tree had gone. 'Remember when we said we would never come back to this place? Well, I'm back, Merryn. Imagine how much you would laugh at me now if you were here. I'll always miss you, my darling.'

The raven squawked and flew off into the sky to find another tree to roost in, and Tamsyn took one last moment to look back out towards the sea, moved by the certainty that anything could be possible if she was prepared to work hard for it, and then made her way towards The Poldore Hall Hotel to celebrate her beloved brother's wedding and, as her youngest sister put it, get ratted.

Chapter Twenty-eight

The twins were demon dancers, and for some reason had decided that it was their Aunty Tamsyn they wanted most to dance with, perhaps because she had been preoccupied for the last few days with someone else's baby, and finally they had her to themselves, which seemed a less terrible prospect to Tamsyn, especially after she had had four glasses of champagne.

'We want you to twirl around and around and clap your hands,' Joe instructed her over the noise of the band.

'Don't be ridiculous, I shall do no such thing,' Tamsyn said, complying at once, following each extra outlandish dance move with the trademark mixture of defiance and obedience that they enjoyed, and discovering that she was actually quite good at the moonwalk.

'And now hop like a kangaroo,' Jamie told her.

'Over my dead body,' Tamsyn said as she did just that.

Before she knew it, Alex's very tall ginger friend, Marcus, had swept her into his arms and was whirling her around until both of them were giggling like loons, until she caught the eye of a very tanned woman, in a very small dress, who seemed to be sharpening her talons as she watched them.

'If that's your wife, I think you should go to her,' Tamsyn told Marcus breathlessly. 'I'm too young to die.'

Chuckling to herself, Tamsyn found her way out of the party and into the cool of the foyer. She smiled as an older lady, a guest at the hotel, came in, accompanied by a cab driver who was carrying her bag for her. She made her way to an open door that led out onto a veranda and breathed in the perfect view. How could she ever have believed that anywhere else in the world could be a better place to be than this place?

'You clocking off now?' she heard the receptionist ask the cabby.

'No, love, I got a pickup in half an hour, taking the vicar to the train station.'

Tamsyn turned on her heel and looked at him. He was the same cabby who had brought her here that first night.

'Hello,' she said. 'It's me, do you remember? Back for my brother's wedding?'

He blinked at her.

'I had straight hair, and a really great case,' she prompted him.

'Oh yes, nice to see you,' he said, a little uncertain as to why she was pestering him.

'That vicar, is that Reverend Hayward, by any chance?' Tamsyn asked him.

'That's the feller,' the cabby said.

'Only he told me to tell you he's cancelling the cab.'

'Well, he should phone the office. They'll radio it through,' he said.

'Yes, but he didn't. He told me to tell you,' Tamsyn nodded emphatically. '"You tell that taxi driver, I don't need that cab any more", he said.'

'But how did he know you'd see me to tell me?' the cabby persisted.

'I don't know. Who are you, Sherlock?' Tamsyn flung her arms wide.

'I'll be back here to pick him up in thirty minutes,' the cabby told her, eyeing her warily. 'Looks like he's got a good reason to leg it from where I'm standing.'

'What?' Tamsyn asked the receptionist, who just happened to be the very same one that had seen her spectacular goodbye to Bernard. 'I'm only trying to help the man! That cab is getting cancelled one way or another.'

The rectory already looked abandoned, and if it hadn't been for the light in the upstairs window Tamsyn would have thought that she had somehow missed Jed. She pulled on the rather old-fashioned-looking doorbell, which didn't seem to ring, and banged on the door a few times too for good measure, but there was no reply.

Perhaps he'd snuck a look out of the window. Maybe he knew she was here and was hiding in a wardrobe, hoping she would just go away. Tamsyn paced up and down the hill four or five times while she thought through was she was going to do.

'No, you can't do that,' she told herself. 'That is mental . . . Yes, but time is running out,' she answered herself. 'What if this is your only chance to have what Alex and Ruan have?' She paced some more. 'There's a really big difference between a romantic gesture and the sort of behaviour that results in a restraining order. You're a role model now; think of Kirsten. Think of Mo, how's she going to feel, getting to know her adopted aunty from the other side of prison bars.' She let out a heavy sigh. 'Oh, sod it, what have I got to lose, apart from all self-worth, dignity and possibly my freedom?'

And with her mind made up, Tamsyn used some skills she had learnt as a younger woman and broke in through Jed's back door.

The downstairs of the house was in darkness and completely quiet. Tamsyn slipped off her shoes and padded across the polished wooden floor to the base of the stairs.

'Hello?' she called out softly, reasoning that a person who introduced themselves couldn't possibly be legally accused of intruding. 'Hello?'

Well, it was hardly her fault if he didn't answer her then, was it?

Tension shot through her chest and shoulders as she crept up the stairs, desperately trying to rationalise exactly what it was that she was doing. What *was* she doing? What on earth did she hope to achieve by surprising Jed in this way?

She pushed open the door to his bedroom. The walls now were bare of even the few photos that had been tacked to them and the posters were gone. His desk was cleared and the bed stripped, and leaning against the wall was a large, military-style backpack. There was a change of clothes neatly folded on the bed. And in that moment, Tamsyn knew why she was behaving like such an out-and-out lunatic.

Jed could not leave Poldore, the place that had taken him to its heart and made him feel at home, because of her. She wouldn't let him.

Walking out into the hallway, she heard the shower running in the bathroom. Taking a breath, Tamsyn knocked on the door. She knocked twice, but there was no response, and then the sound of the water stilled.

'Hello? Is there someone there?'

'It's me,' Tamsyn called through the door, 'Tamsyn. I knocked but there was no answer, and the back door was open. Sort of.'

'Tamsyn? I'm in the shower.'

'I know, I'm sorry. But you're leaving in, like, fifteen

minutes and I . . . I have to see you. It's OK, I'll wait for you to come out of the shower.'

There was a silence, and then Jed said, 'I packed my towel.'

Tamsyn pressed her hands over her mouth and closed her eyes, opening them again quickly when she discovered the image of a glistening, golden, naked vicar waiting behind them.

'I'll get it for you,' she called. 'Is it in your backpack?'

'Yes,' he answered, his discomfort evident in his tone.

It only took Tamsyn a few seconds to retrieve the towel.

'Are you . . .?'

'I'm behind the shower curtain,' he said. 'I'm pretty sure it's not see-through.'

'I once oversaw a photo shoot of twenty male models who were all naked except for their hats,' Tamsyn told him.

'Are you deliberately trying to make me feel inadequate?' Jed asked her as she pushed open the door into the steam-filled room.

'No; all I'm saying is that I have seen it all before,' Tamsyn said, 'lots of times. That didn't come out quite how I wanted it to.'

Jed's hand appeared from the other side of the shower curtain.

'Give me the towel, please.'

'No,' Tamsyn said. 'Not yet. Not until you've heard what I've got to say.'

'Tamsyn,' Jed said. 'I think we've said everything, haven't we?'

'No, not everything,' Tamsyn said. 'I'm a Thorne, and we've never finished saying anything. We're famous for being able to go on and on for as long as it takes.'

'Tamsyn, you're such a wonderful . . .'

'Please don't give me that speech again,' Tamsyn took a few steps nearer to the shower. She could see the outline of his naked form on the other side of the curtain, hear his breathing.

'This isn't about the way I feel about you,' Tamsyn said. 'Even I don't understand the way I feel about you yet, or why it is I seem to have fallen so completely in love with a man that I barely know . . . I expect it's probably hormones, or food poisoning or something. I'm sure it will blow over, eventually. This is about you: Jed, don't go. You don't have to go, just because people know about your past now. You're the only person who seems to think that any of that matters.'

'This town deserves a better, stronger vicar than me.'

'No, it doesn't,' Tamsyn said. 'Well, it does, but only because it's got the best vicar it can possibly have. It's got a person who is willing to live at the heart of a community and care about everyone in it. I wish you had been in yesterday when everyone came round to tell you how much they care about you.'

'That sounds a bit like a lynching. Did they have torches and pitchforks?' Jed said drily. 'Please let me have that towel, I'm starting to get a bit cold.'

'No, not until you tell me, honestly. Do you really want to go?'

She heard a long sigh from the other side of the curtain and took another step towards it. Now only a few inches, and a plastic sheet with ducks printed on it, separated her from him. Could he feel her longing for him she wondered, seeping into the steam that found its way through the gaps in the curtain?

'No,' Jed said. 'I don't want to go, of course I don't. But life isn't about what you want. It's about what's right.'

'It's also about what's right for you – and this place is the best thing for you,' Tamsyn said. 'You've been happy here – and well. And Jed, if you're leaving because you're worried that I am going to harass you constantly with my schoolgirl crush, then . . .' Tamsyn grimaced on her side of the curtain. 'Well, I know the fact that I've just broken into your house and am currently holding you hostage, naked in your shower, doesn't look good, but I promise I won't do that again. In fact, if it means you'll stay, I will go. I can find somewhere else to make wedding dresses. Gretna Green, maybe. Alaska.'

Jed said something from behind the curtain that Tamsyn didn't catch.

'Pardon?' she said.

'I said, I don't want you to go. Please don't go.'

'But I know that what happened between us makes you uncomfortable, and I don't want to ruin things for you. I know you don't have those sorts of feeling for me, and it's OK, it's not the first time a man hasn't fancied me. I don't even blame you. I've looked like a knackered toilet brush for most of my visit here, and . . .'

'Tamsyn, shut up.' Jed pulled aside the shower curtain, just enough to reveal his face, and muscular shoulders beaded with water, shining like jewels on his skin.

'Sorry,' she managed to say.

'I do like you,' he said. 'I do desire you, I do want you, I do think about that kiss, all of the time. I do. But how can we be together? You're you and I'm me, and we don't fit, Tamsyn.'

'Are you sure about that?' she said, taking a step closer to him. Her hand trembled as she reached out and touched his cheek. 'I seem to remember our lips fitting together pretty well, and I remember how our bodies filled in all the spaces between us. It felt pretty much like a perfect fit.'

Jed closed his eyes, his hand that wasn't securing his modesty covering hers. 'Tamsyn, don't.'

'I can't help it, though,' her voice was thick with emotion. 'I don't even know why.' She stood on her tiptoes, resting one of her palms against his damp shoulder, looking into his silver eyes, and kissed him, not gently, or demurely, but with all the hunger and longing that seemed to be building like a flood behind a dam, in her chest. And for a few wonderful, heady, perfect seconds Jed kissed her back, before breaking the kiss.

'Please, don't,' he whispered.

'Why not?' Tamsyn asked him. 'You are allowed to be happy, you know; you are allowed to have someone.'

'But could I have you?' Jed took his hand from hers. 'You don't even believe in God, Tamsyn.'

'I-I believe in you,' she replied hotly. 'Isn't that enough?'

'Even so, can you really see yourself at my side for the rest of your life? Can you see yourself as a vicar's wife, hosting the fairs, and being at every service? Don't you see, Tamsyn? That's the reason I can't let myself fall for you. Because when I do, it will be for ever, and I can't lose you. So if you can't promise me you're for ever, right now, right here, then please, just go.'

Tamsyn took a step back from him: everything he had just said was everything she had wanted to hear, and yet . . . for ever seemed like a very long time. The last time Tamsyn had decided to dedicate her life to something she had once been just as passionate and committed to, she'd discovered she'd been making a mistake. What if loving Jed meant messing up the life he had here, the life he loved so much? And she didn't suppose his bosses would take too kindly to the vicar's wife being an agnostic with more faith in the benefits of a good lipstick than the Man Upstairs.

'Don't leave Poldore,' Tamsyn said, handing him the towel. 'Please don't go. This place needs you. Promise me that you won't leave.'

'Does that mean you can't promise me for ever?' Jed asked her.

'I'm not sure that I know how to.' The words caught in Tamsyn's throat. 'Are you staying?'

'I'm staying,' Jed said. 'I'm staying for you, because maybe one day I hope you will look at me, and you will think that for ever is possible.'

Sadly, Tamsyn handed him the towel and left the room, walking into the cool air of the bedroom. She heard Jed coming out from the bathroom, heard his bare feet on the floorboards behind her and closed her eyes, and he put his arms around her. Turning to face him, she buried her face in his neck.

'So if I can't believe in God, and you can't believe that love is enough, then I suppose this has to be goodbye, doesn't it? But just between us, being this way. Not to the town, not to your life.'

She pulled away to look him in the eye. 'I feel so stupid for feeling so heartbroken.'

'You're not stupid,' Jed said, kissing her gently on the mouth. 'You're the best woman I have ever met, Tamsyn.'

'So,' she said, taking a step back from him and lifting

her chin, 'I will see you around, Vicar. Better get back to that wedding. I've got an appointment with the karaoke machine.'

'Goodbye Tamsyn,' Jed said as she walked away, determined not to look back. 'See you around.'

Chapter Twenty-nine

St Piran's was still full of the wedding decorations as the congregation filed in for the Sunday service, which was billed as a service of thanks for no loss of life during the floods. It was just as packed as it had been for the wedding, one week and one day before. The only two people who weren't there this time were Alex and Ruan, who had disappeared to the lighthouse at some point after their wedding, and no one expected them to show their faces again for some time.

It had been an interesting week, one in which Tamsyn had kept herself very busy so that she didn't have to think about the fact that she'd fallen in love with the one man she couldn't have. Laura and Keira had stayed on a little longer to help her find a place to rent, a top-floor apartment with views looking out over the estuary and a balcony where she could sit and eat croissants, assuming another hurricane-force wind wasn't about to sweep through the poor battered town and take her with it.

She had been in touch with Bernard again, emailing him her official letter of resignation, and then making sure he emailed his carefully worded press release about her to all the relevant trade press and fashion magazines. And she helped anyone and everyone who needed it. She helped Sue clear up Castle House after the sick and the homeless gradually began to return back home. She helped Eddie, Rosie and Lucy clean the pub and pump water out of the cellar. She'd gone to Kirsten to see her room in the hostel and bought her a new pair of curtains and a second-hand TV, and when Sue said Jed was looking for people to coordinate a clothes drive for those who had lost everything except what they were standing up in, she'd turned up at the church hall and worked quietly and methodically, organising all the donations into groups according to size, age and gender.

Jed had paused by the table she was working at for a moment, and their eyes had met. She thought he might have been about to saying something to her, but there was just so much that couldn't be said that small talk seemed pointless. Instead he nodded and went on his way.

Which was when it hit Tamsyn, rather like a bolt from above, and she knew what she had to do.

'Are you sure about this?' Laura whispered in her daughter's ear as they slid into a pew at the back.

'Yes,' Tamsyn said. 'Yes, I'm sure.'

'Yes, but are you really, though?' Cordelia leant over from the pew behind, where Keira was attempting to entertain the twins with an iPad, even though one iPad between two four-year-olds was never going to cut it.

'Are you sure that you want to be a singer?' Tamsyn asked her.

'Yes,' Cordelia said.

'And are you sure that you loved Dad from the first moment you set eyes on him?' she asked her mother.

'Yes,' Laura said. 'But . . .'

'And are you now sure,' Tamsyn turned to Keira, 'that you should have just forked out for two iPads?'

'I really am,' Keira said with a resigned sigh.

'There you are then,' Tamsyn said. 'I'm sure this is the right thing to do. I've even googled it, and everything.'

The three other Thorne women exchanged glances, but they all knew, because they were all exactly the same, that once a Thorne had made up their mind to do something, they couldn't be dissuaded. No matter how foolish their actions might be.

Tamsyn waited for the end of the service, the part where the school band that was standing in for the wrecked organ was due to strike up, but the school band happened to be led by one of the girls she had spoken to on that first night at Castle House, and she knew not to start playing when Jed signalled to her.

This was it, Tamsyn thought. This was the defining moment of her life.

'I have something to say.' She got to her feet and

then realised that the words hadn't actually come out, out loud. Clearing her throat, she tried again.

'Um, hello, everyone!' she called out, so that everyone in the church twisted in their pews to look at her. 'Hi!'

She waved, and then regretted it.

'I have something I'd like to say to the vicar, does anyone mind? If I say something to him, the vicar?'

She was met by a chorus of curious no's.

'Tamsyn . . .' Jed's gesture was rather hopeless; it seemed he was starting to get to know the resolve of the Thorne women too.

Tamsyn made her way into the aisle and walked up to the front.

'Jed Hayward, you are a vicar and I am a fashion designer. And you believe in God and I might believe in some sort of design in the fabric of the universe, maybe. You have principles, and I've shopped there once. You are a good, decent, kind, strong and frankly damn gorgeous man. And I'm . . . well, I'm just me, really, a woman who for more than a week now has not been able to find a pair of hair straighteners in the whole of Poldore. But I have helped a baby and a mum get back together, got a teenager back on her feet and I have made beautiful dresses for my brother's wedding. And I have held you in my arms and known what it was like to find pure joy.'

There was gasp, and a scandalised murmur ran around the church.

'Yesterday you asked me if I could promise for ever. And I'm here to tell you the answer, and the answer is no. I can't promise for ever. Not if for ever means one more second not at your side, one more minute when I can't take your hand, another second when you don't know that, for reasons known only to your boss and the universe, I have fallen in love with you and I can't live without you. Jed, I love you, I do. And I know we are two very different people, but did someone say that the greatest of all things was love, and I really think we have that. I really think we have love.'

'Tamsyn,' he spoke her name, but she gestured for him to let her go on.

Tamsyn paused and took a deep breath, fear coursing through her veins as she prepared herself for the greatest gamble of her life. 'Did you know if we start posting our banns now, we could be married in six weeks' time?'

This time the gasps were accompanied by shrieks, and a yell or two.

'Tamsyn?' Jed smiled at her, shaking his head. 'What are you saying?'

'I guess I'm saying let's try this your way. Let's try for ever,' Tamsyn said. 'And I'm asking you to marry me, no wait, get married to me, in this church, in six weeks' time, because I don't want to wait one second longer than that to be your wife.'

A pin could have dropped in the church and you

would have heard its metallic chime as it hit the floor, as everyone turned to look expectantly at Jed.

'Do you mean it?' he asked her, walking down the aisle towards her.

'I've honestly never been more serious about anything in my life,' Tamsyn said.

'Then yes, Tamsyn Thorne,' Jed took her hands as he reached her. 'Yes, I will marry you.'

And that might have been the first time in the four-hundred-year history of St Piran's that the congregation went wild.

Epilogue

It was warm, very warm, and Tamsyn could feel the heat of the day on the back of her neck, having piled all her hair into a bundle of loose curls, which Keira had threaded through with flowers for her, pink sorrel and white daisies.

'Are you thinking of doing a runner?' Ruan asked her as they stood outside the church in near silence. It couldn't have been a more placid day; there wasn't a hint of wind, and the sea was the purest sapphire blue. Most of the town was inside St Piran's already, and they'd had to bring in extra seating. Everyone wanted to be there on the day that the vicar married an agnostic he'd only just met. They were the talk of the town, or more likely the county – no, actually, they'd been talked about even further afield than that. Bishops had discussed them, and Tamsyn's status as a non-believer; they had travelled to meet with senior clergy, who counselled them in marriage, and what their life would be like together, and how it might be impossible for them to make it work when at their core they were so different, finally meeting with Jed's boss, the Bishop of the Diocese.

'But we're not that different,' Jed had said, reaching

out to take Tamsyn's hand. 'And I'm not the first clergyman to marry someone who isn't devout. We both believe in the same things: community, decency, faith, caring for others and, above all, love. Tamsyn believes in those things too, as she's shown more than once in the weeks that I've known her. She's totally revitalised the Youth Homeless Project in Poldore, she's getting the kids work experience, mentors . . . She's done so much to help the town get back on its feet after the storm; she's supported my verger during her recent difficulties, and is helping her settle into life as a mother. And all while she is setting up her own business . . . And more than that,' Jed had turned to look at Tamsyn, and she felt the heat rise through her from her toes upward, and wouldn't have been at all surprised if there was steam coming out of the top of her head, 'I love her. More every day.'

The Bishop had said a little more about how very quick it was, and what was the hurry. He'd pointed out that although there was no actual rule against marrying someone of a different faith or no faith, he was more worried about the pressures that might be put on the marriage as time went by. And then it was Tamsyn's turn to speak.

'I believe in him,' she said, looking at Jed. 'He's been through so much. He's still overcoming so much, and yet look at everything he does for the people around him. As well as being really quite gorgeous.'

Jed closed his eyes, but luckily the Bishop laughed.

Tamsyn continued, 'I admire the way he lives his life, I admire his values. And I will be a really good vicar's wife. I will; I've found a blog on it already, where there are loads of vicars' wives offering tips and a support group. I don't doubt we'll have hard times, because everybody does. But I also don't doubt that we will find a way through them, together.'

The Bishop sat back in his chair, smiled and wished them the very best of luck, which wasn't a blessing, exactly, but it was what Jed had needed to hear, and Tamsyn was grateful.

The days before that meeting, and afterwards, had been days of wonder, truly.

On the day she had proposed to him, Tamsyn had sat on a pew at the front of the church and waited as the congregation, slowly, very slowly, because they all wanted to see what would happen next, filed out of the church. Almost half an hour passed as Jed said goodbye to his flock, answered questions, fended off jokes, and Tamsyn sat perfectly still watching the sunlight dappling through the stained glass.

Eventually she heard the mended door close behind her and Jed's footsteps walking up the aisle towards her.

'I put you on the spot a bit, didn't I?' she said. But he said nothing, taking her hand and leading her out of the church and through the vestry, out through the funny little door and into Kissing Alley.

'You asked me to marry you,' he said finally as they stood there in the shade of the secluded spot.

'I did a bit, yes,' Tamsyn admitted.

'Because you are in love with me?' Jed said. 'I mean really, like, for life? It's not just the lure of the dog collar?'

Tamsyn had laughed a lot, and Jed had flushed red, smiling as he waited for her to stop.

'Is that a thing? Vicar-fancying?'

'Oh, you'd be surprised,' he said.

'Well, no, it's not just that,' Tamsyn took a step back from him, turning away a little. 'No one expects to fall in love with a vicar she's only just met; no one. But you . . . you make me believe in life, and in people, and in possibilities. And you make me want to be better, to be true to myself, to be happy. And you make me want to take your clothes off, quite a lot, if I'm honest. And to be with you, I have to be brave, braver than I have ever been. To be with you I have to be certain, and now that I know I am, then what else is there to do but to ask you to marry me?'

'Even knowing what you know, about the PTSD, knowing it's still there? Because I want you to be sure.'

'The way you handle that only makes me love you more,' Tamsyn told him. 'And if you'll let me, I'll be there with you, helping you get better.'

There was silence behind her, and Tamsyn closed her eyes for a moment.

And then she felt Jed's fingers in her hair, sweeping it aside as he kissed the back of her neck, turning her to face him.

'I didn't think I could ever be this happy,' he told her. 'I love you, Tamsyn.'

'You do know we are standing in Kissing Alley, right?' Tamsyn smiled. 'Be rude not to.'

What wonderful weeks had followed, what blissful times, getting to know more about the man that she felt she already knew in the truest way: they argued over films and music, debated long into the night about books and politics and told each other all of their secrets, all of their hopes and dreams. And best of all, there had been a lot more kissing, headier, glorious, delirious kissing, so much so that sometimes Tamsyn worried that when they were actually married, nothing would get done.

And when she thought about what she'd had with Bernard, and what she had found with Jed, she laughed at how naive she had been to think that Bernard could ever have made her happy. She was making him happy, though, as her coats had featured in all the previews of his new ready-to-wear range in the fashion magazines across two continents, and he had been photographed in Milan with an Italian movie star who was a foot taller than him, looking like the cat that got the cream. And yet when Tamsyn looked at her designs with someone else's name on them, she discovered that she couldn't care less. Because she knew it wasn't her best work; her best work, her career-defining work, was yet to come.

Catriona turned out to be a natural mother. Mo had stayed with Tamsyn for another two weeks, as she recovered; one week while Catriona was in hospital, although Tamsyn took the baby to see her mother every day, and one week after she was discharged. And then for the first few nights Tamsyn had stayed with Catriona in her newly decorated house, the first of the wrecked cottages to be put right, the townspeople of Poldore having made sure it would be ready for Catriona to bring her baby home. And although Tamsyn remained as one of Mo's official carers, until Tess decided to sign her off completely, she felt like her job was done. In the weeks since she and Buoy had first found the baby, Mo had blossomed, putting on weight, hand over chubby fist, smiling at everyone, guzzling milk like there was no tomorrow and becoming really quite a beauty. And as she flowered, so did her mother, and as Catriona's confidence grew, so did her happiness. And before long, she could be seen going about her verger duties again, with Mo tucked cheerfully into a sling, the pair of them inseparable. At some point, Tamsyn didn't know when, Catriona must have decided to do what Jed had advised, which was to contact Mo's father, and to his credit he had arrived in Poldore only a few days later to meet his daughter. Between them they were working out the best way for him to be part of Mo's life, and the more Tamsyn saw of him and Catriona together, the less she found herself surprised if he didn't end up being part of Catriona's life too.

'You know, we have to go in there at some point, otherwise Jed's going to take it personally,' Ruan said. 'I don't think they usually marry people when the bride is standing outside of the church . . .'

'I'm sorry.' Tamsyn took a deep breath and looked at her brother. 'I'm sorry, I was just taking stock, working out how I came to be standing here on this day in this frankly stunning Regency-inspired Tamsyn Thorne organza gown about to get married to the most amazing man I've ever met.'

'Does it matter how?' Ruan asked her. 'You're here, and that's what's important. And I don't just mean *here*, taking a really long time to make your way up the aisle, but I mean here, in Poldore. Home again. Now if I can only find a way to lure Mum and Keira back for good, I'll have a complete set.'

'You don't want the twins living permanently in Poldore,' Tamsyn assured him. 'What that storm did to the town, it's nothing compared to what destruction they can bring.'

'Seriously,' Ruan said, 'it's good to have you back, sis.'

'It's good to have you back too,' Tamsyn said. 'And thank you for giving me away.'

'Are you kidding me?' Ruan chuckled as they entered the church at last. 'I've been waiting all my life to get rid of you.'

It was Kirsten, dressed in a simple rose-coloured, knee-length bridesmaid's dress that Tamsyn had designed for her, who was waiting with her flowers, as she walked into the church. Tamsyn had asked her sisters if they would mind not being bridesmaids, because she wanted the wedding to be as simple as possible, and they had been really rather glad to get out of the duty. In the end she'd asked Kirsten, because Mo was not big enough, and because since she had got to know the girl in the last six weeks, they had become friends, despite the age difference, which Kirsten liked to tease her about as much as possible, and it turned out that she had a flair for design, not to mention needlework. She had virtually made the dress she was wearing herself.

'You look like you might throw up,' Kirsten told her as she handed her the flowers, arranged especially by Keira.

'Really? I was going for luminous and serene,' Tamsyn whispered.

'Oh yeah, that's what I meant,' Kirsten assured her. 'Seriously, you look lovely, and all of the Poldore girls are totally pig-sick about me being your bridesmaid, plus Ben texted me this morning to see if I fancied a coffee. What do you think? Should I go?'

'I think I'm getting married, and that we should discuss your love life a bit later,' Tamsyn suggested.

'Totally,' Kirsten nodded, falling into place behind Tamsyn, who hooked her arm through Ruan's to steady herself.

And there he was, waiting for her at the end of the aisle, and Tamsyn discovered that Ruan had to slow her down at bit, as she was rather trotting up the aisle to be at his side.

'You look stunning,' Jed whispered, taking her hand. 'And you're here. I'm so glad that you are here.'

'Of course I am,' Tamsyn said. 'Where else would I be, but at your side?'

Acknowledgements

With lots of love and thanks to my brilliant team at Ebury who works so hard on my behalf, especially my wonderful editor Gillian Green and the lovely Emily Yau. Also Amelia Harvell and Louise Jones.

Thank you to my agent and friend Lizzy Kremer; also to Harriet Moore and Laura West; and all at David Higham Associates, who I feel very lucky to be represented by.

Once again, a warm thank you to the people of Fowey, Cornwall, where I wrote a good deal of this book, and especially to the staff at Fowey Hall Hotel who are always unfailingly kind and brilliant, and bring me cream teas in a constant stream. Thanks especially to Robin Ashley who gave me some help with constructing a corset out of thin air!

Love and thanks to my lovely family, who let me go to Cornwall to eat cream teas and write a book: my husband Adam and my children Lily, Harry, Freddie, Stanley and Aubrey, who are inspirational, wonderful and delightful – not to mention exhausting.

Enjoyed *Two Weddings and a Baby*?

Read on for a sneak peek at

The Memory Book

The uplifting and beautiful novel about
mothers and daughters

Also by Rowan Coleman

'Painfully real and utterly heartbreaking, every page will leave
you an emotional wreck but, ultimately, this is a wonderfully
uplifting novel about mothers and daughters' Lisa Jewell

'I can't tell you how much I loved this book. It did make
me cry but it also made me laugh. Like *Me Before You*
by Jojo Moyes, I couldn't put it down. A tender
testament to maternal love' Katie Fforde

'Written with great tenderness, *The Memory Book* manages to
be heartbreakingly sad yet uplifting too. You'll hold your loved
ones that little bit closer after reading this novel.
I absolutely loved it!' Lucy Diamond

'*The Memory Book* is warm, sad, and life-affirming, with an
unforgettable heroine who will make you laugh and cry.
It's a tender book about treasuring the past and living
fully in the present; you'll finish it and immediately go
give your loved ones a hug' Julie Cohen

EBURY
PRESS

'Warm, funny and totally heartbreaking, *The Memory Book* is a wonderful read' Polly Williams

'. . . just stunning . . .incredibly beautiful . . . the story took me on a journey that was at turns, devastating and then so uplifting. It made my heart soar at the strength of the human spirit and how capable human beings are of true, selfless love. An unforgettable and courageous story . . . This story has the ingredients to capture the world'
Katy Regan

'A heart-breaking story that will stay with you long after you've finished the book' Carole Matthews

'. . . terrific . . . incredibly moving but also witty and warm'
Kate Harrison

'. . . breath-takingly gut-wrenchingly heart-breakingly wonderful. Exquisitely crafted and with huge emotional depth . . . extraordinary'
Veronica Henry

'An absolutely beautiful, stunningly written story – you HAVE to read *The Memory Book* by Rowan Coleman!'
Miranda Dickinson

'Heartbreakingly good stuff – just be sure to stock up on tissues' *Fabulous Magazine, The Sun on Sunday*

'This is a heart-rending story, but it's also completely absorbing, uplifting, tender, sad and wise'
Sunday Mirror

EBURY PRESS

Prologue

Greg is looking at me; he thinks I don't know it. I've been chopping onions at the kitchen counter for almost five minutes, and I can see his reflection – inside out, convex and stretched – in the chrome kettle we got as a wedding present. He's sitting at the kitchen table, checking me out.

The first time I noticed him looking at me like this I thought I must have had something stuck in my teeth, or a cobweb in my hair, or something, because I couldn't think of any reason my sexy young builder would be looking at me. Especially not on that day when I was dressed in old jeans and a T-shirt, with my hair scraped back into a bun, ready to paint my brand-new attic room – the room that marked the beginning of everything.

It was the end of his last day; he'd been working at the house for just over a month. It was still really hot, especially up there, even with my new Velux windows open. Covered in sweat, he climbed down the newly installed pull-down ladder. I gave him a pint glass of lemonade rattling with ice cubes, which he drank in one go, the muscles in his throat moving as he swallowed. I think I must have sighed out loud at his sheer gloriousness because he looked curiously at me. I laughed and shrugged, and he smiled and then looked at his boots. I poured him another glass of lemonade and went back to my last box – Caitlin's things – yet another box of stuff I couldn't bring myself to throw out and that I knew I'd be clogging up the garage with instead. It was then that I sensed him looking at me. I touched my hair, expecting to find something there, and ran my tongue over my teeth.

'Everything OK?' I asked him, wondering if he was trying to work out how to tell me that my bill had doubled.

'Fine,' he said, nodding. He was – is – a man of few words.

'Good, and are you finished?' I asked, still prepared for bad news.

'Yep, all done,' he said. 'So . . .'

'Oh, God, you want paying. I'm so sorry.' I felt myself blush as I rooted around in the kitchen drawer for my cheque book, which wasn't there – it was never where it was supposed to be. Flustered, I looked around, feeling his gaze on me as I tried to remember where I'd last had it. 'It's around here somewhere . . .'

'There's no hurry,' he said.

'I had it when I was paying some bills, so . . .' I just kept wittering on, desperate, if I'm honest, for him to be gone and for me to be able to breathe out and drink the half bottle of Grigio that was waiting for me in the fridge.

'You can pay me another time,' he said. 'Like maybe when you come out with me for a drink.'

'Pardon?' I said, stopping halfway through searching a drawer that seemed to be full only of rubber bands. I must have misheard.

'Come out with me for a drink?' he asked tentatively. 'I don't normally ask my clients out, but . . . you're not normal.'

I laughed and it was his turn to blush.

'That didn't quite come out the way I thought it,' he said, folding his arms across his chest.

'You're asking me on a date?' I said, just to confirm it, because the whole thing seemed so absurd that I had to say it out loud to test I'd got it right. 'Me?'

'Yes, you coming?'

'OK,' I said. It had all seemed so perfectly plausible to him: him and me, ten years between us, going out on a date. 'Why not?'

That was the first time I noticed him looking at me, looking at me with this sort of mingled heat and joy that I instantly felt mirrored inside me, like my body was answering his call in a way that my conscious mind had no control over. Yes, ever since then I've felt his looks long before I've seen them. I feel the hairs standing up on the back of my neck, and a sense of anticipation washing over me in one long delicious shudder, because I know that soon after he looks at me, he will be touching me, kissing me.

Now I feel his hand on my shoulder and I lean my cheek against his fingers.

'You're crying,' he says.

'I'm chopping onions,' I say, putting down the knife and turning round to face him. 'You know that all Esther will eat is Mummy's homemade lasagne? Here, you should watch me make it, so you know the recipe. First, chop the onions . . .'

'Claire . . .' Greg stops me from picking up the knife again, and turns me towards him. 'Claire, we have to talk about it, don't we?'

He looks so uncertain, so lost and so reluctant, that I want to say no – no, we don't have to talk about it, we can just pretend that today is like yesterday, and all the days before that when we didn't know any better. We can pretend not to know, and who knows how long we might be able to go on like this, so happy, so perfect?

'She likes a lot of tomato purée in the sauce,' I say. 'And also a really big slug of ketchup . . .'

'I don't know what to do or say,' Greg says, his voice breaking on an inward breath. 'I'm not sure how to be.'

'And then, just at the end, add a teaspoon of Marmite.'

'Claire,' he says with a sob, and draws me into his arms. And I stand there in his embrace with my eyes closed, breathing in his scent, my arms at my side, feeling my heart pounding in my chest. 'Claire, how are we going to tell the children?'

Friday, 13 March 1992

Caitlin Is Born

This is the bracelet they gave you in the hospital – pink because you are a girl. It says: 'Baby Armstrong.' They put it on your ankle, and it kept slipping off because you were so tiny, a whole month early, to the day. You were supposed to be an April baby. I had imagined daffodils and blue skies and April showers, but you decided to be born one month early on a cold wet Friday, Friday 13th, no less, not that we were worried about that. If anyone was ever born to overcome bad omens it was you, and you knew it, greeting the world with an almighty shout – not a cry or a wail, but a roar of intent, I thought. A declaration of war.

There wasn't anybody there with us for a long time. Because you were early, and Gran lived far away. So for about the first six hours it was just you and me. You smelled sweet, like a cake, and you felt so warm and . . . exactly right. We were at the end of the ward and we kept the curtain closed around us. I could hear the other mums talking, visitors coming and going, babies crying and fussing, but I didn't want to be part of it. I didn't want to be part of anything ever again except for you and me. I held you, so tiny and scrunched up like a new bud waiting to flower, and I just looked at you, slumbering against my breast, a deep frown on your tiny face, and I told you it was all going to be fine, because you and I were together: we were the whole universe, and that was all that mattered.

1

Claire

I've just got to get away from my mother: she is driving me mad, which would be funny if I wasn't already that way inclined. No, I'm not mad, that's not right. Although I feel pretty angry.

It was the look on her face when we came out of the hospital appointment; the look she had all the way home. Stoical, stalwart, strong but bleak. She didn't say the words, but I could hear them buzzing around in her head: 'This is so typically Claire. To ruin everything just when it's getting good.'

'I'll move in,' she says, even though she blatantly already has, silently secreting herself in the spare bedroom, like I wouldn't notice her, arranging her personal items on the shelf in the bathroom. I knew she would come when she found out. I knew she would and I wanted her to, I suppose; but I wanted to ask her, or for her to ask me. Instead she simply arrived, all hushed tones and sorrowful glances. 'I'll move into the spare room.'

'No, you won't.' I turn to look at her as she drives. She is a very careful driver, slow and exacting. I am not allowed to drive any more, not since I killed that post-box, which carried a far more expensive fine than you would perhaps imagine, because it belongs to Her Majesty. It must be the same if you run over a corgi: if you run over a corgi, you probably get sent to the Tower. My mother is such a careful driver, and yet she never looks in the rear-view mirror when she's reversing. It's like she feels that, in that one aspect, it's safer simply to close her eyes and hope for the best. I used to love driving; I loved the freedom and the independence and knowing that, if I felt like it, I could go anywhere I fancied. I don't like that my car keys have disappeared, gone without me being allowed even to kiss them goodbye, hidden away in a place where I will never find them. I know because I've tried. I could still drive, I think. As long as no one put anything in my way.

'It's not come to you moving in yet,' I insist, although we both know she has already moved in. 'There's still lots of time left when I won't need any help at all. I mean, listen to me. I can still talk and think about . . .' I wave my arm, causing her to duck and look under my hand, which I tuck apologetically back in my lap. 'Things.'

'Claire, this isn't something you can stick your head in the sand about. Trust me, I know.'

Of course she knows: she's lived through this before, and

now, thanks to me, or strictly speaking thanks to my father and his rogue DNA, she has to live through it again. And it's not as if I'll do anything sensible like dying nice and neatly with all my faculties intact, holding her hand and thanking her, with a serene look on my face as I impart words of wisdom to live by to my children. No, my annoyingly quite young, reasonably fit body will linger on long after I've checked out of my mushy little brain, right up until the moment when I forget how to breathe in and out and in again. I know that's what she is thinking. I know the last thing in the world she wants is to watch her daughter fade away and shrivel up, just like her husband did. I know it's breaking her heart and that she's doing her best to be brave, and stand by me, and yet . . . It makes me so angry. Her goodness makes me angry. All my life I've been trying to prove that I can grow up enough to not need her to rescue me all the time. All my life I've been wrong.

'Actually, Mum, I *am* the one who can stick my head in the sand,' I say, staring out of the window. 'I *am* the one who can completely ignore what is happening to me, because most of the time I won't even notice.'

It's funny: I say the words out loud, and feel the fear, there in the pit of my stomach, but it's like it isn't part of me. It really is like it's happening to someone else, this terror.

'You don't mean that, Claire,' Mum says crossly, as if she really thinks that I mean I don't care, and not that I'm just saying it to annoy her. 'What about your daughters?'

I say nothing because my mouth is suddenly thick with words that won't form properly or mean anything like what I need them to mean. So I stay quiet, looking out of the window, at the houses slipping past, one by one. It's almost dark already; living-room lamps are switched on, TVs flicker behind curtains. Of course I care. Of course I'll miss it, this life. Steam-filled kitchens on winter evenings, cooking for my daughters, watching them grow: these are the things I will never experience. I'll never know whether Esther will always eat her peas one by one, and if she will always be blonde. If Caitlin will travel across Central America, like she plans to, or whether she'll do something completely different that she hasn't even dreamed of yet. I won't ever know what that undreamed wish will be. They'll never lie to me about where they are going, or come to me with their problems. These are the things I'll miss, because I'll be somewhere else and I won't even know what I'm missing. Of course I bloody care.

'I suppose they'll have Greg.' My mum sounds sceptical as she ploughs on, determined to discuss what the world will be like after I'm no longer in it, even though it shows a quite spectacular lack of tact. 'That's if he can hold it together.'

'He will,' I say. 'He will. He's a brilliant father.'

I am not sure if that is true, though. I'm not sure if he can take what is happening, and I don't know how to help him. He is such a good man, and a kind one. But lately, ever since the diagnosis, he is becoming a stranger to me day by day. Every time I look at him he is standing further away. It's not his fault. I can tell he wants to be there, to be stalwart and strong for me, but I think perhaps the enormity of it all, of all this happening when really we've only just started out on our life together, is chipping away at him. Soon I won't recognise him at all; I know I already find it hard to recognise the way I feel about him. I know he is the last great love of my life, but I don't feel it any more. Somehow Greg is the first thing I am losing. I remember it, our love affair, but it's as though I've dreamed it, like Alice through the looking glass.

'You, of all people.' Mum cannot help lecturing me, telling me off for being in possession of the family's dark secret, like I brought it on myself by being so damned naughty. 'You, who knew what it was like to grow up without a father. We need to make plans for them, Claire. Your girls are losing their mother and you need to make sure they will be OK when you aren't capable of looking after them any more!'

She brakes suddenly at a zebra crossing, causing a chorus of horns to sound behind her, as a little girl who looks far too young to be out on her own hurries across the road, huddled against the rain. In the glare of Mum's headlights I can see she's carrying a thin blue plastic bag with what looks like four pints of milk inside, bumping against her skinny legs. I hear the break in Mum's voice, hovering just below the frustration and anger. I hear the hurt.

'I do know that,' I say, suddenly exhausted. 'I do know that I have to make plans, but I was waiting, I was hoping. Hoping I might get to enjoy being married to Greg and grow old with him, hoping that the drugs might slow things down for me. Now I know that . . . well, now that I know there is no hope, I'll get a lot more organised, I promise. Make a wall chart, keep a rota.'

'You can't hide from this, Claire.' She insists on repeating herself.

'Don't you think I know that?' I shout. Why does she always do that? Why does she always push me until I shout at her, as if she isn't satisfied I'm really listening until she has made me lose my temper? It's always been that way between us: love and anger mixed up in almost every moment we have together. 'Do you think I don't know what I have done, giving them this shitty life?'

Mum pulls into the drive in front of a house – my house, I realise a second too late – and I feel the tears coming against my will. Slamming out of the car, I don't go into the house, but instead walk into the rain, dragging the edges of my cardigan around me, heading defiantly up the street.

'Claire!' Mum shouts after me. 'You can't do this any more!'

'Watch me,' I say, but not to her, just into the rain, feeling the tiny droplets on my lips and tongue.

'Claire, please!' I just about hear her, but I keep walking. I'll show her; I'll show them all, especially the people that won't let me drive. I can still walk; I can still bloody walk! I haven't forgotten how to do that yet. I'll just go to the end of the road, where the other one crosses over it, and then turn back. I'll be like Hansel following a trail of breadcrumbs.

I won't go far. I just need to do this one thing. Go to the end of the road, turn around and come back. Although it is getting darker now, and the houses round here all look the same: neat, squat 1930s semis. And the end of the road isn't as near as I thought it was.

I stop for a moment, feeling the rain driving into my head, tiny cold needles of icy water. I turn around. My mum isn't behind me: she hasn't followed me. I thought she might, but she hasn't. The street is empty. Did I reach the end of the road and turn around already? I am not sure. Which direction was I walking in? Am I going to or from, and to where? The houses on either side of the road look exactly the same. I stand very still. I left my home less than two minutes ago, and now I am not sure where it is. A car drives past me, spraying freezing water on to my legs. I didn't bring my phone, and anyway I can't always remember how to use it any more. I've lost numbers. Although I look at them and know they are numbers, I've forgotten which ones are which, and which order they come in. But I can still walk, so I begin to walk in the direction that the car that soaked me was going. Perhaps it's a sign. I will know my house when I see it because the curtains are bright-red silk and the light shining through them makes them glow. Remember that: I have red glowing curtains at the front of my house that one of my neighbours said made me look 'loose'. I will remember the red glowing curtains. I'll be home really soon. Everything will be fine.

*

The appointment at the hospital hadn't exactly gone well. Greg had wanted to come but I told him to go and finish the conservatory he was building. I told him that nothing the doctor said would make our mortgage need to be paid any the less, or mean that we don't have to keep feeding the children. It hurt him that I hadn't wanted him there, but he didn't realise that I couldn't cope with trying to guess what the look on his face meant at the same time as guessing what I felt myself. I knew if I took Mum she would just say everything in her head, which is better. It's better than hearing really terrible news and wondering if your husband is sorry that he ever set eyes on you, that of all the people in the world he could have chosen, he chose you. So I wasn't in the best frame of mind – pun intended – when the doctor sat me down to go through the next round of test results. The tests they had given me because everything was happening much faster than they'd thought it would.

I can't remember the doctor's name because it's very long with a great many syllables, which I think is funny. I mentioned this as Mum and I sat there waiting for him to finish looking at the notes on his screen and deliver the bad news, but no one else was amused. There's a time and a place for gallows humour, it seems.

The rain is driving down faster now, and heavier; I wished I'd flounced off with my coat. After a while all the roads round here start to look the same: 1930s semis, in row after row, either side of the street. I'm looking for curtains, aren't I? What colour?

I turn a corner and see a little row of shops, and I stop. I've come out for a coffee, then? This is where I come on a Saturday morning with Greg and Esther for a pain au chocolat and a coffee. It's dark, though, and cold and wet. And I don't seem to have a coat on, and I check my hand, which is empty of Esther's, and for a moment I hold on tight to my chest, worrying that I've forgotten her. But I didn't have her when I started. If I'd had her when I started, I'd be carrying her monkey, which she always insists on taking out but never wants to carry herself. So I've come here for coffee. I'm having some me time. That's nice.

I head across the road, grateful for the rush of warm air that greets me as I enter the café. People look up at me as I walk in through the door. I suppose I must look quite a sight with my hair plastered to my face.

I wait at the counter, belatedly realising that I am shivering. I must have forgotten my coat. I wish I could remember why I came out for coffee. Am I meeting someone? Is it Greg? I come here sometimes with Greg and Esther for a pain au chocolat.

'You all right, love?' the girl, who's about Caitlin's age, asks me. She is smiling, so perhaps I know her. Or perhaps she is just being friendly. A woman sitting with her toddler buggy, just to my left, pushes it a little further away from me. I must look strange, like a lady recently emerged from a lake. Haven't they ever seen a wet person before?

'Coffee, please,' I say. I feel the weight of change in my jeans pocket, and produce it in my fist. I can't remember how much the coffee is here, and when I look at the board over the counter where I know the information is displayed, I am lost. I hold out the coins in the palm of my hand and offer them up.

The girl wrinkles her nose, as if money I've touched might somehow be tainted, and I feel very cold now and very lonely. I want to tell her why I am hesitating, but the words won't come – not the right ones, anyway. It's harder to say things out loud than think them in my head. It makes me scared to say anything to anyone I don't know, in case I say something so ludicrous they just cart me away and lock me up, and by that time I've forgotten my name and . . .

I glance towards the door. Where is this café? I went to the hospital with Mum, we saw the consultant, Mr Thingy, I couldn't remember his name, I thought that was quite funny, and now I am here. But I can't think why I am here, or even where here is. I shudder, taking the coffee and the brown coins that the girl has left on the counter; and then I go and sit down, very still. I feel like if I move suddenly, I might trip some hidden trap, and that something will harm me or I might fall off something. I feel like I might fall very far. I sit still and concentrate hard on how come I am here and how on earth I will leave. And where I will go. Little pieces come back to me – fragments rushing forward with pieces of information that I must somehow decode. The world is shattered all around me.

I'm not responding to the treatment, that much I know. It was always likely. The odds of the drugs doing anything for me were just the same as flipping a coin and calling heads: fifty-fifty. But everyone hoped that, for me, the treatment would make all the difference. Because I am so young, because I have two daughters, and one of them is only three and one will be left to pick up the pieces. They all hoped it would work for me, and work better than anyone – even the doctor with the long and difficult name – ever thought possible. And I too hoped for the groundbreaking miracle that would change everything. It seemed right that fate or God should allow me, of all people, some special dispensation because of my extenuating circumstances. But fate or God has not done that: whichever one it is that is having a good laugh at my expense has done the opposite. Or perhaps it's nothing so personal. Perhaps it's just genealogical accidents stretching back millennia that have brought me to this moment in time when I am the one chosen to bear the consequences. I am deteriorating much faster than anyone thought I would. It's to do with these little emboli. I can remember that word perfectly well, but I have no idea what the metal stirring thing that came with my coffee is called. But the word emboli is quite beautiful, musical almost, poetic. Tiny little blood clots exploding in my brain. It's a new feature, not something the experts expected. It makes me almost unique in the world, and everyone at the hospital is very excited about it, even though they try to pretend they are not. All I know is that every time one pops up, some more of me is gone for good – another memory, a face or a word, just lost, like me. I look around me, feeling colder now than before, and realise I feel afraid. I have no idea how to get home. I'm here, and I feel sane, but leaving this place seems impossible.

There are Christmas decorations hanging from the ceiling, which is odd. I don't remember it being Christmas; I am sure it is not Christmas. But what if I've been here for weeks? What if I left home and just walked and walked and didn't stop, and now I'm miles from anywhere and months have gone by and they all think I am dead? I should call Mum. She'll be angry with me for running off. She tells me that if I want her to treat me like an adult, I need to behave like an adult. She says it's all about trust. And I say, well, don't go through my things, then, bitch. I don't say the bitch bit out loud.

I'd text her, but she doesn't have a phone. I keep telling her, this is the twentieth century, Mum, get with the programme. But she doesn't like them. She doesn't like the fiddly buttons, she reckons. But I wish Mum were here; I wish she were here to take me home, because I am not sure where I am. I look intently around the café. What if she's here and I have forgotten what she looks like?

Wait, I am ill. I am not a girl any more. I am ill and I have come out for a coffee and I can't remember why. My curtains are a colour and they glow. Orange, maybe. Orange rings a bell.

'Hello.' I look up. There's a man. I am not supposed to talk to strangers so I look back down at the table. Perhaps he will go away. He does not. 'Are you OK?'

'I'm fine,' I say. 'Well, I'm cold.'

'Would you mind if I sit here? There's nowhere else.' I look around and the café is busy, although I can see other empty chairs. He looks OK, even nice. I like his eyes. I nod. I wonder if I'll have enough words to be able to talk to him.

'So you came out without a coat?' he asks, gesturing at me.

'Looks like it!' I say carefully. I smile, so as not to scare him. He smiles in return. I could tell him I am ill. He might help me. But I don't want to. He has nice eyes. He is talking to me like I'm not about to drop down dead at any second. He doesn't know anything about me. Neither do I, but that's beside the point.

'So what happened?' He chuckles, looking bemused, amused. I find I want to lean towards him, which I suppose makes him magnetic.

'I only popped out for a pint of milk,' I tell him, smiling. 'And locked myself out. I share a flat with three girls and my . . .' I stop short of saying my baby. For two reasons. First, because I know that this is now, and that it was years ago when I shared a flat with three girls, and back then I didn't even have a baby. Secondly, because I don't want him to know that I've got a baby, a baby who is not a baby any more. Caitlin, I have Caitlin, who is not a baby. She will be twenty-one next year and my curtains are ruby red and glow. I remind myself that I am not in a position to flirt: I'm a married mother of two.

'Can I buy you another coffee?' He signals to the woman behind the counter, who smiles at him as if she knows him. I find it reassuring that the café woman likes him too. I'm losing the ability to judge people by their expressions, and by those little subtle nuances that let you know what a person is thinking and feeling. He might be looking at me like I am a nutter. All I have to go on is his nice eyes.

'Thank you.' He is kind and he is talking to me just like I'm a person. No, not that; I *am* a person. I am still a person. I mean he's talking to me like I'm me, and I like it. It's warming me through, and I feel oddly happy. I miss feeling happy – just happy, without feeling that every moment of joy I experience now must also be tinged with sadness.

'So, you're locked out. Is someone going to ring you when they get back, or bring you a key?'

I hesitate. 'There will be someone in, in a bit.' I have no idea if that's a lie. 'I'll wait a while and then go back.' That *is* a lie. I don't know where I am or how to get to back, wherever that is.

He chuckles, and I look at him sharply. 'Sorry.' He smiles. 'It's just that you do actually look like a drowned rat, and a very pretty one, if you don't mind my saying so.'

'I don't mind you saying so,' I say. 'Say more like that!'

He laughs again.

'I'm a fool,' I say, warming to my new not-ill status. It feels good to be just me, and not me with the disease, the thing that now defines me. I've found a moment of peace and normality in this maelstrom of uncertainty, and it is such a relief. I could kiss him with gratitude. Instead I talk too much. I'm famous for talking too much; it used to be a thing about me that people enjoyed. 'I always have been. If something can go wrong, it happens to me. I don't know why, but it's like I'm a magnet for mishap. Ha, mishap. There's a word you don't hear often enough.' I rattle on and I don't really care what I am saying out loud, conscious only that here I am, a girl talking to a boy.

'I'm a bit like that too,' he says. 'Sometimes I wonder if I will ever grow up.'

'I know that I won't,' I say. 'I know it for sure.'

'Here.' He hands me his paper napkin. 'You look a little bit like you've escaped the apocalypse. Just.'

'A paper napkin?' I take it and laugh, dabbing it on my hair, face, wiping it under my eyes. When I take it away, there is black stuff on it, which means I put some black stuff on my eyes at some point today, a fact I find comforting: black stuff on my lashes means my eyes will look better, I will look better, even if I look like a better panda. 'Better than nothing, I suppose.'

'There's a hand dryer in the toilet,' he says, pointing at a door behind him. 'You could give yourself a quick blast under that. Take the edge off.'

'I'm fine,' I say, patting my damp knees as if to make a

point. I do not want to leave this table, this seat, this coffee, and go anywhere else. Here it feels like I am almost safe, like I'm clinging on to a ledge, and as long as I don't move I will be fine and I won't fall. The longer I can sit here, without having to think about where I am and how to get home, the better. I push away the surge of fear and panic, and concentrate on now. On feeling happy.

'How long have you been married?' He nods at the ring on my finger, which I notice with mild surprise. It feels right there, as if it has bedded into its place on my person, yet somehow it doesn't seem to have anything to do with me.

'It's my father's,' I say, the words coming from a long ago moment in the past, another time when I said them to another boy. 'When he died my mum gave me his ring to wear. I wear it always. One day I'll give it to the man I love.'

There is a moment of silence, awkwardness, I suppose. Once again, present and past converge, and I'm lost. I am so very lost that really all there is in this world is this moment, this table, this person speaking kindly to me, those very nice eyes.

'Perhaps I could take you for another coffee, then?' he says, sounding hesitant, cautious. 'When you are dry and not stuck in the middle of a disaster. I could meet you here or anywhere you like.' He reaches over to the counter and picks up a stumpy writing thing that is not a pen and scrawls on my folded napkin. 'The rain has stopped, shall I walk you home?'

'No,' I say. 'You might be a maniac.'

He smiles. 'So ring me, then? For a coffee?'

'I won't ring you,' I say, apologetically. 'I'm very busy. Chances are I won't remember to.'

He looks at me and laughs. 'Well, if somehow you find the time or the impulse, then ring me. And don't worry; you'll get back into your flat. One of your flatmates will turn up any second, I'm certain.'

'My name is Claire,' I tell him in a rush as he gets up. 'You don't know my name.'

'Claire.' He smiles at me. 'You look like a Claire.'

'What's that supposed to mean?' I laugh. 'And you, what's your name?'

'Ryan,' he says. 'I should have written it on the napkin.'

'Goodbye, Ryan,' I say, knowing that very soon he won't even be a memory. 'Thank you.'

'For what?' He looks perplexed.

'That napkin!' I say, holding up the scrunched-up sodden piece of tissue.

I watch him leave the café, chuckling to himself, and disappear into the dark night. I say his name over and over again. Perhaps if I say his name enough times, it will stick. I will be able to pin it down. A woman on the next table is watching him leave. She is frowning, and her frown is disconcerting. It makes me wonder if everything I thought just happened really did – if it was a nice happy moment or if something bad happened that I hadn't seen, because I've stopped being able to tell the difference. I'm not ready for that to happen yet. I don't want that to be true yet. It's dark outside now, except for a slash of pink sky cutting through the cloud as the sun sets. The woman is still frowning, and I am stuck on this chair.

'Claire?' A woman leans over me. 'Are you OK? What's wrong?'

I look at her, her smooth oval face, long straight brown hair. The frown is concern, I think, and I think she knows me.

'I am not exactly sure how to get home,' I confide in her, for want of any better solution.

She looks towards the door and then obviously thinks better of what she was about to say. Instead she turns back to me, with the frown again. 'You don't remember me, do you? It's fine, I know about your . . . problem. My name is Leslie, and our daughters are friends. My daughter is Cassie, with the pink hair and the nose piercing? And the awful taste in men? There was a time about four years ago when our girls were inseparable.'

'I've got Alzheimer's,' I say. It comes back to me, like the last rays of sun piercing the clouds, and I'm relieved. 'I forget things. They come and go. And sometimes just go.'

'I know, Cassie told me. She and Caitlin met up a few days ago, caught up. I have your Caity's number here, from that time they were supposedly sleeping over at each other's houses, and attempted to go clubbing in London. Remember? You and I waited all night for every single London train that came in, until they finally got home at about two. They hadn't even managed to get into the club. A drunk man had propositioned them on the tube, and they were crying so much we let them off the hook in the end.'

'They sound like a right pair,' I say. The woman frowns again and this time I decide it's concern rather than anger.

'Will you remember Caitlin,' the woman asks me, 'if she comes?'

'Oh, yes,' I say. 'Caitlin, yes, I remember what she looks like. Dark hair and eyes like rock pools under moonlight, black and deep.'

She smiles. 'I forgot you were a writer.'

'I'm not a writer,' I say. 'I do have a writing room, though. I tried it, writing, but it didn't work, and so now I have an empty writing room right at the top of the house. There's nothing in it but a desk and a chair, and a lamp. I was so sure I was going to fill it to the brim with ideas, but instead it just got emptier.' The woman frowns again, and her shoulders stiffen. I'm talking too much and it's making her uncomfortable. 'The thing I'm scared about the most is losing words.'

I've upset her. I should stop saying things. I'm never that sure what I am saying any more. I have to really think. And wait. Talking too much is not a fun or sweet thing about me any more. I close my lips firmly.

'I'll sit with you, shall I? Until she gets here.'

'Oh . . .' I begin to protest, but it peters out. 'Thank you.'

I listen to her make a call to Caitlin. After exchanging a

few words, she gets up and goes outside the café. As I watch her through the window, in the glow of the street lights, and I can see her still talking on the phone. She nods, her free hand gesturing. And then the call ends and she takes a deep breath of cold damp air before she comes back in and sits at my table.

'She'll be here in a few minutes,' she tells me. She seems so nice, I don't have the heart to ask her who she is talking about.